Strebor Quickiez

What is a Strebor Quickiez? Years ago, I decided that I wanted to create a series of short, erotic books that would be designed to be read in the span of one day. Thus, the Strebor Quickiez collection was born. Whether a reader takes in the excitement on the way to and from work on public transportation, or during their lunch break and before bedtime, they can get a "quick fix" in the form of a stimulating read.

Designed to be published in collections of three to six titles per season, Strebor Quickiez will be enticing to those who steer away from larger novels and those who do not have the time to commit to spend a longer span of time to take in a good read. The first set includes *The Raw Essentials of Human Sexuality*, *One Taste* and *Head Bangers: An APF Sexcapade*; the follow-up to my wilder successful novel *The Sisters of APF: The Indoctrination of Soror Ride Dick*. Rounding out the collection is a trilogy featuring three women who receive separate invitations to make their respective sexual fantasies come true: *Obsessed*, *Auctioned* and *Disciplined*.

It is my hope and desire that booksellers embrace Strebor Quickiez and promote them to their consumer base. I am convinced that these books can do a heavy volume in sales and, as always, I appreciate the support shown to all of my efforts throughout the eight years.

Blessings,

Zane

AUCTIONED

AN INVITATION EROTIC ODYSSEY

A NOVEL

KIMBERLY KAYE TERRY

SBI

STREBOR BOOKS

NEW YORK LONDON TORONTO SYDNEY

Strebor Books
P.O. Box 6505
Largo, MD 20792
http://www.streborbooks.com

ISBN-13 978-1-59309-232-0
ISBN-10   1-59309-232-6
LCCN 2008943288

First Strebor Books trade paperback edition March 2009

Cover design: www.mariondesigns.com
Cover photograph: © Keith Saunders/Marion Designs

10 9 8 7 6 5 4 3 2 1

Manufactured in the United States of America

For information regarding special discounts for bulk purchases,
please contact Simon & Schuster Special Sales at 1-800-456-6798
or business@simonandschuster.com

DEDICATION

This is dedicated to my beautiful daughters. The first two,
in heaven, inspired me to begin this journey of writing.
The third, whom I'm blessed to have here on earth,
continually motivates me to be the best that I can be.

Nyame-nti
Imandhan

Nyame-nti is an adinkra symbol of south Africa.
It means by God's grace.

ACKNOWLEDGMENTS

I'd like to first thank Madam Zane for diggin' the concept of an Invitation Erotic Odyssey.

I'd also like to thank Charmaine for all of her hard work and attention to details, that helped to make *Auctioned* the best that it could be!

And last, but not least, to two women whom I love and admire, Delilah Devlin and Allison Hobbs—it was a pleasure to work with you two crazy, talented, erotica divas!

Much love,

Kimberly

CHAPTER 1

"Look, I want that report on my desk now. Not in the next couple of hours, not tomorrow, or the next day. Now." Chase ended the connection in the middle of the new advertising assistant's blabbering and apologizing, not interested in anything the inept man had to say.

Her short, manicured nails flew over her keyboard as she drafted the first marketing plan for the lucrative new account she knew was hers. All of her careful courting would pay off, and the position of president of marketing would be hers once she landed the multimillion-dollar deal.

One corner of her full, mauve-tinted lips hitched up in a smile. Euphoria enveloped her at the thought of occupying the large corner office with the breathtaking view of the downtown Dallas skyline that would come with the promotion.

A near orgasmic shudder of delight coursed through her body.

Her eyes were half-closed behind the small square-framed, designer glasses perched on the bridge of her nose, and a sigh of pleasure escaped from between her pursed lips.

She removed one hand from the keyboard and lightly stroked a hand over the head of the man between her thighs as his head bobbed up and down and his gifted tongue softly lapped the inner lips of her vagina. Although her attention was fully on the screen of her computer, she continued to pet him, encouraging him silently to continue.

She released a very low moan when he captured her plump, blood-engorged clit and suckled it deep into his mouth. When he inserted a finger inside her moist core and pumped in and out, she closed her eyes, bit her fuller bottom lip, but didn't utter a word.

She'd become quite proficient at maintaining silence when needed since her discovery of Javier and his spectacular tongue.

Under her desk, where no one could see—if anyone were to enter her office unannounced, he licked and prodded her, stroked and suckled her cunt with hot delicious strokes, while his fingers delved deep into her core and withdrew her moisture.

He used her juices to rim the puckered hole of her anus, lightly stroking, but not daring to imbed his slender finger all the way inside, plying her pussy and ass until her body began to quake. Her limbs tensed, and the muscles in her vagina clamped in a painful constriction with her orgasm hovering, ready to break free.

But he was careful not to bring her to completion.

He knew better than to do that.

He'd learned over the course of the last months of their association that her release was not his to give.

She no longer had to forcibly move his greedy mouth as he devoured her creaming pussy, desperate to take her to the ultimate little death and to prove something she didn't require from him when she felt the beginnings of her orgasm unfurl.

He'd learned to read the signs her body made when she was dangerously close to orgasm.

She felt the tingling sensation begin to strum through her body, heralding that her release was near.

The walls of her pussy contracted and pulsed in a steady relentless beat, and her limbs began the fine trembling that signaled her body was ready to submit to orgasm.

She moaned, placing her hands in the thick, silky strands of his hair and ground against his face. As he licked her and suckled her clit so hard, her back arched sharply away from her chair with every slick press of his tongue.

"Enough!" She barked the words softly, yet his marauding tongue refused to obey. With an expertise that made her bite the inside of her cheek to prevent a scream from releasing, he hollowed out his tongue and shoved it deep into her creaming core.

Chase's eyes flew open as realization dawned on how close she was, how close *he* had been, to making her come.

"Enough, goddamn it." She forcibly stopped her orgasm. Her jaw clenched and tightened as she fought for control. Her fingers dug into his scalp, and she grasped handfuls of his hair, pulling his head from between her thighs.

She stared down at him angrily as he sat crouched between her thighs with the evidence of his oral activities smeared over his face.

His breathing was uneven, and his eyes glittered almost maniacally with a look she'd never seen before. It vanished as quickly as it appeared, too quick for her to catalogue and process its meaning.

"Bring the bag," she bit out the words, licking dry lips. Her breathing was labored and harsh, mimicking his as she fought to bring her body back under control.

She pushed away from her desk, and her chair nearly toppled

with the force. But she ignored it as she strode around the desk. Her eyes quickly moved to the closed door, making sure the lock was in place before she turned back to Javier.

With her eyes narrowed, she waited for him to bring the small, pink bag to her and withdraw the contents.

"I'm sorry," he said, his voice low and husky. His eyes averted from hers in submission as he handed her the dainty beribboned bag.

"Look at me, Javier," she said in a tight, controlled voice.

When he turned around, she placed a long, slender finger beneath his chin, forcing him to look at her as she ran assessing eyes over his flushed, darkly handsome face, searching for a hint of what she thought she'd seen when she pushed him away.

"Look at me," she demanded again, gentling her voice.

For long moments, their gazes locked, his with a slight fear. She knew her gaze was unflinching and cold.

Slowly she moved her finger down his neck, circled the base of his throat with her long fingers, and applied a slight pressure, until he began to cough.

She smiled, knowing he enjoyed the power play as much as she. Once she asserted her dominance, Chase slowly released her hold.

She feathered her fingers down, past his hard, chiseled chest and stopped at the waistband of his slacks. She kept her eyes glued to his as she unfastened his pants, peeling the edges along the zipper aside and yanked them, along with his briefs, down the length of his legs.

After she removed the bag from his tightly clenched hands, she murmured, "Turn around."

His eyes were bright and shining, an anticipatory gleam in

their dark depths as he licked his lips and did as she requested.

He placed both hands on the edge of the large, mahogany desk and lowered his head, braced himself, and waited.

Lifting her skirt, Chase deftly eased her panties down and attached the long, thick dildo to the harness she wore, nestling the base against her clit, snugly, and grasped him by his lean hips.

Separating the hard, muscled cheeks of his ass, she began to feed him her dick. A low growl of satisfaction came from her lips, accompanied by his moaning cries of welcome.

"Hold on, tight. This won't be easy," Chase promised darkly, her breath fanning the fine hairs at the nape of his neck.

She felt a fine tremor run over his body at her hot words of intent.

Without waiting for a response, her fingers tightened on his hips and drove into him in one deep stroke. Her lips pulled back in a feral grin when he gasped, his body arching sharply against the strength of her invasion.

Once the inner muscles of his walls relaxed, allowing her to press into him as far as she could, Chase allowed him no time to become accustomed to her length. Instead she began to move.

Flexing, surging, and plunging, she rolled her hips, plunging deep into his ass. The feel of the artificial dick spanking against her clit stimulated her and aroused her. As she glanced down at their joined bodies, the sight of her dick easing in and out of him as her hips moved against him aroused her even more.

With her legs braced far apart, she removed one hand from his hip and trailed it around to the front of his body, shoving the ends of his shirt aside to grasp his hard, thick rod in her hand.

She feathered her fingers over the turgid length of his shaft and back to his balls, lightly grasping the twin plum-like spheres in her hands. He moaned when she applied a slight pressure, rolling and massaging them in the palm of her hand before her hand dropped away.

She again grasped his cock in hand, circling the base with her thumb and middle finger, and lightly stroked up the length before using the pad of her thumb to swipe across the tiny eye in the center of the bulbous knob, wiping away his sticky pre-cum.

"Taste it," she encouraged.

After placing her thumb in his mouth, he did as she requested, suckling her thumb and making moaning sounds of delight as he licked her finger clean.

She laughed and removed her thumb from his greedy mouth and grasped his lean hips with both hands, fucking him in long strokes to his accompanying mewling cries of pleasure and pain, so interwoven they blended as one melodious cry of rapture.

Chase delivered a sharp, warning slap on the cheeks of his ass.

Immediately his guttural moans were quieted, becoming small whimpering sighs of pleasure even as he pushed back against her invasion.

Her hips moved with precision, surging in and out of him smoothly, the fire inside of her building, growing, with each drag and pull inside his clenching heat. Chase fucked him in sure, easy glides. He cried out, slamming his hips back against her mound, begging her to do him harder, *deeper*.

Yet she kept her strokes, slow, methodical.

She marinated in him in deliberate, slick strokes, ignoring his fervent moans as he accepted—welcomed—her thrusts, the muscled cheeks of his ass flexing and tensing as she rocked into him.

Chase felt so strong, so alive...so in control as she plunged in and out of Javier. The feeling of being buried deep inside of him was an addictive feeling, downright exhilarating.

She bit the lower rim of her lips to the point of pain, her breathing becoming harsher with each roll of her hips against him.

Her head snapped back, and the corded veins in her neck pulsed and throbbed as she felt her hovering orgasm threatening to break. Instead of pushing it away, as she had when he laved between her thighs, she reached for it.

When her orgasm was seconds from spilling over, she reached around his body with her hand. Gently, yet firmly, she cupped his balls, rolling the spheres in her hand until he released a harsh, keening moan.

She grasped his shaft, ran her hands down the length of the steely pipe, in quick, deadly succession, and he broke. His body jerked and spasmed as his cum—thick, white and hot—spewed like a geyser over her hand.

Chase grit her teeth, clenched her eyes tightly shut, and desperately held on to her control even as her orgasm slammed into her. Unable to hold back, the dam broke, and her cum overflowed, weakening her for that brief moment, so that she had to hang on to his hips as she delivered the last of her thrusts into his quaking body.

When it was over, she laid her chest over his heaving back, blanketing his body for that one moment at peace.

"Thank you," he whispered.

His body fully collapsed on the desk, and Chase's fingers

loosened their death grip on his hips as she drew her body away from his.

"Why...why do you...?" he panted, unable to finish the question as he lay spent and useless, his upper body sprawled on top of her desk.

She ignored his question. She knew he loved having her fat dick working his ass as much as she loved giving it to him.

"Ms. Davidson." Chase's eyes narrowed as she listened to her assistant's voice come over the small discreet intercom on her desk. "I'm sorry to interrupt your...lunch."

"What is it, Christine?"

"Your presence has been requested in the boardroom as soon as you're able."

"I'll be right there," she replied, smoothly easing out of Javier.

She reached inside the dainty, pink bag to lift out a premoistened tissue. Carefully she wiped the length of the dildo and tossed the used wipe in the trash bin under her desk before placing the dildo back inside the bag.

She moved away from the prostrate man, deftly removed the harness from her hips, and placed it in one of the drawers of her desk before skimming her hands down the length of her body and tugging her skirt into place.

Turning to look at her reflection in the small, wall-mounted mirror, she quickly pulled out another desk drawer, withdrew her lipstick, and ran the tinted, bulbous end over her lips before placing it back in the drawer.

She rubbed her lips together, then raised her hands to her hair, smoothing away errant strands that had escaped the tight chignon secured at the nape of her neck.

Once satisfied with her appearance, she lifted her leather

carryall, hooked the strap over her shoulder, and walked toward the door.

With her hand on the knob, she turned back around. Javier had gotten up from his prone position and was fumbling with his slacks.

"Don't ever forget who's in control. If you do that again, I won't go so easy on you the next time," she said, letting him know that she was aware of his transgression. Had she not stopped him, he would have brought her to orgasm.

Even from the distance she was from him, she could see his olive-tinted face blanch and a fine tremor course over his body in response to her threat.

With a smile of satisfaction, she turned and left.

CHAPTER 2

"Have a seat, Chastity." William Buford stood when Chastity entered the boardroom. A wide smile creased his fleshy, rosy face as he motioned for Chase to take a seat.

William Buford was one of three senior managers in the marketing firm of Manhattan Buford, and his being in attendance at the meeting definitely alerted Chastity that indeed, she would be joining the ranks of senior managers.

"Thank you, sir," she replied, her confidence soaring. Not only was William Buford in the room, but the other two senior managers were in attendance as well, reconfirming that she was minutes away from being offered the president of marketing position.

After she sat down and accepted the glass of ice water from a waiting attendant, Chastity glanced around the room. She returned the smiles of Lance Buford and Emily Manhattan, both of whom held key positions at Manhattan Buford.

"I'd like to begin by congratulating you on landing the Stratham deal. It was truly a coup for you and the firm. Well done," William Buford continued.

"Thank you, sir. I'm very pleased with the results as well," she replied, feeling proud of not only what she had accomplished but that she'd done so after several others in her department had failed to acquire the account.

"Yes, well, you should be!" Lance chimed in. "In fact, you've been watched carefully, these last few weeks, by not only the partners but also Mr. Baptiste."

Daemon Baptiste was the man who owned controlling shares in Manhattan Buford. Chase, as well as all of the upper management to most of the secretarial pool, knew of him.

Although he'd never been seen in the Dallas, New York, and California offices of Manhattan Buford, he was the driving force behind Manhattan Buford.

He owned controlling stock and held the position of CEO of the firm, yet no one besides the partners knew much about him. Gossip floated around the office—that he was a hardnosed businessman, one of the richest men in the country, and also one of the most reclusive.

Few images of him were seen publicly, and the available ones were profiles or from a distance. Upon learning about him, Chase had been mildly curious and had sought to find out more about him. No personal information could be found. She found only the bare facts, reports in financial documents, and legal transactions.

What she did know was that Baptiste was a billionaire tycoon who acquired failing businesses, invested money and new management, spearheading the turnaround until the business was not only solvent but also immensely profitable. He then turned around and sold it off to the highest bidder in multi-million, even billion-dollar, deals.

Several years ago, when Manhattan Buford had been in jeopardy of going bankrupt, Baptiste bought the company and within a year, had revitalized it, even taking it beyond its previous levels of success.

However, instead of selling, he'd held on for reasons no one knew. He left the daily operations with the original partners; however, his unseen presence was felt.

"Wow, now *I'm* impressed." Chase brought the crystal goblet to her mouth and took a sip of water, hiding the satisfied smile that hovered around her lips.

As the cold liquid eased down her throat, she fought back the giddy feeling of triumph that threatened to make her lose control. But it was all she could do not to jump up from her chair and turn a series of undignified, joyful cartwheels straight down the middle of the expensive, beautiful mahogany table.

Yes, the position was hers. She knew it.

And the fact that Baptiste knew of her was simply icing on the cake.

"However, before we go into all of that, we have to wait for Mr. Serrano," William finished, catching Chase completely off guard and making her smile slip.

"Mr. Serrano? I'm afraid I don't understand." She carefully placed the goblet on the table, turning questioning eyes to the managers.

"Well—"

The door opened at that moment, interrupting whatever William had been planning to say.

Chastity's eyes narrowed slightly, and a sense of foreboding struck her when the assistant brought Javier into the room and quietly exited.

"I'm sorry I was late, gentlemen…Ms. Davidson." First, he gave his shit-eating, groveling smile to the partners before turning his smile to Chase and slyly giving her a wink, one that no one saw but her.

The sense of foreboding increased, and she watched his narrow ass sit down in the offered seat after fastidiously brushing away imaginary wrinkles from the 800-dollar, charcoal-gray Armani suit she'd gifted him last week. For work well done.

Chase continued to watch him as he straightened the cuffs of his shirt. The overhead light hit the shining, fourteen-carat gold-and-diamond encrusted links—the same ones she gave him for Valentine's Day—so that they seemed to wink at her much as he had, mocking her.

"Well, let's get this started, shall we, gentlemen...Chastity?" William Buford glanced around the table and once he was assured all eyes were on him, began to speak.

"Chastity, again, we want to congratulate you on the deal. Amazing job, well done. Absolutely amazing! We've been trying to get the Stratham business for over two years. You step in and seal the deal in less than two months. Brilliant!" He rubbed his large, beefy hands together. A smile of pure greed spread across his fleshy lips, splitting his lips so wide his canine teeth were exposed, giving his features an uncomplimentary, wolfish appearance.

"Yes, well, I did work hard for it. In fact—" Her words were cut off when Javier broke in.

"Yes, she did. To see her in action, see how she worked it, how she so cunningly manipulated them, worked on their emotions, found their weakness, exploited them...in a good way of course, was *truly* amazing," he said with a laugh. The board members laughed along with him.

Chastity grit her teeth as her heartbeat slammed against her chest. The son-of-a-bitch was making her seem like some damn piranha as though she were nothing more than a cutthroat shark.

"Well, I wouldn't quite put it like that," she said, cutting in.

"I'm sorry! I didn't mean it in a bad way! Not at all! I've learned so much…being under your tutelage, Ms. Davidson," he replied, turning his attention toward her, the expression on his face guileless as though butter wouldn't melt in his conniving mouth.

She nodded her head shortly and gave him a tight smile, while clamping down on the impeding feeling of disaster looming.

"Yes, it definitely shows how well you've learned under Ms. Davidson's mentorship, Javier," Maurice's booming, jovial voice cut in. The feeling of doom amplified when he called Javier by his first name.

"Which is why, in great part, Javier owes you a great deal of gratitude."

Chase cocked her head to the side, raising a brow in question, although she already knew, deep inside, exactly what William Buford meant.

She *damn* well already knew.

"As you know, Maurice Hines recently left Manhattan Buford, and with his departure, the position of president of marketing opened."

Chastity glanced around the room of smiling executives; a scream of denial lodged tightly in her throat.

She listened with distant awareness as they ran down Javier's qualifications—an MBA from Harvard with an emphasis in management, graduating at the top of his class along with his brief tenure working at Manhattan Buford where he'd been promoted due to long hours and his talent.

The same qualifications that she possessed and more.

"Although he's been with us a short time, we believe that Javier has what it takes to take over the position; his leadership and education are above reproach. He—"

"That position is mine." Chase broke into William Buford's spiel not wanting to hear another word of his detailed outline of Javier's qualifications.

William stopped, and all eyes turned to Chastity. She saw a mocking glint spark in Javier's dark gaze as he too looked at her.

"Excuse me, Ms. Davidson?"

"With no disrespect intended, sir...That position should be mine."

"Yes, well..." He stopped, and, for a moment, Chase felt a sharp sense of triumph as he floundered, trying to find the right words to say. "Yes, Ms. Davidson, you are very qualified for the position as well. You've proven how—"

"Then why? And why wasn't I told that Javier was in the running for this?" Her question was sharp, to the point, the muscles in her face sore from the tight control she was keeping on herself.

"It wasn't an easy decision, Chastity. But we feel it's the best one," William replied, almost gently. She gazed angrily at him, hating the look of pity she saw in his watery blue eyes.

"Then why?" She could not look at Javier. To do so would make her falter and lose what little control she desperately held on her emotions.

"To be honest, Javier has what we're particularly looking for, for this position."

"Chase, look, you know how much we've wanted to get a foot

in the Latin market. Javier recently has met Roberto Chavez," he said, mentioning the name of a key player in a successful Hispanic-owned and operated advertising agency whose projects included national commercial print and media ads. "With his courting, they are now considering working with us—"

"*Considering*?"

"Yes. Nothing is confirmed. As I said, we feel confident that Javier will be able to bring us the account." A deep red flushed the man's cheeks, and when he couldn't look directly at Chastity, she turned to stare at Javier before turning back to face Buford.

"What the hell is this about? And don't give me that bullshit line that Javier 'has what it takes' to run the position," she said his name with disdain, jerking a thumb in his direction. "That's a line of crap and we all know that. I worked all day, every day, never took one damn day of vacation time, working long nights, then took work home on weekends...making sure the work was done, and done correctly. No matter *who* the hell took off, I was there, working my ass off! I've just landed...not 'considering'...*landed*...a multi-million dollar account and you have the audacity to tell me this shit?"

The room was silent after her outburst. The proverbial pen could have dropped and all would have heard it. No one said a word, the tension in the room so palpable and thick it felt like a noose around her neck.

"We have another position for you, Chastity. One which we feel you will see the merits of, given time—" William Buford was the first to speak.

"And what would that be?"

There was an ominous moment of silence, and Chase watched them exchange nervous-looking glances. There was a wealth of communication in their silent conversation, one that confused her as much as angered her.

"Mr. Baptiste wants you to work with him."

"What?"

"As his assistant."

"*His assistant*?" Chase narrowed her eyes, spearing them with her glance. She carefully took note of the nervous way William played with the tip of his gold-covered fountain pen, and the way Emily Manhattan avoided her eyes. "So, you're telling me, I'm being *demoted?*"

"No! Not at all, please, Ms. Davidson, listen—"

"This is utter and complete bullshit."

"I'm sorry that you feel that way, Chastity. You are a valuable member of this team."

"If I'm so valuable, why am I being demoted to assistant, William? Tell me that!"

"I'm not at liberty to discuss that with you, at this time. Mr. Baptiste himself will be in contact with you—"

"I don't think so. You can tell Mr. Baptiste he can damn well find himself another lackey. I quit."

There was silence in the room, for long minutes. Chastity turned her head away, and fought back the burn of tears she felt threatening to fall, until she heard the scrape of chairs easing against the plush carpeting, indicating the men were leaving the table.

And that was it. No asking her to reconsider, no negotiating, nothing.

One by one, they left the room. Chastity kept her face averted until she heard the sound of the door opening and closing. When she thought they were all gone, she turned back around, and came face to face with Javier.

He smiled and leaned down, whispering in her ear, "Who got screwed now, bitch?"

She clenched her jaw and said nothing. She simply watched him turn around and saunter toward the door before he left the room.

One lone tear escaped, unnoticed, and trailed down Chastity's cheek.

CHAPTER 3

"Hey lady, what's going on? I ain't seen you in a while."

Chase walked into the dark, deserted bar and offered a smile to the man who stood behind the bar wiping down the counter with another towel.

"Not a whole lot, Mickey. What about you?" she asked as she walked inside, stopping when she reached the bar.

She pulled out one of the high bar stools and climbed onto the seat, placing her bag and laptop on the empty stool beside her.

"Can't complain. Wife is out visiting her mama, got the place to myself for a change," he answered, grinning widely and exposing a shining set of pearly-white dentures that glistened starkly against his charcoal-colored skin.

"Yeah, and what are you going to do with all that freedom?" she asked and nodded her head when he put a glass of whiskey in front of her.

"Hmmm. Don't know. Maybe I'll have that orgy I been thinkin' about," he replied and winked.

Chase offered a small smile in return and swirled the shot glass around, the amber-colored liquid swirling around the small chunks of tinkling ice.

"You gonna play with that or actually drink it?" the old man asked in a hoarse voice, thanks to years of smoking and hard drinking.

She lifted the glass to her lips, drank it in one swallow, and shut her eyes as the alcohol burned and slid down her throat.

After she placed the empty glass down, she raised her eyes and caught Mickey staring at her. A thoughtful expression lined his face.

"Fucked-up day at the office?" he asked, nodding his head toward the empty glass, silently asking if she wanted another.

She shook her head "no" to the refill.

"That's putting it mildly." Her laugh rang hollow even to her own ears.

"Wanna talk about it? I've been told I'm a good listener."

Chase sighed and shook her head, still stunned at the turn of events over the last few hours.

"Have you ever had your dreams snatched from you, Mickey? Have you ever been this close?" she asked, putting up two fingers indicating the length span of an inch. "This close to being number one? And just when the prize is within range, after years of building to that moment, it vanishes. Poof. And you're left freefalling, adrift, and no idea how the fuck it happened?" Chase laughed a harsh-sounding laugh, shaking her head. "Well, that's about how I feel right now. All I wanted to be is number one…is that asking too much?" Although she voiced the question to Mickey, she knew he didn't know the answer to the question, and was speaking to herself more than him.

"Sorry. Yeah…it's been one of those kind of days," she finished. "Look, I'd better go." She glanced up at him as she spoke. The forced smile that she had put on began to slide off her face when she noticed the intent way he was looking at her.

"Hey, why don't you stick around a bit more? Like I said, I'm a good listener," he offered, again, a look of worry creasing his wide forehead.

"No." She wrinkled her nose. "I'm sure you are. I think I've opened up more than enough for one day. But thanks for the offer." She smiled.

He opened his mouth to speak, but promptly closed it. "Why don't you let me make you another drink, one of my specialties? Cures the blues...I even heard it can cure the common cold." He laughed hoarsely.

"Does all that, huh?" She raised a brow. "No, but do you have anything good in the back? Something I can take home with me?"

The surprised look on his face almost made her laugh.

She rarely drank besides an occasional social glass and in the two years she'd known Mickey, he'd never seen her drink more than a shot or two at the most.

"Like I said...It's been a real bitch of a day."

He cocked his head to the side, as though considering something.

"I got just the thing for you. I ordered a few boxes of some real fancy shit last week for some rich guy giving a party: 2001 Cabernet Sauvignon—it just came in. He won't know the difference if I take out a bottle or two."

"For a price, right?"

"You know it, Boo." He laughed, winking at her. His rotund, stout body ambled away toward the back and moments later he returned with a bottle of the wine, offering it to her for her inspection.

"Hmmm. Nice," she murmured, taking the bottle from his

hand and cradling it in her hand, the bottle neck nestled in her palm; the base, cool...soothing...against her inner arm.

"What do I owe you?" she asked, jumping from the barstool and grabbing her things from the stool beside her.

"It's on the house."

"Come on, what do I owe you, Mickey?" She raised incredulous eyes toward him.

"Take it and go before I change my mind." He winked, and with a grin, she thanked him and turned to leave.

She was on her way out of the door when Mickey's voice stopped her.

"You know, being number one can come with a high price. Some would say a harsh price. Are you ready to pay that price, Chase?"

She stared at the door, considering his question. "I've been ready for a long time, Mickey," she answered without turning around.

CHAPTER 4

"What good are you? Can't even fucking tie your goddamn shoe! Come here!"

Chastity's small frame was hauled close to her mother by her collar. With angry, precise movements, her mother tied her shoe, pulling the laces so tightly they dug into the top of her foot. When she was finished, Maybelle shoved her away, and Chastity stumbled, nearly falling.

But, she caught herself, fought for balance, knowing that if she were to fall her mother's anger would escalate.

She controlled her balance as well as the tears burning the back of her throat as she looked at her mother's angry face. Despite her dark complexion, the blush of anger was visible on her jet-black skin.

"You ain't no damn good. Just like *him*," the angry woman muttered, her features tight, her eyes filled with an ugly hatred. The nostrils of her large nose flared in her utter disgust of the small girl.

Chastity carefully avoided her mother's direct stare, casting her eyes aside, staring down at the toe of her scuffed, second-hand sneakers. She was confused and unsure of what she'd done to anger her mother this time.

At the age of seven, Chastity had learned to dare not question her mother. She'd learned to take the insults, the scorn, the smacks, the punches, and the hits all in stride.

She'd also learned to hold herself very still, not look directly into her mother's eyes, and refrain from angering her mother more. The added tears or stupid questions asking what she'd done to make Momma mad, the more likely she was not to get a beating.

The more likely her mother was to just insult her until she grew tired and leave Chastity alone in her room.

She felt Momma's malevolent glare, and her body trembled as it always did.

So afraid.

Her mother was a frightening woman, just one look from her, and Chastity wanted to run and hide. Maybelle was so big, so tall, and so scary when she was angry.

Chastity glanced down at herself, hating how small *she* was, much smaller than the other children in her second-grade class. Her teacher, Ms. Mosley, had told her today that she was so cute and tiny, that she looked like she belonged in pre-school.

Chastity had looked at the woman, without a smile on her small face, and told Ms. Mosley that she wasn't a child.

A strange expression had settled across the woman's pretty face as she stared down at the little girl. Her eyes moved over Chastity's face, her exposed, deep brown-colored, skinny arms with a multitude of healing purplish bruises, down her slight body and legs so skinny the white knee socks she wore bagged helplessly around her little ankles, and the woman's eyes misted.

She remembered how sad she'd felt for Ms. Mosley, feeling bad that she'd somehow made her cry.

Chastity had sought to console her, placing a frail arm around the woman's waist.

The hug Ms. Mosley had given her in return had been the first time anyone had hugged her in her life that she could remember.

It felt good. Warm. Strange, yet…good.

"Are you listening to me, girl? You ain't no damn good!"

Chastity felt her mother's warm, pungent, sour breath fan the hair on the side of her neck as Maybelle leaned down to whisper the ugly words against her ear.

Nodding her head up and down in assent, Chastity immediately spoke when her mother cuffed her face with a closed fist, reminding her that she was to verbally acknowledge to her mother that she was pitiful. That she was less than.

"Yes, ma'am," she spoke, her voice barely above a whisper, and stopped, clearing her throat. "Yes, ma'am, I know."

※▶◎◀※

Chase woke with a start, her heart thudding an erratic beat against her chest. She came to full wakefulness out of a series of vivid dreams, a kaleidoscope of times gone by, times where she was hopeless and afraid.

A time she did her damnedest to never consciously re-visit during her lucid moments. Yet a time that she'd never been able to shake in her dreams.

Her head pounded with pain. She glanced over, barely able to make out the empty wine bottle on her dresser.

"I guess drinking a bottle of wine will do that for you," she mumbled.

In the dark room, the light shafting in through the slates of the wide, wooden blinds on her bedroom's single bay window cast the room in shadows. Shadows that came to blazing life on her wall, grouping and forming lifeless bodies that all seemed to be glaring at her, mocking her with their shadowy, wicked grins.

"Damn," she mumbled, her chest rising and falling heavily.

She untangled the black satin sheets twined around her body, shoved them to the side, and inhaled a deep, calming breath.

After her racing heart had resumed a semblance of normalcy, she reached over and flipped on the dainty bedside lamp on her small, Chippendale nightstand. When the soft light filled her dark bedroom, banishing the shadows, she rested her body against the padded leather headboard.

Before she left the office, after giving her resignation, Chase had gone into her office, walked past her assistant, with her face carefully devoid of any emotion, and told her she was no longer with Manhattan Buford. She had then gone inside, closed the door, and methodically gone through every one of her files.

She removed both paper files and backed up on disc those from her computer before wiping it clean from clients she'd worked with, clients she damn well had every intent of taking with her, wherever that may be.

Then she removed the few personal items in the office, placing them all neatly in her Nike gym bag, and left the office without a backward glance at her astonished assistant.

As soon as she got home from Mickey's, she kicked off her heels, removed her jacket, and tossed it and her leather case on the butcher-block table in the center of the spacious kitchen. She'd quickly stripped down and put on an old pair of running shorts, ripped T-shirt, and her favorite pair of running shoes. Then she took off, running.

She'd had no direction in mind, and to that end, she had simply taken off at a fast clip, running through her small neighborhood. Past the familiar running path she normally took, Chase ran deep into the dense, bushy non-developed area. As she ran, limbs slapped against her legs, the sharp sting going unnoticed as her feet pounded against the dirt and grass, and her long legs carried her across the pavement.

She ran fast and hard, ran until she couldn't run anymore. With her body aching, with every muscle in her body screaming in pain, quivering and shaking, she turned around and slowly jogged the long way back home.

It was late when she got back. Without lights she navigated through her condo and up to her bedroom. The blinking light on the small phone indicated that she had a message. After she stripped out of her clothes, she hit the replay button.

"Did you get it?"

Maybelle did not ask anything else. No greeting, nothing... just those four words.

Yet, those four words, accompanied by the one who asked, made her gut clench, and her hands formed tight fists, her short nails digging small crescent moons into the palms of her hand.

She took the opened bottle of wine Mickey had given her, stripped out of her sweat-drenched clothes and padded naked to the bathroom that joined her bedroom. She lifted the bottle of wine and placed the rim to her lips and drank from it deeply, the spicy, poignant liquid soothing and relaxing her even as it slid down her throat. She finished the bottle, and wearily she had fallen asleep within minutes. And now, here she was awake, restless. And jobless.

"What am I going to do now?" she murmured, turning her head to the small alarm clock with its bright red numbers flashing, and blew out a breath.

Three thirty-five a.m.

Leaning over to the side table, she lifted her glasses, placed them on her nose, and removed her razor-thin laptop from the small stand. Sitting back, she unlatched it and powered up.

"May as well start seeing what's out there, headache or no headache," she said, continuing her one-sided conversation. As secure as she'd been at Manhattan Buford, she always kept her ears opened for what was going on in other firms.

"Not that I thought for one goddamn minute, I'd be in the position I'm in now," she, replied—disgust, anger and a keen sense of betrayal jockeying for position of prominence in her emotions.

Images of her and Javier locked together, his moans and cries of pleasure as she fucked him still ringing in her ears, warred with images of him sitting in the boardroom, a self-satisfied smirk on his handsome face as they named him president of marketing, as he stole her position...her dreams...all of it flashed through her mind's eye.

"The sneaky little son-of-a-bitch." As she bit the words out, she felt her body tense, the muscles in her arms and hands bunch and knot.

She looked down at her hands, balled into fists, and forced her fingers to relax, her hand to open and release the death grip she had on the edges of her laptop.

She shook her head in an attempt to rid her mind of the images, banishing them to the shadow realm, the same place she forced her dreams to go.

She turned her attention to the screen in front of her when she realized her email had turned on when she powered up, a small ding letting her know she had mail. She was seconds from closing down her email server so she could work, when a small envelope appeared with the words *The Invitation* in the subject line.

Something about the simple one-word subject strangely appealed to her.

Despite the thought that it was some bullshit spam email asking her if she was satisfied with the size of her dick, she clicked on the small icon before it could disappear.

The body of the email held a cream-colored envelope, so real looking, so soft in appearance, it appeared as though if she touched the screen, she'd be able to feel the smooth, crisp linen caress her fingers.

Her eyes widened slightly when the envelope became animated, unfurling to reveal a note inside.

The script was one she hadn't seen before, bold, yet feminine in appearance at the same time. Narrowing her eyes she read the contents.

The Invitation…

You are cordially invited to The Island, a place where your strongest desires come to blazing life with just one wish. At The Island, we cater to your most self-indulgent fantasy…where you are number one.

This invitation is given only to a select few, and you've been chosen. Should you choose to accept this invitation, you agree that you are succumbing to your desires, that you are freeing yourself to experience something you've never dared to succumb to. And in doing so, your desire to be number one will manifest deliciously so…

"And the day came when the risk to remain tight in a bud was more painful than the risk it took to blossom."

This invitation will expire in twenty-four hours, Chastity. You can

contact us at 800-555-9860 to experience the fantasy of a lifetime.
We're waiting for your call.

"What kind of scam is this?" Chastity murmured, yet felt shaken after she re-read a line in the invitation.

A place where your strongest desires come to blazing life with just one wish...

Her heart began to race, a dizzy feeling swamping over her as she scanned the invitation once more.

Unknowingly she said aloud the phone number in the corner of the invitation, "8005559860." Surprised, she saw it reanimate, refolding in on itself. It became in appearance the unopened envelope, the ends sealing, and again showing only the red embossed seal with an impression of a flower stamped within.

"Wait..." she cried out, frantically, reaching a hand out as though to physically force the envelope to reopen.

Immediately, she felt heat invade her naked thighs where her computer set on her lap. Hissing, she shoved it off her legs and onto the bed beside her.

"Damn!" she grunted, when the laptop toppled off the bed and onto the floor.

Scrambling off the bed she quickly retrieved it, in time to see the animated card twirl, spinning as though it were a kid's spin toy before it disappeared with a zip.

"No!" she cried out, "800-555-9860, 800-555-9860, 800-555-9860." She chanted the number over and over as she yanked the drawer open on her nightstand and frantically searched for something to write the number down on.

She breathed a sigh of relief when she found a pen and pad, and quickly scribbled the number down.

With her heart racing, her lips partially opened as she blew out a gush of air, she sat back and stared at the number.

She turned her head, looking at her cell phone on the nightstand before glancing out of the bedroom window.

It wasn't even dawn.

No way in hell would someone be there to take her call from the travel agency.

Yet, she knew deep down, this was no ordinary travel agency. And she'd bet her considerable severance pay, it wasn't a typical getaway.

She reached for her cell and punched in the number.

A deep voice with no discernible accent answered, "How may I help you, Ms. Davidson?"

Her stomach clenched.

No, this was definitely something out of the ordinary.

Just what I needed, Chase thought.

CHAPTER 5

Chase flew into the Honolulu airport, and a uniformed man with a sign with her name on it greeted her. He escorted her, one hand solicitously under her elbow, to the waiting charter plane that would take her to her final destination.

Now seated, she glanced at the small group of travelers.

Besides her, there were two other women, the pilot, and one attendant. She had expected there would be more.

Chase thought back over her conversation with the man. After she'd gotten over the shock of her impulsiveness by calling the agency, she had been surprised at how the smooth-voiced man had processed her information as though her early morning call was nothing out of the ordinary.

Although he answered all of her questions, a detailed accounting of her travel plans along with a promise to e-mail the information immediately to her, it hadn't been until Chase had gotten off the phone that she'd realized many of his answers had been vague when she asked about specifics regarding certain aspects of the trip.

He informed her that the resort was exclusive, one that wasn't publicly advertised, yet very high end. When she asked how he'd gotten her name, her information, why her…he smoothly told her that a friend had been her benefactor.

"Benefactor?" she questioned.

If the resort was as high end as he said, Chase wondered which "friend" of hers would do something like that for her. She *had* no friends. Definitely not one who had the means or inclination to be her benefactor. "'Benefactor' in that you must be recommended before you can attend the resort, Ms. Davidson. You are responsible for the fee…and everything included, should you choose to accept the invitation."

He told her the fee, and she blanched at the price. For that amount, she could buy a small resort of her own.

"As I said, if you choose to accept the invitation—"

"I do," she cut in, impulsively making the decision.

She heard the smile in his voice as he continued, finishing the transaction and notifying her that she needed to be ready to go in the next twenty-four hours. She would receive everything she needed in the next thirty minutes, instructions as well as her flight itinerary, at that time.

Once she was off the phone, it hit her that not only had she agreed to everything, she hadn't bothered to ask how he knew she would be available to leave that soon. The entire conversation left her in a bemused state.

"Had to be Mickey," Chastity murmured aloud.

As soon as I return, I'm making a beeline for the bar. I have a few questions for Mickey, Chase thought, settling deeper into the comfortable, leather plane seat.

As the plane headed toward the small, private island of Ka-le'a, she glanced out of the window, staring down at the bright blue water and the cluster of islands. It was a breathtaking view.

Ka-le'a was owned and operated by someone by the name of Merrick. It was the only information she'd been able to find out about the island. Chase had no idea if it was owned by some large corporation, or one owner, or if the owner was male or female. The agent hadn't given her any more information about ownership besides giving her the name Merrick.

What he did tell her was that the island was bought several years ago from the Hawaiian government after years of being vacant. The owner or owners had then transformed the deserted island into a closed resort, exclusively available only to those invited.

For Chase, the fact that it was so exclusive that one had to be invited added a certain appeal.

She turned and glanced at the other two women on the plane, running assessing eyes over the one seated in front of her.

The woman was a prima donna of the first order, from the crown of her shining, straight, dark blonde hair, to the tip of her powder-pink polished toes which peeked out from the metallic-silver, strappy Jimmy Choo sandals.

She was a strangely beautiful, exotic contrast. Her skin, the color of brushed copper, looked just as silky and as soft. Her features were boldly African: large, prominent nose; full, sensual lips; and high cheekbones. Her eyes, an unusual shade of green, were startling in their intensity.

She was the last to enter the plane, arriving at least an hour after the scheduled takeoff, escorted by two large muscle-laden men who strangely complemented her unique appearance: one very Nordic-looking man with long thick blond hair that fell to the middle of his broad shoulders; and the other, equally opposing looking, a fiercely handsome African-American man.

When the woman had been told the men couldn't join her on the plane, she'd angrily fought it, demanding to speak to the pilot. After several exhausting, drama-filled minutes, she relented and, with tears streaming down her face, hugged both men tightly in farewell.

Chase had watched the display with open astonishment.

And with a certain amount of unconscious jealousy as she observed how the two men had seemed to treat the tall woman as though she were a fragile, porcelain doll, escorting her onto the plane, demanding to do so, and reluctantly leaving the weeping woman behind.

"Must be rough," Chase mumbled.

"Excuse me?"

"Nothing." She shook her head when the woman sitting closest to her turned large blue, inquisitive eyes her way.

"Oh, sorry," the woman mumbled, taking a final bite of the éclair she'd been eating. She delicately dusted her powdery fingers on a napkin, her glance falling away from Chase.

Chase watched as "Blue Eyes" fiddled with the handle of her purse, placing it in her lap as she opened it and peered inside. Over and over, she opened and closed the purse, moving the items inside its deep cavernous insides as though searching for something, only to re-close it, and do the same thing again.

And again.

Her strange behavior was beginning to irritate Chase. Chase resisted the urge to reach over and snatch the bag away from her small, pale fingers.

Unlike the obviously rich and exotic beauty in the front seat, this one didn't look as though she could afford to take a trip to the grocery store, much less afford the exclusive resort.

She was pretty in a typical "girl next door" type of way. Long, wavy, blonde hair; overly large blue eyes; a small pink mouth shaped in a bow.

She wore a cheap, two-piece beige suit, complete with pantyhose and bland slip-on pumps, all of which had probably come from a discount retail shop. As Chase's critical gaze ran back up the woman's body, their gazes locked.

The woman bit the bottom rim of her lip as she gaped at Chase.

Purposely, Chase grinned, lowered her lids, and stared at the woman's mouth. She kept her gaze steady on the woman; her desire to fluster the fidgeting woman increased the longer the woman stared at her in open fascination.

Obviously unnerved by the attention, the purse slipped from the woman's grasp and fell to the floor. Chase reached over to retrieve it at the same time that the woman did.

Their heads lightly bumped. Chase boldly licked away the chocolate frosting in the corner of the woman's cupid bow-shaped mouth before she could move away. She held back a laugh when the pale woman's eyes widened comically so. She jumped away, grabbed her purse and held it tightly against her chest.

"You had a bit of icing on your mouth," Chase murmured, her grin widening at the look of fear...and interest...that gleamed in the woman's light-blue gaze.

Bored and more than ready to begin her vacation, Chastity turned away from the woman, and within moments, the tepid blonde was forgotten as her thoughts went to the adventure ahead of her.

Watching the water below, a soothing and comforting feeling enveloped Chase, and a strange sense of euphoria washed over her. She closed her eyes, allowing her mind and body to relax for a moment, the first she'd done in a long time. Within minutes, she was asleep.

"Ms. Davidson, we've landed."

Chase's eyes flew open and she jerked upward, instantly disoriented.

"Wha—what?" she stuttered, staring into the face of the smiling flight attendant.

She straightened her body and fumbled with the clasp of her seatbelt, her face flushing when she realized that she'd fallen asleep.

"The water has that effect on a lot of our travelers—particularly our travelers who have a lot on their minds," the woman replied with a glint of understanding in her eyes.

Chase gave the woman a tight smile in return, neither wanting nor needing her sympathy.

As she gathered her things, she noted that her traveling companions had obviously already de-boarded the plane. Quickly, she grabbed the small carry-on that she'd stashed beneath her seat and stood.

She withdrew her sunglasses from her purse and placed the oversized shades on her face. She strode down the aisle, anticipation and excitement churning in her stomach as she thought of the adventure ahead of her.

As soon as she took the last steps off the plane, she glanced in front of her and saw a long, welcoming line, littered with beautiful women wearing typical Hawaiian apparel of two-piece colorful swimsuits exposing taut, golden skin, wide smiles on their golden-brown faces, and colorful leis in their hands as they waited to welcome her.

At the front of the line, a tall man dressed in all white—slacks, jacket and shirt—was watching her, waiting for her to approach as well. At his side, a woman similarly dressed in all white stood.

He held out a hand as she approached, and she stuck her hand out to shake it. He immediately took her hand and softly kissed her palm, sending electric static through her body. Chase felt her nipples bead against the silk blouse she wore. She quickly withdrew her hand, unnerved by her body's strange reaction.

"Welcome to the Island, Ms. Davidson. We've been eagerly waiting your arrival," he spoke in a low voice, one that she instantly recognized.

"You're the one I spoke with…the one who set up my arrangements," she stated, rather than asked, confident that he and the travel agent were one in the same.

He inclined his head in a slight acknowledgment. His fathomless, dark-brown eyes gave nothing away.

Chase ran her eyes over him. At her height of five feet nine, coupled with the three-inch heels she traditionally wore, she was used to being taller than—or at least as tall as—most men. Not so with this one.

He stood a full head taller than her. If Chase had to guess an age, she'd place him in his mid-to-late fifties, mainly because of the steely gray hair covering his head. Yet, no wrinkles lined his distinguished-looking face, and Chase couldn't detect an ounce of discernible flab on his fit-looking body.

"Welcome to Ka-le'a, Ms. Davidson." The petite woman dressed in white at his side moved as though to place the lei in her hands around Chase's neck.

Chase withdrew, not allowing the woman to do so. The man turned his head toward the woman and shook his head slightly. Without a word, the woman's hands dropped to her sides.

"My name is Merrick. If you need anything throughout your stay, please do not hesitate to ask. If you're ready, please allow one of my assistants to escort you to your lodgings," he said, motioning for one of the few male attendants to come forward.

The mention of his name made Chase turn to him in surprise. This was not only the one she'd called, the one who'd set up her arrangements, but he was also the owner of the island.

"Thank you, Mr. Merrick. And yes, I think I am ready."

A smile stretched across her face as she allowed the handsome waiting attendant to take her bags and gallantly grasp her beneath the elbow and lead her away to a waiting small topless, white Jeep. He stored her bags in the back and opened her door for her before jogging to the driver's side and hopping inside.

Chase sat back with a sigh of contentment, enjoying the late afternoon breeze that gently blew over her and listening with half-hearted attention to the guide's commentary about the island.

It was an idyllic scene, one that could be taken straight out of a movie. The palms on the large trees were lazily fluttering, and the air was thick with nature's perfume of wildly growing hibiscuses that grew alongside the road.

As her thoughts turned inward, her guide continued to drive slowly along the empty roadway, pointing out the flowers and plants indigenous to the island.

I could get used to this, Chase thought. *No worries, no fighting to get to the top, no disappointment over missed opportunities, no wondering what to do next...*She determinedly chased the thoughts away.

No, now was not the time to think about any of that. She planned on enjoying her time here to the fullest and eagerly anticipated what the island had in store for her.

"We're here." The guide interrupted her thoughts.

He came to a smooth halt in front of a quaint, sloped-roof cottage, positioned yards away from the road and nestled between tall palms, a scattering of cylinder-shaped papaya trees, and an abundance of floral bushes and low shrubbery.

Chase stared out at the cottage—eager and apprehensive at the same time. Yet she controlled her excitement, taking deep breaths of air, and remained seated as the guide went around the back of the Jeep and removed her luggage, keeping her gaze on the quaint cottage and lush foliage surrounding it.

After he'd gathered her things and opened the door for her, she allowed him to escort her the short distance to the cottage.

Once he'd unlocked the door, he stepped back and allowed her to enter in front of him into the dark, cool interior.

She walked inside, her eyes taking in the simple yet elegant furnishings in the cottage. The cottage was divided into sections by floor-to-ceiling wood beams. The largest area was the living area, where plush sofas and overstuffed chairs dominated the room, along with ceramic-potted ferns placed on low stands.

"I'll put your bags away," the guide said and disappeared into another sectioned-off area, which Chase assumed was the bedroom.

She walked toward the kitchen, her eyes glancing over the small, efficient room before walking toward a closed patio door.

She opened the doors and walked out into the balcony, smiling when she noted the long stretch of beach visible from where she stood, its pristine whiteness gleaming against the late afternoon sun.

"There is a welcome luau scheduled in the next hour. I can return to pick you up. If you would like to attend, simply dial zero on your phone." Chase turned when the guide spoke directly behind her.

"Thank you—wait," she said when he smiled and turned to go. She opened her purse, searching for money to tip him.

He brought a hand up, stalling her. "No, please…That won't be necessary, Ms. Davidson!" A horrified expression crossed his darkly handsome face, as though she'd committed an act of treason. "I am here to serve *you*. There is no need for recompense."

Chase's hands dropped from her purse, and she carefully placed the bag back on the butcher-block counter. "I'm sorry, I just thought—"

"No, it's no problem. As I said, I'm here to serve you. We all are," he murmured, his dark slumberous eyes raking over her body making her feel naked and exposed. The same feeling she'd gotten, the same prickling heat she'd felt when Merrick had kissed her palm.

"Do you need anything else from me, right now?" he asked in such a way that Chase felt her body respond with a primal inner shout of "yes"…

"No, I think that will be all. Thank you," she replied, instead.

After he left her alone, she exhaled her pent-up breath in one long puff.

She withdrew the long pins holding her hair in the tight chignon, throwing the pins on the table before striding from the room. A long, cool shower was in order.

CHAPTER 6

Her body glistened rosily after the long scrubbing she gave it.

The water from the powerful multi-head shower pounded over Chastity's skin, stimulating her as she luxuriated in the large glassed-in shower. She lathered the sweet-smelling soap over her hair as she scrubbed her body until she felt as though she'd scrubbed every last negative thing away.

Although the water hadn't cooled in the thirty minutes she'd allowed the powerful jetting water to sluice over her skin, she reluctantly turned off the tri-head showerhead, opened the glass door, and reached for the soft, thick, cream-colored robe from a nearby hook and wrapped herself within its warm embrace.

The porcelain floor was cool against her feet as she padded over to the vanity. Chastity peered at herself critically in the gold framed mirror that wrapped around the length of the bathroom.

She noted the minute changes in her appearance. The dark circles underscoring her eyes were fainter; the fine lines of tension that seemed to be a permanent fixture around her small mouth were also softer. She ran one finger beneath the slightly darkened skin underscoring her almond-shaped, light-brown eyes. Surrounding her pupils was a ring of gold around her irises.

Cat eyes.

That's what her mother always told her. She had sly, cat eyes. Just like her father.

Her high cheekbones and a long, oval face, she'd gotten from him.

She stroked her tongue over her small lips and examined herself, feathering her fingers over each of her features, as though she was cataloging them, assessing them, and looking for flaws.

She ran a finger down the short bridge of her nose, over full, naturally blushed lips, and along the slight yet discernible dimple in her chin.

That she'd gotten from her father also.

On the outside, she was the feminine image of her father. She had a tall, athletic body, one she spent hours in the gym to maintain. She lifted one of her heavy breasts, breasts she'd painfully begun developing at an early age, thumbing a finger over the flat disk of her areole, lightly feathering a thumb over her nipple that was becoming stiff and erect with her light touches.

She opened the robe further and stroked her hands down her body, one hand lifting a breast, the other venturing past the tight muscles of her abdomen, the swell of her hips, before traveling to the trimmed thatch of hair between her thighs.

With detached awareness, she watched herself in the mirror as she parted the slick folds and ran one lone finger between the lips, circling her clitoris in tight swirls and back again.

She closed her eyes, and moaned lightly, one hand buried in her pussy, the other molding one of her breasts, pulling on her taut, stiff nipple.

Alone, with no one around, no one to disturb her, no one to make demands on her, she felt free to fondle and pleasure herself as no one else could.

In a way that she *allowed* no one else to do.

Her toying fingers picked up in speed and depth as she plunged them inside her vagina, rotating them, seeking out her inner spot. Once found, she soon felt the tingling sensation that signaled her body was ready to release.

She moaned softly while her body jerked and spasmed when her orgasm took over her body. As her body clenched one final time, she bit her bottom lip to prevent the cry from escalating, panting, taking in deep breaths of air as she finished the climax.

Once her body had calmed, she withdrew her shaky fingers, turned on the gold-tinted faucet taps, and quickly washed her hands.

She saw the deep flush that ran beneath her dark-brown skin and a fine line of sweat bead her brow as she stared at her reflection in the gold-tinted mirror.

Despite the sexual euphoria that enveloped her after her self-given orgasm, Chase felt completely unfulfilled.

Walking toward the bedroom, she quickly unpacked her clothes, carefully hanging the garments inside the ornately carved armoire. Pulling out a colorful sarong, she dressed and took a tour around the cottage, familiarizing herself with her temporary digs.

Feeling anxious, she picked up the phone and called for her attendant, deciding to attend the luau. It was that or go insane as she waited for her *fantasy* to begin.

CHAPTER 7

"Is everything to your satisfaction, Miss?"

Chastity turned from the large bay window where she'd been admiring the view of the moon rising, casting a surreal golden glow over the nearby ocean.

She was startled when she heard the voice behind her speak. She turned to see her guide standing in the doorway of her bedroom.

He'd brought her home from the luau over thirty minutes ago. She'd immediately stripped out her clothes, taken a brisk shower, and had slipped on a long, sheer nightgown, with the intent of sliding into the luxurious, king-sized bed that dominated her temporary bedroom and going to sleep.

"It's beautiful," she replied simply, and turned back around, continuing to admire the scene.

"I'm glad you find your accommodations to your pleasure, Ms. Davidson. However, it's time to go."

"Excuse me?"

"I said, it's time to go. Please come with me." His voice remained pleasant, yet his tone brooked no argument. His tone and his wording raised the hair on the back of her neck.

He walked further into her bedroom, stopping when he

stood several feet away from her. There were no lights on in the cottage, the only illumination came from the glowing moon. Feeling exposed, Chase wrapped her arms around herself.

"Time to go where?" Her forehead creased as she asked the question.

"What you came here for, Ms. Davidson. Your fantasy begins now." His voice didn't rise, and there was little inflection in his tone. Yet, it disturbed her.

He advanced closer. The small, reassuring smile he gave didn't give her any comfort; instead, she felt a sense of anxiety. An odd fear threatened to overwhelm her.

"Let me get dressed. I just stepped out of the shower," she replied after a heartbeat of silence. She motioned a hand over her body, indicating her state of dress.

When she moved to turn away, his hand on her arm stilled her.

"No. It's time now. What you're wearing doesn't matter."

"Look. I said—"

"Now, Ms. Davidson. I believe you have a pair of shoes at the entryway? You can put them on, on our way out."

Although his pleasant smile remained fixed, he directed just a bit more force on her wrist, not enough to hurt, but enough that she felt the added pressure.

"You wouldn't want them to go on without you, would you, Ms. Davidson? You wouldn't want to prolong a moment longer, your desire to be number one?"

They stared at each other and in Chase's mind images of Javier's mocking smile flashed through her mind.

"Don't you want to receive what you deserve?"

She straightened her back, drew in her chest and with one

hand, easily removed the man's hold on her wrist. "Yes. I'm ready."

Ignoring his edict that she not change, Chase grabbed the long, decorative fabric—one of many pieces she'd bought from the small gift store after she'd left the luau—off a chair and wrapped it securely around her body, tying the ends in a knot above her breasts.

With that she followed him, stopping to slip on her strappy sandals before leaving the cottage. She closed the door behind her, and a small grin lifted the corners of her mouth, anticipation replacing the earlier unwanted fear.

⚬

"You mentioned they were all waiting for me. I don't suppose you can tell me what that means?" she asked, doubting the silent man would enlighten her. "And what is your name? I don't think you've ever told me," she said, not knowing if he'd told her and she'd simply not paid attention, or if had never given it.

"My name is Gideon. But, as to the rest of your question, I'm afraid I am not at liberty to give you any information regarding the upcoming events. You'll know soon enough," he replied. Chase was a bit taken aback with his response.

She came out of the house expecting to see the white Jeep he'd driven or at least some type of island-motorized vehicle, but she saw none. She lifted a brow in question when he held her elbow, tugged her along with him, and began to walk along the bushy trail that ran alongside her cottage.

Pushing aside the heavy, abundant foliage in front of them, he cleared a path for her as he walked ahead. Chase was glad she'd wrapped the fabric around her body, saving it from any scratches the branches and foliage would have given her. Thankfully, the ground beneath her was soft. Beneath the delicate soles of her sandals, she couldn't feel sand or rocks, nothing but the soft bed of leaves and grass that carpeted the tropical flooring.

The light from the moon seemed to be the main illumination the further they walked, leaving behind the distant lights from other parts of the resorts that shone brightly near her cottage. Chase glanced behind her in growing concern at the fading lights of the resort the farther they walked along the path.

"How much farther?" Irritably she batted away a low-hanging leafy branch as she continued to follow him. She felt as though she'd been walking for miles, and she saw no end in sight.

The earlier feeling of anticipation began to fade away; trepidation and uncertainty took its place.

It was then the low murmur of a multitude of voices, their hushed tones carrying on the wind, reached her ears.

It was also at that moment that Gideon stepped out into an open stretch of beach. He moved aside and pointed a finger in the direction in front of them.

Further up the beach, near the edge of the shore, was what looked to be a large gathering of people, all seated in front of a raised platform. As soon as she moved around him, a hundred or more heads turned. She suppressed a shiver despite the humid temperature when even in the dark she felt the hungry, lustful stares of a hundred pair of eyes boring into her.

"Please, come forward, Chase. We've been waiting for you," a loud masculine voice invited her. Chase's eyes left the hungry-eyed crowd and sought out the one who spoke.

A man stood on the platform with a microphone in his hand, dressed formally in the tropical paradise, wearing a dark tuxedo, widely smiling at her, holding out a hand, inviting her to join him on the wooden dais.

Her breathing increased, her heart beat out strong staccato thumps against her breasts as Chase allowed Gideon to guide her toward the waiting crowd.

CHAPTER 8

"You're leaving?" Chase asked, turning to the only familiar face in her uncertain world. She felt an almost desperate desire to beg him to stay, to not leave her alone.

"Yes, this is where I leave you on your journey, Ms. Davidson."

"Wha—what do you mean?"

"I have to." She saw a look of sadness enter his eyes as though he wished he did not have to do so. "But you will be in capable hands. I must leave you now to your auctioneer."

"My auctioneer?" Her voice had risen and carried on the wind, seeming to magnify it.

Her head whipped around so swiftly that several strands of hair loosened from the careful topknot she'd created on top of her head, and fell into her eyes. She stared first at the waiting man on the stage, then her gaze went to those who sat in folded chairs in the audience, openly staring…gawking at her.

Her lips partially opened, and her tongue swiped across her now-dry lips. When she turned back to Gideon, it was to find him gone. He'd blended into the darkness as though he was never there.

"Please, come. Join us, Ms. Davidson."

Chase turned reluctantly to face the crowd and the smiling

man on the stage. Swallowing a melon ball-sized lump of fear, she forced her feet to move, slowly walking toward the stage.

She kept her gaze averted from the avid crowd, not ready to face them, unsure of their role in all of this.

As she made the short journey toward the stage, she stared in fascination at the assortment of large, life-sized tiki wooden carvings lining the walkway, some easily depicting males and females, some odd caricatures of both.

When she heard a drum begin to beat, she turned her head toward the sound. Directly in front of her a bare-chested man covered in tribal-looking tattoos over his upper torso, an ornate mask covering the upper half of his face, his long, dark hair flowing down his back, strummed a steady harsh rhythm on the large drum gripped between his thick, muscled thighs.

The closer she drew to the stage, the heavier the beat of his drum.

Chase felt a fine sheen of perspiration trickle down the side of her face.

Once she reached the stage, she grasped the man's opened hand. Solicitously, he helped her up the short flight of stairs that led to the stage.

"She's here, the one we've all been waiting for, the one you all have been eagerly waiting for. Isn't she beautiful?"

The smile he gave her was encouraging, before he gave his attention back to the eager crowd, tugging a bewildered Chase along with him.

"Don't be shy, Ms. Davidson. Come forth and allow them all to see you!"

"I'm not sure this is what I requested." She spoke so low that she doubted the grinning man could hear her. Doubt mingled with trepidation, churning maliciously in her gut. She cast nervous eyes over the murmuring audience.

Again he smiled that strange predatory smile that brought absurd images of Little Red Riding Hood and the wolf to mind.

Chase straightened her back, forcibly bringing herself back in tight control and reining in her fear.

She was no wilting Little Red Riding Hood. She wasn't afraid of the Big Bad Wolf.

"No one is going to bite. At least, not unless you ask them to," he replied, loudly enough for everyone to hear. Despite the loud music and excited crowd, he obviously heard her.

At his quip, she heard a mixture of rumbling male amusement and tinkling feminine laughter.

She turned toward the audience, her eyes sweeping over them. She had to squint her eyes to see them against the beaming lights that circled the stage. On the beach she'd been able to see their faces more clearly. However, now on the stage, with the surrounding tiki lights, all shining down and focused on her, she was unable to see individual people. The bodies and faces in the crowd merged into one homogenous blob.

"We are ready for the final bidding this evening," the man—the auctioneer—began. Bewildered, Chase turned to him, her eyes widening.

"The *what?*"

He ignored her and continued, "What you have all been waiting all evening for, the piece de resistance, I present to you, Chastity Davidson. Ms. Davidson is a prime specimen, isn't she? Look at her, beautiful, intelligent…and talented. For the one who dares to bid on her, untold nights of pleasure will sure to be yours from this dark beauty," he finished with a flourish, stroking a hand down the length of her body, his strokes feather light.

"I don't know what's going on here, but I'm not staying around to find out!" Chase's heart began to pound frantically against her ribcage, as she shoved his hands away from her body. She spun around, her desire to leave paramount, when she tripped and would have gone sprawling off the stage, had he not grabbed her by the arm to prevent her fall.

He brought her up, close to his chest, his dark eyes boring into hers. His stare was so hot, so intense that it seemed to sear a direct path into her soul.

"Isn't this what you wanted, your deepest desire, to be number one?"

"Yes! But not like this!" Chase hissed.

He leaned closer, his warm breath scorching the back of her neck.

She flinched when she felt his lips feather against her neck in a fleeting kiss.

"No?"

The muscles in her jaw tensed. She clenched her teeth so hard together they ached. She moved her head to the side, her breathing harsh, and her face flushed, refusing to look at him.

He placed his hands on her shoulders, forcing her to turn and face the crowd.

"Can't you feel their energy, their excitement?" he whispered against the side of her face, for her ears alone.

Her nostrils flared, her chest rose heavily as her gaze was helplessly, almost against her will, drawn to the nearly invisible faces of the crowd.

"Their desire…it's all for you. And you alone. Only you can appease them."

Chase swallowed deeply.

Although she couldn't see them clearly, she *felt* them. Their lust and sexual energy shot through her body, infusing her with their collective ardor.

The auctioneer's hands slowly moved down her shoulders and over her breasts.

"Only you can satisfy their longings."

She scarcely noticed when he deftly unknotted the ties of the fabric and the cloth fell from her body, leaving her body starkly outlined in the sheer dress.

She felt the crowd's randy anticipation, their excitement.

"They've been waiting for you and you alone, Chastity."

Their lust was a palpable living entity—one so tangible she felt its shadowy, invisible fingers move insidiously down her spine, curl over her body, her breasts, her stomach, and stroke her between her thighs.

Distantly, she felt his hands roam over her body as she stared out, in odd fascination, over the excited crowd.

"Would you deny them the opportunity to make you number one?" he murmured.

The fingers of their combined lust stroked her just as the auctioneer stroked her in a symphonic rhythm. The heavy beat of the drum began to pulse in time with the hammering beat of the walls in her pussy.

She heard the auctioneer lightly chuckle, as though he *knew*...

He continued to skim his hands over her body. He bunched her gown in his fist and slid it up her legs, past her waist, exposing her.

"Who among you is able to tame this beauty? Who can crash through her walls, break down her barriers to reach the hidden treasures she keeps so carefully locked away?"

His words seemed to come from a small distance. She heard them, yet they didn't register in her mind, she was so caught up in the surreal nature of what was happening to her.

He gently pressed a finger into her creaming pussy, adding a second finger while his thumb feathered across her pulsing clit, spreading her own cream around the extended nub.

"Hmmm," he murmured. "So hot." He closed his eyes briefly after bringing the evidence of her arousal to his nostrils and inhaled deeply.

He took his finger into his mouth, licked her cum away, and smiled. "So sweet."

It all felt like a dream to her as she turned her head slightly and watched dispassionately as he licked his finger and smiled.

The air around her grew thick, hotter. Dewy beads of moisture trickled between her breasts.

"Who among you is man…or woman…enough to take on the challenge she lays before you?"

He grabbed the top of her dress and ripped it apart, exposing her fully to the now frantic crowd.

Lifting one heavy breast, he palmed as much as his hand would hold, thumbing a finger over her tight, spiked nipple.

"Who is ready to start bidding on this nubile Amazon?" he laughingly called out.

The crowd began to jump to its feet in a frenzy of sexual energy.

"Are you ready to be number one, Chase?"

The auctioneer's gaze settled on her, his eyes were hot blazing beams of sexual tension.

Nothing about what he was saying, what he was doing, should have appealed to her.

His look, his touch—none of that should have affected her except for disgust and loathing.

Yet, as she stared into his hard, unyielding gaze, it did. *He* did.

She turned to the animated crowd.

They did.

Their frenzy, desire, franticness...It all called to her, called to everything in her that longed to yield.

To give in.

But not just to give in for their bidding.

She turned back to him, seeing the challenge in his dark eyes.

"Who among you is man or woman enough to break her down? To conquer her?"

As her gaze locked with the auctioneer, a delicious, forbidden desire to succumb to the utter madness of the auction rocked her very being.

She turned around, struck out her breasts and dislodged his hands from her body.

She closed her eyes, tilted her head to the side. As her tongue darted out of her mouth to moisten her lips, she boldly ran her hands down her body. With no apology, she showed off her body to those who *thought* they'd be the *one*; the one to break her.

She opened her eyes. raised one single brow at the auctioneer and stepped away from him.

A low laugh tumbled from her lips as she faced the bidding crowd.

The adrenaline coursed fiercely through Chase's veins. Every nerve ending was tingling with anticipation, and the high from the bidding heightened with every call outbidding the last.

She stood before them all, proudly resplendent in her nakedness. She had attended several auctions, but never in her wildest imagination had she ever envisioned the likes of this one. The sheer forbidden quality of it damn near made her giddy, as her head whipped over the crowd, the bids reaching astronomical levels, as each one quickly outbid the other, the bids fast, staccato, hitting hard.

"Five million," a feminine voice rang loudly over the bidding crowd.

A hush fell over the crowd, stilling all action.

Chase squinted against the glare clouding her vision, trying to see who had called out the incredulous amount, but was unable to locate the lone woman.

Her heart thud erratically against her chest, her body drenched with sweat as though she'd just completed a ten mile full out run as she scanned the crowd, wondering just as all the others, if anyone would—could—top the bid.

She turned toward the auctioneer. He held out a hand for her to take.

With her hand trembling, she placed it within his.

"I believe we have—"

Before the auctioneer could end the bidding and declare a winning bid, a deep baritone cut in.

"Twenty-five million."

The crowd's murmuring reached even higher decimals as heads turned in the direction of the voice.

The auctioneer smiled, nodding his head in deference to the direction of the voice.

"I believe we have a winner," he replied simply.

CHAPTER 9

Immediately after the last astonishing bid, Gideon appeared onstage, and Chase was whisked away before she could process all that had transpired. She barely had enough time to gather her ruined garments and re-clothe herself with the torn clothing.

Instead of walking back to her bungalow, as she'd expected, he placed her in the familiar white Jeep, and within minutes they'd arrived back to her temporary home.

Now, with a cigarette clamped between her lips, Chase paced the length of her living area, occasionally walking toward the front door that she'd left opened to peer into the darkness.

She stepped out onto the small porch, one eye narrowing against the curling smoke from the cigarette, searching for signs of someone coming.

"So let the games begin already," she muttered irritably.

She inhaled deeply on the cigarette, holding the smoke deep inside for a moment before blowing it out in a gush of air.

With disgust, she raised a slightly shaky hand to her lips and snatched the half-smoked cigarette out of her mouth and threw it on the ground, stubbing out the burning ember with the heel of her sandal.

She stalked back inside, kicked off her shoes, and slammed the door shut.

Striding through the cottage, she went into the bedroom and stripped off the new fabric wrap she'd worn after returning from the auction. She lay down on the bed, staring up at the ceiling.

Waiting.

Her body was alive and humming in eager anticipation, although what was in store for her, what eroticism she would experience as the night wore on, was an uncertainty.

"Just what in hell I'm waiting for I don't have a damn clue."

As she lay on the bed, she raised a naked arm and noted the fine trembling of her hands as she stared down at it.

Just like a junkie, she was coming down from the high of the auction.

The rush of adrenaline that had pumped through her veins was finally wearing off. Just like any other junkie, she was primed for the next fix.

Frantic for the next high.

But like any good high, this one not only had her jonesing for the next fix, but it had worn her out—so much so that when she closed her eyes, she fell into a restless sleep.

CHAPTER 10

Quietly and with as much stealth as a seasoned cat burglar, Chastity carefully opened, then eased her long legs through her bedroom window. She manipulated and contorted her body to get inside.

She closed the window shut and lightly jumped down into her room, landing with a soft thud on the hardwood floors.

Just as she turned, she bumped against the small nightstand table and bit back a curse.

She quickly righted the stand before it could fall to the floor, afraid the sound would alert her mother that she wasn't in her bed, on the off chance that Maybelle had made it home from work before Chase. There was little chance of that because she hadn't seen Maybelle's beat-up Chevy in the driveway, yet she still remained as quiet as possible.

Chase glanced down at the brightly illuminated dial on her watch.

She had at least an hour before Maybelle would be home from her late-night shift at the nursing home. More than enough time to shower, get dressed, jump into bed, and not risk getting busted for being out.

She quickly shed her clothing and opened a bureau drawer to withdraw her night clothes. Carefully closing the door, she turned around, and blinked her eyes several times when the bright overhead lights in her bedroom came on.

Chastity's heart fell to her stomach when she came face to face with her mother as she stood in her doorway.

"You may as well stop trying to pretend. I know your ass has been out. I got home early from work. Hid the car 'round back."

In her hands, Maybelle held two long strips of leather, slapping them against each other.

Chastity nearly passed out in fear.

"Bet you didn't think that was gonna happen, did you? Imagine my surprise when you weren't here, where you were supposed to be. I told you to stay home, Chastity. And you had to disobey. Now, you goin' to have to pay."

Chastity clutched the gown she held in one hand, the other held out in entreaty, as though to ward off Maybelle. "But, Momma, I *had* to go to the library. I had to finish my report for school. I—"

"*Shut up!* I told you to stay your ass at home."

Maybelle pushed away from the doorframe, walking further inside and casting narrowed eyes around the neat room.

Chastity bit her lip as her mother inspected the room, her eyes following the motion of the leather strips being slapped against Maybelle's stubby, fat hands. She sent a prayer heavenward that was nothing out of order in her room.

"As though I believe you were at the library studying," Maybelle scoffed. Grunting, she lowered her round body to the floor to peer beneath Chastity's bed.

Slowly, she backed away from her mother. "I…I was! I won't get credit if I don't turn in the report," Chastity cried out.

Maybelle whipped her head around from beneath the bed and put a hand out to brace herself as she rose. She pinned

Chastity with a glare. "I said shut the fuck up! I know you were out with some boy, you tramp. Don't lie to me!"

As her mother advanced on her with an evil and crazy glint in her eyes focused directly on her, Chastity slowly backed away until the back of her knees hit the edge of her bed.

"You think you can sneak out of here when I'm hard at work, trying to put food on the goddamn table and a roof over your ungrateful head?" Maybelle yelled. "I know you were out, probably screwing some boy. Stop lying to me, goddamn it!"

Before she could make a run for it, Maybelle grabbed her with a speed and strength that defied the physical limitations of her short, rotund body. She yanked Chastity close and flipped her around, pulling her arms behind her back. Within seconds she had secured the leather straps in her hands around Chastity's wrists.

She shoved Chastity down to the bed, and quickly secured her feet, wrapping the second leather cord around them and secured each ankle to the other before looping the cord around the footboard of the bed.

"No! Don't do this to me, Momma…please!" Chase screamed, tears running down her face as she bucked against the tight restraints.

After she'd secured Chastity to the bed, Maybelle moved away and laughed, her dark face flushed and her large breasts heaving with the exertion.

"Maybe your fast ass will think twice about sneaking out after this!"

"Momma…please! Don't leave me like this! Please, don't let… him." She stopped and swallowed, before choking out in a whisper, "Don't let Daddy come…come," she begged.

Her pleading cries fell on deaf ears.

"He seems to be the only person your lying ass obeys," she replied.

With a look of disgust, Maybelle spun around, shut off the lights and slammed the door shut, leaving Chastity alone, shivering.

She stared at the mocking shadows in the dark, cold room, waiting.

She fell asleep, despite her intent not to, wakening with a cry on her lips when a heavy, putrid-smelling body pressed her into the coarse sheets on her small twin bed.

Chase fought against the dream, fought against the binds that held her as she lay on her small bed, tossing her head back and forth on the pillow as her body bucked against the tight restraints her mother had placed over her limbs.

"Please, Momma...don't leave me like this! I'll be good, I promise!" she cried, tears streaming down her face.

When she felt cool, soft lips fasten over hers and a warm tongue ease between the seams of her lips, she moaned as she fought her attacker, determined that she wouldn't let him do it again.

She would rather die than allow her father to force himself on her again.

When she felt hands stroking up her thighs, a hard body snaking up the length of her body, a pair of hands stroking a hot caress along her instep, her eyes snapped open.

She struggled against the drugging kisses and dregs of the nightmare that held her an unwilling captive.

She forced her head away and shoved against the hands, tongues, and fingers that ran over her body.

Struggling to sit up, she tried to push the body that covered hers away and found that her wrists were clamped together by a pair of strong hands, pinning them above her head.

"What the hell is this?" She choked out the words, shaking off the last sediment of the long-ago nightmare as she fought her unknown assailant.

She saw nothing more than the shadowy imprint of bodies in the midnight darkness of the room, blanketing her body, pressing her into the silk sheets of the bed.

"Sssh, it's okay, just—"

"Hell no, it's not okay! Get the hell off of me! All of you!" Chase interrupted, renewing her struggles to free herself from the restraining hold and the hot bodies that covered and stroked her naked body.

She raised her body and snatched her hands from the tight, masculine hands that held her. Although she could see nothing in the unnaturally dark room, she swung her hand in a wild arc. Satisfaction coursed through her body when she heard the satisfying crack of her hand meeting flesh.

When she felt hands on the opposite end of her body grab her thighs, she pulled her legs up and kicked out.

"Fuck!" she cursed when she missed her intended target.

Her legs were grabbed and held at the same moment that her body was slammed back to the mattress, knocking the wind out of her and stunning her for a moment.

It was enough time for one of her attackers to regain hold of her wrists.

"That's what we're trying to do," a second voice bit the words out. Seconds later she heard a discernible click and felt cold, steel handcuffs lock into place.

Her bound wrists were manacled to one of the wrought-iron poles of the headboard.

The same mouth that brought her out of sleep, again slanted over hers, pushing against her lips to slide a tongue deep inside.

This time she was awake and aware, not caught in the dream world of sleep, not some helpless little girl who had to submit to the tyranny of someone bigger and stronger than her.

She bit the lip kissing her. As the assailant broke the kiss with a curse, she felt the coppery feel of blood fill her mouth.

"He said she wouldn't be easy to conquer," someone said, the voice coming from the lower end of the bed.

He? Who were they talking about? Chase wondered. *God, what was this madness?*

"At twenty-five mil, hope it's worth the price to find out," a silky voice murmured, his voice coming from the side of the bed. Chase realized that there were at least three men in the dark room, all trying to conquer her.

"Whoever the hell *he* is...he was right," Chase spoke behind clenched teeth. "And I should have known."

"You should have known?" the one nearest to her, the one who'd awakened and assaulted her without her permission, spoke.

"That it would take more than one to answer the challenge," she scoffed. "That it took three of you to pool your money... and your dicks...together to win."

A finger reached out and stroked down her cheek, down her throat and onward, caressing down the line of her cleavage. A large hand cupped one of her breasts, thumbing a callused finger over her nipple. Despite her anger, her body reacted, her nipples beading and seeking the rough caress.

"Ah, that's where you're wrong. We're simply one of your appetizers," he said and stopped talking.

She felt his slick, long tongue snake the same path his fingers had—down her throat, licking a hot path to the crest of one breast, tugging the nipple into his mouth, while the fingers of his other hand palmed and caressed the other heavy orb. He clamped his warm mouth over the upper swell of her breast, pulling and sucking her nipple until it spiked hard and tight.

"You're not ready for the main meal, yet," he murmured after releasing her breast and moving away.

"What...what are you talking—" Her stumbling was cut off mid-question when she felt a balmy breath blow across her sex, followed by a tongue stroking deep into her cunt.

Her body arched sharply off the mattress, and Chase bit back a moan. Her cream eased from her pussy despite her resistance. Wet kisses scored down her inner leg, licking over her knees, and down her leg, lightly grasping one of her feet.

She struggled against the invasion. Her nails scored deep grooves into her palms as she clenched her fists, unsuccessfully trying to escape the bonds that held her hands securely in place.

With a strangled breath, she struggled against the deceptively soft kisses, refusing to give in to her body's demands and the sexual lethargy that threatened to overwhelm her.

"How do you feel?" a deep, husky voice asked, jerking her away from the sensations flooding her body and the internal fight she was having with her mind and body.

She gasped when she felt the man blanketing her back reach across her body and scrape his thumb against her clit.

"I...it feels...good." The admission was torn from her tightly clenched lips.

The hand playing with her clit moved, and she felt a firm-stinging slap to her backside, followed by him running his hand over the stinging flesh to ease the sting.

She gasped, tugging against the restraints with renewed fervor.

"No. You didn't answer the question. How do *you* feel?"

"Out of control." The admission filled her with shame.

When nubile fingers separated the lips of her vagina and a finger caressed the flesh between the dripping folds, Chase growled from deep within her throat.

She heard a myriad of satisfied murmurs at her response.

"We've just begun," one of the deep, husky voices replied.

Her lips were captured again, in a hot, nasty kiss that set her body tingling. "You need to succumb, Chastity. You need to give in to the pleasure. Stop trying to exert your will. The sooner you do so, the sooner you'll be ready for him."

"Him? Who...what are you talking about?"

In the dark, she sought out the man's gaze but was given no time to consider his words before he was on her again, before they all converged back on her with a myriad of tongues, lips, teeth, and hands.

She moved, seeking out the firm yet sensually soft lips of the one kissing her.

The man drank deeply from her; his hands stroked the smooth fleshy mounds of her ass, and another set caressed and fondled her body in a series of nips, licks, and kisses, all of which brought Chase to a feverish pitch of wanton desire. She was drunk with lust, her body on fire.

A slick tongue parted her lips and pressed hotly inside, push-ing past her teeth to ravage her mouth, devouring her in hot strokes and darting away before Chase's tongue could capture his.

His lips captured the lower rim of her lip and bit; the sting caused a sharp zing directly to her pussy.

Simultaneously, she felt strong, masculine hands press her thighs apart, while a rock-hard chest hovered behind her pressing insistently against her back.

God, how many of them are there? Chase thought, her mind in a sexual fog of lust and desire.

Long, lean fingers grasped her breasts, palming and toying with the orbs before tugging on her spiked nipples.

Her nipples tightened painfully, elongating, begging for more attention.

Hands lifted her, rolling her body until she was lying on her side, all done without any break in contact; the multiple hands continued to stroke, pet and caress her.

"Lift your body," a deep voice, different than one kissing her, commanded, and Chase obeyed. A soft pillow eased between her and the mattress, cushioning and raising her hips.

Her outer leg was raised, and her big toe slid past a set of full lips before being engulfed in a warm mouth that pulled on the toe and suckled it deeply. Chase whimpered against the lips slashing over hers.

There was a deep answering laugh, and her toe was released. That tongue now trailed a path from her foot up her legs before landing between her thighs.

She felt a shift; bodies moved on hers in an easy exchange, and the face between her legs settled between her thighs. When a slick tongue flicked out, capturing her blood-turgid clit, she cried out.

His fingers quickly joined his tongue, in a symphony of moves that soon had Chase bucking against his face, her moans now loud and harsh in the dark room.

The man kissing her mouth pulled away, and Chase leaned forward to try and recapture the connection, angry when the bonds restricted her from doing so.

Her body and mind strained against the onslaught of sensations. She grew restless, her skin felt too tight, and her breath came out in strangled gasps when suddenly the broad, fleshy knob of a penis pressed insistently against her lips with a silent but obvious command for her to open.

She opened her mouth wide and allowed him to feed her his shaft slowly until the tip bumped the back of her throat.

Her tongue hollowed. She cupped the soft, slick underside of the silky skin of his dick, wrapping her tongue around it and stroking from side to side before curling her tongue over the top of his cock, repeating the same careful movements.

She felt his hands on each side of her face, the rough pads of twin thumbs softly stroking her cheeks as her head bobbed up and down on his shaft. He withdrew from her in small increments. Chase followed his lead, licking her way to the top of his dick, circling the thick ridge around the knob and greedily lapping the drip of pre-cum away from the tiny eye in the center before deep-throating him again.

She felt hands on her hips, smoothly moving her to lay on her side. As she was moved, she never lost connection with the stiff rod in her mouth or the tongue suckling deeply into her cunt. The cheeks of her buttocks were gently spread, and a body settled behind her.

Feeling overwhelmed, she began to fight against the onslaught of sensation; squirming against the restraints that held her hands immobile and the strong hands that securely held the rest of her body firmly in place.

Seconds later a hot tongue slid around the puckered hole of her anus, flickering in short, tight swirls against her before easing inside, along with a long index finger. Her heart pounded against her chest and despite the cool fan swirling a breeze over her naked flesh, Chase was unbearably hot. A pool of sweat eased down her face, between her breasts, and the cream from her pussy gushed down her leg. She grunted against the cock in her mouth in sensual agony when a tongue joined the finger playing against her puckered hole.

Her skin felt as though it were wrapped in flames.

When a small pencil-thin object replaced the finger and tongue stroking her, and a cool gel filled deep inside, she inhaled a sharp breath. She hissed in painful pleasure when oily fingers rubbed more of the gel over and around her puckered hole, before pressing deeply into her ass.

Seconds later, a thick, hot cock took the place of fingers and began to work slowly into her ass. The pressure was intense despite the lubricant and Chase moaned around the cock in her mouth. The pressure continued to build, and she helplessly released a scream as the multitude of sensations rained down on her.

Every part of her body was being suckled...laved...fucked. When the man between her thighs reached a hand up and began to fondle her breasts, Chase drew in a deep breath before slowly releasing the pent-up hair in a harsh whimper.

Moaning, mentally she fought against her own body's reaction, fought against the pleasure being forced on her. Yet, she continued to undulate her hips against the dual invasion below and suckle the cock in her mouth.

Her body now had a mind of its own. No longer was she in control of it.

She moaned even as she accepted the strokes and thrusts—pussy, breasts, ass—every part of her was being catered to, propelling her to a fevered pitch of mindless lust.

Sliding back and forth, her ass sought the pleasure of the dick plunging deep inside her buttocks. Her thighs were shaking, quivering around the head between her legs as a fevered tongue continued to stroke and suckle her cunt. The sound of a multitude of harsh breaths and moans of delights combined into one melodious song of rapture.

When Chase felt the orgasm slamming into her, she fought against it.

She ripped her mouth away, twisting and bucking her body against the dual invasion of pussy and ass. She was unable to stop the incredulous orgasm that threatened to break her, she screamed as she released.

Her body bowed down on itself as the orgasm washed over her as violent as a tsunami and just as devastating.

As her orgasm reached its pinnacle, a strange feeling enveloped her, one she'd never felt. Her body tingled, and a queasy, disorienting feeling swamped her.

Damn. She was going to faint. The reality hit her, stunning her.

Before losing consciousness, she felt hot cum splash against her body in a multitude of jetting streams.

Down her face, running down her chin, its sticky path ran between her breasts.

Over the rounded cheek of her ass, it slowly, slowly trickled down her body. Against her mound, it ran in hot streams, mingling with her own cum.

Coating, marking, claiming her.

Dominating her.

Chase gasped when she was harshly awakened when a slender but long cock pressed deep into her ass while a thick shaft pushed into her vagina.

Her stomach clenched as the burning pressure she felt on both ends tore through her. Panting, her eyes fluttered open.

She had only passed out for mere moments, but it was enough time for the men to reposition her and remove the bonds.

In the midnight darkness of the room, she was barely able to see a man whose strong muscled ass was near her face, his body bracketing her upper torso. Yet she felt his long dick tap against her lips, silently demanding that she open, again.

Flat on her back, with her legs bent, raised and spread, two men were steadily pumping into her, fucking her to full wakefulness—one in her pussy. the other stroking deep into her ass.

The one straddling her face with his shaft at her lips was perched with his head at the top of her mound, his wicked tongue flicking against her clit.

Moaning, she spread her legs further apart and opened her lips to allow him to ease his rod deep into her mouth. She swallowed it deeply.

In a smooth rhythm, her head bobbed up and down on his shaft, sliding it nearly out of her mouth before she swallowed him again.

Oh God, what am I doing? Chase thought as she milked his cock of the sweet cum that eased down her throat.

She was caught in some type of mad dream. A dream where her body and mind were no longer hers to command as she eagerly lapped her tongue around him, swallowing his cum even as her hips began to undulate, meeting, matching, and eagerly greeting the powerful thrusts of each man between her legs.

She rolled her hips against the dual invasion below, even as her mouth fastened hungrily on the cock in her mouth, her teeth lightly scraping the soft underskin of his shaft, her tongue delicately fondling the twin plum-like testicles.

Chase willingly let go of thoughts about what was right, what was wrong, who was in control...None of that mattered in that moment.

Instead, she fully participated in the wild loving.

CHAPTER 11

C hase opened her eyes and blinked her eyes rapidly against the bright glare of the sun that shafted through the sheer, ivory-colored curtains.

The curtains softly swayed as the early morning, warm breeze wafted past them to whisper over her, cooling her naked skin.

She slowly eased her sore body into a sitting position and turned again to gaze at the billowing curtains, idly wondering when the window had been opened. She glanced down at her body, cringing when she saw the evidence of last night's excess on her dark-brown skin.

She ran her fingers over her breasts and down her stomach. Her fingers came away sticky as she removed the remnants of white cum that was plastered to her skin like glue.

After the first time, they had continued to fuck her, long into the night, even when she thought no other response could be wrung from her, when she thought her body was exhausted, beyond satiated...

Chase winced, ashamed of what she'd allowed to happen.

She gave in to every one of their demands, as they stroked, licked, and fucked every part of her body, finding places on her she hadn't known were hot spots, to bring her to a screaming climax long through the night and into the early morning hours.

With only token protests from her initially, they managed to break her down, had conquered her.

"Damn," she whispered.

They had broken down her physical barriers, and had her accepting...

"Shit, who am I kidding? They had me begging for it." She sighed, blowing a breath that fanned the curls of hair lying limply against her cheek.

She threw her legs over the edge of the bed to get up and hissed when the muscles in her legs screamed out in protest, shaking and failing, due to the extreme and unnatural positions her body had been placed in throughout most of the night.

Bending her sore body to pick up the wrap that lay in a heap on the floor near the bed, Chase tied the ends over her breasts and padded barefoot into the adjoining bathroom.

She stared at herself in the smoky-glass-tinted mirror, seeing the dark rings under her eyes and her hair that curled wildly. She fingered the curls that lay in a sweaty riot over her head, long ago sweated out from their original flat-iron straightness.

"God, I'm a mess," she mumbled, pulling her hair back tightly with one hand while searching with the other hand for something to hold it, before she allowed her hands to drop.

She laughed, lightening her dark mood, and left her hair alone.

Here she was thinking about her hair when she'd just had one of the most out-of-control sexual experiences of her life.

Turning away, she walked the short distance to the shower and turned the knobs to the far left to allow hot water to come pouring from the jets before stepping inside.

She leisurely washed. Carefully, she soaped between her legs, gently separating her vaginal lips, wincing when her fingers touched the still-tender flesh. She turned her face fully into the stinging overhead spray, scrubbing her face, body, and hair... She futilely attempted to scrub away the memory of what she'd done the night before, shying away from delving too deeply into her thoughts on what she'd fully participated in.

After the shower, she donned a two-piece swimsuit and again wrapped the fabric around herself, securely it around her hips—this time, fashioning a skirt.

Walking out of the bedroom, she was hit with a delicious, aromatic smell wafting from the kitchen. Curious, she walked over and saw several dome-covered platters on the counter.

Lifting one of the lids, she discovered an array of breakfast delicacies of thinly sliced ham, fat little sausages, petit croissants, and an assortment of fruits.

Just as with the window, someone had come into her cottage without her knowledge, anticipating her needs in a way that she found uncomfortable.

Although her stomach growled, and the food looked amazing, she found the thought of eating unappealing and instead lifted the small carafe of coffee to pour into one of the mugs set out for her use. Then she caught sight of a second carafe alongside a wine goblet.

Curious, she poured from the second carafe and took a careful sip before realizing it was a mimosa. The sweet juice had been spiked with enough champagne that she'd easily discerned its taste.

After last night, she needed something much stronger than caffeine.

She drank the glass in one long, thirsty gulp, and placed the goblet down on the counter. She poured another glass, carrying it with her through the kitchen and staring out the opened windows to the welcoming, deserted beach below.

She walked toward the living area and grabbed the chenille blanket casually placed over the arm of a corner chair and tossed it over her shoulder, then walked back into the kitchen.

Donning the sandals she left near the entry, Chase decided to walk to the beach before it became populated with any other island guests. She needed the tranquility and peace that came only when she could be completely alone.

A time she desperately needed to come to grips with the wild curveballs life had thrown her over the last few days.

"Beautiful morning, isn't it?"

Startled, Chase jumped and twisted her upper body around as a deep, melodic voice intruded her solitary thoughts.

"Yes, it is," she murmured in response and glanced up.

She brought her hand to her forehead to shield the blazing sun from her eyes, wishing she'd thought to bring her sunglasses to the beach. She inhaled a swift breath.

She stared up into the face of one of the most beautiful men she'd ever seen.

His skin, the color of smooth, rich cream, was flawless. She ran her eyes over the perfect symmetry of his features: his deeply set, gray eyes; sharply cut cheekbones; bold, aquiline nose, and full, sensual lips—lips that were perfectly sculpted. Lips made for sin.

Taken separately, his features were bold, aristocratic, and at odds with one another. But together, they fit, beautifully so, as though a master artesian had, with careful precision, sculpted each one.

It was him.

The man who'd been watching her so intently at the welcome luau she'd attended upon arriving at the island.

When she'd been invited to attend the luau she'd gone, knowing good and well that if she stayed in her cottage, the anxiety of waiting for her fantasy to begin would work her nerves.

She arrived after the luau had already been in full swing. She had lucked out and found an unoccupied table, slightly tucked away from the crowd yet close enough to enjoy the festively garbed hula group entertaining the crowd with Hawaiian folk music.

Gratefully, she sat at the table alone, neither seeking nor wanting any companionship. Despite the many invitations from the occasional earnest man who asked within moments of her sitting down.

She felt a prickling down her spine, and, with the uncanny ability that women had, felt an intent stare. She casually turned in her chair, her eyes scanning the crowd, and had discovered a set of intense gray eyes intently observing her. As Chase caught eyes with him, she hadn't been able to look away. For that brief moment a wave of electric awareness seem to arc between them.

More than a bit disturbed, she forced herself to look away and blindly gave her attention to the musicians on the stage. After their song ended, she was to turn around, only to discover the man gone. She dismissed the accompanying feeling of disappointment as soon as she felt it.

She only had that one moment to see him, yet she wouldn't forget his piercing stare, or the moment of connection between them.

"Is this seat taken?" he asked, looking down at her.

One side of his wide mouth hitched up in a smile as he indicated the throw she had spread over the sand as a makeshift beach blanket.

"No," she murmured, clearing her throat as she shifted her body to allow him room on the blanket. "Feel free."

She nonchalantly studied him as he hunkered down, situating his long body on the throw.

He was casually dressed in a simple white cotton shirt, the top buttons undone to reveal a sprinkling of silky dark hair on his broad, muscled chest, and a pair of snug dark jeans molding his hard thighs.

Chase moved her eyes over the large bulge between his legs that strained his zipper and the slightly more worn area around his crotch before allowing her eyes to reverse their trail up his body, just as he was turning toward her after sitting down.

He faced her, and twin, small creases slashed his lean cheeks— the small smile which hitched one side of his lips upward still in place.

Chase returned the slight smile before she turned away and wrapped her arms around her bent knees.

Gazing out at the cerulean blue water that sparkled like diamonds against the rays of the early morning sun, she said, "I've never seen anything so breathtaking. It's beautiful."

"It is," he agreed.

Chase turned slightly, only to discover that his eyes weren't on the water, but instead, watching her with that same intent concentration she'd felt at the luau. She stared at him, unable to move her eyes away. Tingling awareness shot down her body again. She shivered despite the warm, early morning sun beating down on her.

Forcing herself to look away from him, she turned back toward the water, and adjusted the fabric wrap more securely around her body.

"Is it everything you expected?"

Chase frowned, glancing at him from the corner of her eye. "What do you mean?"

"This—" He waved, sweeping a hand out, encompassing the beach, the water, the island.

"I don't know that I knew what to expect." The sigh escaped her before she could prevent it.

He released a low, deep chuckle, one that caused a rash of goosebumps to dance along her skin. She tightened her hold around her knees. "It is quite a different experience, isn't it? A very…unique experience."

Chase turned considering eyes on him. "What did *you* expect?" She wondered if he too were here for a fantasy getaway, and if so, what his fantasy was.

He was silent for so long that she doubted he'd answer. When he did, his answer was different than she'd expected.

"The same thing as you, I would imagine."

"And that would be?"

When he said nothing, she prodded further. "You're here for…" She allowed the question to dangle, not satisfied with his lack of a real answer.

"To have a fantasy fulfilled. A fantasy that if it does become fulfilled, it will not be for me alone."

"Oh? So you're a philanthropist?" She turned and faced him, raising a sardonic brow in question.

He laughed. "I wouldn't go that far. Let's just say that in fulfilling a fantasy of mine, it will also help fulfill the...un-known...fantasy of another."

"They don't know what they want?" Chase quickly picked up on his slight emphasis on fulfilling an *unknown* fantasy of another.

"On some level, perhaps."

Chastity pondered his statement. Before she could comment, he continued, "Do you always know what you want, Chastity?"

She bit her bottom lip, considering. "The same thing a lot of people want. I want to be on top. I've worked hard for every-thing I have achieved. I want recognition for it," she replied without thinking and immediately wondered what he thought of her bold statement.

He said nothing, but simply continued to stare out at the ocean. Although he didn't ask for any more information, Chase felt a need to explain.

"Is it so bad to want to be on the top? Is there anything wrong with wanting to be number one?"

"No, nothing wrong with that. But, before that happens, Chastity, you have to know yourself. You'll never get what you really want...what you deserve, if you don't free yourself of the demons of your past."

"What—what are you talking about?" Nearly speechless, Chase stammered the question.

He raised a long, lean finger and caressed a path down her face, his gaze locked with hers for long moments. Instead of flinching away, Chase found herself leaning into his touch. The moment she realized what she was doing, she brought herself up short and turned her head away, licking the bottom rim of her tongue in a state of confusion.

She heard him stand to leave and felt him staring down at her. She, however, forced herself not to look at him. After long moments, he turned and walked away.

Once she was sure he was gone, Chase turned her body to watch his retreating back as he walked toward the other end of the beach before disappearing behind the line of shrubbery, completely from her sight.

As she sat staring after him, it dawned on Chase that he'd called her by her first name. Her brows lowered and her forehead creased as she wondered how he knew her name.

A shiver of unknown awareness trickled down her spine.

CHAPTER 12

"We're here to bathe you."

Chastity's eyes snapped open with a start.

"Bathe me?" she muttered, licking her dry lips as she struggled to sit up.

She lifted her body from the sofa, where she'd fallen asleep after returning home from the beach. The warm sun and the mimosa she'd drunk had mingled to put her into such a relaxed state that she had dozed off to sleep within minutes of lying on the sofa.

Standing before her were two women wearing identical pleasant expressions on their beautiful faces and identical clothing of short, sheer, white gowns. But that was where the similarities ended.

One was tall, nearly as tall as Chase, and appeared to be of Asian heritage. Her dark, slanted eyes stared at Chase as she tightened the ties of her wrap around her body. Chase ran her eyes over the woman, from head to toe. She had porcelain-white, pale skin, yet beneath the sheer gown she wore, Chase could clearly see the imprint of her small, high breasts, tipped with small, cherry-wine-colored nipples that pressed against the sheer fabric.

Her eyes trailed down the woman's body, noting the small indenture of her waist and soft flaring of slender hips. At the juncture of her thighs, barely discernible, she saw a sprinkling of light-colored hair that covered her mound, which matched the color of her long, waist-length, rich, sable-colored hair.

Chase turned to the other woman, who silently appraised her as well. This one was petite and African American. The top of her closely cropped, curly hair barely reached her companion's shoulder.

Where her companion was boyishly slender, this one was the exact opposite. Her body was lushly curved beneath the sheer gown. Her waist was small and tightly nipped in with richly curved hips, and thick, toned legs. Chase's eyes rolled over her unbound breasts.

The large, perfectly rounded globes appeared firm, although they gently hung low, no doubt due to their massive size. Her chocolate-brown nipples, several shades darker than her creamy café au lait complexion, strained against the fabric.

A bloom of fiery lust unfurled deep in her belly as she surveyed the two beautiful attendants standing before her.

"My name is Aisha," the petite, brown beauty spoke in a low, husky voice. "This is LuAhn," she said, nodding her head toward the tall woman at her side, smiling a dazzling smile, exposing tiny, perfectly white teeth.

Chase swallowed the hazy desire threatening to overcome her as she surveyed the women before her. "What do you mean 'bathe me'?"

Neither woman replied. The one named LuAhn offered a hand, and Chase hesitantly placed hers within the woman's, allowing her to help her to rise.

Once she stood, both women bracketed her, one in front, the other in back, and quickly divested her of her clothing. Deft fingers moved over Chase's body with such cool efficiency that they had her completely nude before she could utter a protest.

"Come, let's go." The smaller one—Aisha—grasped her hand again and tugged, leading Chase toward the bedroom. Both women laid her on the bed and quickly joined her.

"I don't need you to bathe me. I—"

Soft hands pressed her down to the bed, and the women followed, lying on either side of her, front and back, sandwiching her. She felt the lushness of Aisha's body against her breasts, the soft curls covering her mound hotly pressed against Chase's own, and one muscular leg knifed Chase's thighs apart as her body molded and conformed to Chase's.

At the same time, the hard-body LuAhn pressed tightly against Chase's back, her mound contouring to Chase's buttocks, and her thighs nestled against the back of Chase's legs. One long, lean leg wrapped securely around one of Chase's calves.

"You will," the soft promise came from behind her.

A pair of pale hands firmly cupped Chase's breasts, tugging on her sensitive nipples, as a dark hand reached between her thighs, and numbly able fingers delved deep inside her core.

Chase moaned, and pressed closer to Aisha and her driving fingers. LuAhn lifted one of her breasts. Aisha's greedy mouth fastened on, making wet, kittenish sounds of delight as she feasted on Chase, her tongue lapping around the flat disk of her areole before tugging on Chase's tightening nipple.

After one final, sweet lick, the smaller woman released her hold on Chase's breast. Chase's body was slightly repositioned, so that she lay against LuAhn, while Aisha snaked her nimble body down the length of Chase's body until she reached the juncture of her legs.

Chase's eyes flew opened as the woman nipped her clit with the tips of her small teeth before using her tongue to soothe and stroke once, deeply into her cunt.

"Sssh, it's okay," LuAhn whispered hotly against Chase's ear as Chase began to fight against it, pushing away from LuAhn and leaning down to try and bring the dark beauty back toward her.

"No...stop." She breathed the words while trying again to pull the woman's bobbing head away from her, only to have LuAhn grab her hands and anchor them to her sides, forcing her to allow the other to continue.

"I...I...can't—" Chase bit the words out. "Not again."

"Give in to it," LuAhn encouraged.

Chase moved her head to look away, but LuAhn wouldn't allow her. She turned her face so that she had no choice but to watch.

Aisha placed both of her small hands beneath the globes of Chastity's buttocks, her eyes glued to Chase's, and with agonizing slowness leaned down toward the dark, curly thatch of hair at the apex of Chase's thighs.

Chase's nostrils flared, her heart slammed a staccato beat against her chest as she waited to feel her tongue against her pussy.

Her pointed tongue speared directly into Chase, her tongue hollowing as she scooped out a measure of her sweet cream.

A sigh of pleasure whispered past Chase's lips before she could prevent its escape.

She swallowed, her breath coming out in harsh gasps as she fought against the panic she felt begin to swamp her mind. It was too soon. She couldn't do this again...

Closing her eyes, she inhaled a deep, calming breath.

She then leaned back against LuAhn, forcing her body, her mind, to relax and gradually allowed her legs to relax as well, giving the woman and her devouring tongue silent acquiesce to continue.

"It's good?" LuAhn whispered the words, more of a statement than question, against Chase's neck. "You're enjoying this, yes?" Her tone was eager, as though her only wish, her only thought, was to please Chase.

Chase was silent, unable to say anything, warring emotions rendering her speechless. Aisha turned her head, looking to LuAhn for approval. She felt LuAhn nod her head, and like the eager pup she appeared to be, Aisha smiled happily and returned to feast between Chase's legs.

LuAhn's hands began to mold and massage Chase's breasts as Aisha devoured and lapped at her pussy in exquisite perfect orchestration.

LuAhn's firm but soft hands firmly massaged and played with her breasts, tugging and pulling on nipples that were taut and blood-filled, while Aisha's lips caressed her down below in slick, hot glides.

When the eager Aisha slipped a finger inside her ass, still going at her pussy with her velvet tongue, Chase gasped, pushing back into LuAhn's embrace.

LuAhn removed one hand from Chase's breasts and turned her face and slanted her mouth over Chase's, swallowing her whimpers of protests and pleasure.

The woman struck her tongue deep into Chase's mouth, and Chase eagerly latched on, their tongues dueling, chasing each other, as the kiss exploded.

"Yes, I think she is enjoying it," Chase heard the dark woman between her thighs murmur in response to the question she'd asked. She felt the woman's smile against her thighs, but no longer cared. She simply wanted her to keep doing what she was doing.

Chase reached a hand down and planted it at the top of the dark woman's head, not to draw away from her, as she'd done in the past; instead to draw her nearer, shamelessly grinding her vagina against the woman's face.

She bucked and ground her lower body while exchanging hot, torrid kisses with the beautiful Asian woman, the pleasure humming through her body was so strong, so...intense, tears burned the back of her eyes.

When Aisha lifted her thighs higher, placing them over her shoulder, and fucked her in tight licks, adding a second finger to dig further into her clenching ass, Chase clenched her eyes shut. Yet she continued to allow the women to work her, fuck her, fully participating in the threesome as the women catered to her, doing her so good, a cry of pleasure ripped from her throat.

With determined licks and prods of her tongue, the woman between her thighs continued to eat and suck, devouring her pussy in earnest. Humming softly buzzed in Chase's ears as her body began to tremble, the beginnings of an orgasm unfurling.

She swallowed, her muscles tensing; the legs she had around Aisha clamped down on either side of her face.

Panicking, Chase grunted in protest against the woman's mouth when she tried to escape the passionate clutches of both women.

She broke the kiss, and frantically shoved against the woman between her thighs, pulling at her head, desperately trying to escape the impeding orgasm.

But neither woman allowed her to escape.

The one holding her captive grasped her arms and pulled them behind her head. With smooth dexterity, she grabbed the gown she'd discarded near the floor and knotted Chase's hands together, effectively securing them above her head.

In desperation, realizing what was happening, Chase fought against the makeshift restraints to no avail.

LuAhn slammed her mouth over Chase's, roughly grasped her blood-tightened nipples between her fingers and pulled. The painful tug caused electric pulses to radiate through her body. At the same time, Aisha pulled her clit deep into her mouth and lightly bit the engorged nub before releasing it. She peeled back the lips of her vagina, laving her inner lips, and immediately began to feed Chase her fingers, one at a time until she'd imbedded them all, stuffing her small, balled fist deep into Chase's cunt.

The woman returned to a slow screwing, her balled fists dragging in and out of Chase's core as her mouth gave short, almost delicate swipes to her outer vaginal lips.

The orgasm hit, without warning, slamming her back against the woman who cradled her in her arms.

She screamed into LuAhn's mouth as she ground herself, impaled herself on Aisha's fist, grinding against her; her body bucked and spasmed as the release washed over her.

Once her body completed, drowsy, she lay back, exhausted against LuAhn's body, her chest moving in and out in deep breaths at the lazily swirling overhead fan.

She didn't protest as they lifted her as though her weight was nothing and carried her into the bathroom.

After filling the large, Jacuzzi-styled tub, the three women, as though in a rehearsed erotic play, climbed into the tub.

The women immediately began to wash her. Aisha began to clean her feet, as she lay against LuAhn, both of their soft hands feathering over her body in caresses so light they felt like butterflies whispering over Chase's skin.

She closed her eyes and allowed them to cater to her. When she felt the soapy towel between her thighs, nudging against them, she opened her legs, willingly, knowing what the women wanted.

She moaned when she felt the sponge slip between the swollen lips of her vagina, yet didn't stop her.

LuAhn ran a twin sponge down her breasts, and with a detached awareness, Chase watched the soapy trail of suds trickle between the valley of her breasts, down the mid line of her body, before disappearing in the water near her hips.

"I think you're ready for him," LuAhn whispered against her ear.

Chase's eyes snapped opened, the relaxing nearly euphoric feeling evaporating at the woman's words.

CHAPTER 13

With methodical precision, Chase folded her clothes neatly, placing them in her opened suitcase. After she'd finished, she placed her toiletry bag on top, and with a definitive snap, she closed her suitcase, snapping the lock into place.

She glanced around the room, making sure she hadn't forgotten anything, before lifting the case from the bed, placing it on the bedroom floor.

She exhaled a long breath.

She had to get out.

Enough was damn enough.

After the women had left, LuAhn's words rang into her head, long into the day, and the following night. *"I think you're ready for him..."*

She'd been on edge, waiting and wondering what was to come next. In the end, she decided that she no longer wanted to play puppet in someone's twisted game.

"This is *my* fantasy. I didn't come here to be a pawn or made to submit to someone else's agenda," she murmured out loud.

She picked up the phone and not knowing what else to do, merely going on blind instinct, punched the number for the operator. Immediately she was connected with a woman who identified her by name, and solicitously asked how she could serve her.

"You can *serve* me by getting me the hell out of this place. Now."

There was a long pause before the woman replied in a cheerful voice, "I'm sorry, Ms. Davidson, but your fantasy has not reached its natural conclusion. You—"

"Natural conclusion, my ass. Bitch, if you do *not* get me off this island, *now*…" Chase clamped her mouth shut and took in deep breaths, futilely attempting to bring her temper under control.

There was deafening silence, then a series of clicks…

"Is there a problem, Ms. Davidson?" the smooth deep voice of the man she knew to be Merrick asked.

"Yes. You could say that!" Chase proceeded to outline, in precise detail, what the problem was, concluding with, "I didn't sign up for this, Merrick. I didn't sign up to be gang-raped and forced to do shit—"

"You were gang-raped? Forced to do things against your will, Ms. Davidson?" he smoothly interjected, his voice calm, neutral.

Chase shut her eyes and gritted her teeth.

Chase sighed. She sat down on the bed, shoving the suitcase to the side.

She refused to give him the satisfaction by admitting she had become an all-too-willing participant in the sexual games. "This isn't what I thought it would be. Nothing has been as I thought it would be."

"Did you not ask to be number one? Wasn't that your desire, to be in demand, every need catered to…to be number one?" he asked, his voice silky and smooth.

"Not like this! I—"

"Do you *not* remember what your invitation stated, Ms. Davidson?"

Chase opened her mouth to tell him exactly what she thought of the *invitation*, but before she could, he continued to speak.

"Should you choose to accept this invitation, you agree that you are succumbing to your desires, that you are freeing your-self to experience something you've never dared to yield to," he reminded her of the last clause in the invitational contract.

"So does that mean I'm forced to stay here? Is *that* what the hell you're telling me?" she spat in agitation.

"Ms. Davidson, at the conclusion of your fantasy, your charter plane will arrive to safely escort you off the island."

Seconds later, a buzzing tone hummed in her ear, indicating he'd disconnected the line, leaving a bemused Chase on the other end.

She'd pressed the dial button ready to call him back, to let him know just what she thought of his island. This was supposed to be a fantasy where she was number one, where she called the shots.

"Damn it!" she snarled.

She hurled the phone against the wall and in satisfaction watched it break into a hundred shattered pieces and fall to the floor.

CHAPTER 14

"I don't think I've ever seen water so blue."

Chase experienced a thrill when she heard the deep voice from behind her. She hadn't heard his approach, yet she wasn't surprised that he was there.

She turned, glancing over her shoulder, and made eye contact with the man who stood near.

Not only was his appearance anticipated, Chase had hoped she would see him. In her subconscious she knew she would come to the beach again, at the same time in the hope of seeing him again.

She didn't want to leave the island without seeing him one final time. And she had every intent on leaving the island today, even if that meant she had to swim across to the main island.

"No, I can't say that I have. But then again, everything about this island is...*different*."

"Magical?"

"Hmmm," she hummed the non-committal response.

"May I?"

He didn't wait for a reply, but simply folded his large frame down to sit closely beside her.

"Different in what way?"

She turned, her features twisting, eyebrows scrunched as she considered his response. After he'd settled, she turned away, staring at the sun as it settled behind the calm, dark, azure waters.

"Maybe surreal is a more apt way to describe it," she replied and shrugged. "Damned if I know." She laughed without any real humor.

They sat in companionable silence for long moments as they gazed at the gentle waves slapping against one another in the otherwise calm ocean waters.

"Have you ever worked so hard for something only to have it snatched away from you, along with all of your dreams crashing down around you?" Chase asked, shivering when the wind rose and wrapping her arms more snuggly around her bent knees.

She felt him shift on the blanket and draw nearer. When one strong arm wrapped around her shoulders, it felt good to lean against him, to soak in his warmth. It seemed natural to allow him the intimacy. To allow the intimacy of a stranger.

"I have." His answer, although short, increased the feeling of *rightness* she'd felt around him, from the moment they'd met.

As though they were kindred spirits, of sorts. She shrugged off the uncomfortable thought and shifted her body so that his arm fell away. He made no response, yet she felt his gaze.

"Well, welcome to my world." She laughed, without humor, turning back to look at him. "I guess that's why I jumped at the chance to come here. Nothing like mindless sex to take your mind off your problems," she finished flippantly.

His eyes intently roamed over her face as though seeking the answer to some unknown question. Chase shivered beneath his intent stare.

"No. That's not why you came. There had to be more to it than mindless sex."

Chase exhaled a long breath. Closing her eyes, her hands flattened on the blanket as she leaned back in thought. "No. That's not why I came."

He said nothing, and the silence, the semi-deserted beach, and his strangely comforting presence aided in creating an atmosphere that compelled Chase to speak out loud about the things that were on her mind—easily.

"I lost something that I'd been working all my life for." She released a humorless laugh. "I suppose it was something I was able to measure myself against, to measure my success against. When I didn't get it, a lot of things changed for me, things I'm still trying to understand and get a grasp on it. Hell, I'm still not sure what or why it all happened." She began to tell him of the events that had transpired over the last week of her life, events that had turned her world upside down.

"It's in those moments that you have to take a hard look at your life. You know, when your world comes crashing in. When you—" She stopped.

Self-conscious, realizing that she'd just told a complete stranger things she'd never discussed with anyone, things she'd kept hidden away from herself.

The thought was disconcerting. "God, I'm sorry. Didn't mean to deliver a diatribe."

"No need to apologize. I suppose that's a good enough reason as any to re-evaluate your life," he replied smoothly, the genuine warmth in his voice reassuring.

She continued to speak, finding it easy to talk to him, to unload things she'd kept buried deep inside for years. She told him things she'd never spoken out loud, things she never documented in a personal journey. Things she normally tried to avoid all thoughts of.

In doing so, she felt a portion of her curious burden lift from her shoulders.

"You grew up alone." Chase turned to look at him. He offered the question more like a statement.

"It was just me and my mother for a long time. When I was a bit older, my mother remarried. My father didn't re-enter the picture until I was older," she answered, swallowing against the bile that rose to her throat immediately. She ruthlessly suppressed the revulsion…the fear.

"Did things change when he came back into your life?"

Chase laughed, harshly, no longer seeing the handsome, enigmatic man beside her. Instead she saw the mocking image of the one who was supposed to protect her, the one who'd been the one who had hurt her, had been instrumental in damaging her in ways that went far beyond the physical.

"Yes," she answered softly, painful memories of just how well she'd gotten to know her father piercing her heart.

She ground her teeth together, batting her eyelashes and frantically forcing to prevent the tears she felt threatening to break through, to remain tightly leashed.

"Look, I need to go," she said, feeling a desperate need to get away from him and his intent stare.

She hastily got to her feet and quickly retrieved her things after he moved away from the blanket. Silently, he watched her as she dumped the blanket inside the tote bag she'd carried to the beach.

"Thanks for the free therapy," she said glibly and ignored

the look he gave her. "But, I think it's time for me to go." She said the words with finality. It was not only time for her to get away from him and her strange attraction to him, but to get as far away from the island as she could get.

She turned to leave, not waiting—not wanting—to hear his reply. She'd only taken a few steps away when his words stopped her.

"Success comes with a price, Chastity. What price are you willing to pay?"

Chase faltered in her steps at his words, and stopped. She turned her head, so that she could see him in her peripheral vision.

"I'm willing to pay whatever price is necessary."

CHAPTER 15

Chase sat in one of the swivel-backed chairs of the kitchen's small dinette table, staring out of one of the windows, overlooking the beach.

"What price am I willing to pay to succeed?" she said out loud in a low voice, recalling his words.

She didn't need a trip to her therapist to know that her need to be in control had long been an obsession and was what drove her every action, her every step. The obsession had invaded not only her professional life. Her unquenchable desire and thirst to be successful had also shaped her personal life, twisting her in ways she hadn't realized.

It went beyond the sexual. Chase knew that the root of her problem was embedded in her childhood, yet it had been something she'd refused to acknowledge, much less try and get resolution for.

She'd allowed her past to shape her present—to the point that her world was now tumbling down around her.

Before the events of the last few days, Chase had been confident of who she was, had been so confident that there wasn't a man...or woman...who could control or manipulate her.

First, there'd been Javier. She had been certain he was well controlled, that she was the one in charge...*Overly so, obviously*, she thought and laughed harshly. She picked up the coffee and took a careful sip of the steaming brew before thoughtfully placing it back down on the glass table.

She'd been confident that he was faithful to her, assured that she could trust him. That she'd *trained* him well. She had molded him, carefully manipulated the relationship, ensuring his dependence on her, dominating him to ensure his dependence on her. And in the end...

"In the damn end, he screwed me. Just like he said." She laughed without humor.

She pushed herself away from the table and stood. *God, what was she going to do?*

Padding barefoot over to the small sink, she placed the mug inside and turned on the tap, rinsing out the cup and stopped herself.

Even now, she had to have everything neat, in order. Everything in her world always had to neat, exact, orderly.

After leaving the beach, her conversation with—*God, she didn't even know the man's name*, she thought—ran through her mind.

She had no idea what would await her when she accepted the invitation to come to Ka-le'a. Her only thought had been to get away from the devastation that had become her life, in a matter of hours. The very enticing thought of being number one, even sexually, had swayed her, at a time when she needed a quick ego stroke.

Instead, she'd been forced to deal with her own demons, had been forced to submit and allow others to pleasure her. In doing so she'd been forced to release and give up her own power, the power she'd worked her entire life to maintain. And she found pleasure in doing so. As much as she hated to think about it, much less acknowledge it, she found it strangely exhilarating. But, the thought of her "final" adventure, the one that the others hinted at, was unsettling.

She straightened her back. She'd come this far in her journey; there was no way in hell she was going to back out now.

With a sigh, she turned away and as she walked toward the living area, she turned when she heard the back door of the patio open.

Her eyes widened, and her heart slammed against her chest when she saw the man lounging against the doorway, his light-gray eyes staring at her. No emotion crossed his handsome face.

"You. I should have known."

CHAPTER 16

She stood there, immobile, staring at the lounging form of the man in the doorway whose gray-eyed gaze seared a burning, betraying hole that painfully pierced her heart.

Thinking back, it all made sense. Of course it was him. Who else would it be?

"So what—who—are you?" she asked, staring at the man who was a stranger, yet not.

Her question was met with a silence that angered her even more.

"Why me?" The words were torn from behind tightly clenched teeth.

She turned away, unable to look at him. She felt vulnerable... naked, despite that she was fully clothed. Her stomach churned and her head throbbed with a sudden ache as she thought of how she'd exposed herself to him. The way she'd told him some of her deepest thoughts. Thoughts she'd never shared with another living soul.

She'd poured out her heart thinking he was a complete stranger, finding it easy to reveal herself to him, in that way that came easier with strangers, falsely believing she would have no more interaction with him.

And all along he'd *known* who she was. "God damn you."

He had been the one to "buy" her. Her lips curled in a snarl as she spun around to face him, only to find him standing directly behind her. He'd moved silently, further into the room and now stood mere inches away from her. His hands settled on top of her shoulders. Flinching, she tore away from him.

"Don't fucking touch me," she spit the words and turned on her heels to move away. She'd only taken two steps away when his voice stopped her.

"Don't go. Please."

The simple command prevented her from moving.

"And if I do?" she asked, without turning back around.

Silence met her question. She waited, wondering to what lengths he'd go to keep her.

"You can't go, Chase. To do so would be admitting defeat. You're too strong of a woman for that."

"What do you know about me or my strengths?" She hurled the words at him turning to face him. "You don't know shit about me!" She reached out and slapped him as hard as she could, her hand leaving a burning red imprint on his lean cheek.

He swallowed. His jaw tightened so that the muscle twitched. But, he said nothing. That angered Chase even more.

"What? You're just going to take it? Nothing to say?" She pushed him, her anger escalating.

She shoved her flattened hands against the steel wall of his chest, as angry tears ran down her face in rivulets. Balling her fists, in earnest she fought him, until she stumbled and fell to the floor, bringing him down with her.

He swiftly maneuvered their bodies, ripping the fabric wrap dress she wore so that her breasts came tumbling free. He trapped her beneath him.

"Enough!" he bit out, grabbing her hands and securing them above her head; his hard chest blanketing her now naked body.

Her chest heaved as she took in deep breaths. The wood floor was cold against her naked breasts, and his hard back was warm against her back, yet she wasn't going to allow him to dominate her. She'd had enough of that.

Chase waited for long moments, enough to catch her breath, before she renewed her struggles. Surprising him, she slammed her head back, catching the side of his face and snatched her hands away from his grip.

She bucked against him, throwing him off her body, enough so that she was able to get on her hands and knees and crawl away from him.

"Come back here," he growled, grabbing her legs, pulling her roughly back toward him as she crawled along the floor.

Chase didn't waste energy speaking.

She kicked one leg behind her, blindly, and heard the satisfying sound of connecting with some part of his body. He grunted, but kept coming after her.

She rose and made a mad dash toward the patio door. Seconds away from opening the door, she felt him grasp her around the waist. He spun her around, his hold unyielding as he dragged her back against him. Crushing her body to his, he slammed their joined bodies against the wall.

"That's the last time you get away with that." The hard, determined look on his angry face sent thrills of fear and anticipation racing over Chase's body.

His hands roamed over her, familiarizing himself with the lush lines of her curves, running his hands over her back, over the nipped-in indenture of her waist, and over the smooth, muscled contours of her ass.

He grabbed the ties of her dress and tore them, pulling the dress from her body.

"You won't need these, either," he said before ripping her thong off her body, staring into her eyes, his expression intense.

She gasped when he pressed against her, and slipped one thick finger past her creaming folds, plunged deep inside her pussy, and scooped a measure of her cum out, flickering her blood-thickened clit, spreading the dewy moisture around it.

He trailed his finger down her perineum, the sensitive skin between her pussy and ass, and Chase bit back a moan of pleasure when he rimmed her tight, puckered hole, feathering against it, teasing her.

Before she could utter a protest, he had her back down on the floor, she in front of him, on her hands and knees with him behind her.

She heard the hiss of his zipper and glanced over her shoulder to see him impatiently pull his slacks down the length of his legs, far enough so that his angry cock jutted free. His hands quickly went to his shirt, pulling it over his head and exposing his broad, thick, muscled chest before he brought her body back into tight alignment with his.

She swallowed, deeply, when the impressive, hard length of his dick probed impatiently at her pussy, demanding entrance.

He grabbed her hair, fisted the long strands like a rope around his hand and pulled her head back, so that she was forced to look at him. Her heart thudded erratically against her chest, as she took in his tightly drawn features, the look of lust and determination gleaming sharply in his eyes in the dark room. He placed a scorching kiss on the side of her neck, and Chase moaned, her eyes fluttering closed.

He ran his tongue down her neck and the column of her throat before retracing his path. He swirled a delicious, hot pattern inside her ear, taking the fleshy lobe into his mouth, and biting sharply. The sting was negligible, but it was enough for her to feel it. Cream ran down the inside of her thighs.

"You're not angry with me. You're angry with yourself," he whispered the words against the sensitive hollow beneath her ear.

He pushed her back down and clamped a hand over the back of her neck, stilling her. "You're angry because what you *thought* you wanted, you didn't get."

The ends of Chase's nostrils flared; her breathing hitched as she listened to him speak. The words shot a piercing arrow directly to her heart.

"You're angry because you knew that all along."

He began to feed her his dick in painstakingly slow, scorching inches, until he filled her, stuffing her, until she felt every hard inch and he bumped the back of her womb. She shut her eyes tightly; her hands and arms shook as she accepted him deep into her body.

"You had to be broken down. You had to be *forced* to reevaluate who you are. Why you are."

The more he spoke, as his strokes intensified in strength and power, the more her body began to ripple, blossom.

"Only then would you be ready. Only then can you be the true woman you were destined to be."

Chase pushed back against his dick, seeking to devour him as much as he was devouring her with his cock and his words. The scent of sex and lust made her dizzy. Stars began to unfold behind the tightly clenched lids of her eyes.

He pushed her down on the floor and ground into her, riding her ass, fucking her fiercely, her clit rubbing against the wood floor as he rode her. At the angle he had her, with her ass slightly raised off the floor, pressed out so he could fuck her, her pussy and clit mashed against the cold floor, as he ground into her.

"Yes…yes," she cried out against his thrusts as her pussy milked his dick.

"You're so ripe, so juicy," he bit the words out as he pumped into her in long strokes. She heard his breathing, as harsh and loud as her own, as he steadily drove into her.

He jammed her body, driving into her seeping hole until his balls tapped her ass, unrelenting in his dominance over her, surging into her welcoming heat.

"So wet, but so tight," he bit the words out.

His hard hand roughly smoothed over her ass before he separated the round, high cheeks of her ass, running a finger down until he reached her seeping vagina.

"Oh, God…yes, yes…" she moaned as he moved in and out of her in easy, sure glides.

Her body jostled and her knees scraped against the hardwood floors as his strokes became hotter, harder, more demanding. Had he not held on to her, her body would have completely lifted off the floor with the strength of his strokes. Chase pushed back against him, her cunt gripping and milking his rigid cock as he knifed into her with powerful able slices.

Her thighs quivered, her breath came out in strangled gasps, her nostrils flared as the scent of sex and his unique smell covered her. Overwhelmed her.

She moaned and cried out against the power of his thrusts, raising herself onto her elbows as she bucked back against him, loving every minute of the glorious fucking.

His thrusts were so powerful, so harsh, they bordered on painful, yet she shoved back into him, rolled her hips against his marauding cock to capture every thriving thrust. Her breasts swayed, jostling, the tips of her nipples brushing on the floor with each shove of his dick inside.

"Yes, yes...harder....just like that," she gasped, and shouted when she felt the stinging slap of a hard hand against one of her butt cheeks. Her keening cries rang loudly in the room when he delivered another stinging slap to her bottom. She screamed, the pleasure intensifying to incredulous portions, her body on fire, sweat dripping down her face.

As he fucked her, he continued to slap her ass, harder, in rhythm to his corkscrew thrusts until the pain and pleasure mingled into one, sending her body over the edge, shattering her. Crystal-like stars flashed in front of her, her mind and body shattering into a million shards of glass as the power of her release shook her.

Behind her, he continued to dig into her, lifting one of her legs to reposition her as he angled his marauding cock at a new angle. He pumped into her—hard, fast, mercilessly. Chase felt another orgasm rip, tearing into her. She screamed as he held on to her tightly.

As she came a second time, she heard his hoarse shout from behind her and seconds later his cum, hot, scorching, sweet, landed in hot streams on her back.

Chase lay on her stomach, with his body pressing her into the floor, limp and utterly satiated. She shivered as their combined sweat began to cool, shivering in reaction to the wild sex and the man who had thoroughly and completed dominated her.

Later, they lay on the bed, sweaty and exhausted. One of his hard legs was horizontally across hers, pinning her to the bed while an arm rested over her waist. His penis, now softened, lay against her buttocks.

He'd taken her again, on the floor, soon after the first episode. The second time he'd fucked her, his erection had been as rigid, just as unyielding as the first time, as though the sexing he'd given her moments earlier hadn't happened.

It had been quick, hot and hard, as he'd rutted her like a dog. And like a bitch in heat, she'd welcomed him into her body until she'd exploded, taking him with her.

It had been much later that she'd felt him lift her satiated body from the floor and carry her into the bedroom, carefully laying her on the bed, before he'd lain behind her, bringing her body flush against his as they'd drifted to sleep.

Now, as she awoke, and she was no longer caught in the sensual, fiery web of lust and sex, the shame of her complete submission stung.

He moved up her body, snaked his way up her body, and nudged between her legs, pushing them up until her feet were planted on the bed, with her knees bent and raised.

He saw that she was watching, and kept his eyes on hers as he bent his head toward her mound. She inhaled a deep breath, her lips partially opened, her heart thudding, as she waited to feel his mouth on that part of her body that longed for his touch.

"Hmmm," she moaned, arching her back, when he tongued aside the swollen lips of her vagina, the flat of his tongue swiping against her moist folds.

Kneeling between her bent knees, he ran a callused finger

up her inner thigh in soft strokes, until he reached the wiry, closely cut hairs that surrounded her vagina. He drew the finger up the seam of her pussy, gently splitting her open to his watchful gaze. He brought his other hand up, to keep her pussy open, and with the other stroked her distended nub.

Her body responded instantly. Her breath came out in harsh sighs. She felt her face flush in arousal and within seconds, she felt the ease of cream as it dripped from her pussy, and ran down his hand. He lifted his head, one side of his long, sensual mouth hitched. Keeping his eyes trained on hers, he licked his finger of her dewy essence.

"Sweet...bold, enticing. Just like you," he murmured, before turning his gaze back between her thighs.

He fingered her clit, toying and pinching the erect nub until Chase wanted to scream, beg him to take it into his mouth, beg him to bring her to release. But, she stopped herself.

Although every cell in her body, every nerve ending was on fire, begging for him to take her, she clenched her teeth and stopped herself from begging him.

The tormenting pleasure was one she *wanted* to endure.

She wanted him to string her out, wanted him to force her to accept his petting, his teasing. She knew that when he finally gave her what she wanted...*needed*...the release would be that much more pleasurable.

His tongue snaked out and licked her, from the back of her pussy to the front, in one long, hot stroke that had her back peeling off the bed, a cry on her lips.

He leaned back in, and blew a warm breath across her mound, tickling the wiry hairs, and more of her cream eased, running down her thighs. Sounds of pleasure came from his throat as his tongue darted out and quickly lapped her cream.

She clenched her legs in response, only to have him widen them, forcing her knees to spread wide, giving him more room.

This time he used his fingers to separate her, opening the lips of her vagina as he lapped at her streaming core in slick strokes.

Chase leaned back and accepted his oral loving, her hands balled on either side of her body as she fisted the silk sheets in each hand.

He suckled her clit deep into his mouth, his teeth scraping and pulling at the engorged little bud, and then inserted a finger deep inside. Chase bucked against his face, released her hold on the sheets, and grabbed both sides of his face, grinding against him as he continued to lave, suckle, and stroke her.

When the pressure built until she thought she couldn't handle it anymore, he inserted two more fingers deep into her channel; another until he was knuckle deep inside, dragging his curled fingers in and out of her until she broke.

The orgasm slammed into her.

"Yes. Yes!" she screamed, her upper body coming off the bed as she grabbed his head, grinding and pumping her hips against him, as the orgasm slammed into her. He pinched her clit, completely slamming her over the edge, yet continued to eat her pussy.

Even as the tremors began to ease, he lapped at her until she lay spent on the bed.

He delivered one final, hot lick into her core and her body completed its release. He climbed on top of her, leaned down and kissed her, gently on the mouth.

She felt her own essence as he gently kissed her on the mouth.

"Was it worth it?" Chase asked, as she lay next to him.

He looked down at her, raising a dark-brown brow in question.

"Twenty-five million is a lot to pay for a lay."

"Is that all you think this was about?" he asked.

"I don't know anything. You seem to know a lot about me, but I don't know anything about you. Why all of this? Why pay that much money for me?"

"Don't you think you're worth it?"

"Please don't do that."

"What?"

"Turn it around on me. I asked you an upfront question. Or is this something you do often? Pay for sex…"

"No." He laughed lightly. "I've never paid for sex. I didn't pay for sex this time, either." His non-answer thoroughly confused her.

"Do you work for Merrick then? Was all of the bidding, the high bidding, all a part of the fantasy?" she asked, strangely hurt. She remembered how exhilarating it had felt when the price, the "bid," had escalated to millions; recalled the feeling to have a room full of people all desperate for her and her alone.

The thought that it had all been a pretense, that the audience was all actors or whatever…

"It was real, Chase. All of it. The audience, the money, the bidding. All of it was very real, let me assure you."

His answer satisfied her.

"You must think I'm crazy. Wanting to be bought like a piece of merchandise," she said after a long silence, where she lay subdued beneath him, one of his hard legs thrown across her.

He reached down and lifted her chin so that she met his eyes. "No. I don't. Not at all."

Leaning down, he placed a soft kiss on her mouth, and Chase shut her eyes, accepting his kiss. When he broke the kiss, she leaned back down laying her head on his chest.

"You have nothing to be ashamed of. It was a fantasy that many shared with you. There is nothing wrong with you."

She remained quiet and allowed his reassuring words to soak in.

"Do you want me, Chastity?" he asked, his liquid brown eyes locked with hers.

Chase stared at him, uncertain. There was so much more to his question than appeared.

He was waiting for her to acknowledge that she was willing—that she wanted him to pleasure her, yes, but also that she was willing to allow him to break through that final barrier, one she'd kept so firmly in place, one she'd spent years erecting, one that guarded her from ever feeling at the mercy of another.

God, was she ready for that? Was she ready to let go, to allow another control over her body, her mind, her spirit?

Turmoil and anxiety were nothing new to her, particularly over the last few days as she'd been challenged to face the demons of her past.

She swallowed, her eyes roaming over his, before she succumbed.

Unable to speak, she simply nodded her head, in acquiesce.

With her acceptance, peace, serenity, overcame her. She wrapped her leg around his calf, slowly running her foot up his leg, to wrap around over his hard-muscled buttocks, and over his waist.

"Tell me," he demanded, "say it."

She looked in his eyes, desperately, clutching his broad shoulders. "Please…"

"Please what, Chastity?" He was unrelenting in his demands for her full submission.

She closed her eyes against what he was asking of her, what he was demanding for her to say.

He slanted his mouth over hers, swallowing her cry of distress as his tongue shoved past her teeth swiping into her mouth.

"I—I can't," she cried out, breaking away from his mouth.

He brought his hands up to frame her face, forcing her to look at him.

"Tell me, Chastity."

Chase swallowed down the need to rebel, to push him away. To deny him the ultimate access to her. "What makes you think you have a right to demand anything from me?"

"Tell me," he repeated the command, his tone firm, brooking no argument.

She bit her lip and stared at him. Instead of shoving away, she deliberately brought her leg up, running it slowly along his calf, the heel of her foot scraping along his calf, his thighs, before she wrapped her leg around his lean waist pulling their bodies closer.

"I want you to make me come," she whispered, looking directly into his eyes.

The smile he gave her was one of savage satisfaction.

Keeping eye contact with her, he grasped her hands in his, threading his fingers with hers and began to penetrate her.

He eased inside, gently and carefully as though she was fragile, delicate. As though she was cherished.

The sex was different this time. As he stroked into her, he maintained eye contact, taking her hands in his and threading their fingers together. He wouldn't allow her to look away as his hips rolled in slow, leisurely thrusts. He leaned down and kissed her, sliding his tongue as deeply into her mouth as his shaft was inside her body. He broke the kiss, his breath coming out in shallow pants that mimicked hers.

Carefully, he ground into her, setting a smooth, in-and-out rhythm that was nearly unbearable in its pleasure.

"Oh God, that feels so good." Chase panted the words, her hips matching his, thrust for thrust, as their bodies strained against each other. He reached down to pull one of her breasts deeply into his mouth, and Chase cried out sharply.

Between the hot feel of him shafting her and his tight pulls on her breasts, she didn't know how much longer she could take it. When he reached a hand between them and tugged on her clit, she broke.

She screamed as her orgasm slammed into her, her body jerking as the release took over. As she came, he continued to thrust into her until he too released. Hot streams of his cum washed her womb, as she lay beneath him satisfied and replete. Complete at last.

***

When she'd woken in the morning, she turned over in the bed, seeking him. Instead of his warm, large body cradling hers, she was alone.

She had a thousand questions to ask him. Who was he? Why had he come to the island? Why had he chosen her?

But none of those answers would she ever know.

She closed her eyes, hugged the pillow that held his unique scent to her body for long moments, and cried.

She didn't cry because he wasn't there. The tears were for

what he'd helped her to release. What he'd helped her achieve had been magical, something unreal, something she'd never forget.

Just as she'd never forget him.

"Ms. Davidson, we hope your stay here with us was pleasurable."

Chastity removed her sunglasses and smiled genuinely at Merrick.

She leaned her head down to allow the woman who stood at his side to present her with the traditional lei.

She laughed lightly, thinking of when she'd arrived, how she'd impatiently waved the woman away as she'd tried to "lei" her.

She grasped the hand he held out, holding onto it as she looked into his eyes. He smiled, his dark-brown eyes held the same hint of mystery she'd seen when she'd met him, yet to her frustration, she had been unable to decipher. Now, she knew. She mentally amended that. She had a small idea as it pertained to her. His job had been to help her free herself from the bonds—invisible bonds that had kept her restrained for so long, bonds that had limited her from fully coming into her own as a woman.

The rest was now up to her.

"Yes, it was indeed," she replied.

He simply nodded his head to her. Moments later, she turned with him, along with the others who stood waiting as the outer doors of the charter plane transporting them to Honolulu opened, ready to take them back.

She turned and ran her eyes over the small group, searching for *him*. Deep inside, she knew she wouldn't see him in the small crowd.

She batted away the tears that threatened to fall again and met Merrick's enigmatic stare. She doggedly forced a smile on her face.

When the attendant came to her side, she gave him her luggage, and with a final glance over the milling crowd, she turned and strode toward the plane.

CHAPTER 17

Chastity sat with her hands clenching the leathered wheel of her Mercedes, her eyes darting over the rundown, two-story, brick townhouse she called home for the first sixteen years of her life.

She released the death-grip she had on the wheel, cut off the softly humming engine, and pocketed her keys in her purse. And sat. Running her eyes back over the house, she knew her mother was home because her car sat in the driveway.

"God, what in hell am I doing here?" she spoke out loud, running a shaky hand over her loose hair, tucking a curl behind her ear.

What she hoped to accomplish, she didn't know.

She leaned back against the seat, thinking of her return from the island.

When she finally got home, her first order of business was to shower and fall into bed. As she went to retrieve one of the Hawaiian outfits she had purchased, an envelope fell out of the bag. She turned it over, and there was the invitation, the same one she'd gotten in email.

With her heart caught in her throat, she ran her fingers gently over the red wax seal with the blossoming hibiscus embossed in the center. She brought the sealed envelope to her nose, and her eyes feathered closed as the fragrant, distinct scent of the flower wafted into her nostrils.

With trembling hands, she split the seal, and pulled out the note. As she withdrew it, a lone hibiscus petal floated to the floor.

"And the day came when the risk to remain tight in a bud was more painful than the risk it took to blossom."

After reading the quote, the bitter tears she'd kept trapped for years fell freely.

She sat on the expensive ceramic tile in the middle of her living room and cried.

She cried tears of anger, humiliation, fear, and regret. The tears made her body jerk in spasms and her back bow in pain. Her plummeting fist pounded against the tile as the tears wracked her body.

She cried for the years she'd endured under her mother's care. She cried for the lost years of her youth. She cried for the little girl who had been forced to grow up before her time.

She cried for the little girl who never had a mother and was victimized. She cried for the little girl who became an abuser and sought to be number one at all costs without realizing that she'd become no better than her mother. She cried as she realized that what she'd been seeking no one could give her. Peace.

Knowing that she'd never allow another to make her feel as though she was nothing, less than, she'd ruthlessly sought to be the one in control, the one to call the shots and to hell with any and everything else.

She'd cried for the little girl who'd grown up to believe that she was no good.

In her quest for control, she'd become lost, adrift...

She'd cried until her throat, her body, her mind and soul screamed out in painful protest.

She'd cried until she'd had no more tears left to cry.

After the tears had dried, she knew what she had to do. Something that was long overdue.

Now, with her hand on the handle of the door, she hesitated, glancing at the dilapidated house.

Taking a deep breath, she opened the door and briskly walked the short distance to the front door. That old familiar fear pooled and tied her gut in knots, yet she forced one foot in front of the other. Forced herself not to turn away and run back in her car and get the hell out of there.

She knocked on the door, and as fear tied her gut in knots, she waited.

CHAPTER 18

"What do you want? I ain't got no money so I can't buy nothin' you selling, so you may as well go on somewhere," the old woman mumbled, her thick fingers wrapped around the edge of the door. She held it opened just far enough for her to peer out.

"It's me." Chastity cleared her throat and spoke louder. "It's Chastity. Can I come in?"

"Chastity?" the woman asked, her watery eyes squinting as though she didn't recognize her.

"Yeah, it's me. Chase."

"Well, I was in the middle of cooking…" Maybelle's mumbles trailed away as she clutched together the ends of her frayed robe.

She spoke as though she didn't know Chase, as though she was being inconvenienced by Chase. As though she was a stranger and not her own daughter.

"I just wanted to talk to you for a minute. It won't take long," Chase replied, clenching her teeth.

She kept a firm grip on the swarm of emotions crowding in on her; thoughts of what it had even taken for her to do this, knowing that she'd come to confront her mother. She now wondered if she would be able to weather the emotional storm that threatened to break if she did.

Even if Maybelle would allow her to.

"Come on in then," Maybelle finally agreed, and Chastity released a sigh of relief.

Maybelle moved aside, opened the door fully and allowed Chase to enter.

"I was in the middle of something, so I ain't got much time to spare," she said again, walking ahead of Chase, her shoulders stooped, giving her an even more frail appearance.

"I know. I won't take much of your time," she replied, following her mother throughout the dark house. There were no lights on until they came to the kitchen. The single light over the oven lit the small room.

Chase entered and stood in the middle of the kitchen, uncertain what to do and where to start.

"Go on and turn on a light, girl," Maybelle said gruffly and glanced away as she walked into the kitchen.

Chase flipped on a light switch and glanced over the kitchen and connecting living room.

Nothing had changed from the last time she'd been there, which had been over ten years ago. The same knick-knacks were set in ornately carved shadow boxes. The same cheap dime-store prints hung on the whitewashed walls. The same old but clean sofa, covered with an afghan, was in the exact same position, still flanked by matching oatmeal-colored chairs. In front of the sofa was a long, cherrywood table where magazines were placed, stacked in the center. Everything was neat and orderly. Everything was pristine. Not an object was out of place.

Chase tugged at the collar of her blouse, pulling it away from her neck. She felt as though she were being choked.

"There's a place for everything, girl, and everything has its place…"

Maybelle's words from years ago came to her mind.

Chase stared at the living room, seeing herself as a young girl, rag in hand as she polished and cleaned the furniture. As she cleaned, she would listen to the kids outside playing and desperately wanted to rebel, to throw the rag away and join them. If she dared to do that, there would be hell to pay.

"What? You too good to sit down at my table? I may not live in that high-siddity uptown place of yours, but my stuff is good enough," Maybelle said gruffly, startling Chase from the long ago images that swam before her eyes.

"Yes, ma'am. I mean, no, ma'am." She stopped. "I'm sorry." The words spilled out of her mouth as though on cue, from some old familiar song. The instant need to apologize was immediate.

She opened her mouth to apologize again for the unknown slight before she clamped her mouth shut. The response had been automatic, one that had reduced her to that little girl she was long ago. The child she'd been, the one who jumped and apologized for any perceived wrong, rather fact or something only in Maybelle's mind.

Chase had to swallow down the bile as her eyes glanced toward the stairs that had once led to her bedroom. Her mother caught her eyes when she turned back around to face her, her dark-brown face flushing before her features hardened and she turned away.

Chase stared at her mother's back as she shuffled over to the oven and removed a tea kettle before filling it with water.

Time hadn't been kind to Maybelle. Barely in her sixties, lines were strongly etched in harsh grooves bracketing her wide, thick lips. Her rheumy eyes were no longer sharp and clear; instead their light-brown depths were worn ragged.

She remembered as a girl how imposing her mother had seemed to her, how indomitable. However, as she watched her mother's slightly stooped form, she now saw her with the eyes of an adult. One no longer afraid of the strident call, harsh tone, or painful blows inflicted on her.

"You want some tea?"

"No. Thank you."

She watched her mother amble around the kitchen, filling the old tea-kettle with water before placing it on the stove to heat.

"So, what do you want? I ain't heard from you in a while. Last time I heard from you, you was working for that place uptown…"

"Manhattan Buford," Chase supplied.

Although she hadn't step foot in the house she grew up in, from the moment she left, there was a small part of her that, despite the years of abuse she'd suffered under her mother's care, hadn't been able to completely divorce her mother from her life.

Like a dutiful daughter, she called her mother every Sunday after she knew Maybelle was home from church to check on her, to find out if there was anything she needed.

The only time Maybelle contacted her was when she needed money. When Chase had offered to bring it to her, Maybelle would cut her short and tell her to wire it although they both lived in the same city.

Chase never questioned why. In truth, she was relieved when she wouldn't have to see her mother. She was able to assuage herself of any guilty feelings by giving her mother money, allowing her money to be the link that kept them connected.

"What you do?" Maybelle turned around, the cup of tea held tightly in her thick fingers.

Chase frowned. "What are you talking about?"

"What you do not to get that promotion you were so sure was yours? What'd you do wrong?" Maybelle asked, her lip curling as she assessed Chase across the room, her watery eyes piercing as she stared at her over the rim of her tea mug. She took a long drink of the tea. Chase stared as the strong column of Maybelle's throat worked the hot liquid down.

"I didn't come here to talk about that." Irritated, unable to keep sitting in the chair, Chase stood and walked toward the living room.

"Sit down somewhere. All that moving around is getting on my nerves. If you didn't come to tell me about that new job, then what you come here for? I already told you, I'm busy," Maybelle mumbled.

Chase didn't bother asking what Maybelle was busy with. She knew it was just her way of trying to get rid of her.

"What did I ever do to you, to make you hate me so, Momma?"

There was a moment of silence after Chase blurted out the words.

"Now look—"

"Why did you let...*him*...do that to me?" She couldn't bring herself to call him father.

Once she started, she couldn't stop.

All the pain, humiliation and fears crowded in on her as her fingers feathered over Maybelle's beloved collectibles all neatly arranged on the shelves. Her fingers slid over the familiar books Maybelle had from the time Chase was a child.

Her eyes zeroed in on the small assortment of photos and bittersweet memories assailed her as she picked up one old photo framed in a chipped ceramic frame.

It was a picture one of the nuns had taken of her at a school outing. Chase remembered she'd been in the first grade and so excited to go on her first field trip. She'd gone to Catholic school and instead of having to wear their traditional plaid skirt and white blouse, the students were allowed to wear street clothes.

Maybelle had carefully dressed Chase, actually buying her a new pair of jeans and T-shirt for the outing. Chase had been so happy, proud of the new clothes, and although she'd wanted to run and play like the other kids, she had been careful not to mess up her new clothes.

She hadn't been looking where she was going and had fallen, tearing the knee of her jeans. When she got home, she'd suffered the consequences.

She placed the picture down and turned to see Maybelle staring at her.

"Why do you hate me so? What did I ever do to make you hate me so bad?"

"What the hell are you going on about, girl? Ain't nobody hate you! I raised you the best I could. I worked night and day to keep a roof over your ungrateful head and all I get is—"

"Why did you let him rape me, over and over, Maybelle? Why?" The words spilled from her in a torrential flood.

"You wasn't listening to me. I thought maybe you'd listen to a man better. You needed discipline. You wasn't listening to me," she mumbled, repeating herself and not looking Chase in the eyes.

"By molesting me? You thought I'd learn *discipline* by allowing my own father to rape me?"

The bitter anger that had been brewing for years overflowed. Tears of anger ran unchecked down her face.

"Shut up! He never did nothing like that, you nasty slut!" Maybelle turned away and fumbled as she began to clumsily attack the dishes, her lined face set in angry lines of denial.

Chase left the living room and strode into the kitchen, staring at Maybelle. She stood several feet away to stare at Maybelle, watching her hands shake as she sank her hands in the soapy water and began to wash the dishes methodically, scrubbing and re-scrubbing the shining plate. Maybelle's eyes were glued to the shining plate.

She threw the dish down in the sink, splattering it in half and moved as though to leave.

Chase reached out a hand and grasped her mother's shoulder, preventing her from leaving.

"Momma, you *knew* what he was doing! Don't stand there and fucking lie to me!"

"Don't you talk to me like that! You shut your lying, filthy mouth!" Maybelle yelled back and with a strength that amazed Chase, shoved at her. In Maybelle's earnest washing, water had overlapped, spilling on the floor, and Chase slipped on it. Before she could right herself, she fell, desperately grasping the handle on a nearby cabinet to stop her fall.

Maybelle stood before her with a sneer on her face.

"See, this is why you needed discipline. You could never control yourself. You was always a deceitful, lying, devious little bitch, and you needed someone to keep you in check."

Chase narrowed her eyes, staring into the malevolent face of her mother.

"Always crying, whining about something. Even as a baby, you were always demanding. I couldn't have a free moment to myself, always sick. There was always *something* with you! You're the reason why he left." Maybelle's ample bosom heaved. Her dark face was flushed in anger as she stared down at Chase.

Chase remained in the half-crouched position, staring into her mother's reddened, angry face.

"If it hadn't been for you, Charlie would have never left. We were fine before you came along, and then when you came, it was never the same. He always found a reason to be gone, said you crying was getting on his nerves. Told me if I didn't get you under control, if I didn't get you to shut up, he was gone."

Her large nostrils flared angrily as she stared down at Chase. Chase knew she was locked in the past and although her eyes were on hers, she didn't see her.

"When he came back, I promised him it would be different."

"It isn't my fault. It was never my fault." Chase slowly rose, a burden being lifted off of her, falling like the useless weight it was as she finally allowed the truth to settle in.

As Maybelle continued to stare down at her, pinning Chase with an evil glare, she felt disdain and pity for the old woman rather than fear. She slowly rose from her crouched position and faced her mother.

She'd dreamed of this day. The day she would have the courage to face her mother and demand answers. The day she'd force the old woman to account for her actions.

Judgment day.

And now, as she faced her, staring down at the woman who'd intimidated her, abused her, allowed her to be abused, instead of vindication, she only felt sadness for the creature in front of her.

A strange euphoria wrapped warmly around her, cocooning her in its embrace as she stood.

Her past of pain and neglect, fear and trepidation were over.

She had faced her demon. The demon that had plagued her, making her always feel as though she was less than the fear that dictated her life, forcing her to make herself rigid in her desire for control over every aspect of her life.

"I feel sorry for you, Maybelle."

"What I got to be sorry for?"

Chase stared at her mother, knowing that Maybelle saw the truth in Chase's eyes. There was no need for an answer. Chase walked over and gathered her things.

She opened her purse and withdrew a small stack of bills, laying them on the counter. Maybelle's greedy eyes shifted to the stack as she licked her lips in obvious anticipation. "This will be the last 'loan' you'll get from me. I'm not giving it to you because I think I 'owe you.' I'm giving it to you because it's my way of saying good-bye to you. I don't hate you. I don't love you. You were a part of my past, a past that I don't need to constantly revisit. A past that I will no longer allow to define me. Good-bye, Maybelle."

Without another word or a final glance, Chase turned and walked away.

Chase thought about saying more, thought about all the things she thought she would say, things she wanted to say in her final say with her mother. But she realized they no longer mattered.

As she walked out of the door to her mother's house for the final time, she knew she'd quieted the demons of her past. Her trip to the island had opened her eyes to the possibilities of living her life without constraints, without the overwhelming need to control everything and everyone in her life.

Maybelle no longer had any power over her.

CHAPTER 19

Chase strode through downtown offices of Manhattan Buford with determined steps. She walked past the open area that was cluttered with at least a dozen small cubicles, not sparing a second look for the curious glances that fell her way.

When she reached the outer door of the mid-managerial team where she had her office, she took a deep breath, briefly closed her eyes, and shouldered her way inside.

Christine glanced up when the door opened, her eyes widening in surprise when she saw Chase.

"Ms. Davidson? I wasn't expecting you...I thought..."

"Yes, I know, Christine," she interrupted quietly. "Is my office still available?" Chase asked, unsure if they'd already assigned someone else to the office.

"Of course! Everything is just like you left it. Can I get you anything? Coffee?" Although Christine was clearly confused, she was the epitome of professionalism as she jumped from her seat and scurried around to the front of her desk.

Chase held up a stalling hand.

"No, I'm fine, Christine." Chase stopped. "You know, coffee sounds good. Your coffee is always perfect." She smiled and turned toward her door, biting back a chuckle when Christine's mouth formed a perfect "O" and her pale face blushed at the small compliment. During the two years that Christine worked for her, Chase had never given the woman the slightest bit of praise. She vowed to rectify that.

If she still had the opportunity, Chase thought and opened the door of her office and gently closed it on her blushing assistant's face.

She leaned back against the door frame, feeling a sense of déjà vu.

Two weeks ago, she'd done the same thing after leaving the meeting with the partners and Javier.

Two weeks ago she'd quit her job when she hadn't gotten the promotion she thought she needed, the one she thought would prove her worth. She'd gathered her things and left, feeling betrayed with her tail tucked beneath her and wondering how things had gotten so out of control, how she'd been left with egg on her face.

Now, she was back and determined to start new. Things that she thought were so important in the past, no longer were. With everything she had learned about herself and the complete turnaround in her feelings about who she was, she felt different, felt empowered. *A true "ah ha" moment as Oprah would say*, Chase thought with an inner laugh.

She took the remainder of the week off, thinking of what she would do next. It hadn't taken long before she realized what she wanted—no, what she *needed*—to do.

She'd made a call to one of the partners, and quietly, with dignity, asked if her job was still open for her, apologizing for her behavior. She hadn't known what to expect, had half expected him to laugh and tell her what she could do with her apology. However, she had been pleasantly surprised when he welcomed her back and asked her if she required any more time off before returning.

She'd assured him she had taken all the time she needed and that she would be returning on Monday.

"And now, here I am," she said aloud, in a barely audible voice, her eyes scanning her office.

Nothing had been moved; everything was exactly as it was when she'd left two weeks earlier. She dropped her jacket on the small, leather chair tucked in the corner and walked toward her desk. Immediately, her eyes widened when she saw the large, bountiful hibiscus plant in a gleaming, burnished gold pot.

With her mouth ajar as she approached the plant, she reached a hand out and ran it over one of the petals that were so large and perfectly formed. They almost appeared as if the fragile petals had been crafted from crepe paper. The petals were so delicate.

A smile stretched her mouth wide, and her heart quickened when she saw the small envelope nestled deep within the plant. She lifted it out of the plant and opened the card. Her brow etched in confusion when she read the card's one line.

Your time to blossom has arrived…

Her door opened. Without looking away from the magnificent plant and her mind puzzling over the note attached, she asked Christine to place her coffee on her desk.

"I don't have any coffee…Hopefully what I do have will bring you a bit more pleasure."

Chase's head whipped around. Stunned, she watched as the man from the island entered her office.

"What are you doing here?" she asked and laughed at the look of affront that crossed his face.

"Should I have made an appointment?" he asked, closing the door and striding into her office.

A thousand questions entered her mind, but none seemed important as he held his arms out to her. Without another word, Chase ran into his arms, and when his head descended and his lips slanted over hers, she willingly sank into the deep, explosively hot kiss.

He pulled her tight into his embrace, his hands roaming over her body as she wrapped her arms around his neck, pulling him tighter and closer as their lips crashed and bodies strained against each other.

It was long minutes before the kiss ended. With reluctance, he withdrew his mouth from hers.

"Of course, you don't need an appointment...But how did you know where I worked? How did you know I'd be here when even I didn't know?" she finally asked, completely out of breath.

"Let's sit down. I have a lot to tell you," he replied, stroking a callused thumb over her kiss-swollen lips.

Confused but happy to see him, Chase allowed him to guide her to the small loveseat in the corner of her office.

"My name is Daemon Baptiste."

It took more than a few seconds for the significance to penetrate her brain.

"Daemon Baptiste?"

He said nothing, staring at her. His gaze remained steady, yet she noted the uncertainty in his eyes as though he was unsure of what reception his announcement would have with her.

"*The* Daemon Baptiste? As in the controlling stockholder of Manhattan Buford?" Her eyes narrowed, staring at him.

"Yes. One and the same."

"What was this, some kind of twisted game?" Chase angrily shoved his hands away and tried to leap from the chaise. He stopped her, grabbing her wrists before she could move and forcing her to turn back to face him.

"No. It wasn't a game, Chase. My intent was never to hurt you. It was the exact opposite," he replied. Although his tone remained the same, his pale gray eyes shone brightly with sincerity.

"Then why..." Her voice trailed off, and she stopped speaking.

She closed her eyes and inhaled a deep breath of air before reopening them and stared at him in anger and confusion. "God, I feel like Alice in damn wonderland! I don't understand any of this!" She angrily pulled her wrists away from him, shoving him away. He allowed her to move from him.

"Please, just hear me out. If after I'm done, you don't want to have anything to do with me or my proposition, you're free to go." He held a hand out in entreaty, silently begging her to stay and to hear him out before she ran as far and as fast as she could away from the madness her life had become.

Wetting her lips, she tucked an errant strand of hair behind her ear, carefully examining his face for any clues to what in hell was going on. She nodded her head, agreeing for him to continue speaking, but she warily watched him.

"I make it my job to know about every member of management, even the junior members. Your work ethic is beyond reproach. Your attention to details, your long hours are all... commendable."

"But?"

He smiled. "No 'but.' You reminded me of someone I knew a long time ago. Someone who was just as driven, just as determined to succeed no matter the cost."

He didn't say who the person was, but Chase knew he was referring to himself. She allowed him to speak without interruption.

"I admire those strengths. But those same strengths could be the very things that prevent you from fully blossoming."

She picked up and stroked the hibiscus petal that had fallen onto her desk , tears blurring the image as she stared at it blindly.

"I want more from you, more than you can give. Unless you were freed from the cage you'd placed yourself in, you would never reach your full potential."

"Were you the one to invite me to the island?"

One side of his wide mouth lightly lifted. "I may have had something do with it. The opportunity arose…"

She didn't ask for details she knew he wouldn't give.

"So, I'm to be your assistant?"

He smiled slightly, the lone dimple in one cheek flashing. "You could say that."

"But the position is a bit more than that of an 'assistant,' as the partners led you to believe. I didn't share with them the full scope of what the position would mean."

"So. It's more than making your coffee and taking dictation?"

"You could say that."

To her utter astonishment, he outlined the scope of her duties. Her main one was to run the Dallas office of Manhattan Buford, a position that would give her full autonomy in every final decision the firm had.

"Of course that comes with your own staff, a fantastic raise, of course, an office with an incredible view…"

Chase listened as he detailed entirely the scope of her new job and all the responsibilities that went with it. Her mind was whirling, emotions—astonishment and euphoria—were crashing in on her as she was blown away with the magnitude of his gesture. Of his obvious faith in her as a leader and her abilities to lead the company.

Two weeks ago, her world had closed in on her. Now, she was being handed the golden key. A key that would give her the opportunity to show that she indeed had what it took to run an entire branch of a multibillion-dollar corporation.

She stared at the man who was the catalyst to turmoil in her life. Turmoil was needed to force her to come to terms with her life, to re-evaluate who she was. In doing so, he not only helped to free herself of the demons of her past, but had also helped her realize the possibilities of a future she never dreamed of.

She had plenty of questions—about the position, as well as questions about the man who sat staring at her. But all of those could wait for the moment.

"Does this sound like something you'd be interested in, Ms. Davidson?" he asked, a small smile flirting around his sensual mouth.

Chase laughed out loud, beyond satisfied with the unexpected outcome. "Yes...It is."

ABOUT THE AUTHOR

Kimberly Kaye Terry is a multi-published author who pens interracial and multicultural delicious tales that expertly blend eroticism and true romance, as well as erotic fiction. She lives with her husband, a Lieutenant Colonel in the U.S. Army, their beautiful child, and two ridiculously spoiled poodles who think they're human, in a suburb in Texas.

Although Kimberly has a bachelor's degree in social work and a master's degree in human relations, and has held licenses in social work and mental health therapy in various cities within the United States and abroad, she happily calls writing her full-time job. Kimberly volunteers at various social service agencies and is a longstanding member of Zeta Phi Beta Sorority, Inc., a community-conscious organization.

Kimberly is a naturalist and practices aromatherapy. She believes in embracing the powerful woman within each of us and meditates on a regular basis. You can visit her at www.kimberly kayeterry.com to learn more about her. Or feel free to drop by her MySpace blog, where she occasionally waxes poetic, or shamelessly pimps her books, at www.myspace.com/kimberlykayeterry.

MORALITY
AND
RATIONAL
SELF-INTEREST

edited by

DAVID P. GAUTHIER
University of Toronto

MORALITY
AND
RATIONAL
SELF-INTEREST

Prentice-Hall, Inc., Englewood Cliffs, New Jersey

Library of Congress Catalog Card Number: 78–113847

Printed in the United States of America

C 13–600890–9
P 13–600882–8

Current Printing (last digit):

10 9 8 7 6 5 4 3 2 1

PRENTICE-HALL INTERNATIONAL, INC., London
PRENTICE-HALL OF AUSTRALIA, PTY. LTD., Sydney
PRENTICE-HALL OF CANADA, LTD., Toronto
PRENTICE-HALL OF INDIA PRIVATE LIMITED, New Delhi
PRENTICE-HALL OF JAPAN, INC., Tokyo

CENTRAL ISSUES IN PHILOSOPHY SERIES

BARUCH A. BRODY
series editor

~~~~~~~~~~~~~~~~~~~~~~~~~~~~~~~~~~~~~~~

Foreword

The Central Issues in Philosophy series is based upon the conviction that the best way to teach philosophy to introductory students is to experience or to *do* philosophy with them. The basic unit of philosophical investigation is the particular problem, and not the area or the historical figure. Therefore, this series consists of sets of readings organised around well-defined, manageable problems. All other things being equal, problems that are of interest and relevance to the student have been chosen.

Each volume contains an introduction that clearly defines the problem and sets out the alternative positions that have been taken. The selections are chosen and arranged in such a way as to take the student through the dialectic of the problem; each reading, besides presenting a particular point of view, criticizes the points of view set out earlier.

Although no attempt has been made to introduce the student in a systematic way to the history of philosophy, classical selections relevant to the development of the problem have been included. As a side benefit, the student will therefore come to see the continuity, as well as the breaks, between classical and contemporary thought. But in no case will a selection be included merely for its historical significance; clarity of expression and systematic significance are the main criteria for selection.

BARUCH A. BRODY

Contents

Introduction

I

"Do you really want to convince us that right is in all circumstances better than wrong or not?" [1]

This question begins the serious argument of Plato's *Republic*. But what a strange question it seems to be. For surely what is right is better than what is wrong. What we *mean* by "right" involves "good," and what we *mean* by "wrong" involves "bad." We dispute about what action is right and what action is wrong, but if we reach agreement, we do not then go on to debate whether the right action is better than the wrong one.

Yet Plato does not find the question strange. Indeed, he considers it to be one of the key questions of ethics. What then is the force of the question, and what sort of answer does it require?

As Glaucon and Adeimantus, the questioners in the *Republic*, make clear, to show that right is better than wrong is to show that right is good and wrong is evil "because of what it inevitably does to its possessor." [2] It is the *effect* of acting rightly or wrongly on the *agent* which is in question. Is the action which is right for me also, and necessarily, the action which will most truly be good for me? And is the action which is wrong for me also, and necessarily, the action which will most truly be bad for me? This is what Plato, speaking through Socrates, seeks to demonstrate in the *Republic*.

[1] Plato, *The Republic*, 357. (tr. H. D. P. Lee).
[2] *Ibid.*, 367.

1

Let us say that right and wrong comprise the province of morality. And let us say that what is good for one and bad for one comprise the province of rational self-interest. The moral man does what is right; the rationally self-interested man does what is truly good for him. We see that the question of the *Republic* is this:

"Do you really want to convince us that the dictates of morality are in all circumstances coincident with those of rational self-interest or not?"

This question no longer seems strange. And it is indeed one of the key questions of ethics. The connection—or lack of connection—between morality and self-interest has been debated by philosophers from Plato to the present. The readings we have collected here will, hopefully, illuminate the issue. They will not resolve it.

II

Although four centuries of philosophical writing are represented in this volume, it is nevertheless deliberately restricted in its scope. The problem originates with the Greeks, but they are not directly represented here. In the next section of the Introduction, we shall suggest some of the differences between the Greek view of the problem and our own. H. A. Prichard examines several of Plato's arguments in the selection from "Duty and Interest." But for the student who seeks to understand the Platonic view of the connection between the right (or the just) and the good, there can be no alternative to a full reading of the *Republic*.

Among more recent philosophy, concern with the relation of morality to self-interest has been an especially marked trait of moral philosophy done in the English, rather than the continental tradition. Continental moral philosophy tends to be an offshoot of one (or both) of two much wider studies—metaphysical speculation and social theorizing. One finds an emphasis on the metaphysical status of moral values, or an emphasis on the social bases of morality, but less concern with the position of the individual agent who must decide what it is reasonable to do. English speaking moral philosophers have rarely forgotten this more practical standpoint, so that from Hobbes in the seventeenth century to Hare, Toulmin, and Baier today, we find the great theme of reason occupying the center of concern. Thus in selecting our readings exclusively from this tradition, we are not choosing the philosophy of one language group in preference to that of another, but rather selecting from the philosophical milieu in which our problem has been most thoroughly discussed.

The readings divide into three groups, each of which focuses on a particular problem which arises in discussing the relationship of morality to self-interest.

The first problem arises in the following way. Most of us would agree that if there are moral grounds of action, then it must be reasonable to act on those grounds. If the requirements of morality are not requirements of reason, or at least not compatible with reason, then morality is surely a delusion. Furthermore, most of us find that the requirements of morality are sometimes inconsistent with the dictates of self-interest. But if self-interested grounds of action are also reasonable, then we seem faced with a contradiction—we have two incompatible sets of reasonable grounds of action. We may therefore ask if self-interested grounds of action really are reasonable—if the position of the egoist, who seeks to maximize the satisfaction of his interests, is a rational position.

This problem is posed in our selection from Sidgwick, who finds himself faced with an apparent incompatibility between egoism and utilitarian morality. Moore and Medlin both dispose of this problem by arguing that in fact egoism is not rational: that self-interest does not provide a sufficient basis for reasonable action. However, in the final selection of the first section Kalin restores the initial problem by arguing strongly for the rationality of the egoist's position.

The second problem concerns motivation rather than reason. Most of us would agree that if there are moral grounds of action, then it must be possible for us to be motivated to act on those grounds. In other words, if we ought to do something, then it is psychologically possible for us to do it, or we can do it. Again, the requirements of morality do not, or at least do not seem to coincide always with the dictates of self-interest. But if all motivation is based on self-interest, then we seem faced with a contradiction: moral motivation must be both different from, yet the same as, motivation based on interest.

In the first of the second group of selections, Hutcheson argues that moral motivation is distinct from that of self-interest. Although Hume agrees that we possess a moral sense distinct from that of self-interest or self-love, he argues that nevertheless morality must be in our interest if it is to have practical effect, and endeavors to convince us that it is so. Prichard, finally, stoutly maintains that there is no reason to suppose that the dictates of morality and self-interest coincide, and that any attempt to reduce moral motivation to interested motivation eliminates morality. Prichard rejects any relationship between morality and self-interest—moral motives are utterly distinct from self-interested motives, and moral requirements utterly distinct from the requirements of self-interest.

The third problem concerns reason, without ignoring motivation. Suppose we agree that the requirements of morality do not, or at least do not seem to coincide always with the dictates of self-interest, so that moral action may require the sacrifice of interest. Yet would we not also agree that a community of moral men are better off—do better for themselves—than a community of purely self-interested men? Is not morality beneficial, at least to most people? Again, we seem faced with a contradiction: those who sacrifice their interests may be better off than those who never sacrifice their interests.

If it can be shown that there is no real contradiction here, then perhaps a solution to the two previous problems will be at hand. For if moral men do better for themselves than self-interested men, then surely it is in our interest to act on moral grounds. Moral action will prove both reasonable and psychologically possible, even if we suppose that both reason and motivation rest on interest.

Hobbes, from whom we take the first selection in the third group, does not in fact believe that there can be real opposition between morality and self-interest, but rather treats morality as the best mutual basis of action for self-interested men. His position does, however, suggest Baier's argument that morality overrides self-interest when it is in everyone's interest that it do so, and that therefore morality is the most reasonable basis of action for everyone. Gauthier shows that no contradiction is involved in the claim that those who sacrifice their interests may be better off than those who do not, but that treating morality as a set of principles overriding self-interest does not resolve our earlier problems. For it does not follow from this position either that morality is more reasonable than self-interest, or that moral motivation is compatible with self-interested motivation.

Thus the debate about the relation of morality to rational self-interest will continue. In later sections of this Introduction we shall examine the argument of each of these readings in more detail, and finally suggest one direction which the debate may take.

III

Let us first return briefly to the question of the *Republic*. We shall not consider how it is answered, but rather why it is assumed that it must be answerable. For Plato makes certain assumptions which are characteristic of classical Greek thinking about morality and which many modern philosophers would not accept. And these assumptions affect our understanding of the question.

First of all, Plato and philosophers in the Platonic tradition assume that to discover the good for man, one requires knowledge of the function of man. Man, like everything else in the cosmos, is to be understood in terms of his *telos*, or natural end, and the good man is necessarily the man who most fully actualizes this end. The good for man is then what conduces this actualization.

We may think of the rationally self-interested man as the man who seeks to maximize his satisfaction. But clearly if we are to speak of rational self-interest in the context of Greek ethics—and the Greeks of course did *not* speak of rational self-interest—we must think of the rationally self-interested man as the man who seeks to maximize his actualization or to attain his natural end.

To say this is of course not to deny that, to the Greeks, the man who actualizes himself is also the satisfied, or happy, man. *Ευ.daimonia*, the Greek term we translate, somewhat inadequately, as happiness, is the preeminent quality of the good life. But happiness becomes, then, not the subjective condition of a satisfied individual, but the objective condition of a man who attains his natural end.

Now if we agree that man has a natural end, it seems absurd to deny that man acts rightly in seeking to attain it, and wrongly in seeking to avoid it. It is thus established that right action is connected with the good for man, and so it must be possible to show that it will be better for one to do what is right than what is wrong.

However, if we suppose that the good for man is not man's actualization, but his satisfaction, then it is no longer evident that right action is connected with the good for man. It is not absurd to deny that man acts rightly in seeking his own satisfaction, and wrongly in seeking to avoid it. Indeed, many philosophers and moralists have argued that morality may require one to sacrifice one's own satisfaction to some other end. Even the utilitarian moralist, such as John Stuart Mill, who supposes that happiness is the proper goal of moral action, praises "those who can abnegate for themselves the personal enjoyment of life when by such renunciation they contribute worthily to increase the amount of happiness in the world." [3] But such abnegation is not for the good of the individual concerned; he sacrifices his good for the good of the whole.

Thus for us, although not for the Greeks, the connection between morality and rational self-interest is problematic. For Plato, what is truly moral and what is truly for one's good must coincide, for both must lead to one's actualization. For us there is no such necessary connection.

There is a further assumption of some importance. According to Plato, man actualizes himself as a rational being. Rational action is not only instrumental to the attainment of man's end, but the highest form of rational action—the activity of contemplation—is intrinsic to the end itself. Man's self-interest, then, in leading him to seek his good, leads him toward reason; true self-interest is intrinsically rational.

Our conception of self-interest, on the other hand, may involve only instrumental rationality. The man who acts on rational self-interest is the man whose beliefs about what will benefit him and how this may be attained are rational, and whose actions conform to these beliefs. The rational character of the end is not in question. And so it is possible for us to suppose that rationally self-interested action lacks any further rationality, that it is directed toward an end which is not itself the rational end for men to aim at, because there is no such rational end. For Plato, who takes the end to be reason, such a supposition would be nonsensical.

This very brief discussion may suggest, then, that two questions arise for us which do not arise for the Greeks. First, is it right to aim at what is good for one? And second, is it rational to aim at what is good for one? We may find on reflection that we can answer these questions affirmatively, or we may not. But we cannot simply dismiss the questions. And thus we are led to the themes of our readings: the interrelations of morality, self-interest, and reason.

IV

The first of our selections is from *The Methods of Ethics*, by Henry Sidgwick, who was professor of moral philosophy at the University

---

[3] J. S. Mill, *Utilitarianism*, Chap. II.

of Cambridge in the late nineteenth century. Although contemporary moral philosophers tend to suppose that the modern era began when G. E. Moore asked how "good" is to be defined, it would be equally possible to trace its beginnings to Sidgwick, whose explicit concern with ethical *methodology* marks the transition from the ethical enquiries of utilitarians and idealists in the nineteenth century to the meta-ethical enquiries of analytic philosophers in the twentieth.

The essential features of Sidgwick's position, in so far as they are relevant to our present concerns, seem to be these. First, Sidgwick maintains that what is right is what is reasonable, so that we can show by rational argument what we ought to do. Moral judgments are not supported merely by an appeal to our feelings, or by an appeal to rewards and penalties. The moral faculty may be more akin to perception or to ratiocination, but whichever is the case, it enables us to establish objectively valid moral truths. Second, these truths have a practical force. The cognition that some action ought to be done also provides a motive for doing the action. Thus "X ought to be done" may be taken to indicate an objective rational precept.

How do we arrive at such precepts? Sidgwick distinguishes three principal methods, which he terms *egoism, intuitionism,* and *utilitarianism.* The first and last are types of *hedonism,* and may be distinguished respectively as *egoistic* and *universalistic* hedonism. The underlying principle of egoistic hedonism is "that the rational end of conduct for each individual is the Maximum of his own Happiness or Pleasure".[4] The underlying principle of universalistic hedonism is rather "that the conduct which, under any given circumstances, is objectively right, is that which will produce the greatest amount of happiness on the whole".[5] Thus both of these methods rest on the consideration of consequences. Intuitionism, on the other hand, takes as its fundamental assumption "that we have the power of seeing clearly what actions are in themselves right and reasonable" [6] apart from their consequences.

Sidgwick argues at great length that the utilitarian and intuitionist methods are not only not incompatible, but that the only principles we can really intuit as self-evident provide the rational basis for the utilitarian system. Thus he is left with the problem of relating egoism

[4] Henry Sidgwick, *The Methods of Ethics,* fifth edition (London: Macmillan & Co., 1893), p. xx.

[5] *Ibid.,* p. 411.

[6] *Ibid.,* p. xxiii.

and utilitarianism, and this brings us directly to our own problem.

In the concluding Chapter, which is part of our selection, Sidgwick maintains that it is impossible to show on empirical grounds that the requirements of utilitarianism and egoism coincide. But both are rational; the egoistic and the universalistic principles are equally self-evident. How then may they be reconciled?

The only answer which Sidgwick is able to offer is that if we may assume the existence of God, then we may suppose that he affords adequate rewards and penalties for those who obey or disobey the utilitarian principle, so that they may be assured that their own well-being is in fact maximized by seeking the happiness of all. But may we assume the existence of God? If not, it would seem that we are confronted with an ultimate contradiction in what we find reasonable to do. May we assume that there is no such contradiction, or is perfect rationality too much to expect? Sidgwick gives us no final answer.

The unsatisfactory character of Sidgwick's attempt to reconcile egoism and utilitarianism is fairly evident. For egoism tells us that what we ought to do is to aim at our own maximum well-being, whereas utilitarianism tells us that what we ought to do is to aim at the maximum well-being for all. Even if the same course of action should always achieve both these aims, we would still be faced with two logically different ultimate ethical principles, each of which, in Sidgwick's view, is rationally self-evident. The ultimate precept of reason cannot be both egoistic and universalistic.

G. E. Moore is well aware of this problem. But he considers the contradiction between egoism and utilitarianism to be subsidiary to another contradiction, which he argues vitiates Sidgwick's overall position.

Moore's most noted contribution to moral philosophy is of course the claim that most ethical systems fail because they commit the naturalistic fallacy—the fallacy of supposing that "good" may be defined. This is the argument in his famous book, *Principia Ethica*, which has captured by far the most philosophic attention. However, he also argues in *Principia Ethica* that egoism, or egoistic hedonism, is not a rational doctrine—that Sidgwick was utterly mistaken in considering egoism one of the rational methods of ethics. If Moore is right, then self-interest can be rational only within a wider nonegoistic framework, and rational self-interest is neither a possible ethical system, nor a possible competitor with ethical systems.

Our selection contains Moore's argument against egoism. Moore holds that one ought to aim at whatever is good in itself. Elsewhere in *Principia*, Moore defines "right" as "cause of a good result";[7] hence right action must be directed to the best consequences.

The egoistic principle tells each man to aim at his own maximum pleasure, or well-being. Hence it tells each man that his own pleasure, and only his own pleasure, is good in itself. But this is impossible. For if my pleasure, and only my pleasure, is good in itself, then your pleasure cannot be good in itself. *Each* man's pleasure cannot be the *sole* good. Egoism, therefore, involves a contradiction.

It may seem easy to avoid this contradiction. The egoist may reply that the egoistic principle tells each man that his own pleasure, and only his own pleasure, is good *for him*. But Moore will not accept this reply. To say that a man's pleasure is good *for him* is to say only that *his* pleasure, and perhaps *his* pleasure-seeking, are parts of what is universally good, or good in itself. It may be that a man ought to aim only at his own pleasure, because in so doing he contributes most to realizing what is good in itself. But what is good in itself is the ultimate end of all action, and what is good in itself is universally good, and not good merely in relation to some person or persons.

Moore's position rests on the assumption that the proper objective of human action must be universal in character. Moore does not argue that this is so, but really only asserts it. One may place contrary assertions against Moore such as that of Aristotle, who insists that what is good or bad implies "reference to a particular person." [8] And if one does insist that what is good is good only in relation to or for some person (or perhaps more generally some sentient being), then one will find no logical difficulty in accepting the basic principle of egoism. That each person should aim at what is good for himself may seem the obvious principle of all rational action.

Moore is not the only critic of the rationality of egoism. In a justly famous article, "Ultimate Principles and Ethical Egoism," which constitutes our third selection, the Australian philosopher Brian Medlin tries to show that egoism involves, not a contradiction, but an inconsistency. Medlin takes an emotivist, rather than an objectivist, position in ethics, claiming that moral principles must express our attitudes. Now the principle of what Medlin calls universal categorical egoism—which is the only form ethical egoism can take—is that "we all ought to observe our own interests, because that is what we ought

[7] G. E. Moore, *Principia Ethica* (Cambridge at the University Press, 1903), p. 147.
[8] Aristotle, *De Anima*, 431b 10ff.(tr. J. A. Smith).

to do".[9] This principle must be considered to express the attitudes of those who hold it, and these attitudes, Medlin argues, must be on the one hand favorable to everyone's happiness (since the principle enjoins each individual to observe his own interests, or seek his own happiness), and yet indifferent to everyone's happiness (since the principle enjoins each individual to seek his own happiness whatever the effects on the happiness of others). These attitudes are inconsistent. Hence the principle of egoism rests on inconsistent attitudes.

Medlin's arguments, as well as those of a third critic of egoism, the contemporary American philosopher W. K. Frankena, are subject to intensive criticism in a paper specially written for this volume by Jesse Kalin, a young professor at the State University of New York at Buffalo.

Kalin shows first that egoism, to be consistent, must be formulated so that it is always the self-interest of the prospective *agent* which determines what he is to do. An egoism which required each person to use his own self-interest in determining what anyone ought to do, would of course lead to inconsistency, for *I* would judge that *you* ought to do what was to *my* self-interest, and *you* would judge that *you* ought to do what was to *your* self-interest.

This, Kalin claims, is sufficient to meet Frankena's objections to egoism, but it leads him to a direct confrontation with Medlin's position. Kalin insists that Medlin has failed to make a crucial distinction between the *belief* that someone ought to perform a particular act and the *desire* to perform that act. Kalin appeals to a situation in which we all find ourselves from time to time—the competitive game—to make his point. For surely we believe that our opponent *ought* to do what will lead to his winning, although we do not *want* him to do this.

Kalin does not deny Medlin's insistence that ethical principles express attitudes, although he prefers to argue his case in different terms. Of course the egoist is favorably disposed to his own well-being, and of course this is the root of his egoism. But what concerns Kalin is that Medlin interprets the relation between attitudes and ethical principles in such a way that he supposes one must have a favorable attitude towards whatever conduct is required by one's principle. This, Kalin argues, is to fail to distinguish *material valuations* from *formal valuations*.

Kalin's criticism of Medlin here applies also to Moore. Both suppose that the supreme principle of conduct must reflect a single end, or a single attitude, shared by all. This Kalin terms the material conception of value—that there is a good common to all. On the other hand, the egoist supposes no such common good, but rather believes that what is good differs from person to person. This is the formal conception of value, and it gives rise to a supreme principle of conduct which rests on the different ends, or different attitudes, of each. Thus the egoistic principle, interpreted teleologically, rests on the view that each man's happiness is his end, and interpreted emotively, on the view that each man has a favorable attitude to his own happiness.

This argument may not move Medlin, who can insist that if one holds a supreme ethical principle, one must be favorably disposed to *anyone* acting on it. What this may show, of course, is that *no* principle satisfies both the universality requirement of ethics, and the attitudinal requirement of emotivism. Whether one should reject ethics or emotivism is a question demanding further exploration.

Kalin goes on to observe that egoism, as an ethical position, has certain curious features. The egoist will neither give nor seek moral advice, for it is not in his interest to tell others what they ought to do, and not in their interest to tell him what he ought to do. He will not teach his morality to his children, for it will not benefit him to make them egoists. If these, and other characteristics of egoism, disqualify it as a moral theory, then Kalin insists that "moral" is a mere label, which does not affect the status of egoism as a coherent guide to conduct. And if egoism is a coherent guide to conduct, why is it not reasonable to adopt it? If we suppose morality to be rational yet distinct from ethical egoism, then we are caught once again in Sidgwick's contradiction.

V

Moral philosophy has seldom flourished as it did in eighteenth-century Britain. Today the student is almost certain to be acquainted with the work of David Hume; he may perhaps have read or read about the *Sermons* of Joseph Butler; but little else is likely to have come to his attention. This ignorance matters little to those whose main philosophical interests lie well outside moral philosophy, since ethics was never as free of general metaphysical speculation as in this period. But such an enquiry as ours should tempt us to a greater familiarity with our eighteenth-century predecessors, who discussed many of our problems from viewpoints which we can well appreciate today.

Francis Hutcheson, professor of moral philosophy at Glasgow University, is perhaps the most unjustly neglected of all. We take the first selection in our second section from his *Inquiry concerning Moral Good and Evil*, not to remedy this neglect, but because there are few more thorough discussions of the character of moral motivation.

Hutcheson's primary concern, in the chapter of his work which we are reprinting, is to show that the moral affections cannot be reduced to self-love, or desire of private interest. These affections Hutcheson divides into two pairs—complacence (also called esteem or approbation of others), with its contrary contempt, and benevolence, with its contrary malice. And he begins by observing that hope of benefit may lead a man to seek another's ruin, but not to disapprove of that other. With this, the relation between esteem and self-interest is for the moment dismissed. Hutcheson's main concern is with those who would derive benevolence from self-interest. This is the more important problem, since esteem is directed upon the moral qualities of others, and if we are to esteem others for more than their disposition to esteem also, it must be for their benevolence.

Hutcheson considers two attempts to derive benevolence from self-interest. The first claims that we arouse benevolence in ourselves whenever it is in our interest to do so, whether for direct pleasure, or to enjoy our own esteem, or to receive reward from society or the deity. The second claims that since we tend to sympathize with the pleasure and misery of others, we naturally seek their happiness as a means to our own sympathetic pleasure, and their relief from misery as a means to the relief of our own sympathetic pain, and that this constitutes benevolence.

Hutcheson's principal argument against the first attempt is that we cannot arouse feelings at will. Secondarily he argues that if we could arouse benevolence at will, so that we could feel benevolent and act benevolently whenever it was in our interest to do so, then we should not approve benevolence, since we do not approve affections based solely on our own interests.

He considers the second attempt more plausible, since it does not require us to will our feelings of benevolence. But again, he asks, since we do not approve actions directed at the happiness of others if they are undertaken merely to secure wealth or sensual pleasure, why would we approve them if they were undertaken merely to secure sympathetic pleasure? Further, if our sole aim is to secure sympathetic pleasure or avoid sympathetic pain, then the means should be indifferent to us, so why would we prefer to seek to relieve the sufferings of others than to blot out our awareness of their sufferings? Hutcheson contends that those who suppose we seek the well-being of others solely as means to our own well-being confuse our *intention,* which is to secure the well-being of others, with the delight *consequent* upon achieving that intention. This delight (we may add to his account) cannot be what we seek, since it arises only in so far as we obtain what we seek.

Hutcheson admits that nothing so effectively arouses our esteem of others as their benevolence toward us. But this esteem is not based on self-interest, since it is not the means, but the consequence, of securing the benevolence of others. And it does not cease when benevolence ceases, as it would if the benevolent were esteemed solely because of their advantage to us.

What then is the motive of moral action? Hutcheson considers it an instinct, influencing us to the love of others, and quite separate from that reason based on interest. This instinct is most fully aroused toward those with whom we are most closely associated, but it extends to some extent toward all mankind. It may be overpowered by considerations of self-interest when these conflict with it, but it is always present in all men.

We may doubt the optimistic conclusion just reached. But let us grant Hutcheson his negative arguments—that we cannot derive moral affections, esteem, and benevolence, from considerations of interest. What does this show?

As our next reading suggests, very little. David Hume, the Scotsman who dominates eighteenth-century British philosophy, would agree with Hutcheson that the moral affections or sentiments are not derived from self-love or self-interest. Nevertheless, we must show that considerations of interest oblige us to perform those actions which our moral sentiments prompt.

Hume's argument would seem to have this basis. We have many sentiments or affections, directed at various objects. Some may be selfish, in that their object is some aspect of our own well-being. Some may be altruistic, in that their object is some aspect of the well-being of others. Now we may not be able to satisfy all of these sentiments, since what satisfies one may be incompatible with what satisfies another. How then may we decide what to do? Only by considering what will maximize our happiness.

Perhaps our happiness will be maximized by seeking the well-being of others. For in so far as we are prompted by our moral affections to seek their well-being, we shall be uneasy if we fail to do so. But it may be that we have stronger affections which will lead us to ignore their well-being, and accept the consequent uneasiness as the necessary price of some greater benefit to ourselves.

Hume tries to convince us that self-interest does in fact support morality. He argues that moral approbation extends to what is agreeable and useful, both to its possessor and to others. That we should seek what is agreeable and useful to ourselves will be immediately conceded by self-interest. That we should seek what is agreeable and useful to others will require more argument, but surely we must agree that these social virtues are what we would want to possess, for our own happiness, if we were to have the power of making our own characters. It is only the lack of these affections in sufficient strength which leads us to forgo the unbought pleasures of virtue, which, Hume assures us, are truly beyond all price.

This is rhetoric and not argument. Hume cannot *prove* what he seeks to prove, and he in effect admits this. His intention is to convince us that moral motives are supported by considerations of interest. But instead he shows us that the problem of moral motivation is more complex than it may first appear to be. It is not enough to show that moral motives are not derived from self-interest, since all primary motives are prior to motivation based on considerations of interest. What must be shown is either that moral motives are reinforced by interest, or that conflicts among motives need not be resolved by an appeal to interest.

This latter position is taken by H. A. Prichard, one of the most noted English intuitionist moral philosophers of the first half of the twentieth century. Indeed, Prichard maintains the very strong position that duty and interest are in no way connected.

In our selection Prichard presents two main arguments. The first is directed especially against Plato, although as Prichard indicates it applies to many other philosophers as well. It centers on the claim that if we maintain that an action must be advantageous if it is to be right, then we must maintain that advantageousness alone makes an action right. For we cannot demonstrate any other necessary link between what is advantageous and what is right. Now Prichard takes it to be evidently absurd that advantageousness renders an action right, and so dismisses Plato's argument and all similar arguments. He then asks why Plato seeks to show that what is right must be advantageous. And his answer is that Plato believes that whenever a man acts deliberately, he acts to secure some good for himself.

This brings us to our present problem—moral motivation. Prichard insists, as Hutcheson does, that benevolent actions are not directed only at our own satisfaction, but arise at least in part from a desire to secure satisfaction for someone else. He insists, as Hutcheson does not, we may also perform malicious actions, directed at the frustration or unhappiness of someone else. And he is led to suppose the existence of a desire to do what is right (though not, it should be noted, of a desire to do what is wrong).

However, as we have seen in examining Hume's argument, this is insufficient to show that when we act reflectively, we are moved by anything other than consideration of the maximum self-satisfaction which we can attain. A desire to do what is right may be no more than another particular desire, to be subjected to the scrutiny of self-interest.

But Prichard insists that the desire to be happy, which we may take to be the basis of self-interest, and the desire to do what is right, are incommensurable. We cannot take the desire to do what is right as one among the particular desires, the maximum satisfaction of which constitutes happiness. We cannot even choose between doing what is right, and doing what will make us happy, since there is no basis for such a choice. In a particular situation we may sacrifice our happiness to duty, or our duty to happiness. We must decide, but our decision has and can have no foundation, and so—it seems to follow—must be unmotivated. Man has two fundamental types of motive— prudential and moral—and there is no relation between them.

Let us summarize the argument of this section. None of the philosophers represented maintains that moral motivation can be derived from self-interested motivation. Hutcheson is primarily concerned to refute this view. But it is still possible to hold, as Hume does, that on reflection only considerations of self-love move us, so that we shall act on our moral desires only if in so doing we contribute to our greatest overall satisfaction. Prichard rejects this position, insisting that moral motivation and self-interested motivation are strictly incommensurable.

Can we avoid agreeing with either Hume or Prichard? Is it possible to hold that moral motivation and self-interested motivation are commensurable, without supposing that self-interest provides the standard of commensurability? This is a question which invites further investigation.

VI

The selections in our third section approach the problem of relating morality to rational self-interest from a quite different standpoint. Rather than arguing abstractly about the rationality of egoism, or about the possibility of nonself-interested motivation, they focus on the consequences of self-interested action, and the possibility that morality may develop from the failure of action based on self-interest to achieve its ends.

In *Leviathan,* the seventeenth-century political philosopher Thomas Hobbes paints a grim picture of a world in which men are moved to act only by considerations of interest, without moral, political, or social institutions to modify their behavior. In such a world, which Hobbes terms the *state of nature,* men bent on their own preservation and well-being find themselves in competition for the scarce goods which maintain and enhance life. And from this competition arises hostility, as each man realizes that his best chance of preserving himself is to eliminate his competitors. So although each man seeks to avoid death, all men find themselves in a permanent condition of war of every man against every man, "and the life of man solitary, poor, nasty, brutish, and short." [10]

The result of the unlimited pursuit of self-interest is a war which is in the interest of no one. Yet in this pursuit men have not acted in a foolish or misguided manner; any man who fails to compete with his fellows avoids the war of all against all only by becoming a prey to other men, and so by hastening the death he would avoid. In contemporary terms, an arms race may prove mutually suicidal, but failure to engage in an arms race—unilateral disarmament—is an invitation to more immediate disaster.

In the state of nature, Hobbes says, man has an unlimited right to

[10] P. 135 in this volume.

all things—each may do as he pleases, in order to preserve himself. As long as men retain this unlimited right, so long will the war of all against all continue. Hence it is in the interest of every man to part with this unlimited right, provided others do so as well. If each man accepts certain restraints on his pursuit of self-interest, then peace is possible, and all men will benefit.

The conditions of peace are the *laws of nature,* and the laws of nature constitute the true moral philosophy. Thus it is in the interest of every man to accept the laws of nature and so to be moral, provided every other man does so as well. Although it would be suicidal for an individual to restrain unilaterally his pursuit of self-interest by following the laws of morality, it is reasonable for all individuals to restrain themselves in this way. The moral solution to the arms race is mutual agreement to disarm.

But Hobbes is confronted with a problem. For although it is advantageous for men to agree to give up certain of their rights, is it advantageous for them to carry out their agreements? May it not be more advantageous, and so more reasonable, for a man—more to his interest—only to pretend to accept certain restraints on his pursuit of self-interest?

Hobbes argues that justice—the keeping of covenants or agreements—is in fact always in the true interest of every man. Thus in fact men do not limit their pursuit of self-interest, but rather merely change the circumstances in which they act, so that their pursuit of self-interest ceases to be mutually destructive. And indeed, as Hobbes makes clear in parts of *Leviathan* not reprinted here, what is required to hold men to the laws of nature is a sovereign with power sufficient to ensure that no man can expect to benefit save by adherence to the laws. This power is required to restrain men from destroying each other.

For Hobbes, then, there is no morality beyond prudence—and there can be no such morality because men are necessarily motivated to act only on consideration of what conduces to their preservation and well-being. Hobbes is thus unable to exploit what nevertheless is the basic insight in his approach to morality—that if men act only on considerations of self-interest, they will not end up as well off as if they were to modify their pursuit of self-interest in certain situations.

This insight has been developed by Kurt Baier, who is now professor of philosophy at the University of Pittsburgh. Baier asks the question, "Why should we be moral?" and argues that to answer it we must show that being moral maximizes satisfactions and minimizes frustrations. Following reason must pay; to say that we should be moral is to say that being moral is following reason; hence if we should be moral, being moral must pay.

Baier shows that self-interested considerations provide reasons for acting, since it obviously pays to follow them. But moral considerations are better reasons for acting, because everyone does better if everyone follows moral considerations, rather than if everyone follows only self-interested considerations. Baier admits that an individual may do better if he follows self-interest and not morality. But he regards such a course of action as unreasonable, if others follow morality. It is equally unreasonable for an individual to follow morality, if others follow self-interest. Morality is the most reasonable basis of action for everyone.

Baier's argument rests on an appeal to Hobbes' account of the state of nature, and of the desirability of following the laws of nature. But Baier does not accept Hobbes' account of human motivation, so that he is not forced to conclude that morality can be operative only in so far as it is actually to one's advantage to act on a moral rule in a particular situation. He is able to suppose that people will be prepared to sacrifice their own advantage, when they believe that others will make similar sacrifices, and when they realize that the overall result of such sacrifices will be to everyone's advantage.

But has Baier really shown that it must pay to accept moral considerations as reasons for acting? This question is discussed in the final selection, written by the editor, who is professor of philosophy at the University of Toronto.

Gauthier first tries to clarify just what is involved in the claim that everyone may do better if everyone follows moral considerations rather than self-interested considerations. He shows the formal structure of a fairly simple type of situation in which individuals acting solely on considerations of self-interest will end up worse off than individuals acting otherwise. In terms of this structure, it is clear that whatever other individuals do, *each* person is better off if he acts on considerations of interest than if he does not. Thus in one fairly obvious sense, following moral considerations which override those of self-interest does not, and cannot, pay.

Gauthier suggests that the rationally prudent or rationally self-interested man lacks the capacity for moral behavior. The man who acts morally—in the sense of morality suggested by Baier—must accept certain considerations as reasons for acting, and must be moved by such considerations, without being shown that it pays to do so. There is no nonmoral reason for being moral.

Furthermore, Gauthier argues that Baier's sense of morality omits all considerations such as fairness. If we suppose, as we commonly do, that the moral man is willing to restrain his own self-interested activity to ensure equal opportunities for others, then we are even further from defending morality in terms of what pays—what maximizes satisfactions and minimizes frustrations.

Gauthier agrees with Baier that there is a connection between morality and rational self-interest—that moral men as a community will do better for themselves than self-interested men. What he denies is that this provides a rational defence or justification of morality to the self-interested individual.

If the connection between morality and rational self-interest is clarified by these readings, it is by no means determinately established. Even the outcome of the debate between Baier and Gauthier is far from clear. For although these arguments appear both to be plausible, and to depend on similar views of what is reasonable, yet their conclusions are incompatible:

(a) If it is reasonable for me to accept only self-interested reasons for acting, then it is reasonable for everyone. But if everyone accepted only self-interested reasons for acting, then everyone would do worse than if everyone also accepted moral reasons for acting. But it is not reasonable for everyone to do worse than necessary. Therefore it is not reasonable for everyone to accept only self-interested reasons for acting, and so not reasonable for me.

(b) If it is reasonable for me to accept moral reasons for acting, then I must do better by accepting them. For it is not reasonable for me to do worse than necessary. But whether others accept moral reasons or not, I do better to accept only self-interested reasons, rather than moral reasons as well. Therefore it is reasonable for me to accept only self-interested reasons for acting.

VII

In this final section we shall suggest one direction which discussion of the relation between morality and rational self-interest may take. This suggestion, not surprisingly, may be considered a sequel to some of the arguments advanced in "Morality and Advantage."

In that paper a very limited use is made of formal techniques taken from the mathematical theory of games. The theory of games provides a perspicuous way of representing the structure of conflict situations, in terms of the courses of actions (or strategies) open to the persons (players) involved, and the utility (or benefit) to the persons of the various results of different possible combinations of actions or strategies.

To illustrate this, consider a very simple example. Suppose that Jones and Smith are playing the following game. Smith holds a marble in one of his hands, and Jones must guess which hand. If Jones guesses wrong, then he pays Smith 25 cents. If he guesses right, then if the marble is in Smith's right hand, Smith pays Jones 50 cents, and if it is in Smith's left hand, Smith pays Jones 10 cents.

We represent this "conflict situation" in a matrix, where the numbers in each entry represent the monetary pay-off (assumed proportional to the utility) to Jones and to Smith respectively.

	Smith holds coin	
Jones guesses	in right hand	in left hand
right hand	50¢, −50¢	−25¢, 25¢
left hand	−25¢, 25¢	10¢, −10¢

One of the aims of the theory of games is to provide "solutions" for such games or conflict situations. The solution indicates the strategy that each person should follow in order to maximize his expected pay-off. In the example, it should be clear that neither Jones nor Smith should always select the same hand. If Jones always guessed Smith's right hand, in an effort to win 50 cents, then Smith could always hold the coin in his left hand, and always win 25 cents. On the other hand, if Smith always held the coin in his left hand, to prevent Jones from winning more than 10 cents, Jones could always win the 10 cents by guessing the left hand. The reader may amuse himself by trying to determine how Jones and Smith should play so that, in the long run, each will do as well for himself as possible.

The theory of games is a valuable tool in making more determinate our understanding of rational self-interest. For the "solutions" it provides to conflict situations are solutions for rationally self-interested men—instructions which they may follow in order to maximize their expected utilities, or in other words, their expected well-being.

But as anyone familiar with game theory knows, there are no agreed solutions for more than a very limited class of games. And even where solutions have been established, they do not always meet the conditions which we might have expected to hold, prior to formal analysis. Consider, for example, such a matrix as this:

	Smith holds coin	
Jones guesses	**in** right hand	in left hand
right hand	20¢, 20¢	−25¢, 25¢
left hand	25¢, −25¢	−5¢, −5¢

The game represented by this matrix will require a "bank" which makes and receives payments, so that under certain circumstances both players can gain, and in other circumstances both can lose. An analysis of this matrix, which is a variant of the Prisoner's Dilemma, and is formally similar to the matrix discussed in "Morality and Advantage," reveals that whatever Smith does, Jones does better to guess the left hand than the right hand, and whatever Jones guesses, Smith does better to hold his coin in the left hand rather than the right hand. Game theorists therefore take the solution of this conflict situation to be that Smith holds the coin in his left hand and Jones guesses this. Both players must then pay 5 cents to the bank, instead of both receiving 20 cents from the bank as they would were each to shift to the right hand.

The principle employed in reaching this solution may be expressed, informally, by saying that if one strategy (or course of action) open to a person is *dominant,* that is, better than any other strategy for each possible course of action open to his opponent(s), then it is in his interest, and so rational, for him to select that strategy. This principle seems to follow directly from the general principle that one should seek to maximize one's pay-off or utility.

But there is another principle which, as this example shows, is incompatible with the principle of dominance, and yet may seem equally reasonable. We may express it informally by saying that in a given conflict situation, the solution should be *Pareto-optimal,* that is, there should be no other outcome which is better for some player or players and worse for none.[11] For if the outcome is not Pareto-optimal, then at least some persons, and perhaps every person, will do worse than need be, which is unreasonable.

The principle of *dominance* is related to argument (b) at the end

[11] Note that in our example, *all* of the outcomes *except* the solution are Pareto-optimal.

of the preceding section, whereas the principle of *Pareto-optimality* is related to argument (a). Neither of these principles does more than impose a necessary condition on the solution of most conflict situations. Only rarely is dominance sufficient to determine a solution, and only when there is no real conflict will Pareto-optimality alone suffice. However, we may ask whether more general principles can be found, one of which incorporates dominance, and one of which incorporates Pareto-optimality, which provide general and rival solutions for conflict situations, each of which may be defended as reasonable in that it maximizes well-being.

Game theorists have not agreed on such principles. But this is a field of enquiry which is by no means closed, and the editor's own researches suggest the possibility of devising such principles. To report further on these researches here is impossible; the issues involved are sufficiently complex that any popular account would be far too long, and any brief account far too technical.

If these researches prove successful, they will provide the basis for determining, with respect to the class of situations which may be formalized as two-person games, precisely what is involved *first* in a simple policy of maximizing one's advantage, and *second* in a policy of maximizing one's advantage compatibly with the maximization of advantage for all. The first, we suggest, is the policy of rational self-interest; the second is the policy of what Baier terms morality.

But further questions remain. Even if the difference between Baier's "morality" and rational self-interest may be formalized, we may still question the adequacy of Baier's characterization of morality. The editor would suggest the possibility of appealing again to the theory of games, not to provide maximizing solutions for conflict situations, but to suggest "solutions" which capture our ill-defined notion of fairness or justice.[12] The editor's researches also suggest the possibility of devising a precise principle which will determine fair solutions to conflict situations, and which may therefore be defended as reasonable even though it does not allow each individual to act in that way which would maximize his advantage (or even that way which would maximize his advantage compatibly with the maximization of advantage for all).

These researches will not shed any direct light on the problems we have discussed as problems concerning motivation. All that we can

[12] R. B. Braithwaite, *Theory of Games as a Tool for the Moral Philosopher* (Cambridge at the University Press, 1955), attempts this.

hope to achieve from this study of the theory of games is to be able to make precise the principles of action which correspond to our vague notions of acting in one's interest, and acting morally. But this may be of indirect benefit in discussing problems of motivation, if we can devise experiments—as game theorists with psychological interests do —to determine the actual learning and use of these principles.

The problems remain. Indeed, hopefully, they are your problems, now.

part one

IS

SELF-INTEREST

RATIONAL?

HENRY SIDGWICK

Reason, Egoism, and Utilitarianism

CHAPTER III

Ethical Judgments

§ 1. In the first chapter I spoke of actions that we judge to be
right and what ought to be done as being "reasonable," or "rational,"
and similarly of ultimate ends as "prescribed by Reason:" and I con-
trasted the motive to action supplied by the recognition of such reasonableness with "nonrational" desires and inclinations. This manner of
speaking is employed by writers of different schools, and seems in accordance with the common view and language on the subject. For we
commonly think that wrong conduct is essentially irrational, and can
be shewn to be so by argument; and though we do not conceive that
it is by reason alone that men are influenced to act rightly, we still
hold that appeals to the reason are an essential part of all moral
persuasion, and that part which concerns the moralist or moral philosopher as distinct from the preacher or moral rhetorician. On the
the other hand it is widely maintained that, as Hume says, "Reason,
meaning the judgment of truth and falsehood, can never of itself be
any motive to the Will"—the motive to action being in all cases some

* From *The Methods of Ethics*, Book I, Chap. iii, and Concluding Chapter. The
text used is that of the fifth edition, published by Macmillan Co. in 1893. Students
of Sidgwick's thought will wish to consult the seventh edition, 1907. But the fifth,
although differing only in details, is in my judgment superior for its treatment of
our problems. Certain footnotes, containing cross references to other parts of the
book, are omitted.

feeling of the class that I have characterized as Nonrational Desires. It seems desirable to examine with some care the grounds of this contention, before we proceed any further.

Let us begin by defining the issue raised, as clearly as possible. Everyone, I suppose, has had experience of what is meant by the conflict of nonrational or irrational desires with reason: most of us (*e.g.*) occasionally feel bodily appetite prompting us to indulgences which we judge to be imprudent, and anger prompting us to acts which we disapprove as unjust or unkind. It is when this conflict occurs that the desires are said to be irrational, as impelling us to volitions opposed to our deliberate judgments: sometimes we yield to such seductive impulses, and sometimes not: and it is perhaps when we do *not* yield, that the impulsive force of such irrational desires is most definitely felt, as we have to exert in resisting them a voluntary effort somewhat analogous to that involved in any muscular exertion. Often, again— since we are not always thinking either of our duty or of our interest —desires of this kind take effect in voluntary actions without our having judged such actions to be either right or wrong, either prudent or imprudent; as (*e.g.*) when an ordinary healthy man eats his dinner. In such cases it seems most appropriate to call the desires "nonrational" rather than "irrational." Neither term is intended to imply that the desires spoken of—or at least the more important of them—are not normally accompanied by rational or intellectual processes. It is true that some impulses to action seem to take effect, as we say, "blindly" or "instinctively," without any definite consciousness either of the end at which the action is aimed, or of the means by which the end is to be attained: but this, I conceive, is only the case with impulses that do not occupy consciousness for an appreciable time, and do not require any but very familiar and habitual actions for the attainment of their proximate ends. In all other cases—that is, in the case of the actions with which we are chiefly concerned in ethical discussion— the result aimed at, and usually some part at least of the means by which it is to be realized, are more or less distinctly represented in consciousness, previous to the volition that initiates the movements tending to its realization. Hence the resultant forces of what I call "nonrational" desires, and the volitions to which they prompt, are continually modified by intellectual processes in two distinct ways; first by new perceptions or representations of means conducive to the desired ends, and secondly by new presentations or representations of facts actually existing or in prospect—especially more or less probable consequences of contemplated actions—which rouse new impulses of desire and aversion.

The question, then, is whether the account just given of the influence of the intellect on desire and volition is not exhaustive; and whether the experience which is commonly described as a "conflict of desire with reason" is not more properly conceived as a conflict among desires and aversions; the sole function of reason being to bring before the mind ideas of actual or possible facts, which modify in the manner above described the resultant force of our various impulses.

I hold that this is not the case; that the ordinary moral or prudential judgments which, in the case of all or most minds have some—though too often not a predominant—influence on volition, cannot legitimately be interpreted as judgments respecting the present or future existence of human feelings or any facts of the sensible world; the fundamental notion represented by the word "ought" or "right," which such judgments contain expressly or by implication, being essentially different from all notions representing facts of physical or psychical experience. The question is one on which appeal must ultimately be made to the reflection of individuals on their practical judgments and reasonings: and in making this appeal it seems most convenient to begin by shewing the inadequacy of all attempts to explain the practical judgments or propositions in which this fundamental notion is introduced, without recognizing its unique character as above negatively defined. There is an element of truth in such explanations, in so far as they bring into view feelings which undoubtedly accompany moral or prudential judgments, and which ordinarily have more or less effect in determining the will to actions judged to be right; but so far as they profess to be interpretations of what such judgments mean, they appear to me to fail altogether.

. . . .

[The conclusions reached in this omitted portion are summarized in the following sentence.]

§ 3. It seems then that the notion of "ought" or "moral obligation" as used in our common moral judgments, does not merely import (1) that there exists in the mind of the person judging a specific emotion (whether complicated or not by sympathetic representation of similar emotions in other minds); nor (2) that certain rules of conduct are supported by penalties which will follow on their violation (whether such penalties result from the general liking or aversion felt for the conduct prescribed or forbidden, or from some other source). What then, it may be asked, does it import? What definition can we give of "ought," "right," and other terms expressing the same fundamental notion? To this I should answer that the notion which these terms have in common is too elementary to admit of any formal definition; but if what the questioner wants is a complete account of the relation of what ought to be to what is, I should add that it does not belong to Ethics to furnish this, but to some more comprehensive study: at any rate this task is not undertaken in the present treatise, which only attempts to methodize our practical judgments and reasonings, in which this fundamental notion must, I conceive, be taken as ultimate and unanalysable.

In speaking of this fundamental notion as "unanalysable," I do not mean that it belongs to the "original constitution of the mind;" that is, that its presence in consciousness is not the result of a process of development. I do not doubt that the whole fabric of human thought —including the conceptions that present themselves as most simple and elementary—has been developed, through a gradual process of psychical change, out of some lower life in which thought, properly speaking, had no place. But it is not therefore to be inferred, as regards this or any other notion, that it has not really the simplicity which it appears to have when we now reflect upon it. It is sometimes assumed that if we can shew how thoughts have grown up—if we can point to the psychical antecedents of which they are the natural consequents—we may conclude that the thoughts in question are really compounds containing their antecedents as latent elements. But I know no justification for this transference of the conceptions of chemistry to psychology:[1] I know no reason for considering psychical antecedents as really constitutive of their psychical consequents, in spite of the apparent dissimilarity between the two. In default of such reasons, a psychologist must accept as elementary what introspection carefully performed declares to be so: and, using this criterion, I find the notion

---

[1] In Chemistry we regard the antecedents (elements) as still existing in and constituting the consequent (compound) because the latter is exactly similar to the former in weight, and because we can generally cause this compound to disappear and obtain the elements in its place. But we find nothing at all like this in the growth of mental phenomena: the psychical consequent is in no respect exactly similar to its antecedents, nor can it be resolved into them.

that we have been examining elementary and unanalysable.[2] As it now exists in our thought, it cannot be resolved into any more simple notions: it can only be made clearer by determining its relation to other notions with which it is connected in ordinary thought, especially to those with which it is liable to be confounded.

Thus we have to note and distinguish two different implications with which the word "ought" is used; according as the result which we judge "ought to be" is or is not thought capable of being brought about by the volition of any individual, in the circumstances to which the judgment applies. The former alternative is, I conceive, implied by the strictly ethical "ought": in the narrowest ethical sense I cannot conceive that I "ought" to do anything which at the same time I judge that I cannot do. In a wider sense, however—which cannot conveniently be discarded in ordinary discourse—I sometimes judge that I "ought" to know what a wiser man would know, or feel as a better man would feel, in my place, though I may know that I could not directly produce in myself such knowledge or feeling by any effort of will. In this case the word merely implies an ideal or pattern which I "ought"—in the stricter sense—to seek to imitate as far as possible. And this wider sense seems to be that in which the word is normally used in the precepts of Art generally, and in political judgments: when I judge that the laws and constitution of my country "ought to be" other than they are, I do not of course imply that my own or any other individual's single volition can directly bring about the change.[3] In either case, however, I imply that what ought to be is a possible object of knowledge: that is, that what I judge to be "right" must, unless I am in error, be thought to be so by all rational beings who judge truly of the matter.

In referring such judgments to the "Reason," I do not mean here to prejudge the question whether valid moral judgments are normally attained by a process of reasoning from universal principles or axioms, or by direct intuition of the particular duties of individuals. It is not uncommonly held that the moral faculty deals primarily with individual cases as they arise, applying directly to each case the general

---

[2] I should explain that I am not here arguing the question whether the *validity* of moral judgments is affected by a discovery of their psychical antecedents. This question I reserve for subsequent discussion. See Book III, Chap. i, § 4.

[3] I do not even imply that any combination of individuals could completely realize the state of political relations which I conceive "ought to" exist. My conception would be futile if it had no relation to practice: but it may merely delineate a pattern to which no more than an approximation is practically possible.

notion of duty, and deciding intuitively what ought to be done by this person in these particular circumstances. And I admit that on this view the apprehension of moral truth is more analogous to Sense-perception than to Rational Intuition (as commonly understood):[4] and hence the term Moral Sense might seem more appropriate. But the term Sense suggests a capacity for feelings which may vary from A to B without either being in error, rather than a faculty of cognition[5]: and, as it appears to me fundamentally important to avoid this suggestion, I have thought it better to use the term Reason with the explanation above given, to denote the faculty of moral cognition.

Further, when I speak of the cognition or judgment that "X ought to be done"—in the stricter ethical sense of the term ought[6]—as a "dictate" or "precept" of reason to the persons to whom it relates; I imply that in rational beings as such this cognition gives an impulse or motive to action: though in human beings, of course, this is only one motive among others which are liable to conflict with it, and is not always—perhaps not usually—a predominant motive. In fact, this possible conflict of motives seems to be connoted by the term "dictate" or "imperative"; which describes the relation of Reason to mere inclinations or nonrational impulses by comparing it to the relation between the will of a superior and the wills of his subordinates. This conflict seems also to be implied in the terms "ought," "duty," "moral obligation," as used in ordinary moral discourse: and hence these terms cannot be applied to the actions of rational beings to whom we cannot attribute impulses conflicting with reason. We may, however, say of such beings that their actions are "reasonable," or (in an absolute sense) "right."

§ 4. I am aware that some persons will be disposed to answer all the preceding argument by a simple denial that they can find in their consciousness any such unconditional or categorical imperative as I have been trying to exhibit. If this is really the final result of self-

[4] We do not commonly say that particular physical facts are apprehended by the Reason: we consider this faculty to be conversant in its discursive operation with the relation of judgments or propositions: and the intuitive reason (which is here rather in question) we restrict to the apprehension of universal truths, such as the axioms of Logic and Mathematics.

[5] By cognition I always mean what some would rather call "apparent cognition" —that is, I do not mean to affirm the *validity* of the cognition, but only its existence as a psychical fact, and its claim to be valid.

[6] This is the sense in which the term will always be used in the present treatise, except where the context makes it quite clear that only the wider meaning—that of the political "ought"—is applicable.

examination in any case, there is no more to be said. I, at least, do not know how to impart the notion of moral obligation to any one who is entirely devoid of it. I think, however, that many of those who give this denial only mean to deny that they have any consciousness of moral obligation to actions without reference to their consequences; and would not really deny that they recognize some universal end or ends—whether it be the general happiness, or well-being otherwise understood—as that at which it is ultimately reasonable to aim, subordinating to its attainment the gratification of any personal desires that may conflict with this aim. But in this view, as I have before said, the unconditional imperative plainly comes in as regards the end, which is—explicitly or implicitly—recognized as an end at which all men "ought" to aim; and it can hardly be denied that the recognition of an end as ultimately reasonable involves the recognition of an obligation to do such acts as most conduce to the end. The obligation is not indeed "unconditional," but it does not depend on the existence of any nonrational desires or aversions. And nothing that has been said in the preceding section is intended as an argument in favour of Intuitionism, as against Utilitarianism or any other method that treats moral rules as relative to General Good or Well-being. For instance, nothing that I have said is inconsistent with the view that Truthspeaking is only valuable as a means to the preservation of society: only if it be admitted that it *is* valuable on this ground I should say that it is implied that the preservation of society—or some further end to which this preservation, again, is a means—must be valuable *per se*, and therefore something at which a rational being, as such, ought to aim. If it be granted that we need not look beyond the preservation of society, the primary "dictate of reason" in this case would be "that society *ought* to be preserved"; but reason would also dictate that truth ought to be spoken, so far as truthspeaking is recognized as the indispensable or fittest means to this end: and the notion "ought" as used in either dictate is the unanalysable "ought" which I have been trying to make clear.

So again, even those who hold that moral rules are only obligatory because it is the individual's interest to conform to them—thus regarding them as a particular species of prudential rules—do not thereby get rid of the "dictate of reason," so far as they recognize private interest or happiness as an end at which it is ultimately reasonable to aim. The conflict of Practical Reason with irrational desire remains an indubitable fact of our conscious experience, even if practical reason is interpreted to mean merely self-regarding Prudence. It is, indeed, maintained by Kant and others that it cannot properly be said to be a man's duty to promote his own happiness; since "what everyone inevitably wills cannot be brought under the notion of duty." But even granting[7] it to be in some sense true that a man's volition is always directed to the attainment of his own happiness; it does not follow that a man always does what he believes will be conducive to his own *greatest* happiness, or his "good on the whole." As Butler urges, it is a matter of common experience that men indulge appetite or passion even when, in their own view, the indulgence is as clearly opposed to what they conceive to be their interest as it is to what they conceive to be their duty. "Video meliora proboque, deteriora sequor" is as applicable to the Epicurean as it is to any one else: and in recognizing that he "chooses the worse," a man implicitly, if not explicitly, recognizes that he ought to choose something else. Thus the notion "ought"—as expressing the relation of rational judgment to non-rational impulses—will find a place in the practical rules of any egoistic system, no less than in the rules of ordinary morality, understood as prescribing duty without reference to the agent's interest.

Even, finally, if we discard the belief, that any end of action is unconditionally or "categorically" prescribed by reason, the notion "ought" as above explained is not thereby eliminated from our practical reasonings: it still remains in the "hypothetical imperative" which prescribes the fittest means to any end that we may have determined to aim at. When (*e.g.*) a physician says, "If you wish to be healthy you ought to rise early," this is not the same thing as saying "early rising is an indispensable condition of the attainment of health." This latter proposition expresses the relation of physiological facts on which the former is founded; but it is not merely this relation of facts that the word "ought" imports: it also implies the unreasonableness of adopting an end and refusing to adopt the means indispensable to its attainment. It may perhaps be argued that this is not only unreasonable but impossible: since adoption of an end means the preponderance of a desire for it, and if aversion to the indispensable means causes them not to be adopted although recognized as indispensable, the desire for the end is *not* preponderant and it ceases to be adopted. But this view is due, in my opinion, to a defective psychological analysis. According to my observation of consciousness, the

---

[7] As will be seen from the next chapter, I do not grant this.

adoption of an end as paramount—either absolutely or within certain limits—is quite a distinct psychical phenomenon from desire: it is to be classed with volitions, though it is, of course, specifically different from a volition initiating a particular immediate action. As a species intermediate between the two, we may place resolutions to act in a certain way at some future time: we continually make such resolutions, and sometimes when the time comes for carrying them out, we do in fact act otherwise under the influence of passion or mere habit, without consciously cancelling our previous resolve: in this case the act is, I conceive, clearly irrational as inconsistent with a resolution that still persists in thought. Similarly the adoption of an end logically implies a resolution to take whatever means we may see to be indispensable to its attainment: and if when the time comes we do not take them while yet we do not consciously retract our adoption of the end, it must surely be admitted that we "ought" in consistency to act otherwise than we do. That Reason dictates the avoidance of a contradiction will be allowed even by those who deny that it dictates anything else: and such a contradiction as I have described, between a general resolution and a particular volition, is surely a matter of common experience.

CONCLUDING CHAPTER

The Mutual Relations of the Three Methods

§ 1. In the greater part of the treatise of which the final chapter has now been reached, we have been employed in examining three methods of determining right conduct, which are for the most part found more or less vaguely combined in the practical reasonings of ordinary men, but which it has been my aim to develope as separately as possible. A complete synthesis of these different methods is not attempted in the present work: at the same time it would hardly be satisfactory to conclude the analysis of them without some discussion of their mutual relations. Indeed we have already found it expedient to do this to a considerable extent, in the course of our examination of the separate methods. Thus in the present and preceding books we have directly or indirectly gone through a pretty full examination of the mutual relations of the Intuitional and Utilitarian methods. We have found that the common antithesis between Intuitionists and Utilitarians must be entirely discarded: since such abstract moral principles as we can admit to be really self-evident are not only not incompatible with a Utilitarian system, but even seem required to furnish a rational basis for such a system. Thus we have seen that the essence of Justice or Equity (in so far as it is clear and certain), is that different individuals are not to be treated differently, except on grounds of universal application; and that such grounds, again, are supplied by the principle of Universal Benevolence, that sets before each man the happiness of all others as an object of pursuit no less worthy than his own; while other time-honoured virtues seem to be fitly explained as special manifestations of impartial benevolence under various circumstances of human life, or else as habits and dispositions indispensable to the maintenance of prudent or beneficent behaviour under the seductive force of various nonrational impulses. And although there are other rules which our common moral sense when first interrogated seems to enunciate as absolutely binding; it has appeared that careful and systematic reflection on this very Common Sense, as expressed in the habitual moral judgments of ordinary men, results in exhibiting the real subordination of these rules to the fundamental principles above given. Then, further, this method of systematising particular virtues and duties receives very strong support from a comparative study of the history of morality; as the variations in the moral codes of different societies at different stages correspond, in a great measure, to differences in the actual or believed tendencies of certain kinds of conduct to promote the general happiness of different portions of the human race: while, again, the most probable conjectures as to the prehistoric condition and original derivation of the moral faculty seem to be entirely in harmony with this view. No doubt, even if this synthesis of methods be completely accepted, there will remain some discrepancy in details between our particular moral sentiments and unreasoned judgments on the one hand, and the apparent results of special utilitarian calculations on the other; and we may often have some practical difficulty in balancing the latter against the more general utilitarian reasons for obeying the former: but there seems to be no longer any theoretical perplexity as to the principles for determining social duty.

It remains for us to consider the relation of the two species of Hedonism which we have distinguished as Universalistic and Egoistic. In Chap. ii of this book we have discussed the rational process (called by a stretch of language "proof") by which one who holds it reasonable to aim at his own greatest happiness may be determined to take

Universal Happiness instead, as his ultimate standard of right conduct. We have seen, however, that the application of this process requires that the Egoist should affirm, implicitly or explicitly, that his own greatest happiness is not merely the rational ultimate end for himself, but a part of Universal Good: and he may avoid the proof of Utilitarianism by declining to affirm this. It would be contrary to Common Sense to deny that the distinction between any one individual and any other is real and fundamental, and that consequently "I" am concerned with the quality of my existence as an individual in a sense, fundamentally important, in which I am not concerned with the quality of the existence of other individuals: and this being so, I do not see how it can be proved that this distinction is not to be taken as fundamental in determining the ultimate end of rational action for an individual. And it may be observed that most Utilitarians, however anxious they have been to convince men of the reasonableness of aiming at happiness generally, have not commonly sought to attain this result by any logical transition from the Egoistic to the Universalistic principle. They have relied almost entirely on the Sanctions of Utilitarian rules; that is, on the pleasures gained or pains avoided by the individual conforming to them. Indeed, if an Egoist remains impervious to what we have called Proof, the only way of rationally inducing him to aim at the happiness of all, is to shew him that his own greatest happiness can be best attained by so doing. And further, even if a man admits the self-evidence of the principle of Rational Benevolence, he may still hold that his own happiness is an end which it is irrational for him to sacrifice to any other; and that therefore a harmony between the maxim of Prudence and the maxim of Rational Benevolence must be somehow demonstrated, if morality is to be made completely rational. This latter view, indeed (as I have before said), appears to me, on the whole, the view of Common Sense: and it is that which I myself hold. It thus becomes needful to examine how far and in what way the required demonstration can be effected.

§ 2. Now, in so far as Utilitarian morality coincides with that of Common Sense—as we have seen that it does in the main—this investigation has been partly performed in Chap. v of Book II. It there appeared that while in any tolerable state of society the performance of duties towards others and the exercise of social virtues seem *generally* likely to coincide with the attainment of the greatest possible happiness in the long run for the virtuous agent, still the *universality* and *completeness* of this coincidence are at least incapable of empirical proof: and that, indeed, the more carefully we analyse and estimate the different sanctions—Legal, Social and Conscientious—considered as operating under the actual conditions of human life, the more difficult it seems to believe that they can be always adequate to produce this coincidence. The natural effect of this argument upon a convinced Utilitarian is merely to make him anxious to alter the actual conditions of human life: and it would certainly be a most valuable contribution to the actual happiness of mankind, if we could so improve the adjustment of the machine of Law in any society, and so stimulate and direct the common awards of praise and blame, and so develop and train the moral sense of the members of the community, as to render it clearly prudent for every individual to promote as much as possible the general good. However, we are not now considering what a consistent Utilitarian will try to effect for the future, but what a consistent Egoist is to do in the present. And it must be admitted that, as things are, whatever difference exists between Utilitarian morality and that of Common Sense is of such a kind as to render the coincidence with Egoism still more improbable in the case of the former. For we have seen that Utilitarianism is more rigid than Common Sense in exacting the sacrifice of the agent's private interests where they are incompatible with the greatest happiness of the greatest number: and of course in so far as the Utilitarian's principles bring him into conflict with any of the commonly accepted rules of morality, the whole force of the Social Sanction operates to deter him from what he conceives to be his duty.

§ 3. There are however writers of the Utilitarian school [8] who seem

---

[8] See J. S. Mill's treatise on Utilitarianism (Chap. iii. *passim*): where however the argument is not easy to follow, from a confusion between three different objects of inquiry: (1) the actual effect of sympathy in inducing conformity to the rules of Utilitarian ethics, (2) the effect in this direction which it is likely to have in the future, (3) the value of sympathetic pleasures and pains as estimated by an enlightened Egoist. The first and third of these questions Mill did not clearly separate, owing to his psychological doctrine that each one's own pleasure is the sole object of his desires. But if my refutation of this doctrine (Book I, Chap. iv, § 3) is valid, we have to distinguish two ways in which sympathy operates: it generates sympathetic pleasures and pains, which have to be taken into account in the calculations of Egoistic Hedonism: but it also may cause impulses to altruistic action, of which the force is quite out of proportion to the sympathetic pleasure (or relief from pain) which such action seems likely to secure to the agent. So that even if the average man ever should reach such a pitch of sympathetic development, as never to feel prompted to sacrifice the general good to his own, still this will not prove that it is egoistically reasonable for him to behave in this way.

to maintain or imply, that by due contemplation of the paramount importance of Sympathy as an element of human happiness we shall be led to see the coincidence of the good of each with the good of all. In opposing this view, I am as far as possible from any wish to depreciate the value of sympathy as a source of happiness even to human beings as at present constituted. Indeed I am of opinion that its pleasures and pains really constitute a great part of that internal reward of social virtue, and punishment of social misconduct, which in Book II, Chap. v, I roughly set down as due to the moral sentiments. For, in fact, though I can to some extent distinguish sympathetic from strictly moral feelings in introspective analysis of my own consciousness, I cannot say precisely in what proportion these two elements are combined. For instance: I seem able to distinguish the "sense of the ignobility of Egoism" of which I have before spoken—which, in my view, is the normal emotional concomitant or expression of the moral intuition that the Good of the whole is reasonably to be preferred to the Good of a part—from the jar of sympathetic discomfort which attends the conscious choice of my own pleasure at the expense of pain or loss to others; but I find it impossible to determine what force the former sentiment would have if actually separated from the latter, and I am inclined to think that the two kinds of feeling are very variously combined in different individuals. Perhaps, indeed, we may trace a general law of variation in the relative proportion of these two elements as exhibited in the development of the moral consciousness both in the race and in individuals; for it seems that at a certain stage of this development the mind is more susceptible to emotions connected with abstract moral ideas and rules presented as absolute; while after emerging from this stage and before entering it the feelings that belong to personal relations are stronger.[9] Certainly in a Utilitarian's mind sympathy tends to become a prominent element of all instinctive moral feelings that refer to social conduct; as in his view the rational basis of the moral impulse must ultimately lie in some pleasure won or pain saved for himself or for others; so that he never has to sacrifice himself to an impersonal Law, but always for some being or beings with whom he has at least some degree of fellow feeling.

But besides admitting the actual importance of sympathetic pleasures

[9] I do not mean to imply that the process of change is merely circular. In the earlier period sympathy is narrower, simpler, and more presentative; in the later it is more extensive, complex, and representative.

to the majority of mankind, I should go further and maintain that, on empirical grounds alone, enlightened self-interest would direct most men to foster and develop their sympathetic susceptibilities to a greater extent than is now commonly attained. The effectiveness of Butler's famous argument against the vulgar antithesis between Self-love and Benevolence is undeniable: and it seems scarcely extravagant to say that, amid all the profuse waste of the means of happiness which men commit, there is no imprudence more flagrant than that of Selfishness in the ordinary sense of the term—that excessive concentration of attention on the individual's own happiness which renders it impossible for him to feel any strong interest in the pleasures and pains of others. The perpetual prominence of self that hence results tends to deprive all enjoyments of their keenness and zest, and produce rapid satiety and *ennui:* the selfish man misses the sense of elevation and enlargement given by wide interests; he misses the more secure and serene satisfaction that attends continually on activities directed towards ends more stable in prospect than an individual's happiness can be; he misses the peculiar rich sweetness, depending upon a sort of complex reverberation of sympathy, which is always found in services rendered to those whom we love and who are grateful. He is made to feel in a thousand various ways, according to the degree of refinement which his nature has attained, the discord between the rhythms of his own life and of that larger life of which his own is but an insignificant fraction.

But allowing[10] all this, it yet seems to me as certain as any conclusion arrived at by hedonistic comparison can be, that the utmost development of sympathy, intensive and extensive, which is now possible to any but a very few exceptional persons, would not cause a perfect coincidence between Utilitarian duty and self-interest. Here it seems to me that what was said in Book II, Chap. v, § 4, to shew the insufficiency of the Conscientious Sanction, applies equally, *mutatis mutandis,* to Sympathy. Suppose a man finds that a regard for the general good—Utilitarian Duty—demands from him a sacrifice, or extreme risk, of life. There are perhaps one or two human beings so dear to him that the remainder of a life saved by sacrificing their

[10] I do not however think that we are justified in stating as *universally* true what has been admitted in the preceding paragraph. Some few thoroughly selfish persons appear at least to be happier than most of the unselfish; and there are other exceptional natures whose chief happiness seems to be derived from activity, disinterested indeed, but directed towards other ends than human happiness.

happiness to his own would be worthless to him from an egoistic point of view. But it is doubtful whether many men, "sitting down in a cool hour" to make the estimate, would affirm even this: and of course that particular portion of the general happiness, for which one is called upon to sacrifice one's own, may easily be the happiness of persons not especially dear to one. But again, from this normal limitation of our keenest and strongest sympathy to a very small circle of human beings, it results that the very development of sympathy may operate to increase the weight thrown into the scale against Utilitarian duty. There are very few persons, however strongly and widely sympathetic, who are so constituted as to feel for the pleasures and pains of mankind generally a degree of sympathy at all commensurate with their concern for wife or children, or lover, or intimate friend: and if any training of the affections is at present possible which would materially alter this proportion in the general distribution of our sympathy, it scarcely seems that such a training is to be recommended as on the whole felicific. And thus when Utilitarian Duty calls on us to sacrifice not only our own pleasures but the happiness of those we love to the general good, the very sanction on which Utilitarianism most relies must act powerfully in opposition to its precepts.

But even apart from these exceptional cases—which are yet sufficient to decide the abstract question—it seems that the course of conduct by which a man would most fully reap the rewards of sympathy (so far as they are empirically ascertainable) will often be very different from that to which a sincere desire to promote the general happiness would direct him. For the relief of distress and calamity is an important part of Utilitarian duty: but as the state of the person relieved is on the whole painful, it would appear that sympathy under these circumstances must be a source of pain rather than pleasure, in proportion to its intensity. It is probably true, as a general rule, that in the relief of distress other elements of the complex pleasure of benevolence decidedly outweigh this sympathetic pain: for the effusion of pity is itself pleasurable, and we commonly feel more keenly that amelioration of the sufferer's state which is due to our exertions than we do his pain otherwise caused, and there is further the pleasure that we derive from his gratitude, and the pleasure that is the normal reflex of activity directed under a strong impulse towards a permanently valued end. Still, when the distress is bitter and continued, and such as we can only partially mitigate by all our efforts, the philanthropist's sympathetic discomfort must necessarily be considerable; and the work of combating misery, though not devoid of elevated happiness, will be much less happy on the whole than many other forms of activity; while yet it may be to just this work that Duty seems to summon us. Or again, a man may find that he can best promote the general happiness by working in comparative solitude for ends that he never hopes to see realized, or by working chiefly among and for persons for whom he cannot feel much affection, or by doing what must alienate or grieve those whom he loves best, or must make it necessary for him to dispense with the most intimate of human ties. In short, there seem to be numberless ways in which the dictates of that Rational Benevolence, which as a Utilitarian he is bound absolutely to obey, may conflict with that indulgence of kind affections which Shaftesbury and his followers so persuasively exhibit as its own reward.

§ 4. It seems then that we must conclude, from the arguments given in Book II, Chap. v, supplemented by the discussion in the preceding section, that the inseparable connexion between Utilitarian Duty and the greatest happiness of the individual who conforms to it cannot be satisfactorily demonstrated on empirical grounds. Hence another section of the Utilitarian school has preferred to throw the weight of Duty on the Religious Sanction: and this procedure has been partly adopted by some of those who have chiefly dwelt on sympathy as a motive. From this point of view the Utilitarian Code is conceived as the Law of God, who is to be regarded as having commanded men to promote the general happiness, and as having announced an intention of rewarding those who obey his commands and punishing the disobedient. It is clear that if we feel convinced that an Omnipotent Being has, in whatever way, signified such commands and announcements, a rational egoist can want no further inducement to frame his life on Utilitarian principles. It only remains to consider how this conviction is attained. This is commonly thought to be either by supernatural Revelation, or by the natural exercise of Reason, or in both ways. As regards the former it is to be observed that—with a few exceptions—the moralists who hold that God has disclosed his law either to special individuals in past ages who have left a written record of what was revealed to them, or to a permanent succession of persons appointed in a particular manner, or to religious persons generally in some supernatural way, do not consider that it is the Utilitarian Code that has thus been revealed, but rather the rules of Common Sense morality with some special modifications and additions. Still, as Mill has urged, in so far as Utilitarianism is more rigorous than Common Sense in exacting the sacrifice of the individual's happiness to that of mankind generally, it is strictly in accordance with the most characteristic teaching of Christianity. It seems, however, unnecessary to discuss the precise relation of different Revelational Codes to Utilitarianism, as it would be going beyond our province to investigate the grounds on which a Divine origin has been attributed to them.

In so far, however, as a knowledge of God's law is believed to be attainable by the Reason, Ethics and Theology seem to be so closely connected that we cannot sharply separate their provinces. For, as we saw,[11] it has been widely maintained, that the relation of moral rules to a Divine Lawgiver is implicitly cognized in the act of thought by which we discern these rules to be binding. And no doubt the terms (such as "moral obligation"), which we commonly use in speaking of these rules, are naturally suggestive of Legal Sanctions and so of a Sovereign by whom these are announced and enforced. Indeed many thinkers since Locke have refused to admit any other meaning in the terms Right, Duty, and so forth, except that of a rule imposed by a lawgiver. This view however seems opposed to Common Sense; as may be, perhaps, most easily shewn by pointing out that the Divine Lawgiver is himself conceived as a Moral Agent; that is as prescribing what is right, and designing what is good. It is clear that in this conception at least the notions "right" and "good" are used absolutely, without any reference to a superior lawgiver; and that they are here used in a sense not essentially different from that which they ordinarily bear seems to be affirmed by the *consensus* of religious persons. Still, though Common Sense does not regard moral rules as being *merely* the mandates of an Omnipotent Being who will reward and punish men according as they obey or violate them; it certainly holds that this is a true though partial view of them, and perhaps that it may be intuitively apprehended. If then reflection leads us to conclude that the particular moral principles of Common Sense are to be systematized as subordinate to that preeminently certain and irrefragable intuition which stands as the first principle of Utilitarianism; then, of course, it will be the Utilitarian Code to which we shall believe the Divine Sanctions to be attached.

Or, again, we may argue thus. If—as all theologians agree—we are to conceive God as acting for some end, we must conceive that end to

[11] See Book III, Chap. i, § 2: also Book III, Chap. ii, § 1.

be Universal Good, and, if Utilitarians are right, Universal Happiness: and we cannot suppose that in a world morally governed it can be prudent for any man to act in conscious opposition to what we believe to be the Divine Design. Hence if in any case after calculating the consequences of two alternatives of conduct we choose that which seems likely to be less conducive to Happiness generally, we shall be acting in a manner for which we cannot but expect to suffer.

To this it has been objected, that observation of the actual world shews us that the happiness of sentient beings is so imperfectly attained in it, and with so large an intermixture of pain and misery, that we cannot really conceive Universal Happiness to be God's end, unless we admit that he is not Omnipotent. And no doubt the assertion that God is omnipotent will require to be understood with some limitation; but perhaps with no greater limitation than has always been implicitly admitted by thoughtful theologians. For these seem always to have allowed that some things are impossible to God: as, for example, to change the past. And perhaps if our knowledge of the Universe were complete, we might discern the *quantum* of happiness ultimately attained in it to be as great as could be attained without the accomplishment of what we should then see to be just as inconceivable and absurd as changing the past. This, however, is a view which it belongs rather to the theologian to develop. I should rather urge that there does not seem to be any other of the ordinary interpretations of Good according to which it would appear to be more completely realized in the actual universe. For the wonderful perfections of work that we admire in the physical world are yet everywhere mingled with imperfection, and subject to destruction and decay: and similarly in the world of human conduct Virtue is at least as much balanced by Vice as Happiness is by Misery.[12] So that, if the ethical reasoning that led us to interpret Ultimate Good as Happiness is sound, there seems no argument from Natural Theology to set against it.

§ 5. If, then, we may assume the existence of such a Being, as God, by the *consensus* of theologians, is conceived to be, it seems that Utili-

---

[12] It may perhaps be said that this comparison has no force for Libertarians, who consider the essence of Virtue to lie in free choice. But to say that *any* free choice is virtuous would be a paradox from which most Libertarians—admitting that Evil may be freely chosen no less than Good—would recoil. It must therefore be Free choice of good that is conceived to realise the divine end: and if so, the arguments for the utilitarian interpretation of Good—thus freely chosen—would still be applicable *mutatis mutandis:* and if so, the arguments for regarding rules of utilitarian duty as divinely sanctioned would be similarly applicable.

tarians may legitimately infer the existence of Divine sanctions to the code of social duty as constructed on a Utilitarian basis; and such sanctions would, of course, suffice to make it always everyone's interest to promote universal happiness to the best of his knowledge. It is, however, desirable, before we conclude, to examine carefully the validity of this assumption, in so far as it is supported on ethical grounds alone. For by the result of such an examination will be determined, as we now see, the very important question whether ethical science can be constructed on an independent basis; or whether it is forced to borrow a fundamental and indispensable premiss from Theology or some similar source.[13] In order fairly to perform this examination, let us reflect upon the clearest and most certain of our moral intuitions. I find that I undoubtedly seem to perceive, as clearly and certainly as I see any axiom in Arithmetic or Geometry, that it is "right" and "reasonable" for me to treat others as I should think that I myself ought to be treated under similar conditions, and to do what I believe to be ultimately conducive to universal Good or Happiness. But I cannot find inseparably connected with this conviction, and similarly attainable by mere reflective intuition, any cognition that there actually is a Supreme Being who will adequately[14] reward me for obeying these rules of duty, or punish me for violating them.[15] Or—omitting the strictly theological element of the proposition—I may say that I do not find in my moral consciousness any intuition, claiming to be clear and certain, that the performance of duty will be adequately rewarded and its violation punished. I feel

[13] It is not necessary, if we are simply considering Ethics as a possible independent science, to throw the fundamental premiss of which we are now examining the validity into a Theistic form. Nor does it seem always to have taken that form in the support which Positive Religion has given to Morality. In the Buddhist creed this notion of the rewards inseparably attaching to right conduct seems to have been developed in a far more elaborate and systematic manner than it has in any phase of Christianity. But, as conceived by enlightened Buddhists, these rewards are not distributed by the volition of a Supreme Person, but by the natural operation of an impersonal Law.

[14] It may be well to remind the reader that by "adequate" is here meant "sufficient to make it the agent's interest to promote universal good"; not necessarily "proportional to Desert."

[15] I cannot fall back on the resource of thinking myself under a moral necessity to regard all my duties *as if they were* commandments of God, although not entitled to hold speculatively that any such Supreme Being really exists. I am so far from feeling bound to believe for purposes of practice what I see no ground for holding as a speculative truth, that I cannot even conceive the state of mind which these words seem to describe, except as a momentary half-wilful irrationality, committed in a violent access of philosophic despair.

indeed a desire, apparently inseparable from the moral sentiments, that this result may be realised not only in my own case but universally; but the mere existence of the desire would not go far to establish the probability of its fulfilment, considering the large proportion of human desires that experience shews to be doomed to disappointment. I also judge that in a certain sense this result *ought* to be realized: in this judgment, however, "ought" is not used in a strictly ethical meaning; it only expresses the vital need that our Practical Reason feels of proving or postulating this connexion of Virtue and self-interest, if it is to be made consistent with itself. For the negation of the connexion must force us to admit an ultimate and fundamental contradiction in our apparent intuitions of what is Reasonable in conduct; and from this admission it would seem to follow that the apparently intuitive operation of the Practical Reason, manifested in these contradictory judgments, is after all illusory.

I do not mean that if we gave up the hope of attaining a practical solution of this fundamental contradiction, through any legitimately obtained conclusion or postulate as to the moral order of the world, it would become reasonable for us to abandon morality altogether: but it would seem necessary to abandon the idea of rationalising it completely. We should doubtless still, not only from self-interest, but also through sympathy and sentiments protective of social well-being, imparted by education and sustained by communication with other men, feel a desire for the general observance of rules conducive to general happiness; and practical reason would still impel us decisively to the performance of duty in the more ordinary cases in which what is recognized as duty is in harmony with self-interest properly understood. But in the rarer cases of a recognized conflict between self-interest and duty, practical reason, being divided against itself, would cease to be a motive on either side; the conflict would have to be decided by the comparative preponderance of one or other of two groups of nonrational impulses.

If then the reconciliation of duty and self-interest is to be regarded as a hypothesis logically necessary to avoid a fundamental contradiction in one chief department of our thought, it remains to ask how far this necessity constitutes a sufficient reason for accepting this hypothesis. This, however, is a profoundly difficult and controverted question, the discussion of which belongs rather to a treatise on General Philosophy than to a work on the Methods of Ethics: as it could not be satisfactorily answered, without a general examination of the criteria of true and false beliefs. Those who hold that the edifice of physical science is really constructed of conclusions logically inferred from self-evident premises, may reasonably demand that any practical judgments claiming philosophic certainty should be based on an equally firm foundation. If on the other hand we find that in our supposed knowledge of the world of nature propositions are commonly taken to be universally true, which yet seem to rest on no other grounds than that we have a strong disposition to accept them, and that they are indispensable to the systematic coherence of our beliefs— it will be more difficult to reject a similarly supported assumption in ethics, without opening the door to universal scepticism.

G. E. MOORE

Is Egoism Reasonable?

58. . . . . Egoism, as a form of Hedonism, is the doctrine which holds that we ought each of us to pursue our own greatest happiness as our ultimate end. The doctrine will, of course, admit that sometimes the best means to this end will be to give pleasure to others; we shall, for instance, by so doing, procure for ourselves the pleasures of sympathy, of freedom from interference, and of self-esteem; and these pleasures, which we may procure by sometimes aiming directly at the happiness of other persons, may be greater than any we could otherwise get. Egoism in this sense must therefore be carefully distinguished from Egoism in another sense, the sense in which Altruism is its proper opposite. Egoism, as commonly opposed to Altruism, is apt to denote merely selfishness. In this sense, a man is an egoist, if all his actions are actually directed towards gaining pleasure for himself; whether he holds that he ought to act so, because he will thereby obtain for himself the greatest possible happiness on the whole, or not. Egoism may accordingly be used to denote the theory that we should always aim at getting pleasure for ourselves, because that is the best *means* to the ultimate end, whether the ultimate end be our own greatest pleasure or not. Altruism, on the other hand, may denote the theory that we ought always to aim at other people's happiness, on the ground that this is the best *means* of securing our own as well as theirs. Accordingly an Egoist, in the sense in which I am now going to talk of Egoism, an Egoist, who holds that his own greatest happi-

* From *Principia Ethica*, Cambridge at the University Press, 1903, sections 58–61 and 63. Reprinted with the kind permission of the Cambridge University Press.

ness is the ultimate end, may at the same time be an Altruist: he may hold that he ought to "love his neighbour," as the best means to being happy himself. And conversely an Egoist, in the other sense, may at the same time be a Utilitarian. He may hold that he ought always to direct his efforts towards getting pleasure for himself on the ground that he is thereby most likely to increase the general sum of happiness.

59. I shall say more later about this second kind of Egoism, this anti-altruistic Egoism, this Egoism as a doctrine of means. What I am now concerned with is that utterly distinct kind of Egoism, which holds that each man ought rationally to hold: My own greatest happiness is the only good thing there is; my actions can only be good as means, in so far as they help to win me this. This is a doctrine which is not much held by writers nowadays. It is a doctrine that was largely held by English Hedonists in the seventeenth and eighteenth centuries: it is, for example, at the bottom of Hobbes' Ethics. But even the English school appear to have made one step forward in the present century: they are most of them nowadays Utilitarians. They do recognise that if my own happiness is good, it would be strange that other people's happiness should not be good too.

In order fully to expose the absurdity of this kind of Egoism, it is necessary to examine certain confusions upon which its plausibility depends.

The chief of these is the confusion involved in the conception of "my own good" as distinguished from "the good of others." This is a conception which we all use every day; it is one of the first to which the plain man is apt to appeal in discussing any question of Ethics: and Egoism is commonly advocated chiefly because its meaning is not clearly perceived. It is plain, indeed, that the name "Egoism" more properly applies to the theory that "my own good" is the sole good, than that my own pleasure is so. A man may quite well be an Egoist, even if he be not a Hedonist. The conception which is, perhaps, most closely associated with Egoism is that denoted by the words "my own interest." The Egoist is the man who holds that a tendency to promote his own interest is the sole possible, and sufficient, justification of all his actions. But this conception of "my own interest" plainly includes, in general, very much more than my own pleasure. It is, indeed, only because and in so far as "my own interest" has been thought to consist solely in my own pleasure, that Egoists have been led to hold that my own pleasure is the sole good. Their course of reasoning is as follows: The only thing I ought to secure is my own interest; but my own interest consists in my greatest possible pleasure; and therefore the only thing I ought to pursue is my own pleasure. That it is very natural, *on reflection,* thus to identify my own pleasure with my own interest; and that it has been generally done by modern *moralists,* may be admitted. But, when Prof. Sidgwick points this out (Book III, Chap. xiv, § 5, Div. III.),[1] he should have also pointed out that this identification has by no means been made in ordinary thought. When the plain man says "my own interest," he does *not* mean "my own pleasure"—he does not commonly even include this—he means my own advancement, my own reputation, the getting of a better income and so forth. That Prof. Sidgwick should not have noticed this, and that he should give the reason he gives for the fact that the ancient *moralists* did not identify "my own interest" with my own pleasure, seems to be due to his having failed to notice that very confusion in the conception of "my own good" which I am now to point out. That confusion has, perhaps, been more clearly perceived by Plato than by any other moralist, and to point it out suffices to refute Prof. Sidgwick's own view that Egoism is rational.

What, then, is meant by "my own good"? In what sense can a thing be good *for me?* It is obvious, if we reflect, that the only thing which can belong to me, which can be *mine,* is something which is good, and not the fact that it is good. When, therefore, I talk of anything I get as "my own good," I must mean either that the thing I get is good, or that my possessing it is good. In both cases it is only the thing or the possession of it which is *mine,* and not *the goodness* of that thing or that possession. There is no longer any meaning in attaching the "my" to our predicate, and saying: The possession of this *by me* is *my* good. Even if we interpret this by "My possession of this is what *I* think good," the same still holds: for *what* I think is that my possession of it is good *simply;* and, if I think rightly, then the truth is that my possession of it *is* good simply—not, in any sense, *my* good; and, if I think wrongly, it is not good at all. In short, when I talk of a thing as "my own good" all that I can mean is that something which will be exclusively mine, as my own pleasure is mine (whatever be the various senses of this relation denoted by "possession"), is also *good absolutely;* or rather that my possession of it is *good absolutely.* The *good* of it can in no possible sense be "private" or belong to me; any more than a thing can *exist* privately or *for* one person only. The

---

[1] [All references are to *The Methods of Ethics.*—ed.]

only reason I can have for aiming at "my own good," is that it is *good absolutely* that what I so call should belong to me—*good absolutely* that I should *have* something, which, if I have it, others cannot have. But if it is *good absolutely* that I should have it, then everyone else has as much reason for aiming at *my* having it, as I have myself. If, therefore, it is true of *any* single man's "interest" or "happiness" that it ought to be his sole ultimate end, this can only mean that *that* man's "interest" or "happiness" is *the sole good, the* Universal Good, and the only thing that anybody ought to aim at. What Egoism holds, therefore, is that *each* man's happiness is the sole good—that a number of different things are *each* of them the only good thing there is— an absolute contradiction! No more complete and thorough refutation of any theory could be desired.

60. Yet Prof. Sidgwick holds that Egoism is rational; and it will be useful briefly to consider the reasons which he gives for this absurd conclusion. "The Egoist," he says (last Chap., § 1),² "may avoid the proof of Utilitarianism by declining to affirm," either "implicitly or explicitly, that his own greatest happiness is not merely the ultimate rational end for himself, but a part of Universal Good." And in the passage to which he here refers us, as having there "seen" this, he says: "It cannot be proved that the difference between his own happiness and another's happiness is not *for him* all-important" (Book IV, Chap. ii, § 1). What does Prof. Sidgwick mean by these phrases "the ultimate rational end for himself," and "*for him* all-important"? He does not attempt to define them; and it is largely the use of such undefined phrases which causes absurdities to be committed in philosophy.

Is there any sense in which a thing can be an ultimate rational end for one person and not for another? By "ultimate" must be meant at least that the end is good in itself—good in our undefinable sense; and by "rational," at least, that it is truly good. That a thing should be an ultimate rational end means, then, that it is truly good in itself; and that it is truly good in itself means that it is a part of Universal Good. Can we assign any meaning to that qualification "for himself," which will make it cease to be a part of Universal Good? The thing is impossible: for the Egoist's happiness must *either* be good in itself, and so a part of Universal Good, *or else* it cannot be good in itself at all: there is no escaping this dilemma. And if it is not good at all, what reason can he have for aiming at it? how can it

² [P. 37 in this volume.—ed.]

be a rational end for him? That qualification "for himself" has no meaning unless it implies "*not* for others," and if it implies "not for others," then it cannot be a rational end for him, since it cannot be truly good in itself: the phrase "an ultimate rational end for himself" is a contradiction in terms. By saying that a thing is an end for one particular person, or good for him, can only be meant one of four things. Either (1) it may be meant that the end in question is something which will belong exclusively to him; but in that case, if it is to be rational for him to aim at it, that he should exclusively possess it must be a part of Universal Good. Or (2) it may be meant that it is the only thing at which he ought to aim; but this can only be, because, by so doing, he will do the most he can towards realising Universal Good: and this, in our case, will only give Egoism as a doctrine of *means*. Or (3) it may be meant that the thing is what he desires or thinks good; and then, if he thinks wrongly, it is not a rational end at all, and, if he thinks rightly, it is a part of Universal Good. Or (4) it may be meant that it is peculiarly appropriate that a thing which will belong exclusively to him should also by him be approved or aimed at; but, in this case, both that it should belong to him and that he should aim at it must be parts of Universal Good: by saying that a certain relation between two things is fitting or appropriate, we can only mean that the existence of that relation is absolutely good in itself (unless it be so as a means, which gives case (2)). By no possible meaning, then, that can be given to the phrase that his own happiness is the ultimate rational end for himself can the Egoist escape the implication that his own happiness is absolutely good; and by saying that it is *the* ultimate rational end, he must mean that it is the only good thing—the whole of Universal Good: and, if he further maintains, that each man's happiness is the ultimate rational end for *him,* we have the fundamental contradiction of Egoism—that an immense number of different things are, *each* of them, *the sole good.* And it is easy to see that the same considerations apply to the phrase that "the difference between his own happiness and another's is *for him* all-important." This can only mean either (1) that his own happiness is the only end which will affect him, or (2) that the only important thing for him (as a means) is to look to his own happiness, or (3) that it is only his own happiness which he cares about, or (4) that it is good that each man's happiness should be the only concern of that man. And none of these propositions, true as they may be, have the smallest tendency to shew that if his own happiness is desirable at all, it is not a part of Universal Good. Either his own happiness is a good thing or it is not; and, in whatever sense it may be all-important for him, it must be true that, if it is not good, he is not justified in pursuing it, and that, if it is good, everyone else has an equal reason to pursue it, so far as they are able and so far as it does not exclude their attainment of other more valuable parts of Universal Good. In short it is plain that the addition of "for him," "for me" to such words as "ultimate rational end," "good," "important" can introduce nothing but confusion. The only possible reason that can justify any action is that by it the greatest possible amount of what is good absolutely should be realised. And if anyone says that the attainment of his own happiness justifies his actions, he must mean that this is the greatest possible amount of Universal Good which he can realise. And this again can only be true either because *he* has no power to realise more, in which case he only holds Egoism as a doctrine of means; or else because his own happiness is the greatest amount of Universal Good which can be realised at all, in which case we have Egoism proper, and the flagrant contradiction that every person's happiness is singly the greatest amount of Universal Good which can be realised at all.

61. It should be observed that, since this is so, "the relation of Rational Egoism to Rational Benevolence," which Prof. Sidgwick regards "as the profoundest problem of Ethics" (Book III, Chap. xiii, § 5, *n.* 1), appears in quite a different light to that in which he presents it. "Even if a man," he says, "admits the self-evidence of the principle of Rational Benevolence, he may still hold that his own happiness is an end which it is irrational for him to sacrifice to any other; and that therefore a harmony between the maxim of Prudence and the maxim of Rational Benevolence must be somehow demonstrated, if morality is to be made completely rational. This latter view is that which I myself hold" (last Chap., § 1) .[3] Prof. Sidgwick then goes on to shew "that the inseparable connection between Utilitarian Duty and the greatest happiness of the individual who conforms to it cannot be satisfactorily demonstrated on empirical grounds" (*Ibid.*, § 3).[4] And the final paragraph of his book tells us that, since "the reconciliation of duty and self-interest is to be regarded as a hypothesis logically necessary to avoid a fundamental *contradiction* in one chief department of our thought, it remains to ask how far this necessity constitutes

---

[3] [P. 37 in this volume.—ed.]
[4] [The quotation is from sec. 4, p. 42 in this volume.—ed.]

a sufficient reason for accepting this hypothesis" [5] (*Ibid.*, § 5).[6] To "assume the existence of such a Being, as God, by the *consensus* of theologians, is conceived to be" would, he has already argued, ensure the required reconciliation; since the Divine Sanctions of such a God "would, of course, suffice to make it always everyone's interest to promote universal happiness to the best of his knowledge" (*Ibid.*, § 5).[7]

Now what is this "reconciliation of duty and self-interest," which Divine Sanctions could ensure? It would consist in the mere fact that the same conduct which produced the greatest possible happiness of the greatest number would always also produce the greatest possible happiness of the agent. If this were the case (and our empirical knowledge shews that it is not the case in this world), "morality" would, Prof. Sidgwick thinks, be "completely rational": we should avoid "an ultimate and fundamental contradiction in our apparent intuitions of what is Reasonable in conduct." That is to say, we should avoid the necessity of thinking that it is as manifest an obligation to secure our own greatest Happiness (maxim of Prudence), as to secure the greatest Happiness on the whole (maxim of Benevolence). But it is perfectly obvious we should not. Prof. Sidgwick here commits the characteristic fallacy of Empiricism—the fallacy of thinking that an alteration in *facts* could make a contradiction cease to be a contradiction. That a single man's happiness should be *the sole good,* and that also everybody's happiness should be *the sole good,* is a contradiction which cannot be solved by the assumption that the same conduct will secure both: it would be equally contradictory, however certain we were that that assumption was justified. Prof. Sidgwick strains at a gnat and swallows a camel. He thinks the Divine Omnipotence must be called into play to secure that what gives other people pleasure should also give it to him—that only so can Ethics be made rational; while he overlooks the fact that even this exercise of Divine Omnipotence would leave in Ethics a contradiction, in comparison with which his difficulty is a trifle—a contradiction, which would reduce all Ethics to mere nonsense, and before which the Divine Omnipotence must be powerless to all eternity. That *each* man's happiness should be the *sole good,* which we have seen to be the principle of Egoism, is in itself a contradiction: and that it should also be true that the Happiness of all is the *sole good,* which is the principle of Universalistic Hedonism,

[5] The italics are mine.
[6] [P. 46 in this volume.—ed.]
[7] [Pp. 44–5 in this volume.—ed.]

would introduce another contradiction. And that these propositions should all be true might well be called "the profoundest problem in Ethics": it would be a problem necessarily insoluble. But they *cannot* all be true, and there is no reason, but confusion, for the supposition that they are. Prof. Sidgwick confuses this contradiction with the mere fact (in which there is no contradiction) that our own greatest happiness and that of all do not seem always attainable by the same means. This fact, if Happiness were the sole good, would indeed be of some importance; and, on any view, similar facts are of importance. But they are nothing but instances of the one important fact that in this world the quantity of good which is attainable is ridiculously small compared to that which is imaginable. That I cannot get the most possible pleasure for myself, if I produce the most possible pleasure on the whole, is no more *the* profoundest problem of Ethics, than that in any case I cannot get as much pleasure altogether as would be desirable. It only states that, if we get as much good as possible in one place, we may get less on the whole, because the quantity of attainable good is limited. To say that I have to choose between my own good and that of *all* is a false antithesis: the only rational question is how to choose between my own and that of *others,* and the principle on which this must be answered is exactly the same as that on which I must choose whether to give pleasure to this other person or to that.

·　　·　　·　　·　　·　　·　　·　　·　　·　　·　　·　　·　　·

63. The second cause I have to give why Egoism should be thought reasonable, is simply its confusion with that other kind of Egoism— Egoism as a doctrine of means. This second Egoism has a right to say: You ought to pursue your own happiness, sometimes at all events; it may say: Always. And when we find it saying this we are apt to forget its proviso: But only as a means to something else. The fact is we are in an imperfect state; we cannot get the ideal all at once. And hence it is often our bounden duty, we often *absolutely "ought,"* to do things which are good only or chiefly as means: we have to do the best we can, what is absolutely "right," but not what is absolutely good. Of this I shall say more hereafter. I only mention it here because I think it is much more plausible to say that we ought to pursue our own pleasure as a means than as an end, and that this doctrine, through confusion, lends some of its plausibility to the utterly different doctrine of Egoism proper: My own greatest pleasure is the only good thing.

BRIAN MEDLIN

Ultimate Principles and Ethical Egoism

I believe that it is now pretty generally accepted by professional philosophers that ultimate ethical principles must be arbitrary. One cannot derive conclusions about what should be merely from accounts of what is the case; one cannot decide how people ought to behave merely from one's knowledge of how they do behave. To arrive at a conclusion in ethics one must have at least one ethical premiss. This premiss, if it be in turn a conclusion, must be the conclusion of an argument containing at least one ethical premiss. And so we can go back, indefinitely but not forever. Sooner or later, we must come to at least one ethical premiss which is not deduced but baldly asserted. Here we must be a-rational; neither rational nor irrational, for here there is no room for reason even to go wrong.

But the triumph of Hume in ethics has been a limited one. What appears quite natural to a handful of specialists appears quite monstrous to the majority of decent intelligent men. At any rate, it has been my experience that people who are normally rational resist the above account of the logic of moral language, not by argument—for that can't be done—but by tooth and nail. And they resist from the best motives. They see the philosopher wantonly unravelling the whole fabric of morality. If our ultimate principles are arbitrary, they say, if those principles came out of thin air, then anyone can hold any principle he pleases. Unless moral assertions are statements of fact about the world and either true or false, we can't claim that

* From the *Australasian Journal of Philosophy*, XXXV (1957), 111–118. Reprinted with the kind permission of the author, and of the editors of the *Australasian Journal of Philosophy*.

any man is wrong, whatever his principles may be, whatever his behaviour. We have to surrender the luxury of calling one another scoundrels. That this anxiety flourishes because its roots are in confusion is evident when we consider that we don't call people scoundrels, anyhow, for being mistaken about their facts. Fools, perhaps, but that's another matter. Nevertheless, it doesn't become us to be high-up. The layman's uneasiness, however irrational it may be, is very natural and he must be reassured.

People cling to objectivist theories of morality from moral motives. It's a very queer thing that by doing so they often thwart their own purposes. There are evil opinions abroad, as anyone who walks abroad knows. The one we meet with most often, whether in pub or parlour, is the doctrine that everyone should look after himself. However refreshing he may find it after the high-minded pomposities of this morning's editorial, the good fellow knows this doctrine is wrong and he wants to knock it down. But while he believes that moral language is used to make statements either true or false, the best he can do is to claim that what the egoist says is false. Unfortunately, the egoist can claim that it's true. And since the supposed fact in question between them is not a publicly ascertainable one, their disagreement can never be resolved. And it is here that even good fellows waver, when they find they have no refutation available. The egoist's word seems as reliable as their own. Some begin half to believe that perhaps it is possible to supply an egoistic basis for conventional morality, some that it may be impossible to supply any other basis. I'm not going to try to prop up our conventional morality, which I fear to be a task beyond my strength, but in what follows I do want to refute the doctrine of ethical egoism. I want to resolve this disagreement by showing that what the egoist says is inconsistent. It is true that there are moral disagreements which can never be resolved, but this isn't one of them. The proper objection to the man who says "Everyone should look after his own interests regardless of the interests of others" is not that he isn't speaking the truth, but simply that he isn't speaking.

We should first make two distinctions. This done, ethical egoism will lose much of its plausibility.

1. UNIVERSAL AND INDIVIDUAL EGOISM

Universal egoism maintains that everyone (including the speaker) ought to look after his own interests and to disregard those of other people except in so far as their interests contribute towards his own.

Individual egoism is the attitude that the egoist is going to look after himself and no one else. The egoist cannot promulgate that he is going to look after himself. He can't even preach that he *should* look after himself and preach this alone. When he tries to convince me that he should look after himself, he is attempting so to dispose me that I shall approve when he drinks my beer and steals Tom's wife. I cannot approve of his looking after himself and himself alone without so far approving of his achieving his happiness, regardless of the happiness of myself and others. So that when he sets out to persuade me that he should look after himself regardless of others, he must also set out to persuade me that I should look after him regardless of myself and others. Very small chance he has! And if the individual egoist cannot promulgate his doctrine without enlarging it, what he has is no doctrine at all.

A person enjoying such an attitude may believe that other people are fools not to look after themselves. Yet he himself would be a fool to tell them so. If he did tell them, though, he wouldn't consider that he was giving them *moral* advice. Persuasion to the effect that one should ignore the claims of morality because morality doesn't pay, to the effect that one has insufficient selfish motive and, therefore, insufficient motive for moral behaviour is not moral persuasion. For this reason I doubt that we should call the individual egoist's attitude an ethical one. And I don't doubt this in the way someone may doubt whether to call the ethical standards of Satan "ethical" standards. A malign morality is none the less a morality for being malign. But the attitude we're considering is one of mere contempt for all moral considerations whatsoever. An indifference to morals may be wicked, but it is not a perverse morality. So far as I am aware, most egoists imagine that they are putting forward a doctrine in ethics, though there may be a few who are prepared to proclaim themselves individual egoists. If the good fellow wants to know how he should justify conventional morality to an individual egoist, the answer is that he shouldn't and can't. Buy your car elsewhere, blackguard him whenever you meet, and let it go at that.

2. CATEGORICAL AND HYPOTHETICAL EGOISM

Categorical egoism is the doctrine that we all ought to observe our own interests, *because that is what we ought to do.* For the categorical egoist the egoistic dogma is the ultimate principle in ethics.

The hypothetical egoist, on the other hand, maintains that we all ought to observe our own interests, because. . . . If we want such and such an end, we must do so and so (look after ourselves). The hypothetical egoist is not a real egoist at all. He is very likely an unwitting utilitarian who believes mistakenly that the general happiness will be increased if each man looks wisely to his own. Of course, a man may believe that egoism is enjoined on us by God and he may therefore promulgate the doctrine and observe it in his conduct, not in the hope of achieving thereby a remote end, but simply in order to obey God. But neither is *he* a real egoist. He believes, ultimately, that we should obey God, even should God command us to altruism.

An ethical egoist will have to maintain the doctrine in both its universal and categorical forms. Should he retreat to hypothetical egoism he is no longer an egoist. Should he retreat to individual egoism his doctrine, while logically impregnable, is no longer ethical, no longer even a doctrine. He may wish to quarrel with this and if so, I submit peacefully. Let him call himself what he will, it makes no difference. I'm a philosopher, not a rat-catcher, and I don't see it as my job to dig vermin out of such burrows as individual egoism.

Obviously something strange goes on as soon as the ethical egoist tries to promulgate his doctrine. What is he doing when he urges upon his audience that they should each observe his own interests and those interests alone? Is he not acting contrary to the egoistic principle? It cannot be to his advantage to convince them, for seizing always their own advantage they will impair his. Surely if he does believe what he says, he should try to persuade them otherwise. Not perhaps that they should devote themselves to his interests, for they'd hardly swallow that; but that everyone should devote himself to the service of others. But is not to believe that someone should act in a certain way to try to persuade him to do so? Of course, we don't always try to persuade people to act as we think they should act. We may be lazy, for instance. But in so far as we believe that Tom should do so and so, we have a tendency to induce him to do so and so. Does it make sense to say: "Of course you should do this, but for goodness' sake don't"? Only where we mean: "You should do this for certain reasons, but here are even more persuasive reasons for not doing it." If the egoist believes ultimately that others should mind themselves alone, then, he must persuade them accordingly. If he doesn't persuade them, he is no universal egoist. It certainly makes sense to say: "I know very well that Tom should act in such and such a way. But I know also that it's not to my advantage that he should so act. So I'd better dissuade him from it." And this is just what the egoist must say, if he is to consider his own advantage and disregard everyone else's. That is, he must behave as an individual egoist, if he is to be an egoist at all.

He may want to make two kinds of objection here:

(1) That it will not be to his disadvantage to promulgate the doctrine, provided that his audience fully understand what is to their ultimate advantage. This objection can be developed in a number of ways, but I think that it will always be possible to push the egoist into either individual or hypothetical egoism.

(2) That it is to the egoist's advantage to preach the doctrine if the pleasure he gets out of doing this more than pays for the injuries he must endure at the hands of his converts. It is hard to believe that many people would be satisfied with a doctrine which they could only consistently promulgate in very special circumstances. Besides, this looks suspiciously like individual egoism in disguise.

I shall say no more on these two points because I want to advance a further criticism which seems to me at once fatal and irrefutable.

Now it is time to show the anxious layman that we have means of dealing with ethical egoism which are denied him; and denied him by just that objectivism which he thinks essential to morality. For the very fact that our ultimate principles must be arbitrary means they can't be anything we please. Just because they come out of thin air they can't come out of hot air. Because these principles are not propositions about matters of fact and cannot be deduced from propositions about matters of fact, they must be the fruit of our own attitudes. We assert them largely to modify the attitudes of our fellows but by asserting them we express our own desires and purposes. This means that we cannot use moral language cavalierly. Evidently, we cannot say something like "All human desires and purposes are bad." This would be to express our own desires and purposes, thereby committing a kind of absurdity. Nor, I shall argue, can we say "Everyone should observe his own interests regardless of the interests of others."

Remembering that the principle is meant to be both universal and categorical, let us ask what kind of attitude the egoist is expressing. Wouldn't that attitude be equally well expressed by the conjunction of an infinite number of avowals thus?

I want myself to come out on top	and	I don't care about Tom, Dick, Harry . . .
and		and
I want Tom to come out on top	and	I don't care about myself, Dick, Harry . . .
and		and
I want Dick to come out on top	and	I don't care about myself, Tom, Harry . . .
and		and
I want Harry to come out on top	and	I don't care about myself, Dick, Tom . . .
etc.		etc.

From this analysis it is obvious that the principle expressing such an attitude must be inconsistent.

But now the egoist may claim that he hasn't been properly understood. When he says "Everyone should look after himself and himself alone," he means "Let each man do what he wants regardless of what anyone else wants." The egoist may claim that what he values is merely that he and Tom and Dick and Harry should each do what he wants and not care about what anyone else may want and that this doesn't involve his principle in any inconsistency. Nor need it. But even if it doesn't, he's no better off. Just what does he value? Is it the well-being of himself, Tom, Dick and Harry or merely their going on in a certain way regardless of whether or not this is going to promote their well-being? When he urges Tom, say, to do what he wants, is he appealing to Tom's self-interest? If so, his attitude can be expressed thus:

I want myself to be happy		I want myself not to care
and	and	about Tom, Dick,
I want Tom to be happy		Harry . . .

We need go no further to see that the principle expressing such an attitude must be inconsistent. I have made this kind of move already. What concerns me now is the alternative position the egoist must take up to be safe from it. If the egoist values merely that people should go on in a certain way, regardless of whether or not this is going to promote their well-being, then he is not appealing to the self-interest of his audience when he urges them to regard their own interests. If Tom has any regard for himself at all, the egoist's blandishments will leave him cold. Further, the egoist doesn't even have his own interest in mind when he says that, like everyone else, he should look after himself. A funny kind of egoism this turns out to be.

Perhaps now, claiming that he is indeed appealing to the self-interest of his audience, the egoist may attempt to counter the objection of the previous paragraph. He may move into "Let each man do what he wants and let each man disregard what others want when their desires clash with his own." Now his attitude may be expressed thus:

I want everyone to be happy	and	I want everyone to disregard the happiness of others when their happiness clashes with his own.

The egoist may claim justly that a man can have such an attitude and also that in a certain kind of world such a man could get what he wanted. Our objection to the egoist has been that his desires are incompatible. And this is still so. If he and Tom and Dick and Harry did go on as he recommends by saying "Let each man disregard the happiness of others, when their happiness conflicts with his own," then assuredly they'd all be completely miserable. Yet he wants them to be happy. He is attempting to counter this by saying that it is merely a fact about the world that they'd make one another miserable by going on as he recommends. The world could conceivably have been different. For this reason, he says, this principle is not inconsistent. This argument may not seem very compelling, but I advance it on the egoist's behalf because I'm interested in the reply to it. For now we don't even need to tell him that the world isn't in fact like that. (What it's like makes no difference.) Now we can point out to him that he is arguing not as an egoist but as a utilitarian. He has slipped into hypothetical egoism to save his principle from inconsistency. If the world were such that we always made ourselves and others happy by doing one another down, then we could find good utilitarian reasons for urging that we should do one another down.

If, then, he is to save his principle, the egoist must do one of two things. He must give up the claim that he is appealing to the self-interest of his audience, that he has even his own interest in mind. Or he must admit that, in the conjunction above, although "I want everyone to be happy" refers to ends, nevertheless "I want everyone to disregard the happiness of others when their happiness conflicts with his own" can refer only to means. That is, his so-called ultimate principle is really compounded of a principle and a moral rule subordinate to that principle. That is, he is really a utilitarian who is urging everyone to go on in a certain way so that everyone may be happy. A utilitarian, what's more, who is ludicrously mistaken about the nature of the world. Things being as they are, his moral rule is a very bad one. Things being as they are, it can only be deduced from his principle by means of an empirical premiss which is manifestly false. Good fellows don't need to fear him. They may rest easy that the world is and must be on their side and the best thing they can do is be good.

It may be worth pointing out that objections similar to those I have brought against the egoist can be made to the altruist. The man who holds that the principle "Let everyone observe the interests of others" is both universal and categorical can be compelled to choose between two alternatives, equally repugnant. He must give up the claim that he is concerned for the well-being of himself and others. Or he must admit that, though "I want everyone to be happy" refers to ends, nevertheless "I want everyone to disregard his own happiness when it conflicts with the happiness of others" can refer only to means.

I have said from time to time that the egoistic principle is inconsistent. I have not said it is contradictory. This for the reason that we can, without contradiction, express inconsistent desires and purposes. To do so is not to say anything like "Goliath was ten feet tall and not ten feet tall." Don't we all want to eat our cake and have it too? And when we say we do we aren't asserting a contradiction. We are not asserting a contradiction whether we be making an avowal of our attitudes or stating a fact about them. We all have conflicting motives. As a utilitarian exuding benevolence I want the man who mows my landlord's grass to be happy, but as a slugabed I should like to see him scourged. None of this, however, can do the egoist any good. For we assert our ultimate principles not only to express our own attitudes but also to induce similar attitudes in others, to dispose them to conduct themselves as we wish. In so far as their desires conflict, people don't know what to do. And, therefore, no expression of incompatible desires can ever serve for an ultimate principle of human conduct.

JESSE KALIN

In Defense of Egoism

~~~~~~

I

Ethical egoism is the view that it is morally right—that is, morally permissible, indeed, morally obligatory—for a person to act in his own self-interest, even when his self-interest conflicts or is irreconcilable with the self-interest of another. The point people normally have in mind in accepting and advocating this ethical principle is that of justifying or excusing their own self-interested actions by giving them a moral sanction.

This position is sometimes construed as saying that selfishness is moral, but such an interpretation is not quite correct. "Self-interest" is a general term usually used as a synonym for "personal happiness" and "personal welfare," and what would pass as selfish behavior frequently would not pass as self-interested behavior in this sense. Indeed, we have the suspicion that selfish people are characteristically, if not always, unhappy. Thus, in cases where selfishness tends to a person's unhappiness it is not in his self-interest, and as an egoist he ought not to be selfish. As a consequence, ethical egoism does not preclude other-interested, nonselfish, or altruistic behavior, as long as such behavior also leads to the individual's own welfare.

That the egoist may reasonably find himself taking an interest in others and promoting their welfare perhaps sounds nonegoistic, but it is not. Ethical egoism's justification of such behavior differs from other accounts in the following way: The ethical egoist acknowledges no general obligation to help people in need. Benevolence is never justified unconditionally or "categorically." The egoist has an obligation to promote the welfare only of those whom he likes, loves, needs, or can use. The source of this obligation is his interest in them. No interest, no obligation. And when his interest conflicts or is irreconcilable with theirs, he will reasonably pursue his own well-being at their expense, even when this other person is his wife, child, mother, or friend, as well as when it is a stranger or enemy.

Such a pursuit of one's own self-interest is considered *enlightened*. The name Butler provides for ethical egoism so interpreted is "cool self-love." [1] On this view, a person is to harmonize his natural interests, perhaps cultivate some new interests, and optimize their satisfaction. Usually among these interests will be such things as friendships and families (or perhaps one gets his greatest kicks from working for UNICEF). And, of course, it is a part of such enlightenment to consider the "long run" rather than just the present and immediate future.

Given this account of ethical egoism plus the proper circumstances, a person could be morally justified in cheating on tests, padding expense accounts, swindling a business partner, being a slum landlord, draft-dodging, lying, and breaking promises, as well as in contributing to charity, helping friends, being generous or civic minded, and even undergoing hardship to put his children through college. Judged from inside "standard morality," the first actions would clearly be immoral, while the preceding paragraphs suggest the latter actions would be immoral as well, being done from a vicious or improper motive.

With this informal account as background, I shall now introduce a formal definition of ethical egoism, whose coherence will be the topic of the subsequent discussion:

(i) $(x)(y)(x$ ought to do y if and only if y is in x's overall self-interest)

---

[1] Butler, Joseph, *Fifteen Sermons Preached at the Rolls Chapel,* 1726. Standard anthologies of moral philosophy include the most important of these sermons; or see the Library of Liberal Arts Selection, *Five Sermons* (New York: The Bobbs-Merrill Company, Inc., 1950). See particularly Sermons I and XI. In XI, Butler says of rational self-love that "the object the former pursues is something internal —our own happiness, enjoyment, satisfaction . . . The principle we call "self-love" never seeks anything external for the sake of the thing, but only as a means of happiness or good." Butler is not, however, an egoist for there is also in man conscience and "a natural principle of benevolence" (see Sermon I).

In this formalization, "x" ranges over persons and "y" over particular actions, no kinds of action; "ought" has the sense "ought, all things considered." (i) may be translated as: "A person ought to do a specific action, all things considered, if and only if that action is in that person's overall (enlightened) self-interest."

(i) represents what Medlin calls "universal egoism." [2] The majority of philosophers have considered universalization to be necessary for a sound moral theory, though few have considered it sufficient. This requirement may be expressed as follows: If it is reasonable for A to do s in C, it is also reasonable for any similar person to do similar things in similar circumstances. Since everyone has a self-interest and since the egoist is arguing that his actions are right simply because they are self-interested, it is intuitively plausible to hold that he is committed to regarding everyone as morally similar and as morally entitled (or even morally obligated) to be egoists. His claim that his own self-interested actions are right thus entails the claim that all self-interested actions are right. If the egoist is to reject this universalization, he must show that there are considerations in addition to self-interest justifying his action, considerations making him relevantly different from all others such that his self-interested behavior is justified while theirs is not. I can't imagine what such considerations would be. In any case, egoism has usually been advanced and defended in its universalized form, and it is in this form that it will most repay careful examination. Thus, for the purposes of this paper, I shall assume without further defense the correctness of the universalization requirement.

It has also been the case that the major objections to ethical egoism have been derived from this requirement. Opponents have argued that once egoism is universalized, it can readily be seen to be incoherent. Frankena[3] and Medlin each advance an argument of this sort. In discussing their positions, I shall argue that the universalization of egoism given by (i) is coherent, that there is more than one type of "universalization," and that egoism can, in fact, be universalized in both senses. More importantly, I shall argue that the form of universalization presenting the most problems for the egoist is a form based

[2] Medlin, Brian, "Ultimate Principles and Ethical Egoism," *Australasian Journal of Philosophy*, XXXV (1957), 111–18; reprinted in this volume, pp. 56–63. See pp. 57–8 for Medlin's discussion of universal versus individual egoism.

[3] Frankena, William, *Ethics* (Englewood Cliffs, New Jersey; Prentice-Hall, Inc., 1963), pp. 16–18. References to Frankena in sections II and V are to this book.

upon a certain conception of value which the egoist can coherently reject. The result will be that egoism can with some plausibility be defended as an ultimate practical principle. At the least, if egoism is incorrect, this is not due to any incoherence arising from the universalization requirement.

II

One purpose of a moral theory is to provide criteria for first person moral judgments (such as "I ought to do *s* in C"); another purpose is to provide criteria for second and third person moral judgments (such as "Jones ought to do *s* in C"). Any theory which cannot coherently provide such criteria must be rejected as a moral theory. Can ethical egoism do this? Frankena argues that it cannot.

Frankena formulates egoism as consisting of two principles:

(a) If A is judging about himself, then A is to use this criterion: A ought to do *y* if and only if *y* is in A's overall self-interest.

(b) If A is a spectator judging about anyone else, B, then A is to use this criterion: B ought to do *y* if and only if *y* is in A's overall self-interest.

Frankena thinks that [(a) & (b)] is the only interpretation of (i) "consistent with the spirit of ethical egoism."

But isn't it the case that (a) and (b) taken together produce contradictory moral judgments about an important subset of cases, namely, those where people's self-interests conflict or are irreconcilable? If this is so, egoism as formulated by Frankena is incoherent and must be rejected.

To illustrate, let us suppose that B does *s*, and that *s* is in B's overall self-interest, but not in A's. Is *s* right or wrong? Ought, or ought not B do *s*? The answer depends on who is making the judgment. If A is making the judgment, then "B ought not to do *s*" is correct. If B is making the judgment, then "B ought to do *s*" is correct. And, of course, when both make judgments, both "B ought to do *s*" and "B ought not to do *s*" are correct. Surely any principle which has this result as a possibility is incoherent.

This objection may be put another way. The ethical egoist claims that there is one ultimate moral principle applicable to everyone. This is to claim that (i) is adequate for all moral issues, and that all applications of it can fit into a logically coherent system. Given the above illustration, "B ought to do *s*" does follow from (a), and "B ought not to do *s*" does follow from (b), but the fact that they cannot coherently be included in a set of judgments shows that (a) and (b) are not parts of the same ultimate moral principle. Indeed, these respective judgments can be said to follow from a moral principle at all only if they follow from *different* moral principles. Apparently, the ethical egoist must choose between (i)'s parts if he is to have a coherent ethical system, but he can make no satisfactory choice. If (a) is chosen, second and third person judgments become impossible. If (b) is chosen, first person judgments become impossible. His moral theory, however, must provide for both kinds of judgment. Ethical egoism needs what it logically cannot have. Therefore, it can only be rejected.

The incompatibility between (a) and (b) and the consequent incoherence of (i) manifests itself in still a third way. Interpreted as a system of judgments, [(a) & (b)] is equivalent to: Everyone ought to pursue A's self-interest, and everyone ought to pursue B's self-interest, and everyone ought to pursue C's self-interest, and . . . .[4] When the interests of A and B are incompatible, one must pursue both of these incompatible goals, which, of course, is impossible. On this interpretation, ethical egoism must fail in its function of guiding conduct (one of the most important uses of moral judgments). In particular, it must fail with respect to just those cases for which the guidance is

---

[4] This can be shown as follows:

  i. Suppose A is the evaluator, then

       What ought A to do? A ought to do what's in A's interest. (by (a))
       What ought B to do? B ought to do   "   (by (b))
       What ought C to do? C ought to do   "   (by (b))
       etc.

       Therefore, everyone ought to do what's in A's interest. (by (a) & (b))
  ii. Suppose B is the evaluator, then

       What ought A to do? A ought to do what's in B's interest. (by (b))
       What ought B to do? B ought to do   "   (by (a))
       What ought C to do? C ought to do   "   (by (b))
       etc.

       Therefore, everyone ought to do what's in B's interest. (by (a) & (b))
  iii. Suppose C is the evaluator, then

       .
       .
       .
       etc.

Conclusion: Everyone ought to do what's in A's interest, and everyone ought to do what's in B's interest, and . . . *etc.*

most wanted—conflicts of interests. In such situations, the theory implies that one must both do and not do a certain thing. Therefore, since ethical egoism cannot guide conduct in these crucial cases, it is inadequate as a moral theory and must be rejected.

Ethical egoism suffers from three serious defects if it is interpreted as [(a) & (b)]. These defects are closely related. The first is that the theory implies a contradiction, namely, that some actions are both right *and* wrong. The second defect is that the theory, if altered and made coherent by rejecting one of its parts, cannot fulfill one of its essential tasks: Altered, it can provide for first person moral judgments *or* for second and third person moral judgments, but not for both. The third defect is that the theory cannot guide conduct and must fail in its advice-giving function because it advises (remember: advises, all things considered) a person to do what it advises him not to do.

Any one of these defects would be sufficient to refute the theory, and indeed they do refute ethical egoism when it is defined as [(a) & (b)]. The only plausible way to escape these arguments is to abandon Frankena's definition and reformulate egoism so that they are no longer applicable. Clearly, (a) must remain, for it seems central to any egoistic position. However, we can replace (b) with the following:

(c) If A is a spectator judging about anyone else, B, then A is to use this criterion: B ought to do *y* if and only if *y* is in B's overall self-interest.

The objections to [(a) & (b)] given above do not apply to [(a) & (c)]. [(a) & (c)] yields no contradictions, even in cases where self-interests conflict or are irreconcilable. When we suppose that B is the agent, that *s* is in B's overall self-interest, and that *s* is against A's overall self-interest, both B and A will agree in their moral judgments about this case, that is, both will agree that B ought to do *s*. And, of course, the theory provides for all moral judgments, whether first, second, or third person; since it yields no contradictions, there is no need to make it coherent by choosing between its parts and thereby making it inadequate.

Finally, this interpretation avoids the charge that ethical egoism cannot adequately fulfill its conduct guiding function. Given [(a) & (c)], it will never truly be the case that an agent ought to pursue anyone's self-interest except his own. Any judgment of the form "A ought to pursue B's self-interest" will be false, unless it is understood to mean that pursuit of B's self-interest is a part of the pursuit of A's self-interest (and this, of course, would not contribute to any incoherence in the theory). Thus, the theory will have no difficulty in being an effective practical theory; it will not give contradictory advice, even in situations where interests conflict. True, it will not remove such conflicts—indeed, in practice it might well encourage them; but a conflict is not a contradiction. The theory tells A to pursue a certain goal, and it tells B to pursue another goal, and does this unequivocally. That both cannot succeed in their pursuits is irrelevant to the coherence of the theory and its capacity to guide conduct, since both *can* do what they are advised to do, all things considered—pursue their own self-interests.

(i), when interpreted as [(a) & (c)], is a fully objective moral theory. Therefore, in defending ethical egoism, one need not be driven into the kind of subjectivism which holds that "right," "wrong," "morally justified," and even "true" when used in a moral argument or judgment always mean "right for A," or "right for B," or "wrong for A," or "true ʿor B," or perhaps "right from A's point of view," "wrong from B's point of view," etc.[5] Such usage would be exceedingly peculiar, for in what sense can a judgment or action be said to be justified, all things considered, if it is justified for me and unjustified for you? Thus, interpreting ethical egoism as [(a) & (c)] rather than as [(a) & (b)] has the great merit of making it possible to avoid the temptation to subjectivism.

There remains the question whether [(a) & (c)] is a plausible interpretation of (i), that is, whether it is "consistent with the spirit of ethical egoism." It is certainly consistent with the "spirit" behind the "ethical" part of egoism in its willingness to universalize the doctrine. It is also consistent with the "egoistic" part of the theory in that if a person does faithfully follow (a) he will behave as an egoist. Adding the fact that [(a) & (c)] is a coherent theory adequate to the special ethical chores so far discussed, do we have any reason for rejecting it as an interpretation of (i) and ethical egoism? So far, I think not. Therefore, I conclude that Frankena has failed to refute egoism. It has thus far survived the test of universalization and still remains as a candidate for "the one true moral theory."

[5] As is Gardner Williams in his *Humanistic Ethics* (New York: Philosophical Library, 1951), see Chapter III, particularly pp. 29–31.

III

In his article, "Ultimate Principles and Ethical Egoism," Brian Medlin maintains that ethical egoism cannot be an ultimate moral principle because it fails to guide our actions, tell us what to do, or determine our choice between alternatives.[6] He bases this charge on his view that because ethical egoism is the expression of inconsistent desires, it will always tell people to do incompatible things. Thus:

> I have said from time to time that the egoistic principle is inconsistent. I have not said it is contradictory. This for the reason that we can, without contradiction, express inconsistent desires and purposes. To do so is not to say anything like "Goliath was ten feet tall and not ten feet tall." Don't we all want to have our cake and eat it too? And when we say we do we aren't asserting a contradiction whether we be making an avowal of our attitudes or stating a fact about them. We all have conflicting motives. None of this, however, can do the egoist any good. For we assert our ultimate principles not only to express our own attitudes but also to induce similar attitudes in others, to dispose them to conduct themselves as we wish. In so far as their desires conflict, people don't know what to do. And, therefore, no expression of incompatible desires can ever serve for an ultimate principle of human conduct. (p. 63)

That egoism could not successfully guide one's conduct was a criticism discussed and rebutted in section II. There, it rested upon Frankena's formulation of egoism as equal to [(a) & (b)] and was easily circumvented by replacing principle (b) with principle (c). Medlin's charge is significant, however, because it appears to be applicable to [(a) & (c)] as well [7] and therefore must be directly refuted if egoism is to be maintained.

---

[6] All references to Medlin are to the reprint in this volume, pp. 56–63.

[7] Medlin himself does not distinguish between (b) and (c). Some of his remarks suggest (c). Thus, at one point he says:

> When he [the egoist] tries to convince me that he should look after himself, he is attempting so to dispose me that I shall approve when he drinks my beer and steals Tom's wife. I cannot approve of his looking after himself and himself alone without so far approving of his achieving his happiness, regardless of the happiness of myself and others. (p. 58)

This passage implies that as a spectator assessing another's conduct, I should employ principle (c) and approve of A's doing y whenever y promotes A's interest, even if this is at the expense of my welfare.

But other of his remarks suggest (b). Thus, the above passage continues:

The heart of Medlin's argument is his position that to affirm a moral principle is to express approval of any and all actions following from that principle. This means for Medlin not only that the egoist is committed to approving all egoistic actions but also that such approval will involve wanting those actions to occur and trying to bring them about, even when they would be to one's own detriment.

> But is not to believe that someone should act in a certain way to try to persuade him to do so? Of course, we don't always try to persuade people to act as we think they should act. We may be lazy, for instance. But insofar as we believe that Tom should do so and so, we have a tendency to induce him to do so and so. Does it make sense to say: "Of course you should do this, but for goodness' sake don't"? Only where we mean: "You should do this for certain reasons, but here are even more persuasive reasons for not doing it." If the egoist believes ultimately that others should mind themselves alone, then, he must persuade them accordingly. If he doesn't persuade them, he is no universal egoist. (p. 59)

According to Medlin, if I adopt ethical egoism and am thereby led to approve of A's egoistic actions (as would follow from (c)), I must also *want* A to behave in that way and must want him to be happy, to come out on top, and so forth where wanting is interpreted as setting an end for my own actions and where it tends (according to the intensity of the want, presumably) to issue in my "looking after him."

Of course, I will also approve of my pursuing my own welfare (as would follow from (a)) and will want myself to be happy, to come out on top, and so forth. Since I want my own success, I will want A's noninterference. Indeed, what I will want A to do, and will therefore approve of A's doing, is to pursue my welfare, rather than his own.

It is thus the case that whenever my interest conflicts with A's interest, I will approve of inconsistent ends and will want incompatible things ("I want myself to come out on top and I want Tom to come

---

> So that when he sets out to persuade me that he should look after himself regardless of others, he must also set out to persuade me that I should look after him regardless of myself and others. Very small chance he has! (p. 58)

Here, the implication is that the egoist as spectator and judge of another should assess the other's behavior according to his own interests, not the other's, which would be in accordance with (b).

Perhaps Medlin is arguing that the egoist is committed to accepting both (b) and (c), as well as (a). This interpretation is consistent with his analysis of "approval."

out on top," p. 61). Since I approve of incompatible ends, I will be motivated in contrary directions—both away from and toward my own welfare, for instance. However, this incompatibility of desires is not sufficient to produce inaction and does not itself prove Medlin's point, for one desire may be stronger than the other. If the egoist's approval of his own well-being were always greater than his approval of anyone else's well-being, the inconsistent desires constituting egoism would not prevent (i) from decisively guiding conduct. Unfortunately for the egoist, his principle will in fact lead him to inaction, for in being universal (i) expresses equal approval of each person's pursuing his own self-interest, and therefore, insofar as his desires follow from this principle, none will be stronger than another.

We can now explain Medlin's conclusion that "the proper objection to the man who says 'Everyone should look after his own interests regardless of the interests of others' is not that he isn't speaking the truth, but simply that he isn't speaking" (p. 57). Upon analysis, it is clear that the egoist is "saying" that others should act so that he himself comes out on top and should not care about Tom, Dick, *et al.*, but they should also act so that Tom comes out on top and should not care about himself, Dick, the others, and so forth (p. 61). This person *appears* to be saying how people should act, and that they should act in a definite way. But his "directions" can guide no one. They give one nothing to do. Therefore, such a man has in fact said nothing.

I think Medlin's argument can be shown to be unsuccessful without a discussion of the emotivism in which it is framed. The egoist can grant that there is a correct sense in which affirmation of a moral principle is the expression of approval. The crux of the issue is Medlin's particular analysis of approbation, and this can be shown to be incorrect.

We may grant that the egoist is committed to approving of anyone's egoistic behavior at least to the extent of believing that the person ought so to behave. Such approval will hold of all egoistic actions, even those that endanger his own welfare. But does believing that A ought to do *y* commit one to wanting A to do *y*? Surely not. This is made clear by the analogy with competitive games. Team A has no difficulty in believing that team B ought to make or try to make a field goal while not wanting team B to succeed, while hoping that team B fails, and, indeed, while trying to prevent team B's success. Or consider this example: I may see how my chess opponent can put my king in check. That is how he ought to move. But believing that he ought to move his bishop and check my king does not commit me to wanting him to do that, nor to persuading him to do so. What *I* ought to do is sit there quietly, hoping he does not move as he ought.

Medlin's mistake is to think that believing that A ought to do *y* commits one to *wanting* A to do *y* and hence to encouraging or otherwise helping A to do *y*. The examples from competitive games show that this needn't be so. The egoist's reply to Medlin is that just as team A's belief that team B ought to do so and so is compatible with their not wanting team B to do so and so, so the egoist's belief that A ought to do *y* is compatible with the egoist's not wanting A to do *y*. Once this is understood, egoism has no difficulty in decisively guiding conduct, for insofar as (i) commits the egoist to wanting anything, it only commits him to wanting his own welfare. Since he does not want incompatible goals, he has no trouble in deciding what to do according to (a) and in judging what others ought to do according to (c).

IV

There is in Medlin's paper confusion concerning what the egoist wants or values and why he believes in ethical egoism. The egoist does not believe that everyone ought to pursue their own self-interest merely because *he* wants to get *his* goodies out of life. If this were all there were to his position, the egoist would not bother with (i) or with moral concepts at all. He would simply go about doing what he wants. What reason, then, does he have to go beyond wanting his own welfare to ethical egoism? On Medlin's emotivist account, his reason must be that he also wants B to have B's goodies, and wants D to have his, and so forth, even when it is impossible that everybody be satisfied. But I argued in the preceding section that the egoist is not committed to wanting such states, and that it is not nonsense for him to affirm (i) and desire his own welfare yet not desire the welfare of others. Therefore, the question remains—why affirm egoism at all?

The egoist's affirmation of (i) rests upon both teleological and deontological elements. What *he* finds to be of ultimate value is his own welfare. He needn't be selfish or egocentric in the ordinary sense (as Medlin sometimes suggests by such paraphrases as "Let each man do what he wants regardless of what anyone else wants," p. 61), but he will value his own interest above that of others. Such an egoist would share Sidgwick's view that when "the painful necessity comes for another man to choose between his own happiness and the general happiness, he must as a reasonable being prefer his own." [8] When this occasion does arise, the egoist will want the other's welfare less than he wants his own, and this will have the practical effect of not wanting the other's welfare at all. It is in terms of this personal value that he guides his actions, judging that he ought to do y if and only if y is in his overall self-interest. This is the teleological element in his position.

However, there is no reason that others should find his well-being to be of value to them, less more to be of ultimate value; and it is much more likely that each will find his own welfare to be his own ultimate value. But if it is reasonable for the egoist to justify his behavior in terms of what he finds to be of ultimate value, then it is also reasonable for others to justify their behavior in terms of what they find to be of ultimate value. This follows from the requirement of universalization and provides the deontological element. Interpreted as "Similar things are right for similar people in similar circumstances," the universalization principle seems undeniable. Failing to find any relevant difference between himself and others, the egoist must admit that it can be morally permissible for him to pursue his self-interest only if it is morally permissible for each person to pursue his self-interest. He therefore finds himself committed to (i), even though he does not *want* others to compete with him for life's goods.

Medlin and others have not construed egoism in this way. While they have acknowledged the role of deontological considerations in the production of (i) by noting the universalization requirement, they have given more emphasis to its teleological aspects. In particular, they have thought that at the least (i) states that a certain state of affairs is intrinsically valuable and *therefore* ought to be brought about. If this is so, to affirm the principle is to accept this set of values. Medlin then argues that an egoist cannot accept these values and remain a consistent egoist. He asks of the ethical egoist: "Just what does he value? Is it the well-being of himself, Tom, Dick, and Harry or merely their going on in a certain way regardless of whether or not this is going to promote their well-being?" (p. 61).

[8] Henry Sidgwick, *The Methods of Ethics,* 7th ed. (London: Macmillan and Co., 1907), preface to the 6th edition, p. xvii.

Consider this latter alternative and the result if everyone were to follow (i) and behave as the egoist claims it is most reasonable for them to do. We would have a state wherein everyone disregarded the happiness of others when their happiness clashed with one's own (p. 62). Given the normal condition of the world in which the major goods requisite for well-being (food, clothing, sex, glory, *etc.*) are not in overabundance, we would have a state of competition, struggle, and probably much avoidable misery. Hobbes' overstatement is that it would be a "war of everyman against everyman" in which life is "solitary, poor, nasty, brutish, and short."

Since Medlin holds that acceptance of a moral principle such as (i) rests on valuing that state of affairs which compliance to the principle would bring about, and that acceptance of this principle as ultimate rests on placing ultimate value on that state of affairs (on wanting that state more than any other), it is understandable that ethical egoism should appear to him to be "a funny kind of egoism" (p. 62).

Medlin's point is that a person valuing such a state of affairs is no longer an egoist in any natural sense of that term. An egoist values his own welfare. But the Hobbesian conditions described above include this value only incidentally, if at all. To make his position consistent, therefore, he must choose between the following alternatives. He can accept the actual values promoted by his theory. Since these are not egoistic values (confirmed by the fact that he could not convince others to value and promote such a state of affairs by appealing solely to their self-interest, p. 62), this is to abandon egoism. Or he can accept self-interest as the ultimate value which, because of the universalization requirement, will involve accepting each person's self-interest as of equal value. This will be to abandon egoism and (i) for a form of utilitarianism (p. 63).

Medlin's crucial charge against ethical egoism is not that it is incoherent or unable to fulfill the necessary functions of a moral theory such as decisively guiding conduct in cases where interests conflict, but that principle (i) is simply not an expression of egoism. Egoism is an unformulable moral theory, and hence *no* moral theory.[9] This charge rests, however, on what I shall call the material conception of value. Medlin's criticism rests on the assumption that ethical egoism (*i.e.*, principle (i)) is saying that there is something of intrinsic value

[9] The egoist "must behave as an individual egoist, if he is to be an egoist at all" (p. 60), but since "the individual egoist cannot promulgate his doctrine without enlarging it, what he has is no doctrine at all" (p. 58).

which everyone ought to pursue—that there is one specific state of affairs everyone ought to pursue. This is false, and is the result of not distinguishing *material* valuations from what I shall call *formal* valuations.

In analyzing the teleological basis of (i), Medlin and others have been misled by imposing on the egoist a conception of intrinsic or ultimate value which he does not hold. They suppose that there is *one* value or set of values which is or ought to be *common* to everyone (or they suppose that principles like (i) express the desire that such a set of values be common to everyone). It is characteristic of this position that these values are of such a nature that everyone ought to promote them; they are objective and binding upon everyone. It is in terms of this common goal that each person's actions are to be guided and justified. Furthermore, these values demand and establish a harmony and concert among men's actions. There is some end, some state of affairs, perhaps quite complex, the establishment of which is the goal of all moral actions. The task of a moral theory, and particularly of any ultimate moral principle, is to direct one to such a goal. I call this view the *material conception of value.*

In utilitarianism, the single, though hardly simple, material value is the state of maximum social welfare—"the greatest happiness of the greatest number," "people being as happy as it is possible to make them," or some such variant. For Moore, it is a state in which there is a maximum of intrinsic goods—that is, of pleasure, knowledge, love, the enjoyment of beauty, moral qualities, and so forth.[10] On his view, Jones' pleasure is as valuable as my pleasure, and I have the same obligation to bring about that pleasure as Jones does. Supremacy of the state views are further instances of this conception, as is the view that each man is an end in himself and as such entitled to one's respect, where one sign of this respect is acting always so that any other being could share the ends of one's actions.

The egoist would replace this standard view with the *formal conception of value.* On this account, that which is to have ultimate value for different people will usually be the same only in the sense that it is the same *kind* of good but not the same particular instance of it. What is valued will be similar but normally not identical. In the statement, "Self-interest is the ultimate good," "self-interest" is used in a generic sense. What is specifically valued—the various contents of

[10] Moore, G. E., *Ethics* (London: Oxford University Press, 1912), Chapter VII, "Intrinsic Value," see especially pp. 140, 146–47, 152–53.

these self-interests—is quite different from person to person and sometimes mutually incompatible. What the egoist is saying, of course, is
that his welfare has ultimate (or intrinsic) value to himself, though
not to anyone else, and that Tom's welfare has ultimate (or intrinsic)
value to Tom, but not to himself or others, and that Harry's welfare
has ultimate value to Harry, but not . . . , and so forth. He is saying
that his interests give him a reason for acting but give Tom and Harry
none, and that Tom's interests give Tom a reason for acting but give
him and Harry none, and that . . . , and so forth. Here, there is no
common value shared by the egoist, Tom, Harry, *et al.,* unless by
accident.

According to a teleological moral theory, what a person ought to do
is maximize the good or ultimate value, whatever that might be. If
ultimate value is understood in the material sense, one will naturally
believe that everyone has an obligation to bring about the same particular state of affairs. And since the egoist says everyone ought to act
in a certain way, one will assume that this is because there is something ultimately valuable about everyone acting in that way. This
would be a mistake. A moral theory may be teleological in terms of
merely formal values. Nothing stronger is necessary. One can agree
that people ought to maximize the good, but maintain that there is
nothing which is good to everyone. Thus, people will be justified in
pursuing somewhat different states, and possibly come into conflict.
Moral principles will not have the objective of establishing a concert
and harmony among men's actions nor of expressing a common goal.
(i), in particular, will not have as its purpose the promotion of material values. If everyone does follow (i), states highly disvaluable to
some will result, and there is no assurance that the egoist will succeed
in maximizing value for himself.

In the previous section, I argued that the egoist's belief that other
egoists ought to act in a way harmful to himself could be understood
by noting similar beliefs in competitive games. We can likewise understand how the egoist can construct a coherent moral system not essentially dependent on material values by noting that practical systems
such as professional football can be explained and justified without
assuming a set of ultimate values common to all the parties encom-
passed by them. Thus, the player's ultimate values are, let us say,
winning and being superior, money (for themselves), the satisfaction
of playing the game, and glory; the owner's values are money (for
themselves), promotion of civic or business enterprises, and winning

and being superior; the spectator's values are the pleasures of watching the game and being a fan, both aesthetic and more visceral; the official's values are money (for themselves), and perhaps other goods such as superiority or "love of the game." These values are virtually all only formally the same; but their pursuit by the respective parties is sufficient to produce the game. The players' interests, for instance, do not have to be shared or even mutually compatible—only one team can win, glory is a scarce good requiring the defeat of others, and so forth. One player need not care about the others, or the spectators, except in so far as they figure *as means* necessary to his ends. Since he cannot win, or make a fortune, or even play football without others playing too, he must get together with them to form a league with all its paraphernalia. But even with such cooperation, the ultimate values Tom the football player is pursuing are quite different materially from those pursued by Harry the football player, though probably of the same kind. Similarly, acceptance of the egoist principle requires no more of a commitment to common material values than acceptance of the competitive game does, that is, none.

We began this section with a question suggested by Medlin: Why does the egoist believe that everyone ought to pursue his own self-interest rather than believe that everyone ought to pursue *his* self-interest or simply going off to get his own? Medlin thought that the egoist could not coherently maintain (i) and remain an egoist—that he must in fact simply go off to get his own. I have argued that he can, and have tried to answer Medlin's question as follows: The egoist finds that his own self-interest gives him a reason to act in certain ways, but he does not think that this self-interest *per se* gives any other person a reason to act. Self-interest is an ultimate good in the formal but not the material sense. He therefore holds that what *he* ought to do, all things considered (what it would be most reasonable for him to do), is pursue his own self-interest, even to the harming of others when necessary. But he further acknowledges that if this form of reasoning is sufficient to justify his egoistic behavior, it is sufficient to justify anyone's, or everyone's egoistic behavior. Consequently, he will accept the universalization of his position to "For each person, it is most reasonable for him to pursue his own self-interest, even to the harming of others if necessary," or to "(x)(y)(x ought to do y if and only if y is in x's overall self-interest)." While this is a teleological moral principle because it states that a person ought to maximize value, it is a mistake to think that it points to one particular state of affairs which is valuable and which *therefore* ought to be promoted by everyone. Such a mistake is based on the failure to distinguish between material and formal valuations. Because (i) establishes other's welfare as valuable only in the formal sense, the egoist can affirm (i) without being committed to accepting either their welfare or Hobbesian-like conditions of competition as valuable, thus avoiding Medlin's dilemma.

V

Medlin remarks that the egoist would be a fool to tell other people they should "look after themselves and no one else" (p. 58). He goes on to say:

> Obviously something strange goes on as soon as the ethical egoist tries to promulgate his doctrine. What is he doing when he urges upon his audience that they should each observe his own interests and those interests alone? It he not acting contrary to the egoistic principle? It cannot be to his advantage to convince them, for seizing always their own advantage they will impair his. (p. 59)

So far as Medlin is concerned, I discussed this "strange" aspect of egoism when I argued that it was not necessary either to want or to urge another to do what he ought to do in order to believe that he ought to do it. Behind Medlin's requirement of promulgation was seen to be a commitment to the material conception of value. The difficulties such a commitment entail for the egoist can be avoided if he uses only formal valuations. Thus, Medlin has failed to show that the egoist must violate his principle in the very holding of it because he has failed to show that the egoist *must* promulgate that principle *if* he holds it.

At this point, many philosophers would argue that ethical egoism is an even stranger doctrine than Medlin supposes if it can be consistently held only when it is silently held. In this section, I shall examine their argument. We shall first look at what the egoist must abandon along with the requirement of promulgation. It appears as though this must include most of the activities and emotions characterizing morality as such. According to its critics, this would mean that ethical egoism was not a moral theory. We shall then consider the egoist's reply to this criticism.

Taking the long run fully into account, the egoist must hold his position silently if he is to remain prudent. This restriction is more serious than might be suspected, for it means the egoist must refrain not only from advocating his doctrine, but also from a wide range of behavior typical of any morality. For instance, he will not be able to enter into moral discussions, at least not sincerely or as an egoist, for to debate a moral issue will ultimately require him to argue for (i). This will not be to his interest for at least the reason that others will become suspicious of him and cease to trust him. They will learn he is an egoist and treat him accordingly. It would be even worse if he should win the debate and convince them.

Nor will he be able to give or receive moral advice. If it is objected that he can advise others as long as interests do not conflict, it will do to note that it is not to his interest to have his egoistic views known. Giving of advice involves giving reasons for certain actions; inquiries about the moral principle upon which that advice is based are therefore appropriate. Of course, the egoist can lie. When Harry comes to Tom about his affair with Dick's wife, Tom can approve, professing enlightened views about marriage, noting that there are no children, that both are adults, and so forth, although he knows Harry's behavior will soon lead to a scandal ruining Harry's career—all to Tom's advantage. Tom has advised Harry, but not sincerely; he has not told Harry *what he thinks Harry really ought to do*—what would be most in Harry's overall self-interest. And Tom ought not, since he himself is following (i). This all goes to make the point; the egoist is not sincerely advising Harry, but rather pretending to sincerely advise him while really deceiving and manipulating him.

This use of advice—to manipulate others—is limited, and perhaps bought at a price too great for the egoist to pay. Since advising is a public activity, urging others to be benevolent (in order to benefit from their actions) gives them grounds to require one to be benevolent toward them, and thus to create sanctions restricting the scope of his self-interested behavior.

Worst of all, it will do the egoist himself no good to *ask* for moral advice for he is bound not to get what he wants. If he asks nonegoists, he will be told to do things which might be in his self-interest, but usually won't be. What sort of help could he get from a Kantian or a utilitarian? Their advice will follow from the wrong moral principle. If he asks another egoist, he is no better off, since he cannot be trusted.

Knowing that he is an egoist, he knows that he is following (a), acting in his own self-interest, and lying if he can benefit from it. The egoist is truly isolated from any moral community, and must always decide and act alone, without the help of others.

It will not be to the egoist's self-interest to support his moral principle with sanctions. He will be unable to praise those who do what they ought, unable to blame those who flagrantly shirk their moral tasks. Nor will he be able to establish institutions of rewards and punishments founded on his principle. The egoist cannot sincerely engage in any of these activities. He will punish or blame people for doing what they ought not to do (for doing what is not in their self-interests) only by coincidence and then under some other rubric than violation of (i). To punish people for not being egoists is to encourage them to be egoists, and this is not to his interest. Similarly, the egoist, if he engages in such an activity at all, will praise people for doing what they ought to do only by chance, and always under a different, nonegoistic label.

A corollary to this is the egoist's inability to teach (i) to his children (while himself following it). It is imprudent to raise egoistic children, since among other things, the probability of being abandoned in old age is greatly increased. Therefore, the egoist can give his children no sincere moral instruction, and most likely will be advised to teach them to disapprove of his actions and his character, should they become aware of their true nature.

Finally, one of the points of appealing to a moral principle is to justify one's behavior *to others*—to convince them that their (sometimes forcible) opposition to this behavior is unwarranted and ought to be withdrawn. When we do convince someone of the rightness of our actions, he normally comes onto our side, even if reluctantly. Thus, the teenage daughter tries to convince her father that it is right and proper for sixteen year old girls to stay out until 12:30 (rather than 11:00) because if she is successful and he agrees with her, he then has *no excuse* (other things being equal) for still withholding his permission. For an ethical egoist, this point is doomed to frustration for two reasons: first, because justifying one's behavior in terms of (i) gives an opponent no reason to cease his opposition if maintaining it would be in his own interest; and second, because it will not be to the egoist's interest to publicly justify his behavior to others on egoistic grounds, thereby running the risk of converting them to egoism. Therefore, the egoist is unable to engage in *interpersonal reasoning* with his moral principle as its basis—he can neither justify nor excuse his egoistic actions as such in the interpersonal sense of "justify" and "excuse."

Adherence to the egoistic principle makes it impossible, because imprudent, for one to sincerely engage in any of these moral activities. There are also typical moral attitudes and emotions which, while perhaps not impossible for an egoist to sincerely have, it is impossible for him to sincerely express. I have in mind remorse, regret, resentment, repentance, forgiveness, revenge, outrage and indignation, and the form of sympathy known as moral support. Let us take forgiveness. When can the egoist forgive another, and for what? One forgives the other's wrongs, wrongs which are normally done against oneself. First, it is hard to see how someone could wrong someone else given ethical egoism, for (i) gives one no obligations to others, and hence no way of shirking those obligations. At least, one has no such obligations directly. Second, what is the nature of the wrong action which is to be forgiven? It must be a failure to properly pursue self-interest. Suppose Harry makes this lapse. Can Tom forgive him? In so far as such forgiveness involves nonexpressed beliefs and attitudes, yes. But Tom would be unwise to express this attitude or to forgive Harry in the fuller, public sense. Partly because if their interests conflict, Tom's good will involve Harry's harm; Tom does not want Harry to do what he ought, and Tom ought not to encourage him to do so, which would be involved in overtly forgiving him. And partly because of the general imprudence of making it known that one is an egoist, which would be involved in expressing forgiveness of nonegoistic behavior. If the egoist is to forgive people where this involves the expression of forgiveness, his doing so must be basically insincere.

Similar considerations hold for the expression of the other emotions and attitudes mentioned. As for those which are not so clearly dependent upon some manner of public expression, such as resentment and remorse, it is perhaps not impossible for the egoist to have them (or to be capable of having them), but it is clear that their objects and occasion will be quite different from what they are in the standard morality. Resentment as a moral attitude involves taking offense at someone's failure to do what they ought. But why should the egoist be offended if other people don't look after their interests, at least when their interests are not connected with his own? And when their interests are connected, the offense does not arise from the fact that the other did something wrong—failed to properly pursue his own interests—but because of the further and undesirable consequences of this failure, but consequences for which that person was not liable. Resentment here is very strange, all the more so because of the formal rather than material commitment of the egoist to the obligation to pursue one's own self-interest. Since he doesn't value others' doing what they ought, any resentment he feels must be slight and rather abstract, amounting to little more than the belief that they ought not to behave that way.

Granting that it would not be in his overall self-interest for others to be egoists too, the ethical egoist has compelling reasons not to engage sincerely in any of the activities mentioned above, as well as not to give expression to various typical moral attitudes and emotions. This is strange not because the egoist is in some sense required to promulgate his doctrine while at the same time faithfully follow it, for we saw above that he can coherently reject this demand, but strange because his position seems to have lost most of the features characterizing a morality. When put into practice, ethical egoism discards the moral activities of advocacy, moral discussion, giving and asking of advice, using sanctions to reward and punish, praising and blaming, moral instruction and training, and interpersonal excusing and justification, as well as the expressing of many moral attitudes and emotions. With these features gone, what remains that constitutes a morality? The egoist may, indeed, have a coherent practical system, but since it lacks certain major structural features of a morality, it is not a *moral theory*. Consider a legal theory which, when put into practice, turns out to have neither trials, nor judges, nor juries, nor sentencing, nor penal institutions, nor legislating bodies. Could it still be a legal theory and lack all of these? Isn't the case similar with ethical egoism?

If the above account is correct, its conclusion would be that egoism is a coherent practical theory, able to guide behavior and provide for the critical assessment of the actions of others without contradiction, but simply not a moral theory of conduct. Many philosophers would agree to the basis of this conclusion—that a theory lacking the wide range of typical moral activities and expressions that egoism lacks is not a moral theory—among them Frankena and Medlin. On their views, a morality must be interpersonal in character—if it is not interpersonal through a commitment to material values, at least interpersonal through a commitment to the various public activities mentioned, and perhaps to methods of carrying them out which will tend toward producing harmonious, if not common, values. Since the egoist is committed to a noninterpersonal morality, a private not public morality, and to only formal values, his position is in their view a nonmoral position, many of whose conclusions will be judged immoral by any legitimate moral theory.

Frankena and Medlin agree that a silent theory is not a moral theory. A moral theory requires publicity, and cannot be private. Thus, Frankena says:

> Here we must understand that the ethical egoist is not just taking the egoistic principle of acting and judging as his own private maxim. One could do this, and at the same time keep silent about it or even advocate altruism to everyone else, which might well be to one's advantage. But if one does this, one is not adopting a moral principle, for as we shall see, if one takes a maxim as a moral principle, one must be ready to universalize it. (p. 17)

Here, Frankena connects nonuniversalization with silence, and thereby universalization with promulgation. This is a very strong sense of "universalize" which goes well beyond the principle "What's right for one person is right for similar people in similar circumstances." One can satisfy the universalization requirement in this latter sense by acknowledging that everyone would be justified in behaving as you are. As we have seen, this can be done without either wanting or urging others to do what they ought. But Frankena takes universalization to be much more, as is made clear by this earlier passage:

> Now morality in the sense indicated is, in one aspect, a social enterprise, not just a discovery or invention of the individual for his own guidance . . . it is not social merely in the sense of being a system governing the relations of one individual to others . . . it is also social in its origins, sanctions, and functions. It is an instrument of society as a whole for the guidance of individuals and smaller groups. It makes demands on individuals which are, initially at least, external to them. . . . As a social institution, morality must be contrasted with prudence. (pp. 5–6)

What it is important to note about this conception of universalization and morality is that it can coherently be rejected.[11] Universaliza-

---

[11] This sense of universalization needn't be rejected. One can coherently promulgate (i), but as we saw in section IV, doing so would make one something other than an egoist in the fullest sense. At the least, such a person would appear to value the state wherein everyone pursues their own welfare, wherein everyone tries to come out on top; this is a material, not formal value. ("But perhaps neither

tion in this strong sense is not a rational requirement (not analytic) as it appears to be in the weak sense. Our extended analogy between ethical egoism and competitive games shows just how coherently these strong conditions can be abandoned. At the most, this strong sense (in part explicated in terms of the various moral activities discussed above) may be part of the notion of "morality"; if so, egoism could not correctly label itself "ethical" or claim to be a moral theory. But this fact does not show that egoism as defined by (i) is mistaken, unreasonable, or inferior to any moral theory.

I personally think that it makes sense to speak of egoism as a morality, since I think it makes sense to speak of a "private morality" and of its being superior to "public moralities." The egoist's basic question is "What ought I to do; what is most reasonable for me to do?" This question seems to me a moral question through and through, and any coherent answer to it thereby deserves to be regarded as a moral theory. What is central here is the rational justification of a certain course of behavior. Such behavior will be justified in the sense that its reasonableness follows from a coherent and plausible set of premises. This kind of justification and moral reasoning can be carried out on the desert island and is not necessarily interpersonal—it does not have as one of its goals the minimal cooperation of some second party. Whether one *calls* the result a "morality" or not is of no matter, for its opponents must show it to be a poor competitor to the other alternatives. With respect to egoism, they cannot do this by arguing that (i) is logically incoherent or is incapable of being a practical system or violates any "principles of reason," such as universalization. I have tried to show how all these attempts would fail. I have even suggested in sections III and IV the way the egoist can argue for the reasonable-

---

gain nor loss. For us, there is only the trying. The rest is not our business." T. S. Eliot.) The more one stresses the "moral" aspects of adopting (i) which seem to require sincere participation in the various public activities mentioned above, the more the "egoist" will be committed to the other than egoistic values which will result if everyone heeds him, such as: conflict, struggle, and competition, strength, craft, and strategic ability, excitement, danger, and insecurity. While it is true that strictly speaking these values are not egoistic, even so (i) retains its egoistic "flavor." This is evident when it is applied to situations of irreconcilable conflict. The issue is to be settled by force or craft, or whatever, just in the way that it would be settled under the full-fledged, nonpromulgated egoism. It is perhaps difficult to imagine someone having the outlook needed in order to publicly promulgate (i) in such inhospitable conditions; nonetheless, it seems a possibility, and perhaps the professional soldier or gambler, or Zorba the Greek are approximations. Certainly, he would not be Medlin's misguided utilitarian.

ness of his position (and it has, of course, seemed eminently reasonable to innumerable men, the "common man" not being the least among these). I therefore conclude that ethical egoism is a possible moral theory, not to be lightly dismissed. Its challenge to standard moralities is great, and not easily overcome.

If one insists that egoism is without the pall of morality, the obvious question one must face is: "Why be moral?" It is not at all easy to convincingly show that the egoist should (that it would be most reasonable for him to) abandon his position for one which could require him to sacrifice his self-interest, even to the point of death. What must be shown is not simply that it is to the egoist's interests to *be in* a society structured by various social, moral, and legal institutions, all of which limit categorically certain expressions of self-interest (as do the penalty rules in football), which is Hobbes' point, but that the egoist also has compelling reasons (always) to abide by its rules, to continue to be moral, social, or legal when "the painful necessity comes for a man to choose between his own happiness and the general happiness."

The egoist can acknowledge that it is in his long range self-interest to be in a moral system and thus that there should be categorical public rules restricting his egoistic behavior. Publicly, these rules will be superior to self-interest, and will be enforced as such. But according to his private morality, they will not be superior. Rather, they will be interpreted as hypotheticals setting prices (sometimes very dear) upon certain forms of conduct. Thus, the egoist will believe that, while it is always reasonable to be in a moral system, it is not always reasonable to act morally while within that system (just as it is not always reasonable to obey the rules of football). The opponent of egoism, in order to soundly discredit it, must show that moral behavior is always reasonable. [12] If the conception of "formal value" is admitted as sound, and if the egoist is correct in his claim that there are no material values, I do not see how such attempts could be successful.

---

[12] This brief discussion of the question "Why be moral?" has Baier's attempt to show that egoism is ultimately unreasonable as its specific background, and is formulated in terms most appropriate to his treatment of the problem. See Kurt Baier, *The Moral Point of View* (New York; Random House, 1965), Chapter 7, especially sections 3 and 4. Section 3 reprinted in this volume, pp. 159–65.

part two

IS
MORAL MOTIVATION
BASED ON
INTEREST?

FRANCIS HUTCHESON

Virtuous Affections
and Self-Love

~~~~~~

. . . . . [Introductory remarks]

I

Every action, which we apprehend as either morally good or evil,
is always supposed to flow from some affection toward sensitive natures; and whatever we call virtue or vice is either some such affection,
or some action consequent upon it. Or it may perhaps be enough to
make an action or omission appear vicious, if it argues the want of
such affection toward rational agents as we expect in characters
counted morally good. All the actions counted religious in any country
are supposed, by those who count them so, to flow from some affections
toward the deity; and whatever we call social virtue we still suppose
to flow from affections toward our fellow creatures. For in this all
seem to agree, that external motions, when accompanied with no affections toward God or man, or evidencing no want of the expected
affections toward either, can have no moral good or evil in them.

Ask, for instance, the most abstemious hermit, if temperance of itself
would be morally good, supposing it showed no obedience toward
the deity, made us no fitter for devotion, or the service of mankind, or
the search after truth, than luxury; and he will easily grant that it
would be no moral good, though still it might be naturally good or
advantageous to health. And mere courage, or contempt of danger,
if we conceive it to have no regard to the defence of the innocent, or

---

*From *An Inquiry concerning Moral Good and Evil*, Section II, *Concerning the
immediate motive to virtuous actions*. The text is that of the third edition, 1729.
Spelling and punctuation have been modernized by the Editor.

91

repairing of wrongs, or self-interest, would only entitle its possessor to Bedlam. When such sort of courage is sometimes admired, it is upon some secret apprehension of a good intention in the use of it, or as a natural ability capable of a useful application. Prudence, if it was only employed in promoting private interest, is never imagined to be a virtue: and justice, or observing a strict equality, if it has no regard to the good of mankind, the preservation of rights, and securing peace, is a quality properer for its ordinary gestamen, a beam and scales, than for a rational agent. So that these four qualities, commonly called cardinal virtues, obtain that name because they are dispositions universally necessary to promote public good, and denote affections toward rational agents; otherwise there would appear no virtue in them.

II

Now if it can be made appear that none of these affections which we approve as virtuous, are either self-love, or desire of private interest; since all virtue is either some such affections, or actions consequent upon them, it must necessarily follow that virtue springs from some other affection than self-love, or desire of private advantage. And where self-interest excites to the same action, the approbation is given only to the disinterested principle.

The affections which are of most importance in morals are commonly included under the names love and hatred. Now in discoursing of love, we need not be cautioned not to include that love between the sexes, which, when no other affections accompany it, is only a desire of pleasure, and is never counted a virtue. Love toward rational agents is subdivided into love of complacence or esteem, and love of benevolence. And hatred is subdivided into hatred of displicence or contempt, and hatred of malice. Complacence denotes approbation of any person by our moral sense, and is rather a perception than an affection, though the affection of good will is ordinarily subsequent to it. Benevolence is the desire of the happiness of another. Their opposites are called dislike and malice. Concerning each of these separately we shall consider whether they can be influenced by motives of self-interest.

Complacence, esteem, or good-liking, at first view appears to be disinterested, and so displicence or dislike; and are entirely excited by some moral qualities, good or evil, apprehended to be in the objects, which qualities the very frame of our nature determines us to approve or disapprove, according to the moral sense[1] above explained. Propose to a man all the rewards in the world, or threaten all the punishments, to engage him to esteem and complacence toward a person entirely unknown, or if known, apprehended to be cruel, treacherous, ungrateful. You may procure external obsequiousness, or good offices, or dissimulation, but real esteem no price can purchase. And the same is obvious as to contempt, which no motive of advantage can prevent. On the contrary, represent a character as generous, kind, faithful, humane, though in the most distant parts of the world, and we cannot avoid esteem and complacence. A bribe may possibly make us attempt to ruin such a man, or some strong motive of advantage may excite us to oppose his interest, but it can never make us disapprove him while we retain the same opinion of his temper and intentions. Nay, when we consult our own hearts, we shall find that we can scarce ever persuade ourselves to attempt any mischief against such persons from any motive of advantage, nor execute it without the strongest reluctance and remorse, until we have blinded ourselves into a false opinion about his temper.

III

As to the love of benevolence, the very name excludes self-interest. We never call that man benevolent who is in fact useful to others, but at the same time only intends his own interest, without any ultimate desire of the good of others. If there be any benevolence at all, it must be disinterested; for the most useful action imaginable loses all appearance of benevolence, as soon as we discern that it only flowed from self-love or interest. Thus, never were any human actions more advantageous than the inventions of fire and iron, but if these were casual, or if the inventor only intended his own interest in them, there is nothing which can be called benevolent in them. Wherever then benevolence is supposed, there it is imagined disinterested and designed for the good of others. To raise benevolence, no more is required than calmly to consider any sensitive nature not pernicious to others. Gratitude arises from benefits conferred from good will on ourselves or those we love; complacence is a perception of the moral sense. Gratitude includes some complacence, and complacence still

---

[1] See Sect. i. [Not reprinted here]

raises a stronger good will than that we have toward indifferent characters, where there is no opposition of interests.

But it must be here observed that as all men have self-love as well as benevolence, these two principles may jointly excite a man to the same action, and then they are to be considered as two forces impelling the same body to motion; sometimes they conspire, sometimes are indifferent to each other, and sometimes are in some degree opposite. Thus if a man have such strong benevolence as would have produced an action without any views of self-interest, that such a man has also in view private advantage, along with public good, as the effect of his action, does no way diminish the benevolence of the action. When he would not have produced so much public good had it not been for prospect of self-interest, then the effect of self-love is to be deducted, and his benevolence is proportioned to the remainder of good, which pure benevolence would have produced. When a man's benevolence is hurtful to himself, then self-love is opposite to benevolence, and the benevolence is proportioned to the sum of the good produced added to the resistance of self-love surmounted by it. In most cases it is impossible for men to know how far their fellows are influenced by the one or other of these principles, but yet the general truth is sufficiently certain, that this is the way in which the benevolence of actions is to be computed.

IV

There are two ways in which some may deduce benevolence from self-love, the one supposing that we voluntarily bring this affection upon ourselves whenever we have an opinion that it will be for our interest to have this affection, either as it may be immediately pleasant, or may afford pleasant reflection afterwards by our moral sense, or as it may tend to procure some external reward from God or man. The other scheme alleges no such power in us of raising desire or affection of any kind by our choice or volition, but supposes our minds determined by the frame of their nature to desire whatever is apprehended as the means of any private happiness, and that the observation of the happiness of other persons, in many cases is made the necessary occasion of pleasure to the observer, as their misery is the occasion of his uneasiness: and in consequence of this connection, as soon as we have observed it, we begin to desire the happiness of others as the means of obtaining this happiness to ourselves which we expect from the contemplation of others in a happy state. They allege it to be impossible to desire either the happiness of another, or any event whatsoever, without conceiving it as the means of some happiness or pleasure to ourselves, but own at the same time that desire is not raised in us directly by any volition, but arises necessarily upon our apprehending any object or event to be conducive to our happiness.

That the former scheme is not just may appear from this general consideration, that neither benevolence nor any other affection or desire can be directly raised by volition. If they could, then we could be bribed into any affection whatsoever toward any object, even the most improper. We might raise jealousy, fear, anger, love toward any sort of persons indifferently by a hire, even as we engage men to external actions, or to the dissimulation of passions, but this every person will by his own reflection find to be impossible. The prospect of any advantage to arise to us from having any affection may indeed turn our attention to those qualities in the object which are naturally constituted the necessary causes or occasions of the advantageous affection, and if we find such qualities in the object the affection will certainly arise. Thus indirectly the prospect of advantage may tend to raise any affection, but if these qualities be not found or apprehended in the object, no volition of ours nor desire will ever raise any affection in us.

But more particularly, that desire of the good of others which we approve as virtuous, cannot be alleged to be voluntarily raised from prospect of any pleasure accompanying the affection itself. For it is plain that our benevolence is not always accompanied with pleasure; nay it is often attended with pain when the object is in distress. Desire in general is rather uneasy than pleasant. It is true, indeed, all the passions and affections justify themselves; while they continue . . . we generally approve our being thus affected on this occasion as an innocent disposition or a just one, and condemn a person who would be otherwise affected on the like occasion. So the sorrowful, the angry, the jealous, the compassionate approve their several passions on the apprehended occasion, but we should not therefore conclude that sorrow, anger, jealousy, or pity are pleasant, or chosen for their concomitant pleasure. The case is plainly thus: the frame of our nature on the occasions which move these passions determines us to be thus affected, and to approve our affection at least as innocent. Uneasiness generally attends our desires of any kind, and this sensation tends to fix our attention and to continue the desire. But the desire does not terminate upon the removal of the pain accompanying the desire, but upon some other event. The concomitant pain is what we seldom reflect upon, unless when it is very violent. Nor does any desire or affection terminate upon the pleasure which may accompany the affection; much less is it raised by an act of will with a view to obtain this pleasure.

The same reflection will show that we do not by an act of our will raise in ourselves that benevolence which we approve as virtuous, with a view to obtain future pleasures of self-approbation by our moral sense. Could we raise affections in this manner, we should be engaged to any affection by the prospect of an interest equivalent to this of self-approbation, such as wealth or sensual pleasure, which with many tempers are more powerful; and yet we universally own that that disposition to do good offices to others which is raised by these motives is not virtuous. How can we then imagine that the virtuous benevolence is brought upon us by a motive equally selfish?

But what will most effectually convince us of the truth on this point is reflection upon our own hearts, whether we have not a desire of the good of others, generally without any consideration or intention of obtaining these pleasant reflections on our own virtue. Nay, often this desire is strongest where we least imagine virtue, in natural affection toward offspring, and in gratitude to a great benefactor; the absence of which is indeed the greatest vice, but the affections themselves are not esteemed in any considerable degree virtuous. The same reflection will also convince us that these desires or affections are not produced by choice, with a view to obtain this private good.

In like manner, if no volition of ours can directly raise affections from the former prospects of interest, no more can any volition raise them from prospects of eternal rewards, or to avoid eternal punishments. The former motives differ from these only as smaller from greater, shorter from more durable. If affections could be directly raised by volition, the same consideration would make us angry at the most innocent or virtuous character, and jealous of the most faithful and affectionate, or sorrowful for the prosperity of a friend; which we all find to be impossible. The prospect of a future state may, no doubt, have a greater indirect influence, by turning our attention to the qualities in the objects naturally apt to raise the required affection, than any other consideration.[2]

[2] These several motives of interest, which, some allege, do excite us to benevolence, operate upon us in a very different manner. Prospect of external advantage of any

It is indeed probably true in fact, that those who are engaged by prospect of future rewards to do good offices to mankind, have generally the virtuous benevolence jointly exciting them to action. Because, as it may appear hereafter, benevolence is natural to mankind, and still operates where there is no opposition of apparent interest, or where any contrary apparent interest is overbalanced by a greater interest. Men conscious of this do generally approve good offices, to which motives of a future state partly excited the agent. But that the approbation is founded upon the apprehension of a disinterested desire partly exciting the agent, is plain from this, that not only obedience to an evil deity in doing mischief, or even in performing trifling ceremonies, only from hope of reward or prospect of avoiding punishment, but even obedience to a good deity only from the same motives, without any love or gratitude towards him, and with a perfect indifference about the happiness or misery of mankind, abstracting from this private interest, would meet with no approbation. We plainly see that a change of external circumstances of interest under an evil deity, without any change in the disposition of the agent, would lead him into every cruelty and inhumanity.

Gratitude toward the deity is indeed disinterested, as it will appear hereafter. This affection therefore may obtain our approbation, where it excites to action, though there were no other benevolence exciting the agent. But this case scarce occurs among men. But where the sanction of the law is the only motive of action, we could expect no more benevolence, nor no other affection, than those in one forced by the law to be curator to a person for whom he has not the least

---

kind in this life from our fellows, is only a motive to the volition of external actions immediately, and not to raise desire of the happiness of others. Now being willing to do external actions which we know do in fact promote the happiness of others, without any desire of their happiness, is not approved as virtuous; otherwise it were virtue to do a beneficent action for a bribe of money.

The prospect of rewards from the deity of future pleasures, from the self-approbation of our moral sense, or of any pleasure attending an affection itself, are only motives to us to desire or wish to have the affection of benevolence in our hearts, and consequently, if our volition could raise affections in us, these motives would make us will or choose to raise benevolent affections. But these prospects cannot be motives to us from self-love, to desire the happiness of others, for from self-love we only desire what we apprehend to be the means of private good. Now the having those affections is the means of obtaining these private goods, and not the actual happiness of others, for the pleasure of self-approbation, and divine rewards, are not obtained or lost according as others are happy or miserable, but according to the goodness of our affections. If therefore affections are not directly raised by volition or choice, prospects of future rewards or of self-approbation cannot directly raise them.

regard. The agent would so manage as to save himself harmless if he could, but would be under no concern about the success of his attempts, or the happiness of the person whom he served, provided he performed the task required by law; nor would any spectator approve this conduct.

V

The other scheme is more plausible: that benevolence is not raised by any volition upon prospect of advantage, but that we desire the happiness of others, as conceiving it necessary to procure some pleasant sensations which we expect to feel upon seeing others happy; and that for like reason we have aversion to their misery. This connection between the happiness of others and our pleasure, say they, is chiefly felt among friends, parents and children, and eminently virtuous characters. But this benevolence flows as directly from self-love as any other desire.

To show that this scheme is not true in fact, let us consider that if in our benevolence we only desired the happiness of others as the means of this pleasure to ourselves, whence is it that no man approves the desire of the happiness of others as the means of procuring wealth or sensual pleasure to ourselves? If a person had wagered concerning the future happiness of a man of such veracity that he would sincerely confess whether he were happy or not, would this wagerer's desire of the happiness of another, in order to win the wager, be approved as virtuous? If not, wherein does this desire differ from the former, except that in one case there is one pleasant sensation expected, and in the other case other sensations? For by increasing or diminishing the sum wagered, the interest in this case may be made either greater or less than that in the other.

Reflecting in our minds again will best discover the truth. Many have never thought upon this connection; nor do we ordinarily intend the obtaining of any such pleasure when we do generous offices. We all often feel delight upon seeing others happy, but during our pursuit of their happiness we have no intention of obtaining this delight. We often feel the pain of compassion, but were our sole ultimate intention or desire the freeing ourselves from this pain, would the deity offer to us either wholly to blot out all memory of the person in distress, or to take away this connection, so that we should be easy during the misery of our friend on the one hand, or on the other would relieve him from his misery, we should be as ready to choose the former way as the latter, since either of them would free us from our pain, which upon this scheme is the sole end proposed by the compassionate person. Don't we find in ourselves that our desire does not terminate upon the removal of our own pain? Were this our sole intention we would run away, shut our eyes, or divert our thoughts from the miserable object, as the readiest way of removing our pain. This we seldom do, nay we crowd about such objects, and voluntarily expose ourselves to this pain, unless calm reflection upon our inability to relieve the miserable, countermand our inclination, or some selfish affection as fear of danger overpower it.

To make this yet clearer, suppose that the deity should declare to a good man that he should be suddenly annihilated, but at this instant of his exit it should be left to his choice whether his friend, his children, or his country should be made happy or miserable for the future, when he himself could have no sense of either pleasure or pain from their state. Pray would he be any more indifferent about their state now that he neither hoped or feared anything to himself from it, than he was in any prior period of his life? Nay, is it not a pretty common opinion among us, that after our decease we know nothing of what befalls those who survive us? How comes it then that we do not lose at the approach of death all concern for our families, friends, or country? Can there be any instance given of our desiring anything only as the means of private good as violently when we know that we shall not enjoy this good many minutes, as if we expected the possession of this good for many years? Is this the way we compute the value of annuities?

How the disinterested desire of the good of others should seem inconceivable, it is hard to account. Perhaps it is owing to the attempts of some great men to give definitions of simple ideas. Desire, say they, is uneasiness, or uneasy sensation upon the absence of any good. Whereas desire is as distinct from uneasiness as volition is from sensation. Don't they themselves often speak of our desiring to remove uneasiness? Desire then is different from uneasiness, however a sense of uneasiness accompanies it, as extension does the idea of colour, which yet is a very distinct idea. Now wherein lies the impossibility of desiring the happiness of another without conceiving it as the means of obtaining anything farther, even as we desire our own happiness without farther view? If any allege that we desire our own happiness as the means of removing the uneasiness we feel in the absence of happiness, then at least the desire of removing our own uneasiness is an ultimate desire. And why may we not have other ultimate desires?

But can any being be concerned about the absence of an event which gives it no uneasiness? Perhaps superior natures desire without uneasy sensation. But what if we cannot? We may be uneasy while a desired event is in suspense, and yet not desire this event only as the means of removing this uneasiness. Nay, if we did not desire the event without view to this uneasiness, we should never have brought the uneasiness upon ourselves by desiring it. So likewise we may feel delight upon the existence of a desired event, when yet we did not desire the event only as the means of obtaining this delight, even as we often receive delight from events which we had an aversion to.

VI

. . . . . [A discussion of the purpose of the moral sense.]

VII

. . . . . [A discussion of malice.]

VIII

Having offered what may perhaps prove that neither our esteem nor benevolence is founded on self-love or views of interest, let us see if some other affections, in which virtue may be placed, do arise from self-love, such as fear, or reverence, arising from an apprehension of goodness, power, and justice. For nobody apprehends any virtue in base dread and servitude toward a powerful evil being. This is indeed the meanest selfishness. Now the same arguments which prove esteem to be disinterested will prove this honourable reverence to be so too, for it plainly arises from an apprehension of amiable qualities in the person, and love toward him, which raises an abhorrence of offending him. Could we reverence a being because it was our interest to do so, a third person might bribe us into reverence toward a being neither good nor powerful, which everyone sees to be a jest. And this we might show to be common to all other passions which have been reputed virtuous.

IX

There is one objection against disinterested good will, which occurs from considering that nothing so effectually excites our love toward rational agents as their beneficence, and especially toward ourselves, whence we are led to imagine that our love of persons, as well as irrational objects, flows entirely from self-interest. But let us here examine ourselves more narrowly. Do we only wish well to the beneficent because it is our interest to do so? Or do we choose to love them because our love is the means of procuring their bounty? If it be so, then we could indifferently love any character even to obtain the bounty of a third person, or we could be bribed by a third person to love the greatest villain heartily, as we may be bribed to external offices. Now this is plainly impossible. Nay farther, is not our good-will the consequent of bounty, and not the means of procuring it? External show, obsequiousness, and dissimulation may precede an opinion of beneficence, but real love always presupposes it, and will necessarily arise even when we expect no more, from consideration of past benefits.

Or can anyone say he only loves the beneficent as he does a field or garden, because of its advantage? His love then must cease toward one who has ruined himself in kind offices to him, when he can do him no more, as we cease to love an inanimate object which ceases to be useful. . . . Beneficence then must increase our good-will as it raises complacence, which is still attended with stronger degrees of benevolence, and hence we love even those who are beneficent to others.

In the benefits which we receive ourselves, we are more fully sensible of their value, and of the circumstances of the action, which are evidences of a generous temper in the donor, and from the good opinion we have of ourselves we are apt to look upon the kindness as better employed, than when it is bestowed on others of whom perhaps we have less favourable sentiments. It is however sufficient to remove the objection, that bounty from a donor apprehended as morally evil, or extorted by force, or conferred with some view of self-interest, will not procure real good-will; nay it may raise indignation if we suspect dissimulation of love, or a design to allure us into anything dishonourable. Whereas wisely employed bounty is always approved, and gains love to the author from all who hear of it.

If then no good-will toward persons arises from self-love or views of interest, and all virtue flows from good-will or some other affection equally disinterested, it remains that there must be some other affection than self-love, or interest, which excites us to the actions we call virtuous.

Had we no other ultimate desire but that of private advantage, we must imagine that every rational being acts only for its own advantage; and however we may call a beneficent being a good being because it acts for our advantage, yet upon this scheme we should not be apt to think there is any beneficent being in nature, or a being who acts for the good of others. Particularly, if there is no sense of excellence in public love and promoting the happiness of others, whence should this persuasion arise that the deity will make the virtuous happy? Can we prove that it is for the advantage of the deity to do so? This I fancy will be looked upon as very absurd by many who yet expect mercy and beneficence in the deity. And if there be such dispositions in the deity, where is the impossibility of some small degree of this public love in his creatures? And why must they be supposed incapable of acting but from self-love?

. . . . . [A discussion of divine reward and divine goodness in relation to our moral notions.]

X

Having removed these false springs of virtuous action, let us next establish the true one, namely some determination of our nature to study the good of others, or some instinct, antecedent to all reason from interest, which influences us to the love of others, even as the moral sense . . . determines us to approve the actions which flow from this love in ourselves or others. This disinterested affection may appear strange to men impressed with notions of self-love as the sole spring of action, from the pulpit, the schools, the systems and conversations regulated by them. But let us consider it in its strongest and simplest kinds, and when we see the possibility of it in these instances, we may easily discover its universal extent.

An honest farmer will tell you that he studies the preservation and happiness of his children, and loves them without any design of good to himself. But, say some of our philosophers, the happiness of their children gives parents pleasure, and their misery gives them pain, and therefore to obtain the former and avoid the latter, they study from self-love the good of their children. Suppose several merchants joined in partnership of their whole effects; one of them is employed abroad in managing the stock of the company; his prosperity occasions gain to all and his losses give them pain from their share in the loss. Is this then the same kind of affection with that of parents to their children? Is there the same tender personal regard? I fancy no parent will say so. In this case of merchants there is a plain conjunction of interest, but whence the conjunction of interest between the parent and child? Do the child's sensations give pleasure or pain to the parent? Is the parent hungry, thirsty, sick when his children are so? No, but his naturally implanted desire of their good and aversion to their misery, makes him be affected with joy or sorrow from their pleasures or pains. This desire then is antecedent to the conjunction of interest, and the cause of it, not the effect. It must then be disinterested.

No, says another sophist, children are parts of ourselves, and in loving them we but love ourselves in them. A very good answer! Let us carry it as far as it will go. How are they parts of ourselves? Not as a leg or an arm; we are not conscious of their sensations. But their bodies were formed from parts of ours. So is a fly or a maggot which may breed in any discharged blood or humour: very dear insects surely! There must be something else then which makes children parts of ourselves, and what is this but that affection which nature determines us to have toward them? This love makes them parts of ourselves, and therefore does not flow from their being so before. This is indeed a good metaphor, and wherever we find a determination among several rational agents to mutual love, let each individual be looked upon as a part of a great whole or system, and concern himself in the public good of it.

But a later author observes[3] that natural affection in parents is weak, till the children begin to give evidences of knowledge and affections. Mothers say they feel it strong from the very first, and yet I could wish for the destruction of his hypothesis, that what he alleges was true, as I fancy it is in some measure, though we may find in some parents an affection toward idiots. The observing of understanding and affections in children, which can make them appear moral agents, can increase love toward them without prospect of interest, for I hope this increase of love is not from prospect of advantage from the knowledge or affections of children for whom parents are still toiling, and never intend to be refunded their expenses or recom-

[3] See the *Fable of the Bees*, p. 68, 3rd Edition. [Mandeville]

pensed for their labour but in cases of extreme necessity. If then the observing a moral capacity can be the occasion of increasing love without self-interest, even from the frame of our nature; pray may not this be a foundation of weaker degrees of love where there is no preceding tie of parentage, and extend it to all mankind?

XI

And that this is so in fact will appear by considering some more distant attachments. If we observe any neighbours from whom perhaps we have received no good offices, formed into friendships, families, partnerships, and with honesty and kindness assisting each other, pray ask any mortal if he would not more desire their prosperity when their interests are no way inconsistent with his own, than their misery and ruin, and you shall find a bond of benevolence farther extended than a family and children, although the ties are not so strong. Again, suppose a person, for trade, had left his native country, and with all his kindred had settled his fortunes abroad without any view of returning, and only imagine he had received no injuries from his country. Ask such a man, would he not rather desire the prosperity of his country, or could he, now that his interests are separated from that of his nation, as readily wish that it was laid waste by tyranny or a foreign power. I fancy his answer would show us a benevolence extended beyond neighbourhoods or acquaintances. Let a man of a composed temper, out of the hurry of his private affairs, only read of the constitution of a foreign country, even in the most distant parts of the earth, and observe art, design, and a study of public good in the laws of this association, and he shall find his mind moved in their favour; he shall be contriving rectifications and amendments in their constitution, and regret any unlucky part of it which may be pernicious to their interest; he shall bewail any disaster which befalls them, and accompany all their fortunes with the affections of a friend. Now this proves benevolence to be in some degree extended to all mankind, where there is no interfering interest, which from self-love may obstruct it. And had we any notions of rational agents, capable of moral affections, in the most distant planets, our good wishes would still attend them, and we should desire their happiness. And that all these affections whether more or less extensive are properly disinterested, not even founded on any desire of that happiness we may expect in feeling their prosperous condition, may appear from this, that they would continue even at the instant of our death or entire destruction, as was already observed, Article V of this Section.

XII

. . . . . [A discussion of national love, or patriotism.]

We ought here to observe that the only reason of that apparent want of natural affection among collateral relations, is that these natural inclinations in many cases are overpowered by self-love where there happens any opposition of interests; but where this does not happen, we shall find all mankind under its influence, though with different degrees of strength, according to the nearer or more remote relations they stand in to each other, and according as the natural affection of benevolence is joined with and strengthened by esteem, gratitude, compassion, or other kind affections, or on the contrary, weakened by displicence, anger, or envy.

DAVID HUME

Our Obligation to Virtue

~~~~~~

Having explained the moral *approbation* attending merit or virtue, there remains nothing but briefly to consider our interested *obligation* to it, and to inquire whether every man, who has any regard to his own happiness and welfare, will not best find his account in the practice of every moral duty. If this can be clearly ascertained from the foregoing theory, we shall have the satisfaction to reflect, that we have advanced principles, which not only, it is hoped, will stand the test of reasoning and inquiry, but may contribute to the amendment of men's lives, and their improvement in morality and social virtue. And though the philosophical truth of any proposition by no means depends on its tendency to promote the interests of society; yet a man has but a bad grace, who delivers a theory, however true, which, he must confess, leads to a practice dangerous and pernicious. Why rake into those corners of nature which spread a nuisance all around? Why dig up the pestilence from the pit in which it is buried? The ingenuity of your researches may be admired, but your systems will be detested; and mankind will agree, if they cannot refute them, to sink them, at least, in eternal silence and oblivion. Truths which are *pernicious* to society, if any such there be, will yield to errors which are salutary and *advantageous*.

But what philosophical truths can be more advantageous to society, than those here delivered, which represent virtue in all her genuine and most engaging charms, and makes us approach her with ease,

---

* From *An Enquiry Concerning the Principles of Morals,* Section IX, Part II. First published 1751.

familiarity, and affection? The dismal dress falls off, with which many divines, and some philosophers, have covered her; and nothing appears but gentleness, humanity, beneficence, affability; nay, even at proper intervals, play, frolic, and gaiety. She talks not of useless austerities and rigours, suffering and self-denial. She declares that her sole purpose is to make her votaries and all mankind, during every instant of their existence, if possible, cheerful and happy; nor does she ever willingly part with any pleasure but in hopes of ample compensation in some other period of their lives. The sole trouble which she demands, is that of just calculation, and a steady preference of the greater happiness. And if any austere pretenders approach her, enemies to joy and pleasure, she either rejects them as hypocrites and deceivers; or, if she admit them in her train, they are ranked, however, among the least favoured of her votaries.

And, indeed, to drop all figurative expression, what hopes can we ever have of engaging mankind to a practice which we confess full of austerity and rigour? Or what theory of morals can ever serve any useful purpose, unless it can show, by a particular detail, that all the duties which it recommends, are also the true interest of each individual? The peculiar advantage of the foregoing system seems to be, that it furnishes proper mediums for that purpose.

That the virtues which are immediately *useful* or *agreeable* to the person possessed of them, are desirable in a view to self-interest, it would surely be superfluous to prove. Moralists, indeed, may spare themselves all the pains which they often take in recommending these duties. To what purpose collect arguments to evince that temperance is advantageous, and the excesses of pleasure hurtful, when it appears that these excesses are only denominated such, because they are hurtful; and that, if the unlimited use of strong liquors, for instance, no more impaired health or the faculties of mind and body than the use of air or water, it would not be a whit more vicious or blameable?

It seems equally superfluous to prove, that the *companionable* virtues of good manners and wit, decency and genteelness, are more desirable than the contrary qualities. Vanity alone, without any other consideration, is a sufficient motive to make us wish for the possession of these accomplishments. No man was ever willingly deficient in this particular. All our failures here proceed from bad education, want of capacity, or a perverse and unpliable disposition. Would you have your company coveted, admired, followed; rather than hated, despised, avoided? Can any one seriously deliberate in the case? As no enjoyment is sincere, without some reference to company and society; so no society can be agreeable, or even tolerable, where a man feels his presence unwelcome, and discovers all around him symptoms of disgust and aversion.

But why, in the greater society or confederacy of mankind, should not the case be the same as in particular clubs and companies? Why is it more doubtful, that the enlarged virtues of humanity, generosity, beneficence, are desirable with a view of happiness and self-interest, than the limited endowments of ingenuity and politeness? Are we apprehensive lest those social affections interfere, in a greater and more immediate degree than any other pursuits, with private utility, and cannot be gratified, without some important sacrifice of honour and advantage? If so, we are but ill-instructed in the nature of the human passions, and are more influenced by verbal distinctions than by real differences.

Whatever contradiction may vulgarly be supposed between the *selfish* and *social* sentiments or dispositions, they are really no more opposite than selfish and ambitious, selfish and revengeful, selfish and vain. It is requisite that there be an original propensity of some kind, in order to be a basis to self-love, by giving a relish to the objects of its pursuit; and none more fit for this purpose than benevolence or humanity. The goods of fortune are spent in one gratification or another: the miser who accumulates his annual income, and lends it out at interest, has really spent it in the gratification of his avarice. And it would be difficult to show why a man is more a loser by a generous action, than by any other method of expense; since the utmost which he can attain by the most elaborate selfishness, is the indulgence of some affection.

Now if life, without passion, must be altogether insipid and tiresome; let a man suppose that he has full power of modelling his own disposition, and let him deliberate what appetite or desire he would choose for the foundation of his happiness and enjoyment. Every affection, he would observe, when gratified by success, gives a satisfaction proportioned to its force and violence; but besides this advantage, common to all, the immediate feeling of benevolence and friendship, humanity and kindness, is sweet, smooth, tender, and agreeable, independent of all fortune and accidents. These virtues are besides attended with a pleasing consciousness or remembrance, and keep us in humour with ourselves as well as others; while we retain the agreeable reflection of having done our part towards mankind and society.

And though all men show a jealousy of our success in the pursuits of avarice and ambition; yet are we almost sure of their good will and good wishes, so long as we persevere in the paths of virtue, and employ ourselves in the execution of generous plans and purposes. What other passion is there where we shall find so many advantages united; an agreeable sentiment, a pleasing consciousness, a good reputation? But of these truths, we may observe, men are, of themselves, pretty much convinced; nor are they deficient in their duty to society, because they would not wish to be generous, friendly, and humane; but because they do not feel themselves such.

Treating vice with the greatest candour, and making it all possible concessions, we must acknowledge that there is not, in any instance, the smallest pretext for giving it the preference above virtue, with a view of self-interest; except, perhaps, in the case of justice, where a man, taking things in a certain light, may often seem to be a loser by his integrity. And though it is allowed that, without a regard to property, no society could subsist; yet according to the imperfect way in which human affairs are conducted, a sensible knave, in particular incidents, may think that an act of iniquity or infidelity will make a considerable addition to his fortune, without causing any considerable breach in the social union and confederacy. That *honesty is the best policy,* may be a good general rule, but is liable to many exceptions; and he, it may perhaps be thought, conducts himself with most wisdom, who observes the general rule, and takes advantage of all the exceptions.

I must confess that, if a man think that this reasoning much requires an answer, it would be a little difficult to find any which will to him appear satisfactory and convincing. If his heart rebel not against such pernicious maxims, if he feel no reluctance to the thoughts of villainy or baseness, he has indeed lost a considerable motive to virtue; and we may expect that this practice will be answerable to his speculation. But in all ingenuous natures, the antipathy to treachery and roguery is too strong to be counterbalanced by any views of profit or pecuniary advantage. Inward peace of mind, consciousness of integrity, a satisfactory review of our own conduct; these are circumstances, very requisite to happiness, and will be cherished and cultivated by every honest man, who feels the importance of them.

Such a one has, besides, the frequent satisfaction of seeing knaves, with all their pretended cunning and abilities, betrayed by their own maxims; and while they purpose to cheat with moderation and secrecy, a tempting incident occurs, nature is frail, and they give into the snare; whence they can never extricate themselves, without a total loss of reputation, and the forfeiture of all future trust and confidence with mankind.

But were they ever so secret and successful, the honest man, if he has any tincture of philosophy, or even common observation and reflection, will discover that they themselves are, in the end, the greatest dupes, and have sacrificed the invaluable enjoyment of a character, with themselves at least, for the acquisition of worthless toys and gewgaws. How little is requisite to supply the *necessities* of nature? And in a view to *pleasure,* what comparison between the unbought satisfaction of conversation, society, study, even health and the common beauties of nature, but above all the peaceful reflection on one's own conduct; what comparison, I say, between these and the feverish, empty amusements of luxury and expense? These natural pleasures, indeed, are really without price; both because they are below all price in their attainment, and above it in their enjoyment.

H. A. PRICHARD

Duty and Interest

∿∿∿∿∿∿∿∿∿∿∿∿∿∿∿∿∿∿∿∿∿∿∿∿∿∿∿

. . . . . [Opening paragraph of the lecture.]

A general but not very critical familiarity with the literature of Moral
Philosophy might well lead to the remark that much of it is occupied
with attempts either to prove that there is a necessary connexion between duty and interest or in certain cases even to exhibit the connexion as something self-evident. And the remark, even if not strictly
accurate, plainly has some truth in it. It might be said in support that
Plato's treatment of justice in the *Republic* is obviously such an attempt, and that even Aristotle in the *Ethics* tries to do the same thing,
disguised and weak though his attempt may be. As modern instances,
Butler and Hutcheson might be cited; and to these might be added
not only Kant, in whom we should perhaps least expect to find such
a proof, but also Green.

When we read the attempts referred to we naturally cannot help in
a way wishing them to succeed; and we might express our wish in the
form that we should all like to be able to believe that honesty is the
best policy. At the same time we also cannot help feeling that somehow they are out of place, so that the real question is not so much
whether they are successful, but whether they ought ever to have been
made. And my object is to try to justify our feeling of dissatisfaction
by considering what these attempts really amount to, and more es-

* From Prichard's inaugural lecture, *Duty and Interest,* as White's Professor of
Moral Philosophy, 1928. Excerpted and reprinted with the kind permission of the
Clarendon Press, Oxford.

pecially what they amount to in view of the ideas which have prompted them. For this purpose, the views of Plato, Butler, and Green, may, I think, be taken as representative, and I propose to concentrate attention on them.

One preliminary remark is necessary. It must not be assumed that what are thus grouped together as attempts either to prove or to exhibit the self-evidence of a connexion between duty and interest are properly described by this phrase, or even that they are all attempts to do one and the same thing. And in particular I shall try to show that the attempts so described really consist of endeavours, based on mutually inconsistent presuppositions, to do one or another of three different things.

On a casual acquaintance with the *Republic*, we should probably say without hesitation that, apart from its general metaphysics, what it is concerned with is justice and injustice, and that, with regard to justice and injustice, its main argument is an elaborate attempt, continued to the end of the book, to show in detail that if we look below the surface and consider what just actions really consist in and also the nature of the soul, and, to a minor degree, the nature of the world in which we have to act, it will become obvious, in spite of appearance to the contrary, that it is by acting justly that we shall really gain or become happy.

Further, if we were to ask ourselves, "What are Plato's words for right and wrong?"—and plainly the question is fair—we should have in the end to give as the true answer what at first would strike us as a paradox. We should have to allow that Plato's words for right and wrong are not to be found in such words as χρή or δεῖ and their contraries, as in χρή δίκαιον εἶναι or ὅντινα τρόπον χρή ζῆν, where the subject is implied by the context to be τὸν μέλλοντα μακάριον ἔσεσθαι, but in δίκαιον and ἄδικον themselves. When he says of some action that it is δίκαιον, that is his way of saying that it is right, or a duty, or an act which we are morally bound to do. When he says that it is ἄδικον, that is his way of saying that it is wrong. And in the sense in which we use the terms "justice" and "injustice," it is less accurate to describe what Plato is discussing as justice and injustice than as right and wrong. Our previous statement, therefore, might be put in the form that Plato is mainly occupied in the *Republic* with attempting to show it is by doing our duty, or what we are morally bound to do, that we shall become happy.

This is the account of his object which we are more particularly inclined to give if we chiefly have in mind what Socrates in the fourth Book is made to offer as the solution of the main problem. But this solution is preceded by an elaborate statement of the problem itself, put into the mouth of Glaucon and Adeimantus; and if we consider this statement closely, we find ourselves forced to make a substantial revision of this account of Plato's object. Glaucon and Adeimantus make it quite clear that whatever it is that they are asking Socrates to show about what they refer to as justice, their object in doing so is to obtain a refutation of what may be called the Sophistic theory of morality. Consequently, if we judge by what Glaucon and Adeimantus say, whatever Plato is trying to prove must be something which Plato would consider as affording a refutation of the Sophistic theory. But what is this theory as represented by Plato? It almost goes without saying that in the first instance men's attitude towards matters of right and wrong is an unquestioning one. However they have come to do so, and in particular whether their doing so is due to teaching or not, they think, and think without having any doubt, that certain actions are right and that certain others are wrong. No doubt in special cases, they may be doubtful; but, as regards some actions, they have no doubt at all, though to say this is not the same as to say that they are certain. But there comes a time when men are stirred out of this unquestioning frame of mind; and in particular the Sophists, as Plato represents them, were thus stirred by the reflection that the actions which men in ordinary life thought right, such as paying a debt, helping a friend, obeying the government, however they differed in other respects, at least agreed in bringing directly a definite loss to the agent. This reflection led them to wonder whether men were right in thinking these actions duties, that is, whether they thought so truly. Then, having failed to find indirect advantages of these actions which would more than compensate for the direct loss, that is, such advantages as are found in what we call prudent actions, they drew the conclusion that these actions cannot really be duties at all, and that therefore what may roughly be described as the moral convictions which they and others held in ordinary life were one gigantic mistake or illusion. Finally, they clinched this conclusion by offering something which they represented as an account of the origin of justice, but which is really an account of how they and others came to make the mistake of thinking these actions just, that is, right.

This is the theory which on Plato's own showing he wants to refute. It is a theory about certain actions, and, on his own showing, what he has to maintain is the opposite theory about these same actions. But how, if our language is to be accurate, should these actions be referred to? Should they be referred to as *just,* that is, right, actions, or should they be referred to as those actions which in ordinary life we *think* just, that is, right? The difference, though at first it may seem unimportant, is really vital. In the unquestioning attitude of ordinary life we must either be *knowing* that certain actions are right or not knowing that they are right, but doing something else for which "*thinking* them right" is perhaps the least unsatisfactory phrase. There is no possibility of what might be suggested as a third alternative, namely, that our activity is one of thinking, which in instances where we are thinking truly is also one of knowing. For, as Plato realized, to think truly is not to know, and to discover that in some particular case we were thinking truly is not to discover that in doing so we were knowing. Moreover, when we are what is described as reflecting on the activity involved in our unquestioning attitude of mind, we are inevitably thinking of it as having a certain definite character, and, in so thinking of it, we must inevitably be implying either that the activity is one of knowing or that it is not. For we must think of this attitude either as one of thinking, or as one of knowing, and if we think of it as one of thinking, we imply that it is not one of knowing, and *vice versa.* In fact, however we think of the activity, we are committed one way or the other. Now the Sophists clearly implied that this unquestioning attitude is one of thinking and not one of knowing; for it would not have been sense to maintain that those actions which in ordinary life we know to be right are really not right. Their theory, then, must be expressed by saying that those actions which in ordinary life we think, and so do not know, to be right are not really right. Consequently Plato also, since he regards this as the theory to be refuted, is implying that in ordinary life we think, and do not know, that certain actions are right, and that, to this extent, he agrees with the Sophists. And for this reason, if we are to state accurately the problem which he is setting himself, we must represent it as referring not to *just* actions but to those actions which he and others in ordinary life *think* just.

It is clear then that when Plato states through the medium of Glaucon and Adeimantus the problem which he has to solve, he is guilty of an inaccuracy, which, though it may easily escape notice, is important. For Glaucon and Adeimantus persistently refer to the actions of which they ask Socrates to reconsider the profitableness as just and unjust actions, whereas they should have referred to them as the actions which men in ordinary life think just and unjust.

I shall now take it as established that when we judge from Plato's own statement of his problem, worked out as it is by reference to the Sophists, we have to allow that he is presupposing that ordinarily we do not know but think that certain actions are right and that he is thinking of his task as that of having to vindicate the truth of these thoughts against the Sophists' objection. And this is what must be really meant when it is said that Plato's object is to vindicate *morality* against the Sophistic view of it, for here "morality" can only be a loose phrase for our ordinary moral thoughts or convictions.

Glaucon and Adeimantus, however, do not simply ask Socrates to refute the Sophistic view; they ask him to do so in a particular way, which they imply to be the only way possible, namely, by showing that if we go deeper than the Sophists and consider not merely the gains and losses of which they take account, namely, gains and losses really due to the reputation for doing what men think just and unjust, but also those which these actions directly bring to the man's own soul, it will become obvious that it is by doing what we think just that we shall really gain. And so far as the rest of the *Republic* is an attempt to satisfy this request, this must be what it is an attempt to show.

Now on a first reading of the *Republic*, it is not likely to strike us that there is anything peculiar or unnatural about this part of the request. Just because Plato takes for granted that this is the only way to refute the Sophists, we are apt in reading him to do the same, especially as our attention is likely to be fully taken up by the effort to follow Plato's thought. But if we can manage to consider Plato's endeavour to refute the Sophists with detachment, what strikes us most is not his dissent from their view concerning the comparative profitableness of the actions which men think just and unjust—great, of course, as his dissent is—but the identity of principle underlying the position of both. The Sophists in reaching their conclusion were presupposing that for an action to be really just, it must be advantageous; for it was solely on this ground that they concluded that what we ordinarily think just is not really just. And what in the end most strikes us is that at no stage in the *Republic* does Plato take the line, or even suggest as a possibility, that the very presupposition of the Sophists' arguments is false, and that therefore the question whether some action which men think just will be profitable to the agent has really nothing to do with the question whether it is right, so that Thrasymachus may enlarge as much as he pleases on the losses incurred by doing the actions we think just without getting any nearer to showing that it is a mere mistake to think them just. Plato, on the contrary, instead of urging that the Sophistic contention that men lose by doing what they think just is simply irrelevant to the question whether these actions are just, throughout treats this contention with the utmost seriousness; and he implies that unless the Sophists can be met on their own ground by being shown that, in spite of appearances to the contrary, these actions will really be for the good of the agent, their conclusion that men's moral convictions are mere conventions must be allowed to stand. He therefore, equally with the Sophists, is implying that it is impossible for any action to be really just, that is a duty, unless it is for the advantage of the agent.

This presupposition, however, as soon as we consider it, strikes us as a paradox. For though we may find ourselves quite unable to state what it is that does render an action a duty, we ordinarily think that, whatever it is, it is not conduciveness to our advantage; and we also think that though an action which is a duty may be advantageous it need not be so. And while we may not be surprised to find the presupposition in the Sophists, whose moral convictions are represented as at least shallow, we are surprised to find it in Plato, whose moral earnestness is that of a prophet. At first, no doubt, we may try to mitigate our surprise by emphasizing the superior character of the advantages which Plato had in mind. But to do this does not really help. For after all, whatever be meant by the "superiority" of the advantages of which Plato was thinking, it is simply as advantages that Plato uses them to show that the actions from which they follow are right.

Yet the presupposition cannot simply be dismissed as obviously untrue. For one thing, any view of Plato's is entitled to respect. For another, there appear to be moments in which we find the presupposition in ourselves. There appear to be moments in which, feeling acutely the weight of our responsibilities, we say to ourselves, "Why *should* I do all these actions, since after all it is others and not I who will gain by doing them?"

Moreover, there at least seems to be the same presupposition in the mind of those preachers whose method of exhortation consists in appeal to rewards. When, for instance, they commend a certain mode of life on the ground that it will bring about a peace of mind which the pursuit of worldly things cannot yield, they appear to be giving a resulting gain as the reason why we ought to do certain actions, and therefore to be implying that in general it is advantageousness to ourselves which renders an action one which we are bound to do. In fact the only difference between the view of such preachers and that of the Sophists seems to be that the former, in view of their theological beliefs, think that the various actions which we think right will have certain specific rewards the existence of which the Sophists would deny. And the identity of principle underlying their view becomes obvious if the preacher goes on to maintain, as some have done, that if he were to cease to believe in heaven, he would cease to believe in right and wrong. Again, among philosophers, Plato is far from being alone in presupposing that an action, to be right, must be for the good or advantage of the agent. To go no further afield than a commentator on Plato, we may cite Cook Wilson, whose claim to respect no one in Oxford will deny, and who was, to my mind, one of the acutest of thinkers. In lecturing on the *Republic* he used to insist that when men begin to reflect on morality they not only demand, but also have the right to demand, that any action which is right must justify its claim to be right by being shown to be for their own good; and he used to maintain that Plato took the right and only way of justifying our moral convictions, by showing that the actions which we think right are for the good of the society of which we are members, and that at the same time the good of that society *is* our good, as becomes obvious when the nature of our good is properly understood.

Moreover Plato, if he has been rightly interpreted, does not stand alone among the historical philosophers in presupposing the existence of a necessary connexion between duty and interest. At least Butler, whose thoughtfulness is incontestable, is with him. In fact in this matter he seems at first sight only distinguished from Plato by going further. In a well-known passage in the eleventh *Sermon,* after stating that religion always addresses itself to self-love when reason presides in a man, he says: "Let it be allowed, though virtue or moral rectitude does indeed consist in affection to and pursuit of what is right and good, as such; yet that when we sit down in a cool hour, we can neither justify to ourselves this or any other pursuit, till we are convinced that it will be for our happiness, or at least not contrary to it."

Here, if we take the phrase "justify an action to ourselves" in its natural sense of come to know that we ought to do the action by apprehending a reason why we ought to do it, we seem to have to allow that Butler is maintaining that in the last resort there is one, and only one, reason why we ought to do anything whatever, namely, the conduciveness of the action to our happiness or advantage. And if this is right, Butler is not simply presupposing but definitely asserting a necessary connexion between duty and interest, and going further than Plato by maintaining that it is actually conduciveness to the agent's interest which renders an action right.

Nevertheless, when we seriously face the view that unless an action be advantageous, it cannot really be a duty, we are forced both to abandon it and also to allow that even if it were true, it would not enable us to vindicate the truth of our ordinary moral convictions.

It is easy to see that if we persist in maintaining that an action, to be right, must be advantageous, we cannot stop short of maintaining that it is precisely advantageousness and nothing else which renders an action right. It is impossible to rest in the intermediate position that, though it is something other than advantageousness which renders an action right, nevertheless an action cannot really be right unless it be advantageous. For if it be held that an action is rendered a duty by the possession of some other characteristic, then the only chance of showing that a right action must necessarily be advantageous must consist either in showing that actions having this other characteristic must necessarily be advantageous or in showing that the very fact that we are bound to do some action, irrespectively of what renders us bound to do it, necessitates that we shall gain by doing it. But the former alternative is not possible. By "an action" in this context must be meant an activity by which a man brings certain things about. And if the characteristic of an action which renders it right does not consist in its bringing about an advantage to the agent, which we may symbolize by "an X," it must consist in bringing about something of a different kind, which we may symbolize by "a Y," say, for the sake of argument, an advantage to a friend, or an improvement in someone's character. There can, however, be no means of showing that when we bring about something of one kind, for example, a Y, we must necessarily bring about something of a different kind, for example, an X. The nature of an action as being the bringing about a Y cannot require, that is, necessitate, it to be also the bringing about an X, that is, to have an X as its consequence; and whether bringing about a Y in any particular case will bring about an X will depend not only on the nature of the act as being the bringing about a Y, but also on the nature of the agent and of the special circumstances in which the act is done. It may be objected that we could avoid the necessity of having to admit this on one condition, namely that we knew the existence of a Divine Being who would intervene, where necessary, with rewards. But this knowledge would give the required conclusion only on one condition, namely, that this knowledge was really the knowledge that the fact of being bound to do some action itself necessitated the existence of such a Being as a consequence. For if it were the knowledge of the existence of such a Being based on other grounds, it would not enable us to know that the very fact that some action was the bringing about a Y *itself* necessitated that it would also be the bringing about an X, that is, some advantage to the agent. No doubt if we could successfully maintain not only that an action's being the bringing about a Y necessitated its being a duty, but also that an action's being a duty necessitated as a consequence the existence of a Being who would reward it, we could show that an action's being the bringing about a Y necessitated its being rewarded. But to maintain this is really to fall back on the second alternative; and this alternative will, on consideration, turn out no more tenable than the first. It cannot successfully be maintained that the very fact that some action is a duty necessitates, not that the agent will *deserve* to gain—a conclusion which it is of course easy to draw, but that he *will* gain, unless it can be shown that this very fact necessitates, as a consequence, the existence of a being who will, if necessary, reward it. And this obviously cannot be done.

No doubt Kant maintained, and thought it possible to prove, not indeed that the obligation to do *any* action, but that the obligation to do a *certain* action, involves as a consequence that men will gain by carrying out their obligations.[1] In effect he assumed that we know that one of our duties is to endeavour to advance the realization of the highest good, namely, a state of affairs in which men both act morally, that is, do what they think right, purely from the thought that it is right, and at the same time attain the happiness which in consequence they deserve. And he maintained that from this knowledge we can conclude *first* that the realization of the highest good must be possible, that is, that so far as we succeed in making ourselves and others more moral, we and others will become proportionately happier; and *second* that, therefore, since the realization of this conse-

---

[1] Kant, *Critique of Practical Reason* (Book II, Chap. ii, § 5).

quence requires, as the cause of the world in which we have to act, a supreme intelligent will which renders the world such as to cause happiness in proportion to morality, there must be such a cause. But his argument, although it has a certain plausibility, involves an inversion. If, as he rightly implied, an action can only be a duty if we *can* do it, and if we can only even in a slight degree advance a state of affairs in which a certain degree of morality is combined with a corresponding degree of happiness, *provided* there be such a supreme cause of nature, it will be impossible to know, as he assumed that we do, that to advance this state of affairs is a duty, *until* we know that there is such a supreme cause. So far, therefore, from the connexion which he thought to exist between right action and happiness being demonstrable from our knowledge of the duty in question, knowledge of the duty, if attainable at all, will itself require independent knowledge of the connexion.

We are therefore forced to allow that in order to maintain that for an action to be right, it must be advantageous, we have to maintain that advantageousness is what renders an action right. But this is obviously something which no one is going to maintain, if he considers it seriously. For he will be involved in maintaining not only that it is a duty to do whatever is for our advantage, but that this is our only duty. And the fatal objection to maintaining this is simply that no one actually thinks it.

Moreover, as it is easy to see, if we were to maintain this, our doing so, so far from helping us, would render it impossible for us to vindicate the truth of our ordinary moral convictions. For wherever in ordinary life we think of some particular action as a duty, we are not simply thinking of it as right, but also thinking of its rightness as constituted by the possession of some definite characteristic other than that of being advantageous to the agent. For we think of the action as a particular action *of a certain kind,* the nature of which is indicated by general words contained in the phrase by which we refer to the action, that is, *"fulfilling* the *promise* which we made to X yesterday," or *"looking after* our *parents."* And we do not think of the action as right *blindly,* that is, irrespectively of the special character which we think the act to possess; rather we think of it as being right in virtue of possessing a particular characteristic of the kind indicated by the phrase by which we refer to it. Thus in thinking of our keeping our promise to X as a duty, we are thinking of the action as rendered a duty by its being the keeping of our promise. This is obvious because we should never, for instance, think of using as an illustration of an action which we think right, telling *X* what we think of him, or meeting him in London, even though we thought that if we thought of these actions in certain other aspects we should think them right. Consequently if we were to maintain that conduciveness to the agent's advantage is what renders an action right, we should have to allow that any of our ordinary moral convictions, so far from being capable of vindication, is simply a mistake, as being really the conviction that some particular action is rendered a duty by its possession of some characteristic which is not that of being advantageous.

The general moral is obvious. Certain arguments, which would ordinarily be referred to as arguments designed to prove that doing what is right will be for the good of the agent, turn out to be attempts to prove that the actions which in ordinary life we think right will be for the good of the agent. There is really no need to consider in detail whether these arguments are successful; for even if they are successful, they will do nothing to prove what they are intended to prove, namely, that the moral convictions of our ordinary life are true. Further the attempts arise simply out of a presupposition which on reflection anyone is bound to abandon, namely, that conduciveness to personal advantage is what renders an action a duty. What Plato should have said to the Sophists is: "You may be right in maintaining that in our ordinary unquestioning frame of mind we do not know, but only think, that certain actions are right. These thoughts or convictions may or may not be true. But they cannot be false for the reason which you give. You do nothing whatever to show that they are false by urging that the actions in question are disadvantageous; and I should do nothing to show that they are true, if I were to show that these actions are after all advantageous. Your real mistake lies in presupposing throughout that advantageousness is what renders an action a duty. If you will only reflect you will abandon this presupposition altogether, and then you yourself will withdraw your arguments."

I next propose to contend that there is also to be found both in Plato and Butler, besides this attempt to show that actions which we *think* right will be for our good, another attempt which neither of them distinguishes from it and which *is* accurately described as an attempt to prove that *right* actions will be for our good. I also propose to ask what is the idea which led them to make the attempt, and to consider whether it is tenable.

When Plato raises the question "What is justice?" he does not mean by the question "What do we *mean* by the terms 'justice' and 'just,' or, in our language, 'duty' and 'right'?," as we might ask "What do we *mean* by the term 'optimism,' or again, by the phrase 'living thing'?" And as a matter of fact if he had meant this, he would have been raising what was only verbally, and not really, a question at all, in that any attempt to ask it would have implied that the answer was already known and that therefore there was nothing to ask. He means "What is the characteristic the possession of which by an action necessitates that the action is just, that is, an act which it is our duty, or which we ought, to do?" In short he means "What renders a just or right action, just or right?"

Now this question really means "What is the characteristic common to particular just acts which renders them just?" And for anyone even to *ask* this question is to imply that he already *knows* what particular actions are just. For even to *ask* "What is the character common to certain things?" is to imply that we already *know* what the things are of which we are wanting to find the common character. Equally, of course, any attempt to *answer* the question has the same implication. For such an attempt can only consist in considering the particular actions which we know to be just and attempting to discover what is the characteristic common to them all, the vague apprehension of which has led us to apprehend them to be just. Plato therefore, both in representing Socrates as raising with his hearers the question "What is justice?" and also in representing them all as attempting to answer it, is implying, whether he is aware that he is doing so or not, that they all know what particular acts are, and what particular acts are not, just. If on the contrary what he had presupposed was that the members of the dialogue think, instead of knowing, that certain actions are just, his question—whether he had expressed it thus or not—would really have been, not "What *is* justice?" but "What do we *think* that justice is?"; or, more clearly, not "What renders an act just?" but "What do we think renders an act just?" But in that case an answer, whatever its character, would have thrown no light on the question "What is justice?"; and apart from this, he is plainly not asking "What do we *think* that justice is?"

As has been pointed out, however, the view which Plato attributes to the Sophists presupposes that ordinary mankind, which of course includes the members of the dialogue, only thinks and does not know that certain actions are just. Therefore, when Plato introduces this view as requiring refutation and, in doing so, represents the members of the dialogue as not questioning the presupposition, he ought in consistency to have made someone point out that in view of the acceptance of this presupposition Socrates' original question "What is justice?" required to be amended to the question "What do we think that justice is?" But Plato does not do so. In the present context the significant fact is that even after he has introduced the view of the Sophists he still represents the question to be answered as being "What is justice?" and therefore still implies that the members of the dialogue know what is just in particular. Even in making Glaucon and Adeimantus ask Socrates to refute the Sophists, what he, inconsistently, makes them ask Socrates to exhibit the nature of is not the acts which men think just but just acts. And when Plato in the fourth book goes on to give Socrates' answer, which, of course, is intended to express the truth, he in the same way represents Socrates as offering, and the others as accepting, an account of the nature of *just* acts, namely, that they consist in conferring those benefits on society which a man's nature renders him best suited to confer, and then makes Socrates argue in detail that it is *just* action which will be profitable. In doing so he is of course implying, inconsistently with the implication of his treatment of the Sophists' view, that the members of the dialogue, and therefore also mankind in ordinary life, *know* what is just in particular. For in the end the statement "Justice is conferring certain benefits on society" can only mean that conferring these benefits is the characteristic the vague apprehension of which in certain actions leads us to know or apprehend them to be just; and the acceptance of this statement by the members of the dialogue must be understood as expressing their recognition that this characteristic is the common character of the particular acts which they already know to be just.

It therefore must be allowed that, although to do so is inconsistent with his view of the way in which the Sophistic theory has to be refuted, Plato is in the fourth book (and of course the same admission must be made about the eighth and ninth) endeavouring to prove that *just*, that is *right*, action, will be for the good or advantage of the agent.

Given that this is what Plato wants to prove in the fourth book, the general nature of what he conceives to be the proof is obvious. His idea is that if we start with the knowledge of what right actions consist in, namely, to put it shortly, serving the state, and then consider what the effects of these and other actions will be by taking into account not only the circumstances in which we are placed, but also the various desires of the human soul and the varying amounts of satisfaction to which the realization of these objects will give rise, it will be obvious that it is by doing what is right that, at any rate in the long run, we shall become happy.

Now a particular proof of this kind, such as Plato's, naturally provokes two comments. The first is that there is no need to consider its success in detail, since we know on general grounds that it must fail. For it can only be shown that actions characterized by being the bringing about things of one kind, in this case benefits to society, will always have as their consequence things of another kind, in this case elements of happiness in the agent, provided that we can prove, as Plato makes no attempt to do, the existence of a Being who will intervene to introduce suitable rewards where they are needed. The second is that though the establishment of this conclusion, whether with or without the help of theological arguments, would be of the greatest benefit to us, since we should all be better off if we knew it to be true, yet it differs from the establishment of the corresponding conclusion against the Sophists in that it would throw no light whatever on the question "What is our duty in detail, and why? " And this second comment naturally raises the question which seems to be the important one to ask in this connexion, namely, "*Why* did Plato think it important to prove that right action would benefit the agent?"

The explanation obviously cannot be simply, or even mainly, that the combination in Plato of a desire to do what is right and of a desire to become happy led him to try to satisfy himself that by doing what is right he would be, so to say, having it both ways. The main explanation must lie in a quite different direction. There is no escaping the conclusion that when Plato sets himself to consider not what *should,* but what *actually does* as a matter of fact, lead a man to act, when he is acting deliberately, and not merely in consequence of an impulse, he answers "The desire for some good to himself and that only." In other words we have to allow that, according to Plato, a man pursues whatever he pursues simply as a good to himself, that is, really as something which will give him satisfaction, or, as perhaps we ought to say, as an element in what will render him happy. In the *Republic* this view comes to light in the sixth book. He there speaks of τὸ ἀγαθόν as that which every soul pursues and for the sake of which it does all it does, divining that it is something but being perplexed and unable to grasp adequately what it is; and he goes on to say of things that are good (τὰ ἀγαθά) that while many are ready to do and to obtain and to be what only *seems* just, even if it is not, no one is content with obtaining what *seems* good, but endeavours to obtain what is *really* good. It might be objected that these statements do not bear out the view which is attributed to Plato, since Plato certainly did not mean by an ἀγαθόν a source of satisfaction or happiness to oneself. But to this the answer is that wherever Plato uses the term ἀγαθά (goods) elsewhere in the *Republic* and in other dialogues, such as the *Philebus*, the context always shows that he means by a good a good to oneself, and, this being so, he must really be meaning by an ἀγαθόν, a source of satisfaction, or perhaps, more generally, a source of happiness. The view, however, emerges most clearly in the Gorgias, where Plato, in order to show that rhetoricians and tyrants do not do what they really wish to do, maintains that in all actions alike, and even when we kill a man or despoil him of his goods, we do what we do because we think it will be better for us to do so.

Now if we grant, as we must, that Plato thought this, we can find in the admission a natural explanation of Plato's desire to prove that just action will be advantageous. For plainly he passionately wanted men to do what is right, and if he thought that it was only desire of some good to themselves which moved them in all deliberate action, it would be natural, and indeed necessary, for him to think that if men are to be induced to do what is just, the only way to induce them is to convince them that thereby they will gain or become better off.

. . . . . [Discussion of Butler's arguments.]

I propose now to take it as established (1) that both Plato and Butler in a certain vein of thought are really endeavouring to prove that right actions, in the strict sense of "right actions," will be for the agent's advantage; (2) that their reason for doing so lies in the conviction that even where we know some action to be right, we shall not do it unless we think that it will be for our advantage; and (3) that behind this conviction lies the conviction of which it is really a corollary, namely, the conviction that desire for some good to oneself is the only motive of deliberate action.

But are these convictions true? For if it can be shown that they are not, then at least Plato and Butler's reason for trying to prove the advantageousness of right action will have disappeared.

The conviction that even where we know some action to be right, we shall not do it unless we think we shall be the better off for doing it, of course, strikes us as a paradox. At first no doubt we are apt to misstate the paradox. We are apt to say that the conviction, implying as it does that we only act out of self-interest, really implies that it is impossible for us to do anything which we ought to do at all, since if we did some action out of self-interest we could not have done anything which was a duty. But to say this is to make the mistake of thinking that the motive with which we do an action can possibly have something to do with its rightness or wrongness. To be morally bound is to be morally bound to *do* something, that is, to bring something about; and even if it be only from the lowest of motives that we have brought about something which we ought to have brought about, we have still done something which we ought to have done. The fact that I have given *A* credit in order to spite his rival *B*, or again, in order to secure future favours from *A*, has, as we see when we reflect, no bearing whatever on the question whether I ought to have given *A* credit. The real paradox inherent in the conviction lies in its implication that there is no such thing as moral goodness. If I give *A* credit solely to obtain future favours, and even if I gave him credit either thinking or knowing that I ought to do so, but in no way directly or indirectly influenced by my either so thinking or knowing, then even though it has to be allowed that I did something which I was morally bound to do, it has to be admitted that there was no moral goodness whatever about my action. And the conviction in question is really what is ordinarily called the doctrine that morality needs a sanction, that is, really the doctrine that, to stimulate a man into doing some action, it is not merely insufficient but even useless to convince him that he is morally bound to do it, and that, instead, we have to appeal to his desire to become better off.

Now we are apt to smile in a superior way when in reading Mill we find him taking for granted that morality needs a sanction, but we cannot afford to do so when we find Butler, and still more when we find Plato, really doing the same thing. Moreover when Plato and Butler maintain the doctrine that lies at the back of this conviction, namely, the doctrine that we always aim at, that is, act from the desire of, some good to ourselves, they are in the best of company. Aristotle is practically only repeating the statement quoted from the sixth book of the *Republic* when he says in the first sentence of the *Ethics*, that every deliberate action seems to aim at something good, and that therefore the good has rightly been declared to be that at which all things aim. For this to become obvious it is only necessary to consider what meaning must be attributed to the term ἀγαθόν in the early chapters of the *Ethics*. Again, to take a modern instance, Green says: "The motive in every imputable act for which the agent is conscious on reflection that he is answerable, is a desire for personal good in some form or other. . . . It is superfluous to add good to *himself*, for anything conceived as good in such a way that the agent acts for the sake of it, must be conceived as *his own* good, though he may conceive it as his own good only on account of his interest in others, and in spite of any amount of suffering on his own part incidental to its attainment." [2] Moreover the doctrine seems plausible enough, if we ask ourselves in a purely general way "How are we to be led into doing something?" For the natural answer is: "Only by thinking of some state of affairs which it is in my power to bring about and by which I shall become better off than I am now"; and the answer implies that only in this way shall we come to desire to do an action, and that, unless we desire to do it, we shall not do it.

Nevertheless it seems difficult, and indeed in the end impossible, to think that the doctrine will stand the test of instances. It seems impossible to allow that in what would usually be called disinterested actions, whether they be good or bad, there is not at least some element of disinterestedness. It strikes us as absurd to think that in what would be called a benevolent action, we are not moved at least in part by the desire that someone else shall be better off and also by the desire to *make* him better off, even though we may also necessarily have, and be influenced by, the desire to have the satisfaction of thinking that he is better off and that we have made him so. It seems equally absurd to maintain that where we are said to treat someone maliciously, we are not moved in part by the desire of his unhappiness and also partly by the desire to *make* him unhappy. Again when we are said to be pursuing scientific studies without a practical aim, it seems mere distortion of the facts to say that we are moved solely by the desire to have the satisfaction of knowing some particular thing and not, at least in part, by the desire to know it. And we seem driven to make a similar admission when we consider actions in which we are said to have acted conscientiously.

In this connexion it should be noted that the doctrine under consideration, namely, that our motive in doing any action is desire for some good to ourselves to which we think the action will lead, has

[2] *Prolegomena to Ethics*, §§ 91–2.

two negative implications. The first is that the thought, or, alternatively, the knowledge, that some action is right has no influence on us in acting, that is, that the thought, or the knowledge, that an action is a duty can neither be our motive nor even an element in our motive. The existence of this implication is obvious, since if our motive is held to be the desire for a certain good to ourselves, it is implied that the thought that the action is a duty, though present, is neither what moves us, nor an element in what moves us, to do the action. The second implication is that there is no such thing as a *desire* to do what is right, or more fully, a desire to do some action in virtue of its being a duty. The existence of this second implication is also obvious, since if such a desire were allowed to exist, there would be no reason for maintaining that when we do some action which we think to be a duty, our motive is necessarily the desire for a certain good to ourselves. The truth of the doctrine could therefore be contested in one of two alternative ways. We might either deny the truth of the former implication; or, again, we might deny the truth of the latter. The former is, of course, the line taken by Kant, at any rate in a qualified form. He maintained in effect that the mere thought that an action is a duty, apart from a desire to do what we ought to do—a desire the existence of which he refused to admit—is at any rate in certain instances the motive, or at least an element in the motive, of an action. No doubt he insisted that the existence of this fact gave rise to a problem, and a problem which only vindication of freedom of the will could resolve; but he maintained that the problem was soluble, and that therefore he was entitled to insist on this fact. Now this method of refutation has adherents and at first sight it is attractive. For it seems mere wild paradox to maintain that in no case in which we do what we think of as right, do we ever in any degree do it *because* we think it right; and to say that we do some action *because* we think it right seems to imply that the thought that it is right is our motive. Again the statement seems natural that where we are said to have acted thus, we obviously did not want to do what we did but acted against our desires or inclinations. Nevertheless we are, I think, on further reflection bound to abandon this view. For one reason, to appeal to a consideration of which the full elucidation and vindication would take too long, the view involves that where we are said to have done some action because we thought it right, though we had a motive for what we did, we had no purpose in doing it. For we really mean by our purpose in doing some action that the *desire* of which for its own sake leads us to do the action. Again, if we face the purely general question "Can we really do anything whatever unless in some respect or other we desire to do it?" we have to answer "No." But if we allow this, then we have to allow that the obvious way to endeavour to meet Plato's view is to maintain the existence of a desire to do what is right. And it does not seem difficult to do so with success. For we obviously are referring to a fact when we speak of someone as possessing a sense of duty and, again, a strong sense of duty. And if we consider what we are thinking of in these individuals whom we think of as possessing it, we find we cannot exclude from it a desire to do what is a duty, as such, or for its own sake, or, more simply, a desire to do what is a duty. In fact it is hard to resist the conclusion that Kant himself would have taken this line instead of the extreme line which he did, had he not had the fixed idea that all desire is for enjoyment. But if we think this—as it seems we must—we, of course, have no need to admit the truth of Plato's reason for trying to prove that right actions must be advantageous. For if we admit the existence of a desire to do what is right, there is no longer any reason for maintaining as a general thesis that in any case in which a man knows some action to be right, he must, if he is to be led to do it, be convinced that he will gain by doing it. For we shall be able to maintain that his desire to do what is right, if strong enough, will lead him to do the action in spite of any aversion from doing it which he may feel on account of its disadvantages.

It may be objected that if we maintain the existence of a desire to do what is right, we shall become involved in an insoluble difficulty. For we shall also have to allow that we have a desire to become well-off or happy, and that therefore men have two radically different desires, that is, desires the object of which are completely incommensurable. We shall therefore be implying that in those instances—which of course must exist—in which a man has either to do what is right or to do what is for his happiness he can have no means of choosing which he shall do, since there can be no comparable characteristic of the two alternative actions which will enable him to choose to do the one rather than, or in preference to, the other. But to this objection there is an answer which, even if it be at first paradoxical, is in the end irresistible, namely, that in connexion with such instances it is wholly inappropriate to speak of a *choice*. A choice is, no doubt, necessarily a choice between comparable alternatives, for example between an afternoon's enjoyment on the river and an afternoon's enjoyment at a cinema. But it is purely arbitrary to maintain that wherever we have two alternative courses of action before us we have necessarily to *choose* between them. Thus a man contemplating retirement may be offered a new post. He may, on thinking it over, be unable to resist the conclusion that it is a duty on his part to accept it and equally convinced that if he accepts it, he will lose in happiness. He will either accept from his desire to do what is right in spite of his aversion from doing what will bring himself a loss of happiness, or he will refuse from his desire of happiness, in spite of his aversion from doing what is wrong. But whichever he does, though he will have *decided* to do what he does, he will not have chosen to do it, that is, chosen to do it in preference to doing the alternative action.

For the reasons given I shall treat it as established that, though there is to be found in Plato and Butler what is really an attempt to prove that right action is advantageous, the question of its success or failure can be ignored, since the attempt is based on a fundamental mistake about actual human nature.

. . . . . [The remainder of the lecture is omitted.]

~~~~~~

part three

IS

MORALITY

ADVANTAGEOUS?

THOMAS HOBBES

The Natural Condition of Mankind and the Laws of Nature

～～～～～～～～～～～～～～～～～～～～～～～～

CHAPTER XIII

Of the Natural Condition of Mankind as
Concerning Their Felicity, and Misery

MEN BY NATURE EQUAL. Nature hath made men so equal, in the faculties of the body, and mind; as that though there be found one man sometimes manifestly stronger in body, or of quicker mind than another; yet when all is reckoned together, the difference between man, and man, is not so considerable, as that one man can thereupon claim to himself any benefit, to which another may not pretend, as well as he. For as to the strength of body, the weakest has strength enough to kill the strongest, either by secret machination, or by confederacy with others, that are in the same danger with himself.

And as to the faculties of the mind, setting aside the arts grounded upon words, and especially that skill of proceeding upon general, and infallible rules, called science; which very few have, and but in few things; as being not native faculty, born with us; nor attained, as prudence, while we look after somewhat else, I find yet a greater equality amongst men, than that of strength. For prudence, is but experience; which equal time, equally bestows on all men, in those things they equally apply themselves unto. That which may perhaps make such equality incredible, is but a vain conceit of one's own wisdom, which almost all men think they have in a greater degree, than the vulgar; that is, than all men but themselves, and a few

---

* Excerpted from *Leviathan,* Chap. XIII–XV. First published 1651.

others, whom by fame, or for concurring with themselves, they approve. For such is the nature of men, that howsoever they may acknowledge many others to be more witty, or more eloquent, or more learned; yet they will hardly believe there be many so wise as themselves; for they see their own wit at hand, and other men's at a distance. But this proveth rather that men are in that point equal, than unequal. For there is not ordinarily a greater sign of the equal distribution of any thing, than that every man is contented with his share.

FROM EQUALITY PROCEEDS DIFFIDENCE. From this equality of ability, ariseth equality of hope in the attaining of our ends. And therefore if any two men desire the same thing, which nevertheless they cannot both enjoy, they become enemies; and in the way to their end, which is principally their own conservation, and sometimes their delectation only, endeavour to destroy, or subdue one another. And from hence it comes to pass, that where an invader hath no more to fear, than another man's single power; if one plant, sow, build, or possess a convenient seat, others may probably be expected to come prepared with forces united, to dispossess, and deprive him, not only of the fruit of his labour, but also of his life, or liberty. And the invader again is in the like danger of another.

FROM DIFFIDENCE WAR. And from this diffidence of one another, there is no way for any man to secure himself, so reasonable, as anticipation; that is, by force, or wiles, to master the persons of all men he can, so long, till he see no other power great enough to endanger him: and this is no more than his own conservation requireth, and is generally allowed. Also because there be some, that taking pleasure in contemplating their own power in the acts of conquest, which they pursue farther than their security requires; if others, that otherwise would be glad to be at ease within modest bounds, should not by invasion increase their power, they would not be able, long time, by standing only on their defence, to subsist. And by consequence, such augmentation of dominion over men being necessary to a man's conservation, it ought to be allowed him.

Again, men have no pleasure, but on the contrary a great deal of grief, in keeping company, where there is no power able to overawe them all. For every man looketh that his companion should value him, at the same rate he sets upon himself: and upon all signs of contempt, or undervaluing, naturally endeavours, as far as he dares, (which amongst them that have no common power to keep them in quiet, is far enough to make them destroy each other), to extort a greater value from his contemners, by damage; and from others, by the example.

So that in the nature of man, we find three principal causes of quarrel. First, competition; secondly, diffidence; thirdly, glory.

The first, maketh men invade for gain; the second, for safety; and the third, for reputation. The first use violence, to make themselves masters of other men's persons, wives, children, and cattle; the second, to defend them; the third, for trifles, as a word, a smile, a different opinion, and any other sign of undervalue, either direct in their persons, or by reflection in their kindred, their friends, their nation, their profession, or their name.

OUT OF CIVIL STATES, THERE IS ALWAYS WAR OF EVERY ONE AGAINST EVERY ONE. Hereby it is manifest, that during the time men live without a common power to keep them all in awe, they are in that condition which is called war; and such a war, as is of every man, against every man. For WAR, consisteth not in battle only, or the act of fighting; but in a tract of time, wherein the will to contend by battle is sufficiently known: and therefore the notion of *time,* is to be considered in the nature of war; as it is in the nature of weather. For as the nature of foul weather, lieth not in a shower or two of rain; but in an inclination thereto of many days together: so the nature of war, consisteth not in actual fighting; but in the known disposition thereto, during all the time there is no assurance to the contrary. All other time is PEACE.

THE INCOMMODITIES OF SUCH A WAR. Whatsoever therefore is consequent to a time of war, where every man is enemy to every man; the same is consequent to the time, wherein men live without other security, than what their own strength, and their own invention shall furnish them withal. In such condition, there is no place for industry; because the fruit thereof is uncertain: and consequently no culture of the earth; no navigation, nor use of the commodities that may be imported by sea; no commodious building; no instruments of moving, and removing, such things as require much force; no knowledge of the face of the earth; no account of time; no arts; no letters; no society; and which is worst of all, continual fear, and danger of violent death; and the life of man, solitary, poor, nasty, brutish, and short.

It may seem strange to some man, that has not well weighed these things; that nature should thus dissociate, and render men apt to invade, and destroy one another: and he may therefore, not trusting to this inference, made from the passions, desire perhaps to have the same confirmed by experience. Let him therefore consider with himself, when taking a journey, he arms himself, and seeks to go well accompanied; when going to sleep, he locks his doors; when even in his house he locks his chests; and this when he knows there be laws, and public officers, armed, to revenge all injuries shall be done him; what opinion he has of his fellow subjects, when he rides armed; of his fellow citizens, when he locks his doors; and of his children, and servants, when he locks his chests. Does he not there as much accuse mankind by his actions, as I do by my words? But neither of us accuse man's nature in it. The desires, and other passions of man, are in themselves no sin. No more are the actions, that proceed from those passions, till they know a law that forbids them: which till laws be made they cannot know: nor can any law be made, till they have agreed upon the person that shall make it.

It may peradventure be thought, there was never such a time, nor condition of war as this; and I believe it was never generally so, over all the world: but there are many places, where they live so now. For the savage people in many places of America, except the government of small families, the concord whereof dependeth on natural lust, have no government at all; and live at this day in that brutish manner, as I said before. Howsoever, it may be perceived what manner of life there would be, where there were no common power to fear, by the manner of life, which men that have formerly lived under a peaceful government, use to degenerate into, in a civil war.

But though there had never been any time, wherein particular men were in a condition of war one against another; yet in all times, kings, and persons of sovereign authority, because of their independency, are in continual jealousies, and in the state and posture of gladiators; having their weapons pointing, and their eyes fixed on one another; that is, their forts, garrisons, and guns upon the frontiers of their kingdoms; and continual spies upon their neighbours; which is a posture of war. But because they uphold thereby, the industry of their subjects; there does not follow from it, that misery, which accompanies the liberty of particular men.

IN SUCH A WAR NOTHING IS UNJUST. To this war of every man, against every man, this also is consequent; that nothing can be unjust. The notions of right and wrong, justice and injustice have there no place. Where there is no common power, there is no law: where no law, no injustice. Force, and fraud, are in war the two cardinal virtues. Justice, and injustice are none of the faculties neither of the body, nor mind. If they were, they might be in a man that were alone in the world, as well as his senses, and passions. They are qualities, that relate to men in society, not in solitude. It is consequent also to the same condition, that there be no propriety, no dominion, no *mine* and *thine* distinct; but only that to be every man's, that he can get: and for so long, as he can keep it. And thus much for the ill condition, which man by mere nature is actually placed in; though with a possibility to come out of it, consisting partly in the passions, partly in his reason.

THE PASSIONS THAT INCLINE MEN TO PEACE. The passions that incline men to peace, are fear of death; desire of such things as are necessary to commodious living; and a hope by their industry to obtain them. And reason suggesteth convenient articles of peace, upon which men may be drawn to agreement. These articles, are they, which otherwise are called the Laws of Nature: whereof I shall speak more particularly, in the two following chapters.

CHAPTER XIV

Of the First and Second Natural Laws, and of Contracts

RIGHT OF NATURE WHAT. The RIGHT OF NATURE which writers commonly call *jus naturale,* is the liberty each man hath, to use his own power, as he will himself, for the preservation of his own nature; that is to say, of his own life; and consequently, of doing any thing, which in his own judgment, and reason, he shall conceive to be the aptest means thereunto.

LIBERTY WHAT. By LIBERTY, is understood, according to the proper signification of the word, the absence of external impediments: which impediments, may oft take away part of a man's power to do what he would; but cannot hinder him from using the power left him, according as his judgment, and reason shall dictate to him.

A LAW OF NATURE WHAT. DIFFERENCE OF RIGHT AND LAW. A LAW OF NATURE, *lex naturalis,* is a precept or general rule, found out by reason, by which a man is forbidden to do that, which is destructive of his life, or taketh away the means of preserving the same; and to omit that, by which he thinketh it may be best preserved. For though they that speak of this subject, use to confound *jus,* and *lex, right* and *law*: yet they ought to be distinguished; because RIGHT, consisteth in liberty to do, or to forbear: whereas LAW, determineth, and bindeth to one of them: so that law, and right, differ as much, as obligation, and liberty; which in one and the same matter are inconsistent.

NATURALLY EVERY MAN HAS RIGHT TO EVERY THING. THE FUNDAMENTAL LAW OF NATURE. And because the condition of man, as hath been declared in the precedent chapter, is a condition of war of every one against every one; in which case every one is governed by his own reason; and there is nothing he can make use of, that may not be a help unto him, in preserving his life against his enemies; it followeth, that in such a condition, every man has a right to every thing; even to one another's body. And therefore, as long as this natural right of every man to every thing endureth, there can be no security to any man, how strong or wise soever he be, of living out the time, which nature ordinarily alloweth men to live. And consequently it is a precept, or general rule of reason, *that every man, ought to endeavour peace, as far as he has hope of obtaining it; and when he cannot obtain it, that he may seek, and use, all helps, and advantages of war.* The first branch of which rule, containeth the first, and fundamental law of nature; which is, *to seek peace, and follow it.* The second, the sum of the right of nature; which is, *by all means we can, to defend ourselves.*

THE SECOND LAW OF NATURE. From this fundamental law of nature, by which men are commanded to endeavour peace, is derived this second law; *that a man be willing, when others are so too, as farforth, as for peace, and defence of himself he shall think it necessary, to lay down this right to all things; and be contented with so much liberty against other men, as he would allow other men against himself.* For as long as every man holdeth this right, of doing any thing he liketh; so long are all men in the condition of war. But if other men will not lay down their right, as well as he; then there is no reason for any one, to divest himself of his: for that were to expose himself to prey, which no man is bound to, rather than to dispose himself to peace. This is that law of the Gospel; *whatsoever you require that others should do to you, that do ye to them.* And that law of all men, *quod tibi fieri non vis, alteri ne feceris.*

WHAT IT IS TO LAY DOWN A RIGHT. To *lay down* a man's *right* to any thing, is to *divest* himself of the *liberty*, of hindering another of the benefit of his own right to the same. For he that renounceth, or passeth away his right, giveth not to any other man a right which he had not before; because there is nothing to which every man had not right by nature: but only standeth out of his way, that he may enjoy his own original right, without hindrance from him; not without hindrance from another. So that the effect which redoundeth to one man, by another man's defect of right, is but so much diminution of impediments to the use of his own right original.

RENOUNCING A RIGHT, WHAT IT IS. TRANSFERRING RIGHT WHAT. OBLIGATION. DUTY. INJUSTICE. Right is laid aside, either by simply renouncing it; or by transferring it to another. By *simply* RENOUNCING; when he cares not to whom the benefit thereof redoundeth. By TRANS-FERRING; when he intendeth the benefit thereof to some certain person, or persons. And when a man hath in either manner abandoned, or granted away his right; then he is said to be OBLIGED, or BOUND, not to hinder those, to whom such right is granted, or abandoned, from the benefit of it: and that he *ought,* and it is his DUTY, not to make void that voluntary act of his own: and that such hindrance is INJUS-TICE, and INJURY, as being *sine jure*; the right being before renounced, or transferred. So that *injury*, or *injustice*, in the controversies of the world, is somewhat like to that, which in the disputations of scholars is called *absurdity*. For as it is there called an absurdity, to contradict what one maintained in the beginning: so in the world, it is called injustice, and injury, voluntarily to undo that, which from the be-ginning he had voluntarily done. The way by which a man either simply renounceth, or transferreth his right, is a declaration, or sig-nification, by some voluntary and sufficient sign, or signs, that he doth so renounce, or transfer; or hath so renounced, or transferred the same, to him that accepteth it. And these signs are either words only, or actions only; or, as it happeneth most often, both words, and ac-tions. And the same are the BONDS, by which men are bound, and obliged: bonds, that have their strength, not from their own nature, for nothing is more easily broken than a man's word, but from fear of some evil consequence upon the rupture.

NOT ALL RIGHTS ARE ALIENABLE. Whensoever a man transferreth his right, or renounceth it; it is either in consideration of some right reciprocally transferred to himself; or for some other good he hopeth for thereby. For it is a voluntary act: and of the voluntary acts of every man, the object is some *good to himself*. And therefore there be some rights, which no man can be understood by any words, or other signs, to have abandoned, or transferred. As first a man cannot lay down the right of resisting them, that assault him by force, to take away his life; because he cannot be understood to aim thereby, at any good to himself. The same may be said of wounds, and chains, and imprisonment; both because there is no benefit consequent to such patience; as there is to the patience of suffering another to be wounded, or imprisoned: as also because a man cannot tell, when he seeth men proceed against him by violence, whether they intend his death or not. And lastly the motive, and end for which this renouncing, and transferring of right is introduced, is nothing else but the security of a man's person, in his life, and in the means of so preserving life, as not to be weary of it. And therefore if a man by words, or other signs, seem to despoil himself of the end, for which those signs were intended; he is not to be understood as if he meant it, or that it was his will; but that he was ignorant of how such words and actions were to be interpreted.

CONTRACT WHAT. The mutual transferring of right, is that which men call CONTRACT.

There is difference between transferring of right to the thing; and transferring, or tradition, that is delivery of the thing itself. For the thing may be delivered together with the translation of right; as in buying and selling with ready money; or exchange of goods, or lands: and it may be delivered some time after.

COVENANT WHAT. Again, one of the contractors, may deliver the thing contracted for on his part, and leave the other to perform his part at some determinate time after, and in the mean time be trusted; and then the contract on his part, is called PACT, or COVENANT: or both parts may contract now, to perform hereafter: in which cases, he that is to perform in time to come, being trusted, his performance is called *keeping of promise,* or faith; and the failing of performance, if it be voluntary, *violation of faith.*

• • • • • [Discussion of free-gift and promise.]

COVENANTS OF MUTUAL TRUST, WHEN INVALID. If a covenant be made, wherein neither of the parties perform presently, but trust one another; in the condition of mere nature, which is a condition of war of every man against every man, upon any reasonable suspicion, it is void: but if there be a common power set over them both, with right and force sufficient to compel performance, it is not void. For he that performeth first, has no assurance the other will perform after; because the bonds of words are too weak to bridle men's ambition, avarice, anger, and other passions, without the fear of some coercive power; which in the condition of mere nature, where all men are equal, and judges of the justness of their own fears, cannot possibly be supposed. And therefore he which performeth first, does but betray himself to his enemy; contrary to the right, he can never abandon, of defending his life, and means of living.

But in a civil estate, where there is a power set up to constrain those that would otherwise violate their faith, that fear is no more reasonable; and for that cause, he which by the covenant is to perform first, is obliged so to do.

The cause of fear, which maketh such a covenant invalid, must be always something arising after the covenant made; as some new fact, or other sign of the will not to perform: else it cannot make the covenant void. For that which could not hinder a man from promising, ought not to be admitted as a hindrance of performing.

RIGHT TO THE END, CONTAINETH RIGHT TO THE MEANS. He that transferreth any right, transferreth the means of enjoying it, as far as lieth in his power. As he that selleth land, is understood to transfer the herbage, and whatsoever grows upon it: nor can he that sells a mill turn away the stream that drives it. And they that give to a man the right of government in sovereignty, are understood to give him the right of levying money to maintain soldiers; and of appointing magistrates for the administration of justice.

NO COVENANT WITH BEASTS. To make covenants with brute beasts, is impossible; because not understanding our speech, they understand not, nor accept of any translation of right; nor can translate any right to another: and without mutual acceptation, there is no covenant.

NOR WITH GOD WITHOUT SPECIAL REVELATION. To make covenant with God, is impossible, but by mediation of such as God speaketh to, either by revelation supernatural, or by his lieutenants that govern under him, and in his name: for otherwise we know not whether our covenants be accepted, or not. And therefore they that vow anything contrary to any law of nature, vow in vain; as being a thing unjust to pay such vow. And if it be a thing commanded by the law of nature, it is not the vow, but the law that binds them.

No Covenant, but of Possible and Future. The matter, or subject of a covenant, is always something that falleth under deliberation; for to covenant, is an act of the will; that is to say, an act, and the last act of deliberation; and is therefore always understood to be something to come; and which is judged possible for him that covenanteth, to perform.

And therefore, to promise that which is known to be impossible, is no covenant. But if that prove impossible afterwards, which before was thought possible, the covenant is valid, and bindeth, though not to the thing itself, yet to the value; or, if that also be impossible, to the unfeigned endeavour of performing as much as is possible: for to more no man can be obliged.

Covenants How Made Void. Men are freed of their covenants two ways; by performing; or by being forgiven. For performance, is the natural end of obligation; and forgiveness, the restitution of liberty; as being a retransferring of that right, in which the obligation consisted.

Covenants Extorted by Fear Are Valid. Covenants entered into by fear, in the condition of mere nature, are obligatory. For example, if I covenant to pay a ransom, or service for my life, to an enemy; I am bound by it: for it is a contract, wherein one receiveth the benefit of life; the other is to receive money, or service for it; and consequently, where no other law, as in the condition of mere nature, forbiddeth the performance, the covenant is valid. Therefore prisoners of war, if trusted with the payment of their ransom, are obliged to pay it: and if a weaker prince, make a disadvantageous peace with a stronger, for fear; he is bound to keep it; unless, as hath been said before, there ariseth some new, and just cause of fear, to renew the war. And even in commonwealths, if I be forced to redeem myself from a thief by promising him money, I am bound to pay it, till the civil law discharge me. For whatsoever I may lawfully do without obligation, the same I may lawfully covenant to do through fear: and what I lawfully covenant, I cannot lawfully break.

THE FORMER COVENANT TO ONE, MAKES VOID THE LATER TO ANOTHER. A former covenant, makes void a later. For a man that hath passed away his right to one man today, hath it not to pass tomorrow to another: and therefore the later promise passeth no right, but is null.

A MAN'S COVENANT NOT TO DEFEND HIMSELF IS VOID. A covenant not to defend myself from force, by force, is always void. For, as I have showed before, no man can transfer, or lay down his right to save himself from death, wounds, and imprisonment, the avoiding whereof is the only end of laying down any right; and therefore the promise of not resisting force, in no covenant transferreth any right; nor is obliging. For though a man may covenant thus, *unless I do so, or so, kill me*; he cannot covenant thus, *unless I do so, or so, I will not resist you, when you come to kill me*. For man by nature chooseth the lesser evil, which is danger of death in resisting; rather than the greater, which is certain and present death in not resisting. And this is granted to be true by all men, in that they lead criminals to execution, and prison, with armed men, notwithstanding that such criminals have consented to the law, by which they are condemned.

NO MAN OBLIGED TO ACCUSE HIMSELF. A covenant to accuse oneself, without assurance of pardon, is likewise invalid. For in the condition of nature, where every man is judge, there is no place for accusation: and in the civil state, the accusation is followed with punishment; which being force, a man is not obliged not to resist. The same is also true, of the accusation of those, by whose condemnation a man falls into misery; as of a father, wife, or benefactor. For the testimony of such an accuser, if it be not willingly given, is presumed to be corrupted by nature; and therefore not to be received: and where a man's testimony is not to be credited, he is not bound to give it. Also accusations upon torture, are not to be reputed as testimonies. For torture is to be used but as means of conjecture, and light, in the further examination, and search of truth: and what is in that case confessed, tendeth to the ease of him that is tortured; not to the informing of the torturers: and therefore ought not to have the credit of a sufficient testimony: for whether he deliver himself by true, or false accusation, he does it by the right of preserving his own life.

THE END OF AN OATH. THE FORM OF AN OATH. The force of words, being, as I have formerly noted, too weak to hold men to the performance of their covenants; there are in man's nature, but two imaginable helps to strengthen it. And those are either a fear of the consequence of breaking their word; or a glory, or pride in appearing not to need to break it. This latter is a generosity too rarely found to be presumed on, especially in the pursuers of wealth, command, or sensual pleasure; which are the greatest part of mankind. The passion to be reckoned upon, is fear; whereof there be two very general objects: one, the power of spirits invisible; the other, the power of those men they shall therein offend. Of these two, though the former be the greater power, yet the fear of the latter is commonly the greater fear. The fear of the former is in every man, his own religion: which hath place in the nature of man before civil society. The latter hath not so; at least not place enough, to keep men to their promises; because in the condition of mere nature, the inequality of power is not discerned, but by the event of battle. So that before the time of civil society, or in the interruption thereof by war, there is nothing can strengthen a covenant of peace agreed on, against the temptations of avarice, ambition, lust, or other strong desire, but the fear of that invisible power, which they every one worship as God; and fear as a revenger of their perfidy. All therefore that can be done between two men not subject to civil power, is to put one another to swear by the God he feareth: which *swearing,* or OATH, is a *form of speech, added to a promise; by which he that promiseth, signifieth, that unless he perform, he renounceth the mercy of his God, or calleth to him for vengeance on himself.* Such was the heathen form, *Let* Jupiter *kill me else, as I kill this beast.* So is our form, *I shall do thus, and thus, so help me God.* And this, with the rites and ceremonies, which every one useth in his own religion, that the fear of breaking faith might be the greater.

NO OATH BUT BY GOD. By this it appears, that an oath taken according to any other form, or rite, than his, that sweareth, is in vain; and no oath: and that there is no swearing by any thing which the swearer thinks not God. For though men have sometimes used to swear by their kings, for fear, or flattery; yet they would have it thereby understood, they attributed to them divine honour. And that swearing unnecessarily by God, is but profaning of his name: and swearing by other things, as men do in common discourse, is not swearing, but an impious custom, gotten by too much vehemence of talking.

AN OATH ADDS NOTHING TO THE OBLIGATION. It appears also, that the oath adds nothing to the obligation. For a covenant, if lawful, binds in the sight of God, without the oath, as much as with it: if unlawful, bindeth not at all; though it be confirmed with an oath.

CHAPTER XV

Of Other Laws of Nature

THE THIRD LAW OF NATURE, JUSTICE. From that law of nature, by which we are obliged to transfer to another, such rights, as being retained, hinder the peace of mankind, there followeth a third; which is this, *that men perform their covenants made*: without which, covenants are in vain, and but empty words; and the right of all men to all things remaining, we are still in the condition of war.

JUSTICE AND INJUSTICE WHAT. And in this law of nature, consisteth the fountain and original of JUSTICE. For where no covenant hath preceded, there hath no right been transferred, and every man has right to every thing; and consequently, no action can be unjust. But when a covenant is made, then to break it is *unjust*: and the definition of INJUSTICE, is no other than *the not performance of covenant*. And whatsoever is not unjust, is *just*.

JUSTICE AND PROPRIETY BEGIN WITH THE CONSTITUTION OF COMMONWEALTH. But because covenants of mutual trust, where there is a fear of not performance on either part, as hath been said in the former chapter, are invalid; though the original of justice be the making of covenants; yet injustice actually there can be none, till the cause of such fear be taken away; which while men are in the natural condition of war, cannot be done. Therefore before the names of just, and unjust can have place, there must be some coercive power, to compel men equally to the performance of their covenants, by the terror of some punishment, greater than the benefit they expect by the breach of their covenant; and to make good that propriety, which by mutual contract men acquire, in recompense of the universal right they abandon: and such power there is none before the erection of a commonwealth. And this is also to be gathered out of the ordinary definition of justice in the Schools: for they say, that *justice is the constant will of giving to every man his own*. And therefore where there is no *own*, that is no propriety, there is no injustice; and where there is no coercive power erected, that is, where there is no commonwealth, there is no propriety; all men having right to all things: therefore where there is no commonwealth, there nothing is unjust. So that the nature of justice, consisteth in keeping of valid covenants: but the validity of covenants begins not but with the constitution of a civil power, sufficient to compel men to keep them: and then it is also that propriety begins.

JUSTICE NOT CONTRARY TO REASON. The fool hath said in his heart, there is no such thing as justice; and sometimes also with his tongue; seriously alleging, that every man's conservation, and contentment, being committed to his own care, there could be no reason, why every man might not do what he thought conduced thereunto: and therefore also to make, or not make; keep, or not keep covenants, was not against reason, when it conduced to one's benefit. He does not therein deny, that there be covenants; and that they are sometimes broken, sometimes kept; and that such breach of them may be called injustice, and the observance of them justice: but he questioneth, whether injustice, taking away the fear of God, for the same fool hath said in his heart there is no God, may not sometimes stand with that reason, which dictateth to every man his own good; and particularly then, when it conduceth to such a benefit, as shall put a man in a condition, to neglect not only the dispraise, and revilings, but also the power of other men. The kingdom of God is gotten by violence: but what if it could be gotten by unjust violence? were it against reason so to get it, when it is impossible to receive hurt by it? and if it be not against reason, it is not against justice; or else justice is not to be approved for good. From such reasoning as this, successful wickedness hath obtained the name of virtue: and some that in all other things have disallowed the violation of faith; yet have allowed it, when it is for the getting of a kingdom. And the heathen that believed, that Saturn was deposed by his son Jupiter, believed nevertheless the same Jupiter to be the avenger of injustice: somewhat like to a piece of law in Coke's *Commentaries on Littleton*; where he says, if the right heir of the crown be attainted of treason; yet the crown shall descend to him, and *eo instante* the attainder be void: from which instances a man will be very prone to infer; that when the heir apparent of a kingdom, shall kill him that is in possession, though his father; you may call it injustice, or by what other name you will; yet it can never be against reason, seeing all the voluntary actions of men tend to the benefit of themselves;

and those actions are most reasonable, that conduce most to their ends. This specious reasoning is nevertheless false.

For the question is not of promises mutual, where there is no security of performance on either side; as when there is no civil power erected over the parties promising; for such promises are no covenants: but either where one of the parties has performed already; or where there is a power to make him perform; there is the question whether it be against reason, that is, against the benefit of the other to perform, or not. And I say it is not against reason. For the manifestation whereof, we are to consider; first, that when a man doth a thing, which notwithstanding any thing can be foreseen, and reckoned on, tendeth to his own destruction, howsoever some accident which he could not expect, arriving may turn it to his benefit; yet such events do not make it reasonably or wisely done. Secondly, that in a condition of war, wherein every man to every man, for want of a common power to keep them all in awe, is an enemy, there is no man who can hope by his own strength, or wit, to defend himself from destruction, without the help of confederates; where every one expects the same defence by the confederation, that any one else does: and therefore he which declares he thinks it reason to deceive those that help him, can in reason expect no other means of safety, than what can be had from his own single power. He therefore that breaketh his covenant, and consequently declareth that he thinks he may with reason do so, cannot be received into any society, that unite themselves for peace and defence, but by the error of them that receive him; nor when he is received, be retained in it, without seeing the danger of their error; which errors a man cannot reasonably reckon upon as the means of his security: and therefore if he be left, or cast out of society, he perisheth; and if he live in society, it is by the errors of other men, which he could not foresee, nor reckon upon; and consequently against the reason of his preservation; and so, as all men that contribute not to his destruction, forbear him only out of ignorance of what is good for themselves.

As for the instance of gaining the secure and perpetual felicity of heaven, by any way; it is frivolous: there being but one way imaginable; and that is not breaking, but keeping of covenant.

And for the other instance of attaining sovereignty by rebellion; it is manifest, that though the event follow, yet because it cannot reasonably be expected, but rather the contrary; and because by gaining it so, others are taught to gain the same in like manner, the attempt thereof is against reason. Justice therefore, that is to say, keeping of covenant, is a rule of reason, by which we are forbidden to do any thing destructive to our life; and consequently a law of nature.

There be some that proceed further; and will not have the law of nature, to be those rules which conduce to the preservation of man's life on earth; but to the attaining of an eternal felicity after death; to which they think the breach of covenant may conduce; and consequently be just and reasonable; such are they that think it a work of merit to kill, or depose, or rebel against, the sovereign power constituted over them by their own consent. But because there is no natural knowledge of man's estate after death; much less of the reward that is then to be given to breach of faith; but only a belief grounded upon other men's saying, that they know it supernaturally, or that they know those, that knew them, that knew others, that knew it supernaturally; breach of faith cannot be called a precept of reason, or nature.

. . . . [Further discussion of justice, and deduction of the remaining laws of nature.]

These are the laws of nature, dictating peace, for a means of the conservation of men in multitudes; and which only concern the doctrine of civil society. There be other things tending to the destruction of particular men; as drunkenness, and all other parts of intemperance; which may therefore also be reckoned amongst those things which the law of nature hath forbidden; but are not necessary to be mentioned, nor are pertinent enough to this place.

A Rule, by Which the Laws of Nature May Easily Be Examined. And though this may seem too subtle a deduction of the laws of nature, to be taken notice of by all men; whereof the most part are too busy in getting food, and the rest too negligent to understand; yet to leave all men inexcusable, they have been contracted into one easy sum, intelligible even to the meanest capacity; and that is, *Do not that to another, which thou wouldest not have done to thyself*; which sheweth him, that he has no more to do in learning the laws of nature, but, when weighing the actions of other men with his own, they seem too heavy, to put them into the other part of the balance, and his own into their place, that his own passions, and self-love, may add nothing to the weight; and then there is none of these laws of nature that will not appear unto him very reasonable.

THE LAWS OF NATURE OBLIGE IN CONSCIENCE ALWAYS, BUT IN EFFECT THEN ONLY WHEN THERE IS SECURITY. The laws of nature oblige *in foro interno*; that is to say, they bind to a desire they should take place: but *in foro externo*; that is, to the putting them in act, not always. For he that should be modest, and tractable, and perform all he promises, in such time, and place, where no man else should do so, should but make himself a prey to others, and procure his own certain ruin, contrary to the ground of all laws of nature, which tend to nature's preservation. And again, he that having sufficient security, that others shall observe the same laws towards him, observes them not himself, seeketh not peace, but war; and consequently the destruction of his nature by violence.

And whatsoever laws bind *in foro interno*, may be broken, not only by a fact contrary to the law, but also by a fact according to it, in case a man think it contrary. For though his action in this case, be according to the law; yet his purpose was against the law; which, where the obligation is *in foro interno*, is a breach.

THE LAWS OF NATURE ARE ETERNAL. The laws of nature are immutable and eternal; for injustice, ingratitude, arrogance, pride, iniquity, acception of persons, and the rest, can never be made lawful. For it can never be that war shall preserve life, and peace destroy it.

AND YET EASY. The same laws, because they oblige only to a desire, and endeavour, I mean an unfeigned and constant endeavour, are easy to be observed. For in that they require nothing but endeavour, he that endeavoureth their performance, fulfilleth them; and he that fulfilleth the law, is just.

THE SCIENCE OF THESE LAWS, IS THE TRUE MORAL PHILOSOPHY. And the science of them, is the true and only moral philosophy. For moral philosophy is nothing else but the science of what is *good*, and *evil*, in the conversation, and society of mankind. *Good*, and *evil*, are names that signify our appetites, and aversions; which in different tempers, customs, and doctrines of men, are different: and divers men, differ not only in their judgment, on the senses of what is pleasant, and unpleasant to the taste, smell, hearing, touch, and sight; but also of what is conformable, or disagreeable to reason, in the actions of common life. Nay, the same man, in divers times, differs from himself; and one time praiseth, that is, calleth good, what another time he dispraiseth, and calleth evil: from whence arise disputes, controversies, and at last war. And therefore so long as a man is in the condition of mere nature, which is a condition of war, as private appetite is the measure of good, and evil: and consequently all men agree on this, that peace is good, and therefore also the way, or means of peace, which, as I have shewed before, are *justice, gratitude, modesty, equity, mercy,* and the rest of the laws of nature, are good; that is to say; *moral virtues*; and their contrary *vices,* evil. Now the science of virtue and vice, is moral philosophy; and therefore the true doctrine of the laws of nature, is the true moral philosophy. But the writers of moral philosophy, though they acknowledge the same virtues and vices; yet not seeing wherein consisted their goodness: nor that they come to be praised, as the means of peaceable, sociable, and comfortable living, place them in a mediocrity of passions: as if not the cause, but the degree of daring, made fortitude; or not the cause, but the quantity of a gift, made liberality.

These dictates of reason, men used to call by the name of laws, but improperly: for they are but conclusions, or theorems concerning what conduceth to the conservation and defence of themselves; whereas law, properly, is the word of him, that by right hath command over others. But yet if we consider the same theorems, as delivered in the word of God, that by right commandeth all things; then are they properly called laws.

KURT BAIER

Why Should
We Be Moral?

~~~~~~

We are now in a position to deal with the various problems we shelved earlier. In Chapter Two we had to postpone the examination of how we verify those fundamental propositions which serve as major premises in our practical arguments. We must now deal with this. The examination of the prevailing consideration-making beliefs used at the first stage of our practical deliberations leads naturally to the examination of our rules of superiority used at the second stage. This in turn involves our investigating whether moral reasons are superior to all others and whether and why we should be moral. That opens up the most fundamental issue of all, whether and why we should follow reason.

1. THE TRUTH OF CONSIDERATION-MAKING BELIEFS

Let us begin with our most elementary consideration-making belief: the fact that if I did x I would enjoy doing x is a reason for me to do x. There can be little doubt that this is one of the rules of reason recognized in our society. Most people would use the knowledge of the fact that they would enjoy doing something as a pro in their deliberations whether to do it. When we wonder whether to go to the pictures or to a dinner dance, the fact that we would enjoy the dinner dance but not the pictures is regarded as a reason for going to the

---

* From *The Moral Point of View*, by Kurt Baier, abridged edition, Chap. 7, Secs. 1–3. © Copyright 1958 by Cornell University. © Copyright 1965 by Random House. Reprinted by permission.

dinner dance rather than to the pictures. We are now asking whether this widely held belief is correct or true, whether this fact really is a reason or is merely and falsely believed to be so.

What exactly are we asking? Is our question empirical? Obviously it cannot be answered by direct inspection. We cannot see, hear, or smell whether this belief is true, whether this fact is a reason or not. The nature of our question becomes clearer if we remind ourselves of the function of consideration-making beliefs, namely, to serve as major premises in practical arguments. These arguments are supposed to yield true answers to questions of the form "What shall I do?" or "What is the best course of action open to me?" The matter is considerably simplified by the fact that at this point, we are dealing merely with *prima facie* reasons. In order to determine the truth of the premise, we have only to find out whether the conclusion based on it is the best, *other things being equal,* that is, whether it is better than the conclusions based on its contradictory or its contrary.

The problem of the truth or falsity of consideration-making beliefs is thus reduced to the question whether it is better that they, rather than their contraries or contradictories, should be used as rules of reason, that is, as major premises in practical arguments. How would we tell?

Our practical argument runs as follows:

> (i) The fact that if I did *x* I would enjoy doing *x* is a reason for me to do *x*.
> (ii) I would enjoy doing *x* if I did *x*.
> (iii) Therefore I ought to do *x* (other things being equal).

It is not difficult to see that the contrary of our rule of reason is greatly inferior to it. For if, instead of the presently accepted belief (see above (i)), its contrary became the prevailing rule, then anyone trying to follow reason would have to conclude that whenever there is something that he would enjoy doing if he did it then he ought *not* to do it. "Reason" would counsel everyone always to refrain from doing what he enjoys, from satisfying his desires. "Reason" would counsel self-frustration for its own sake.

It is important to note that such an arrangement is possible. To say that we would not now *call* it "following reason" is not enough to refute it. We can imagine two societies in which English is spoken and which differ only in this, that in one society (i) is accepted, in the other the contrary of (i). It would then be correct to say in one society that doing what one would enjoy doing was following reason, in the other society that it was acting contrary to it. The "tautologousness" of the first remark *in our society* is not incompatible with the "tautologousness" of the contrary remark *in another society*. From the fact that the proposition "Fathers are male" is analytic, we can infer that "fathers are male" is necessarily true. But this is so only because we would not correctly *call* anything "father" that we would correctly call "not male." And it is perfectly in order to say that in any society in which English was spoken but in which the words "father" and/or "male" were not used in this way those words did not mean quite the same as in our society. And with this, the matter is ended, for we are not concerned to settle the question which verbal arrangement, ours or theirs, is the better. Nothing of importance follows from the fact that a society has our usage of "father" and "male" or theirs. But in the case of the use of "reason," much depends on which usage is accepted. The real difficulty only begins when we have concluded, correctly, that the word "reason" is used in a different sense in that other society. For the practical implications of the word "reason" are the same in both societies, namely, that people are encouraged to follow reason rather than to act contrary to it. However, *what* is held in one society to be in accordance with reason is held to be contrary to it in the other. Hence, we must say that in practical matters nothing fundamental can be settled by attention to linguistic proprieties or improprieties.

What, then, is relevant? We must remember what sort of a "game" the game of reasoning is. We ask the question "What shall I do?" or "What is the best course of action?" Following reasons is following those hints which are most likely to make the course of action the best in the circumstances. The criteria of "best course of action" are linked with what we mean by "the good life." In evaluating a life, one of the criteria of merit which we use is how much satisfaction and how little frustration there is in that life. Our very purpose in "playing the reasoning game" is to maximize satisfactions and minimize frustrations. Deliberately and for no further reason to frustrate ourselves and to minimize satisfaction would certainly be to go counter to the very purpose for which we deliberate and weigh the pros and cons. These criteria are, therefore, necessarily linked with the very purpose of the activity of reasoning. Insofar as we enter on that "game" at all, we are therefore bound to accept these criteria. Hence we are bound to agree that the consideration-making belief which is prevalent in our society is better than its contrary.

But need we accept that purpose? Is this not just a matter of taste or preference? Could not people with other tastes choose the opposite purpose, namely, self-frustration and self-denial rather than satisfaction of desires and enjoyment? The answer is No, it is not just a matter of taste or preference. Whether we like or don't like oysters, even whether we prefer red ink to claret, is a matter of taste, though to prefer red ink is to exhibit a very eccentric taste. Whether we prefer to satisfy our desires or to frustrate them is not, however, a matter of taste or preference. It is not an eccentricity of taste to prefer whatever one does *not* enjoy doing to whatever one does enjoy doing. It is perverse or crazy if it is done every now and then, mad if it is done always or on principle.

It might be objected that these people would merely be *called* mad by us—this does not prove that they really are, any more than the fact that they might well call us mad proves that we are. This objection seems to take the sting out of the epithet "mad." However, it only seems to do so, because it is misconstrued on one of the following two models.

(i) "They are called artesian wells, but that's only what we call them in this country." In this case, the distinction is between what we all, quite universally but incorrectly, call them in this country and what they really are, that is, what they are properly and correctly called. The difference is between an established but incorrect usage, and the correct but possibly not established usage. However, people who prefer whatever they do not enjoy doing to whatever they do would not merely generally (though incorrectly) but quite correctly be called mad.

(ii) "When two people quarrel and call each other 'bastard,' that does not prove that they are bastards." On this model, it might be argued that the word "mad" has no established usage, that we use it only in order to insult people who are not average. But this is untenable. Admittedly we often use the word "mad" to insult people who are not mad, just as we use the word "bastard" to insult people who were born in wedlock. But we could not use these words for these purposes unless they were correctly used to designate characteristics generally regarded as highly undesirable. When a person is certified insane, this is done not just because he differs from average, but because he is different in certain fundamental and undesirable respects. To prove the undesirability of these differences, it is enough here to point out that no one *wants* to become mad. Our conclusion must be that there is a correct use of the word "mad" and that people who prefer whatever they do not enjoy doing to whatever they do differ from normal people in just such fundamental and undesirable respects as would make the word "mad" correctly applicable to them.

The contradictory of our most fundamental consideration-making belief is also less satisfactory than *it* is. If it were to be believed that the fact that one would enjoy doing *x* was not a reason for doing it (a belief which is the contradictory of our most fundamental consideration-making belief), then people wishing to follow reason would be neither advised to do what they would enjoy doing nor advised not to do it. Reason would simply be silent on this issue. Never to do what one would enjoy doing would be as much in accordance with reason (other things being equal) as always to do it. In such a world, "following reason" might in the long run be less rewarding than following instinct or inclination. Hence this cannot *be* following reason, for in the long run it *must* pay to follow reason at least as much as to follow instinct or inclination, or else it is not reason.

To sum up. People who replace our most fundamental consideration-making belief by its contrary or contradictory will not do as well as those who adhere to it. Those who adopt its contrary must even be said to be mad. This seems to me the best possible argument for the preferability of our fundamental consideration-making belief to its contrary and contradictory. And this amounts to a proof of its correctness or truth. I lack space to examine whether the other consideration-making beliefs prevalent in our society are also true. Perhaps enough has been said to enable readers to conduct this investigation for themselves.

2. THE HIERARCHY OF REASONS

How can we establish rules of superiority? It is a *prima facie* reason for me to do something not only that *I* would enjoy it if *I* did it, but also that *you* would enjoy it if *I* did it. People generally would fare better if this fact were treated as a pro, for if this reason were followed, it would create additional enjoyment all round. But which of the two *prima facie* reasons is superior when they conflict? How would we tell?

At first sight it would seem that these reasons are equally good, that there is nothing to choose between them, that no case can be made out for saying that people generally would fare better if the one or the other were treated as superior. But this is a mistake.

Suppose I could be spending half an hour in writing a letter to Aunt Agatha who would enjoy receiving one though I would not enjoy writing it, or alternatively in listening to a lecture which I would enjoy doing. Let us also assume that I cannot do both, that I neither enjoy writing the letter nor dislike it, that Aunt Agatha enjoys receiving the letter as much as I enjoy listening to the lecture, and that there are no extraneous considerations such as that I deserve especially to enjoy myself there and then, or that Aunt Agatha does, or that she has special claims on me, or that I have special responsibilities or obligations to please her.

In order to see which is the better of these two reasons, we must draw a distinction between two different cases: the case in which someone derives pleasure from giving pleasure to others and the case where he does not. Everyone is so related to certain other persons that he derives greater pleasure from doing something together with them than doing it alone because in doing so he is giving them pleasure. He derives pleasure not merely from the game of tennis he is playing but from the fact that in playing he is pleasing his partner. We all enjoy pleasing those we love. Many of us enjoy pleasing even strangers. Some even enjoy pleasing their enemies. Others get very little enjoyment from pleasing anybody.

We must therefore distinguish between people with two kinds of natural make-up: on the one hand, those who need not always choose between pleasing themselves and pleasing others, who can please themselves *by* pleasing others, who can please themselves more by not merely pleasing themselves, and, on the other hand, those who always or often have to choose between pleasing themselves and pleasing others, who derive no pleasure from pleasing others, who do not please themselves more by pleasing not merely themselves.

If I belong to the first kind, then I shall derive pleasure from pleasing Aunt Agatha. Although writing her a letter is not enjoyable in itself, as listening to the lecture is, I nevertheless derive enjoyment from writing it because it is a way of pleasing her and I enjoy pleasing people. In choosing between writing the letter and listening to the lecture, I do not therefore have to choose between pleasing her and pleasing myself. I have merely to choose between two different ways of pleasing myself. If I am a man of the second kind, then I must choose between pleasing myself and pleasing her. When we have eliminated all possible moral reasons, such as standing in a special relationship to the person, then it would be strange for someone to prefer pleasing someone else to pleasing himself. How strange this is can be seen if we substitute for Aunt Agatha a complete stranger.

I conclude from this that the fact that I would enjoy it if *I* did *x* is a better reason for doing *x* than the fact that you would enjoy it if *I* did *x*. Similarly in the fact that I would enjoy doing *x* if I did it I have a reason for doing *x* which is better than the reason for doing *y* which I have in the fact that you would enjoy doing *y* as much as I would enjoy doing *x*. More generally speaking, we can say that self-regarding reasons are better than other-regarding ones. Rationally speaking, the old quip is true that everyone is his own nearest neighbor.

This is more obvious still when we consider the case of self-interest. Both the fact that doing *x* would be in my interest and the fact that it would be in someone else's interest are excellent *prima facie* reasons for me to do *x*. But the self-interested reason is better than the altruistic one. Of course, interests need not conflict, and then I need not choose. I can do what is in both our interests. But sometimes interests conflict, and then it is in accordance with reason (*prima facie*) to prefer my own interest to someone else's. That my making an application for a job is in *my* interest is a reason for me to apply, which is better than the reason against applying, which I have in the fact that my not applying is in *your* interest.

There is no doubt that this conviction is correct for all cases. It is obviously better that everyone should look after his own interest than that everyone should neglect it in favor of someone else's. For whose interest should have precedence? It must be remembered that we are considering a case in which there are no special reasons for preferring a particular person's interests to one's own, as when there are no special moral obligations or emotional ties. Surely, in the absence of any *special* reasons for preferring someone else's interests, *everyone's* interests are best served if *everyone* puts his own interests first. For, by and large, everyone is himself the best judge of what is in his own best interest, since everyone usually knows best what his plans, aims, ambitions, or aspirations are. Moreover, everyone is more diligent in the promotion of his own interests than that of others. Enlightened egoism is a possible, rational, orderly system of running things, enlightened altruism is not. Everyone can look after himself, no one can look after everyone else. Even if everyone had to look after only two others, he could not do it as well as looking after himself alone. And if he has to look after only one person, there is no advantage in making that person someone other than himself. On the contrary, he is less likely to know as well what that person's interest is or to be as zealous in its promotion as in that of his own interest.

For this reason, it has often been thought that enlightened egoism is a possible rational way of running things. Sidgwick, for instance, says that the principle of egoism, to have as one's ultimate aim one's own greatest happiness, and the principle of universal benevolence, to have as one's ultimate aim the greatest happiness of the greatest number, are equally rational.[1] Sidgwick then goes on to say that these two principles may conflict and anyone who admits the rationality of both may go on to maintain that it is rational not to abandon the aim of one's own greatest happiness. On his view, there is a fundamental and ultimate contradiction in our apparent intuitions of what is reasonable in conduct. He argues that this can be removed only by the assumption that the individual's greatest happiness and the greatest happiness of the greatest number are both achieved by the rewarding and punishing activity of a perfect being whose sanctions would suffice to make it always everyone's interest to promote universal happiness to the best of his knowledge.

The difficulty which Sidgwick here finds is due to the fact that he regards reasons of self-interest as being no stronger and no weaker than moral reasons. This, however, is not in accordance with our ordinary convictions. It is generally believed that when reasons of self-interest conflict with moral reasons, then moral reasons override those of self-interest. It is our common conviction that moral reasons are superior to all others. Sidgwick has simply overlooked that although it is *prima facie* in accordance with reason to follow reasons of self-interest and also to follow moral reasons nevertheless, when there is a conflict between these two types of reason, when we have a self-interested reason for doing something and a moral reason against doing it, there need not be an ultimate and fundamental contradiction in what it is in accordance with reason to do. For one type of reason may be *stronger* or *better* than another so that, when two reasons of different types are in conflict, it is in accordance with reason to follow the stronger, contrary to reason to follow the weaker.

[1] Henry Sidgwick, *The Methods of Ethics*, 7th ed. (London: Macmillan and Co., 1907), concluding Chapter, par. 1. [Pp. 36–7 in this volume.]

3. THE SUPREMACY OF MORAL REASONS

Are moral reasons really superior to reasons of self-interest as we all believe? Do we really have reason on our side when we follow moral reasons against self-interest? What reasons could there be for being moral? Can we really give an answer to "Why should we be moral?" It is obvious that all these questions come to the same thing. When we ask, "Should we be moral?" or "Why should we be moral?" or "Are moral reasons superior to all others?" we ask to be given a reason for regarding moral reasons as superior to all others. What is this reason?

Let us begin with a state of affairs in which reasons of self-interest are supreme. In such a state everyone keeps his impulses and inclinations in check when and only when they would lead him into behavior detrimental to his own interest. Everyone who follows reason will discipline himself to rise early, to do his exercises, to refrain from excessive drinking and smoking, to keep good company, to marry the right sort of girl, to work and study hard in order to get on, and so on. However, it will often happen that people's interests conflict. In such a case, they will have to resort to ruses or force to get their own way. As this becomes known, men will become suspicious, for they will regard one another as scheming competitors for the good things in life. The universal supremacy of the rules of self-interest must lead to what Hobbes called the state of nature. At the same time, it will be clear to everyone that universal obedience to certain rules overriding self-interest would produce a state of affairs which serves everyone's interest much better than his unaided pursuit of it in a state where everyone does the same. Moral rules are universal rules designed to override those of self-interest when following the latter is harmful to others. "Thou shalt not kill," "Thou shalt not lie," "Thou shalt not steal" are rules which forbid the inflicting of harm on someone else even when this might be in one's interest.

The very *raison d'être* of a morality is to yield reasons which overrule the reasons of self-interest in those cases when everyone's following self-interest would be harmful to everyone. Hence moral reasons are superior to all others.

"But what does this mean?" it might be objected. "If it merely means that we do so regard them, then you are of course right, but your contention is useless, a mere point of usage. And how could it mean any more? If it means that we not only do so regard them, but *ought* so to regard them, then there must be *reasons* for saying this.

But there could not be any reasons for it. If you offer reasons of self-interest, you are arguing in a circle. Moreover, it cannot be true that it is always in my interest to treat moral reasons as superior to reasons of self-interest. If it were, self-interest and morality could never conflict, but they notoriously do. It is equally circular to argue that there are moral reasons for saying that one ought to treat moral reasons as superior to reasons of self-interest. And what other reasons are there?"

The answer is that we are now looking at the world from the point of view of *anyone*. We are not examining particular alternative courses of action before this or that person; we are examining two alternative worlds, one in which moral reasons are always treated by everyone as superior to reasons of self-interest and one in which the reverse is the practice. And we can see that the first world is the better world, because we can see that the second world would be the sort which Hobbes describes as the state of nature.

This shows that I ought to be moral, for when I ask the question "What ought I to do?" I am asking, "Which is the course of action supported by the best reasons?" But since it has just been shown that moral reasons are superior to reasons of self-interest, I have been given a reason for being moral, for following moral reasons rather than any other, namely, they are better reasons than any other.

But is this always so? Do we have a reason for being moral whatever the conditions we find ourselves in? Could there not be situations in which it is not true that we have reasons for being moral, that, on the contrary, we have reasons for ignoring the demands of morality? Is not Hobbes right in saying that in a state of nature the laws of nature, that is, the rules of morality, bind only *in foro interno?*

Hobbes argues as follows.

(i) To live in a state of nature is to live outside society. It is to live in conditions in which there are no common ways of life and, therefore, no reliable expectations about other people's behavior other than that they will follow their inclination or their interest.

(ii) In such a state reason will be the enemy of cooperation and mutual trust. For it is too risky to hope that other people will refrain from protecting their own interests by the preventive elimination of probable or even possible dangers to them. Hence reason will counsel everyone to avoid these risks by preventive action. But this leads to war.

(iii) It is obvious that everyone's following self-interest leads to a state of affairs which is desirable from no one's point of view. It is, on the contrary, desirable that everybody should follow rules overriding self-interest whenever that is to the detriment of others. In other words, it is desirable to bring about a state of affairs in which all obey the rules of morality.

(iv) However, Hobbes claims that in the state of nature it helps nobody if a single person or a small group of persons begins to follow the rules of morality, for this could only lead to the extinction of such individuals or groups. In such a state, it is therefore contrary to reason to be moral.

(v) The situation can change, reason can support morality, only when the presumption about other people's behavior is reversed. Hobbes thought that this could be achieved only by the creation of an absolute ruler with absolute power to enforce his laws. We have already seen that this is not true and that it can also be achieved if people live in a society, that is, if they have common ways of life, which are taught to all members and somehow enforced by the group. Its members have reason to expect their fellows generally to obey its rules, that is, its religion, morality, customs, and law, even when doing so is not, on certain occasions, in their interest. Hence they too have reason to follow these rules.

Is this argument sound? One might, of course, object to step (i) on the grounds that this is an empirical proposition for which there is little or no evidence. For how can we know whether it is true that people in a state of nature would follow only their inclinations or, at best, reasons of self-interest, when nobody now lives in that state or has ever lived in it?

However, there is some empirical evidence to support this claim. For in the family of nations, individual states are placed very much like individual persons in a state of nature. The doctrine of the sovereignty of nations and the absence of an effective international law and police force are a guarantee that nations live in a state of nature, without commonly accepted rules that are somehow enforced. Hence it must be granted that living in a state of nature leads to living in a state in which individuals act either on impulse or as they think their interest dictates. For states pay only lip service to morality. They attack their hated neighbors when the opportunity arises. They start preventive wars in order to destroy the enemy before he can deliver his knockout blow. Where interests conflict, the stronger party usually has his way, whether his claims are justified or not.

And where the relative strength of the parties is not obvious, they usually resort to arms in order to determine "whose side God is on." Treaties are frequently concluded but, morally speaking, they are not worth the paper they are written on. Nor do the partners regard them as contracts binding in the ordinary way, but rather as public expressions of the belief of the governments concerned that for the time being their alliance is in the interest of the allies. It is well understood that such treaties may be canceled before they reach their predetermined end or simply broken when it suits one partner. In international affairs, there are very few examples of *Nibelungentreue,* although statesmen whose countries have kept their treaties in the hope of profiting from them usually make such high moral claims.

It is, moreover, difficult to justify morality in international affairs. For suppose a highly moral statesman were to demand that his country adhere to a treaty obligation even though this meant its ruin or possibly its extinction. Suppose he were to say that treaty obligations are sacred and must be kept whatever the consequences. How could he defend such a policy? Perhaps one might argue that someone has to make a start in order to create mutual confidence in international affairs. Or one might say that setting a good example is the best way of inducing others to follow suit. But such a defense would hardly be sound. The less skeptical one is about the genuineness of the cases in which nations have adhered to their treaties from a sense of moral obligation, the more skeptical one must be about the effectiveness of such examples of virtue in effecting a change of international practice. Power politics still govern in international affairs.

We must, therefore, grant Hobbes the first step in his argument and admit that in a state of nature people, as a matter of psychological fact, would not follow the dictates of morality. But we might object to the next step that knowing this psychological fact about other people's behavior constitutes a reason for behaving in the same way. Would it not still be immoral for anyone to ignore the demands of morality even though he knows that others are likely or certain to do so, too? Can we offer as a justification for morality the fact that no one is entitled to do wrong just because someone else is doing wrong? This argument begs the question whether it *is* wrong for anyone in this state to disregard the demands of morality. It cannot be wrong to break a treaty or make preventive war if we have no reason to obey the moral rules. For to say that it is wrong to do so is to say that we ought not to do so. But if we have no reason for obeying the moral rule, then we have no reason overruling self-interest, hence no reason for keeping the treaty when keeping it is not in our interest, hence it is not true that we have a reason for keeping it, hence not true that we ought to keep it, hence not true that it is wrong not to keep it.

I conclude that Hobbes' argument is sound. Moralities are systems of principles whose acceptance by everyone as overruling the dictates of self-interest is in the interest of everyone alike, though following the rules of a morality is not of course identical with following self-interest. If it were, there could be no conflict between a morality and self-interest and no point in having moral rules overriding self-interest. Hobbes is also right in saying that the application of this system of rules is in accordance with reason only under social conditions, that is, when there are well-established ways of behavior.

The answer to our question "Why should we be moral?" is therefore as follows. We should be moral because being moral is following rules designed to overrule reasons of self-interest whenever it is in the interest of everyone alike that such rules should be generally followed. This will be the case when the needs and wants and aspirations of individual agents conflict with one another and when, in the absence of such overriding rules, the pursuit of their ends by all concerned would lead to the attempt to eliminate those who are in the way. Since such rules will always require one of the rivals to abandon his pursuit in favor of the other, they will tend to be broken. Since, *ex hypothesi* it is in everyone's interest that they should be followed, it will be in everyone's interest that they should not only be taught as "superior to" other reasons but also adequately enforced, in order to reduce the temptation to break them. A person instructed in these rules can acknowledge that such reasons are superior to reasons of self-interest without having to admit that he is always or indeed ever attracted or moved by them.

But is it not self-contradictory to say that it is in a person's interest to do what is contrary to his interest? It certainly would be if the two expressions were used in exactly the same way. But they are not. We have already seen that an enlightened egoist can acknowledge that a certain course of action is in his enlightened long-term, but contrary to his narrow short-term interest. He can infer that it is "in his interest" and according to reason to follow enlightened long-term interest, and "against his interest" and contrary to reason to follow short-term interest. Clearly, "in his interest" and "against his interest" here are used in new ways. For suppose it is discovered that the probable long-range consequences and psychological effects on others do not work out as predicted. Even so we need not admit that, in this new and extended sense, the line of action followed merely seemed but really was not in his interest. For we are now considering not merely a single action but a policy.

All the same, we must not make too much of this analogy. There is an all-important difference between the two cases. The calculations of the enlightened egoist properly allow for "exceptions in the agent's favor." After all, his calculus is designed to promote his interest. If he has information to show that in his particular circumstances it would pay to depart from a well-established general canon of enlightened self-interest, then it is proper for him to depart from it. It would not be a sign of the enlightened self-interest of a building contractor, let us say, if he made sacrifices for certain subcontractors even though he knew that they would or could not reciprocate, as subcontractors normally do. By contrast, such information is simply irrelevant in cases where moral reasons apply. Moral rules are not designed to serve the agent's interest directly. Hence it would be quite inappropriate for him to break them whenever he discovers that they do not serve his interest. They are designed to adjudicate primarily in cases where there is a conflict of interests so that from their very nature they are bound to be contrary to the interest of one of the persons affected. However, they are also bound to serve the interest of the other person, hence his interest in the other's observing them. It is on the assumption of the likelihood of a reversal of roles that the universal observation of the rule will serve everyone's interest. The principle of justice and other principles which we employ in improving the moral rules of a given society help to bring existing moralities closer to the ideal which is in the interest of everyone alike. Thus, just as following the canons of enlightened self-interest is in one's interest only if the assumptions underlying it are correct, so following the rules of morality is in everyone's interest only if the assumptions underlying it are correct, that is, if the moral rules come close to being true and are generally observed. Even then, to say that following them is in the interest of everyone alike means only that it is better for everyone that there should be a morality generally observed than that the principle of self-interest should be acknowledged as supreme. It does not of course mean that a person will not do better for himself by following self-interest than by doing what is morally right, when others are doing what is right. But of course such a person cannot *claim* that he is following a superior reason.

It must be added to this, however, that such a system of rules has the support of reason only where people live in societies, that is, in conditions in which there are established common ways of behavior. Outside society, people have no reason for following such rules, that is, for being moral. In other words, outside society, the very distinction between right and wrong vanishes.

DAVID P. GAUTHIER

Morality and Advantage

I

Hume asks, rhetorically, "what theory of morals can ever serve any useful purpose, unless it can show, by a particular detail, that all the duties which it recommends, are also the true interest of each individual?"[1] But there are many to whom this question does not seem rhetorical. Why, they ask, do we speak the language of morality, impressing upon our fellows their duties and obligations, urging them with appeals to what is right and good, if we could speak to the same effect in the language of prudence, appealing to considerations of interest and advantage? When the poet, Ogden Nash, is moved by the muse to cry out:

> O Duty,
> Why hast thou not the visage of a sweetie or a cutie?[2]

we do not anticipate the reply:

> O Poet,
> I really am a cutie and I think you ought to know it.

The belief that duty cannot be reduced to interest, or that morality may require the agent to subordinate all considerations of advantage,

---

* From *The Philosophical Review*, LXXVI, No. 4, October, 1967, 460–75. Reprinted with the kind permission of the editors.

[1] David Hume, *An Enquiry Concerning the Principles of Morals,* sec. ix, pt. ii. [Reprinted in this volume, p. 107.]

[2] Ogden Nash, "Kind of an Ode to Duty."

is one which has withstood the assaults of contrary-minded philosophers from Plato to the present. Indeed, were it not for the conviction that only interest and advantage can motivate human actions, it would be difficult to understand philosophers contending so vigorously for the identity, or at least compatibility, of morality with prudence.

Yet if morality is not true prudence it would be wrong to suppose that those philosophers who have sought some connection between morality and advantage have been merely misguided. For it is a truism that we should all expect to be worse off if men were to substitute prudence, even of the most enlightened kind, for morality in all of their deliberations. And this truism demands not only some connection between morality and advantage, but a seemingly paradoxical connection. For if we should all expect to suffer, were men to be prudent instead of moral, then morality must contribute to advantage in a unique way, a way in which prudence—following reasons of advantage—cannot.

Thomas Hobbes is perhaps the first philosopher who tried to develop this seemingly paradoxical connection between morality and advantage. But since he could not admit that a man might ever reasonably subordinate considerations of advantage to the dictates of obligation, he was led to deny the possibility of real conflict between morality and prudence. So his argument fails to clarify the distinction between the view that claims of obligation reduce to considerations of interest and the view that claims of obligation promote advantage in a way in which considerations of interest cannot.

More recently, Kurt Baier has argued that "being moral is following rules designed to overrule self-interest whenever it is in the interest of everyone alike that everyone should set aside his interest." [3] Since prudence is following rules of (enlightened) self-interest, Baier is arguing that morality is designed to overrule prudence when it is to everyone's advantage that it do so—or, in other words, that morality contributes to advantage in a way in which prudence cannot.[4]

Baier does not actually demonstrate that morality contributes to

[3] Kurt Baier, *The Moral Point of View: A Rational Basis of Ethics* (Ithaca, 1958), p. 314. [This passage does not appear in the abridged edition. But cf. "Moralities are systems of principles whose acceptance by everyone as overruling the dictates of self-interest is in the interest of everyone alike, . . .", p. 163 in this volume.]

[4] That this, and only this, is what he is entitled to claim may not be clear to Baier, for he supposes his account of morality to answer the question "Why should we be moral?" interpreting "we" distributively. This, as I shall argue in Sec. IV, is quite mistaken.

advantage in this unique and seemingly paradoxical way. Indeed, he does not ask how it is possible that morality should do this. It is this possibility which I propose to demonstrate.

II

Let us examine the following proposition, which will be referred to as "the thesis": *Morality is a system of principles such that it is advantageous for everyone if everyone accepts and acts on it, yet acting on the system of principles requires that some persons perform disadvantageous acts.*[5]

What I wish to show is that this thesis *could be true*, that morality could possess those characteristics attributed to it by the thesis. I shall not try to show that the thesis is true—indeed, I shall argue in Section V that it presents at best an inadequate conception of morality. But it is plausible to suppose that a modified form of the thesis states a necessary, although not a sufficient, condition for a moral system.

Two phrases in the thesis require elucidation. The first is "advantageous for everyone." I use this phrase to mean that *each* person will do better if the system is accepted and acted on than if *either* no system is accepted and acted on *or* a system is accepted and acted on which is similar, save that it never requires any person to perform disadvantageous acts.

Clearly, then, the claim that it is advantageous for everyone to accept and act on the system is a very strong one; it may be so strong that no system of principles which might be generally adopted could meet it. But I shall consider in Section V one among the possible ways of weakening the claim.

The second phrase requiring elucidation is "disadvantageous acts." I use this phrase to refer to acts which, in the context of their performance, would be less advantageous to the performer than some other act open to him in the same context. The phrase does not refer to acts which merely impose on the performer some short-term disadvantage that is recouped or outweighed in the long run. Rather it refers to acts which impose a disadvantage that is never recouped. It follows that the performer may say to himself, when confronted with the re-

[5] The thesis is not intended to state Baier's view of morality. I shall suggest in Sec. V that Baier's view would require substituting "everyone can expect to benefit" for "it is advantageous to everyone." The thesis is stronger and easier to discuss.

quirement to perform such an act, that it would be better *for him* not to perform it.

It is essential to note that the thesis, as elucidated, does not maintain that morality is advantageous for everyone in the sense that each person will do *best* if the system of principles is accepted and acted on. Each person will do better than if no system is adopted, or than if the one particular alternative mentioned above is adopted, but not than if any alternative is adopted.

Indeed, for each person required by the system to perform some disadvantageous act, it is easy to specify a better alternative—namely, the system modified so that it does not require *him* to perform any act disadvantageous to himself. Of course, there is no reason to expect such an alternative to be better than the moral system for everyone, or in fact for anyone other than the person granted the special exemption.

A second point to note is that each person must gain more from the disadvantageous acts performed by others than he loses from the disadvantageous acts performed by himself. If this were not the case, then some person would do better if a system were adopted exactly like the moral system save that it never requires *any* person to perform disadvantageous acts. This is ruled out by the force of "advantageous for everyone."

This point may be clarified by an example. Suppose that the system contains exactly one principle. Everyone is always to tell the truth. It follows from the thesis that each person gains more from those occasions on which others tell the truth, even though it is disadvantageous to them to do so, than he loses from those occasions on which he tells the truth even though it is disadvantageous to him to do so.

Now this is not to say that each person gains by telling others the truth in order to ensure that in return they tell him the truth. Such gains would merely be the result of accepting certain short-term disadvantages (those associated with truth-telling) in order to reap long-term benefits (those associated with being told the truth). Rather, what is required by the thesis is that those disadvantages which a person incurs in telling the truth, when he can expect neither short-term nor long-term benefits to accrue to him from truth-telling, are outweighed by those advantages he receives when others tell him the truth when they can expect no benefits to accrue to them from truth-telling.

The principle enjoins truth-telling in those cases in which whether one tells the truth or not will have no effect on whether others tell the truth. Such cases include those in which others have no way of knowing whether or not they are being told the truth. The thesis requires that the disadvantages one incurs in telling the truth in these cases are less than the advantages one receives in being told the truth by others in parallel cases; and the thesis requires that this holds for everyone.

Thus we see that although the disadvantages imposed by the system on any person are less than the advantages secured him through the imposition of disadvantages on others, yet the disadvantages are real in that incurring them is *unrelated* to receiving the advantages. The argument of long-term prudence, that I ought to incur some immediate disadvantage *so that* I shall receive compensating advantages later on, is entirely inapplicable here.

III

It will be useful to examine in some detail an example of a system which possesses those characteristics ascribed by the thesis to morality. This example, abstracted from the field of international relations, will enable us more clearly to distinguish, first, conduct based on immediate interest; second, conduct which is truly prudent; and third, conduct which promotes mutual advantage but is not prudent.

A and *B* are two nations with substantially opposed interests, who find themselves engaged in an arms race against each other. Both possess the latest in weaponry, so that each recognizes that the actual outbreak of full scale war between them would be mutually disastrous. This recognition leads *A* and *B* to agree that each would be better off if they were mutually disarming instead of mutually arming. For mutual disarmament would preserve the balance of power between them while reducing the risk of war.

Hence *A* and *B* enter into a disarmament pact. The pact is advantageous for both if both accept and act on it, although clearly it is not advantageous for either to act on it if the other does not.

Let *A* be considering whether or not to adhere to the pact in some particular situation, whether or not actually to perfom some act of disarmament. *A* will quite likely consider the act to have disadvantageous consequences. *A* expects to benefit, not by its own acts of disarmament, but by *B*'s acts. Hence if *A* were to reason simply in terms of immediate interest, *A* might well decide to violate the pact.

But *A*'s decision need be neither prudent nor reasonable. For suppose first that *B* is able to determine whether or not *A* adheres to the pact. If *A* violates, then *B* will detect the violation and will then consider what to do in the light of *A*'s behavior. It is not to *B*'s advantage to disarm alone; *B* expects to gain, not by its own acts of disarmament, but by *A*'s acts. Hence *A*'s violation, if known to *B*, leads naturally to *B*'s counterviolation. If this continues, the effect of the pact is entirely undone, and *A* and *B* return to their mutually disadvantageous arms race. *A*, foreseeing this when considering whether or not to adhere to the pact in the given situation, must therefore conclude that the truly prudent course of action is to adhere.

Now suppose that *B* is unable to determine whether or not *A* adheres to the pact in the particular situation under consideration. If *A* judges adherence to be in itself disadvantageous, then it will decide, both on the basis of immediate interest and on the basis of prudence, to violate the pact. Since *A*'s decision is unknown to *B*, it cannot affect whether or not *B* adheres to the pact, and so the advantage gained by *A*'s violation is not outweighed by any consequent loss.

Therefore if *A* and *B* are prudent they will adhere to their disarmament pact whenever violation would be detectable by the other, and violate the pact whenever violation would not be detectable by the other. In other words, they will adhere openly and violate secretly. The disarmament pact between *A* and *B* thus possesses two of the characteristics ascribed by the thesis to morality. First, accepting the pact and acting on it is more advantageous for each than making no pact at all. Second, in so far as the pact stipulates that each must disarm even when disarming is undetectable by the other, it requires each to perform disadvantageous acts—acts which run counter to considerations of prudence.

One further condition must be met if the disarmament pact is to possess those characteristics ascribed by the thesis to a system of morality. It must be the case that the requirement that each party perform disadvantageous acts be essential to the advantage conferred by the pact; or, to put the matter in the way in which we expressed it earlier, both *A* and *B* must do better to adhere to this pact than to a pact which is similar save that it requires no disadvantageous acts. In terms of the example, *A* and *B* must do better to adhere to the pact than to a pact which stipulates that each must disarm only when disarming is detectable by the other.

We may plausibly suppose this condition to be met. Although *A* will gain by secretly retaining arms itself, it will lose by *B*'s similar acts, and its losses may well outweigh its gains. *B* may equally lose more by *A*'s secret violations than it gains by its own. So, despite the fact that prudence requires each to violate secretly, each may well do better if both adhere secretly than if both violate secretly. Supposing this to be the case, the disarmament pact is formally analogous to a moral system, as characterized by the thesis. That is, acceptance of and adherence to the pact by *A* and *B* is more advantageous for each, either than making no pact at all or than acceptance of and adherence to a pact requiring only open disarmament, and the pact requires each to perform acts of secret disarmament which are disadvantageous.

Some elementary notation, adapted for our purposes from the mathematical theory of games, may make the example even more perspicuous. Given a disarmament pact between *A* and *B*, each may pursue two pure strategies—adherence and violation. There are, then, four possible combinations of strategies, each determining a particular outcome. These outcomes can be ranked preferentially for each nation; we shall let the numerals 1 to 4 represent the ranking from first to fourth preference. Thus we construct a simple matrix,[6] in which *A*'s preferences are stated first:

		B	
		adheres	*violates*
	adheres	2,2	4,1
A			
	violates	1,4	3,3

The matrix does not itself show that agreement is advantageous to both, for it gives only the rankings of outcomes given the agreement. But it is plausible to assume that *A* and *B* would rank mutual violation on a par with no agreement. If we assume this, we can then indicate the value to each of making and adhering to the pact by reference to the matrix.

[6] Those familiar with the theory of games will recognize the matrix as a variant of the Prisoner's Dilemma. In a more formal treatment, it would be appropriate to develop the relation between morality and advantage by reference to the Prisoner's Dilemma. This would require reconstructing the disarmament pact and the moral system as proper games. Here I wish only to suggest the bearing of game theory on our enterprise.

The matrix shows immediately that adherence to the pact is not the most advantageous possibility for either, since each prefers the outcome, if it alone violates, to the outcome of mutual adherence. It shows also that each gains less from its own violations than it loses from the other's, since each ranks mutual adherence above mutual violation.

Let us now use the matrix to show that, as we argued previously, public adherence to the pact is prudent and mutually advantageous, whereas private adherence is not prudent although mutually advantageous. Consider first the case when adherence—and so violation—are open and public.

If adherence and violation are open, then each knows the strategy chosen by the other, and can adjust its own strategy in the light of this knowledge—or, in other words, the strategies are interdependent. Suppose that each initially chooses the strategy of adherence. *A* notices that if it switches to violation it gains—moving from 2 to 1 in terms of preference ranking. Hence immediate interest dictates such a switch. But it notices further that if it switches, then *B* can also be expected to switch—moving from 4 to 3 on its preference scale. The eventual outcome would be stable, in that neither could benefit from switching from violation back to adherence. But the eventual outcome would represent not a gain for *A* but a loss—moving from 2 to 3 on its preference scale. Hence prudence dictates no change from the strategy of adherence. This adherence is mutually advantageous; *A* and *B* are in precisely similar positions in terms of their pact.

Consider now the case when adherence and violation are secret and private. Neither nation knows the strategy chosen by the other, so the two strategies are independent. Suppose *A* is trying to decide which strategy to follow. It does not know *B*'s choice. But it notices that if *B* adheres, then it pays *A* to violate, attaining 1 rather than 2 in terms of preference ranking. If *B* violates, then again it pays *A* to violate, attaining 3 rather than 4 on its preference scale. Hence, no matter which strategy *B* chooses, *A* will do better to violate, and so prudence dictates violation.

B of course reasons in just the same way. Hence each is moved by considerations of prudence to violate the pact, and the outcome assigns each rank 3 on its preference scale. This outcome is mutually disadvantageous to *A* and *B*, since mutual adherence would assign each rank 2 on its preference scale.

If *A* and *B* are both capable only of rational prudence, they find themselves at an impasse. The advantage of mutual adherence to the agreement when violations would be secret is not available to them, since neither can find it in his own overall interest not to violate secretly. Hence, strictly prudent nations cannot reap the maximum advantage possible from a pact of the type under examination.

Of course, what A and B will no doubt endeavor to do is eliminate the possibility of secret violations of their pact. Indeed, barring additional complications, each must find it to his advantage to make it possible for the other to detect his own violations. In other words, each must find it advantageous to ensure that their choice of strategies is interdependent, so that the pact will always be prudent for each to keep. But it may not be possible for them to ensure this, and to the extent that they cannot, prudence will prevent them from maximizing mutual advantage.

IV

We may now return to the connection of morality with advantage. Morality, if it is a system of principles of the type characterized in the thesis, requires that some persons perform acts genuinely disadvantageous to themselves, as a means to greater mutual advantage. Our example shows sufficiently that such a system is possible, and indicates more precisely its character. In particular, by an argument strictly parallel to that which we have pursued, we may show that men who are merely prudent will not perform the required disadvantageous acts. But in so violating the principles of morality, they will disadvantage themselves. Each will lose more by the violations of others than he will gain by his own violations.

Now this conclusion would be unsurprising if it were only that no man can gain if he alone is moral rather than prudent. Obviously such a man loses, for he adheres to moral principles to his own disadvantage, while others violate them also to his disadvantage. The benefit of the moral system is not one which any individual can secure for himself, since each man gains from the sacrifices of others.

What is surprising in our conclusion is that no man can ever gain if he is moral. Not only does he not gain by being moral if others are prudent, but he also does not gain by being moral if others are moral. For although he now receives the advantage of others' adherence to moral principles, he reaps the disadvantage of his own adherence. As long as his own adherence to morality is independent of what others do (and this is required to distinguish morality from prudence), he must do better to be prudent.

If all men are moral, all will do better than if all are prudent. But any one man will always do better if he is prudent than if he is moral. There is no real paradox in supposing that morality is advantageous, even though it requires the performance of disadvantageous acts.

On the supposition that morality has the characteristics ascribed to it by the thesis, is it possible to answer the question "Why should we be moral?" where "we" is taken distributively, so that the question is a compendious way of asking, for each person, "Why should I be moral?" More simply, is it possible to answer the question "Why should I be moral?"

I take it that this question, if asked seriously, demands a reason for being moral other than moral reasons themselves. It demands that moral reasons be shown to be reasons for acting by a noncircular argument. Those who would answer it, like Baier, endeavor to do so by the introduction of considerations of advantage.

Two such considerations have emerged from our discussion. The first is that if all are moral, all will do better than if all are prudent. This will serve to answer the question "Why should we be moral?" if this question is interpreted rather as "Why should we all be moral —rather than all being something else?" If we must all be the same, then each person has a reason—a prudential reason—to prefer that we all be moral.

But, so interpreted, "Why should we be moral?" is not a compendious way of asking, for each person, "Why should I be moral?" Of course, if everyone is to be whatever I am, then I should be moral. But a general answer to the question "Why should I be moral?" cannot presuppose this.

The second consideration is that any individual always does better to be prudent rather than moral, provided his choice does not determine other choices. But in so far as this answers the question "Why should I be moral?" it leads to the conclusion "I should not be moral." One feels that this is not the answer which is wanted.

We may put the matter otherwise. The individual who needs a reason for being moral which is not itself a moral reason cannot have it. There is nothing surprising about this; it would be much more surprising if such reasons could be found. For it is more than apparently paradoxical to suppose that considerations of advantage could ever of themselves justify accepting a real disadvantage.

V

I suggested in Section II that the thesis, in modified form, might provide a necessary, although not a sufficient, condition for a moral system. I want now to consider how one might characterize the man who would qualify as moral according to the thesis—I shall call him the "moral" man—and then ask what would be lacking from this characterization, in terms of some of our commonplace moral views.

The rationally prudent man is incapable of moral behavior, in even the limited sense defined by the thesis. What difference must there be between the prudent man and the "moral" man? Most simply, the "moral" man is the prudent but trustworthy man. I treat trustworthiness as the capacity which enables its possessor to adhere, and to judge that he ought to adhere, to a commitment which he has made, without regard to considerations of advantage.

The prudent but trustworthy man does not possess this capacity completely. He is capable of trustworthy behavior only in so far as he regards his *commitment* as advantageous. Thus he differs from the prudent man just in the relevant respect; he accepts arguments of the form "If it is advantageous for me to agree[7] to do *x*, and I do agree to do *x*, then I ought to do *x*, whether or not it then proves advantageous for me to do *x*."

Suppose that *A* and *B*, the parties to the disarmament pact, are prudent but trustworthy. *A*, considering whether or not secretly to violate the agreement, reasons that its advantage in making and keeping the agreement, provided *B* does so as well, is greater than its advantage in not making it. If it can assume that *B* reasons in the same way, then it is in a position to conclude that it ought not to violate the pact. Although violation would be advantageous, consideration of this advantage is ruled out by *A*'s trustworthiness, given the advantage in agreeing to the pact.

---

[7] The word "agree" requires elucidation. It is essential not to confuse an advantage in agreeing to do *x* with an advantage in saying that one will do *x*. If it is advantageous for me to agree to do *x*, then there is some set of actions open to me which includes both saying that I will do *x* and doing *x*, and which is more advantageous to me than any set of actions open to me which does not include saying that I will do *x*. On the other hand, if it is advantageous for me to say that I will do *x*, then there is some set of actions open to me which includes saying that I will do *x*, and which is more advantageous to me than any set which does not include saying that I will do *x*. But this set need not include doing *x*.

The prudent but trustworthy man meets the requirements implicitly imposed by the thesis for the "moral" man. But how far does this "moral" man display two characteristics commonly associated with morality—first, a willingness to make sacrifices, and second, a concern with fairness?

Whenever a man ignores his own advantage for reasons other than those of greater advantage, he may be said to make some sacrifice. The "moral" man, in being trustworthy, is thus required to make certain sacrifices. But these are extremely limited. And—not surprisingly, given the general direction of our argument—it is quite possible that they limit the advantages which the "moral" man can secure.

Once more let us turn to our example. *A* and *B* have entered into a disarmament agreement and, being prudent but trustworthy, are faithfully carrying it out. The government of *A* is now informed by its scientists, however, that they have developed an effective missile defense, which will render *A* invulnerable to attack by any of the weapons actually or potentially at *B*'s disposal, barring unforeseen technological developments. Furthermore, this defense can be installed secretly. The government is now called upon to decide whether to violate its agreement with *B*, install the new defense, and, with the arms it has retained through its violation, establish its dominance over *B*.

A is in a type of situation quite different from that previously considered. For it is not just that *A* will do better by secretly violating its agreement. *A* reasons not only that it will do better to violate no matter what *B* does, but that it will do better if both violate than if both continue to adhere to the pact. *A* is now in a position to gain from abandoning the agreement; it no longer finds mutual adherence advantageous.

We may represent this new situation in another matrix:

		B	
		adheres	*violates*
	adheres	3,2	4,1
A			
	violates	1,4	2,3

We assume again that the ranking of mutual violation is the same as that of no agreement. Now had this situation obtained at the outset, no agreement would have been made, for *A* would have had no reason to enter into a disarmament pact. And of course had *A* expected this situation to come about, no agreement—or only a temporary agreement—would have been made; *A* would no doubt have risked the short-term dangers of the continuing arms race in the hope of securing the long-run benefit of predominance over *B* once its missile defense was completed. On the contrary, *A* expected to benefit from the agreement, but now finds that, because of its unexpected development of a missile defense, the agreement is not in fact advantageous to it.

The prudent but trustworthy man is willing to carry out his agreements, and judges that he ought to carry them out, in so far as he considers them advantageous. *A* is prudent but trustworthy. But is *A* willing to carry out its agreement to disarm, now that it no longer considers the agreement advantageous?

If *A* adheres to its agreement in this situation, it makes a sacrifice greater than any advantage it receives from the similar sacrifices of others. It makes a sacrifice greater in kind than any which can be required by a mutually advantageous agreement. It must, then, possess a capacity for trustworthy behavior greater than that ascribed to the merely prudent but trustworthy man (or nation). This capacity need not be unlimited; it need not extend to a willingness to adhere to any commitment no matter what sacrifice is involved. But it must involve a willingness to adhere to a commitment made in the expectation of advantage, should that expectation be disappointed.

I shall call the man (or nation) who is willing to adhere, and judges that he ought to adhere, to his prudentially undertaken agreements even if they prove disadvantageous to him, the trustworthy man. It is likely that there are advantages available to trustworthy men which are not available to merely prudent but trustworthy men. For there may be situations in which men can make agreements which each expects to be advantageous to him, provided he can count on the others' adhering to it whether or not their expectation of advantage is realized. But each can count on this only if all have the capacity to adhere to commitments regardless of whether the commitment actually proves advantageous. Hence, only trustworthy men who know each other to be such will be able rationally to enter into, and so to benefit from, such agreements.

Baier's view of morality departs from that stated in the thesis in that it requires trustworthy, and not merely prudent but trustworthy, men. Baier admits that "a person might do better for himself by following enlightened self-interest rather than morality." [8] This admission seems to require that morality be a system of principles which each person may expect, initially, to be advantageous to him, if adopted and adhered to by everyone, but not a system which actually is advantageous to everyone.

Our commonplace moral views do, I think, support the view that the moral man must be trustworthy. Hence, we have established one modification required in the thesis, if it is to provide a more adequate set of conditions for a moral system.

But there is a much more basic respect in which the "moral" man falls short of our expectations. He is willing to temper his single-minded pursuit of advantage only by accepting the obligation to adhere to prudentially undertaken commitments. He has no real concern for the advantage of others, which would lead him to modify his pursuit of advantage when it conflicted with the similar pursuits of others. Unless he expects to gain, he is unwilling to accept restrictions on the pursuit of advantage which are intended to equalize the opportunities open to all. In other words, he has no concern with fairness.

We tend to think of the moral man as one who does not seek his own well-being by means which would deny equal well-being to his fellows. This marks him off clearly from the "moral" man, who differs from the prudent man only in that he can overcome the apparent paradox of prudence and obtain those advantages which are available only to those who can display real restraint in their pursuit of advantage.

Thus a system of principles might meet the conditions laid down in the thesis without taking any account of considerations of fairness. Such a system would contain principles for ensuring increased advantage (or expectation of advantage) to everyone, but no further principle need be present to determine the distribution of this increase.

It is possible that there are systems of principles which, if adopted and adhered to, provide advantages which strictly prudent men, however rational, cannot attain. These advantages are a function of the sacrifices which the principles impose on their adherents.

Morality may be such a system. If it is, this would explain our

[8] Baier, *op. cit.*, p. 314. [This passage does not appear in the abridged edition. But cf. "to say that following them [the rules of morality] is in the interest of everyone alike . . . does not of course mean that a person will not do better for himself by following self-interest than by doing what is morally right, . . ." p. 164 in this volume.]

expectation that we should all be worse off were we to substitute prudence for morality in our deliberations. But to characterize morality as a system of principles advantageous to all is not to answer the question "Why should I be moral?" nor is it to provide for those considerations of fairness which are equally essential to our moral understanding.

Bibliographical Essay

This guide to further reading is partial in two senses—it is incomplete, and it reflects the tastes and prejudices of the editor. A bibliographical study of the literature on the relation between morality and rational self-interest could occupy another volume. This list only offers the reader a point of departure.

A. THE GREEK BEGINNINGS

PLATO's *Republic* is indispensable. ARISTOTLE's *Nicomachean Ethics* provides a clear statement of the assumptions and arguments which underlie the proof that right action is truly beneficial to the agent—Book I and Book X, Chaps. vi–viii are particularly relevant.

B. IS SELF-INTEREST RATIONAL?

Negative answers may be found in BAIER's *The Moral Point of View*, Chap. v, § 3 of the abridged edition, RICHARD B. BRANDT's *Ethical Theory* (Englewood Cliffs, N.J.: Prentice-Hall, Inc., 1958), Chap. xiv § 2, JOHN HOSPERS' *Human Conduct: an introduction to the problems of ethics* (New York: Harcourt, Brace & World, Inc., 1961), Chap. iv, and JAN NARVESON's *Morality and Utility* (Baltimore: The Johns Hopkins Press, 1967), last chapter.

SIDGWICK's *The Methods of Ethics* provides a lengthy account of egoism, and a defence of its rationality. C. D. BROAD supports Sidgwick in *Five Types of Ethical Theory* (London: Routledge & Kegan Paul Ltd., 1930), pp. 240–46. J. A. BRUNTON defends individualistic egoism in "Egoism and Morality," *Philosophical Quarterly*, 6 (1956).

C. IS MORAL MOTIVATION BASED ON INTEREST?

JOHN CLARKE of Hull defends the derivation of morality from self-love against HUTCHESON in *The Foundation of Morality in Theory and Practice considered,* excerpted in L. A. SELBY-BIGGE, ed., *British Moralists,* Vol. II (Oxford: The Clarendon Press, 1897). BERNARD MANDEVILLE'S *Fable of the Bees* has recently been interpreted as an attempt to explain morality as a system of mutual self-interest whose acceptance is motivated by pride, in an article by M. J. SCOTT-TAGGART, "Mandeville —Cynic or Fool?", *Philosophical Quarterly,* 16 (1966).

DAVID HUME opposes the derivation of morality from self-love in the *Enquiry Concerning the Principles of Morals,* § 5 and appendix II. JOSEPH BUTLER examines the relations of passions, self-interest, benevolence, and conscience in *Fifteen Sermons Preached at the Rolls Chapel.* BROAD offers a favourable appraisal of Butler's achievements in *Five Types of Ethical Theory.* An unfavorable appraisal is found in M. J. SCOTT-TAGGART, "Butler on Disinterested Actions," *Philosophical Quarterly,* 18 (1968).

Utilitarianism is the classic attempt to found a universalistic ethics on psychological egoistic hedonism. The most consistent statement is found in the early chapters of JEREMY BENTHAM's *An Introduction to the Principles of Morals and Legislation,* but JOHN STUART MILL's *Utilitarianism* has received greater popular and philosophical attention.

Sidgwick endeavors to refute psychological hedonism in *The Methods of Ethics*; his arguments are supported by Broad in *Five Types of Ethical Theory.*

The connection between duty and motivation developed by PRICHARD in "Duty and Interest" is challenged by W. D. FALK's " 'Ought' and Motivation," *Proceedings of the Aristotelian Society,* new series XLVIII (1948). WILLIAM K. FRANKENA's "Obligation and Motivation in Recent Moral Philosophy," in A. I. Melden, ed., *Essays in Moral Philosophy* (Seattle: University of Washington Press, 1958), provides an extensive exposition of the issues which underlie questions about moral motivation.

D. IS MORALITY ADVANTAGEOUS?

F. H. BRADLEY defends the Greek view in "Why Should I Be Moral?", *Ethical Studies* (Oxford: The Clarendon Press, 1876), but relates morality to the end for man, and not to advantage. W. T. STACE also defends the Platonic position in Chaps. xi and xii of *The Concept of Morals* (New York: The Macmillan Company, 1937), insisting that morality is necessary to happiness, but that this happiness is altruistic and not egoistic. PHILIPPA FOOT's "Moral Beliefs," *Proceedings of the Aristotelian Society,* new series LIX (1958–59) agrees with Plato that virtues must benefit their possessors, and PETER WERTHEIM's "Morality and advantage," *Australasian Journal of Philosophy,* XLII (1964), argues that vices affect the agent in ways he can not want. D. Z. PHILLIPS' "Does It Pay to Be Good?", *Proceedings of the Aristotelian Society,* new series LXV (1964–65), criticizes Foot from the standpoint of Kierkegaard.

J. C. THORNTON's "Can the moral point of view be justified?" *Australasian Journal of Philosophy,* XLII (1964), rejects the attempts of both Baier and Foot to relate morality to self-interest, arguing that 'Why should I be moral?' is not a genuine question. KAI NIELSEN's important paper "Why Should I Be Moral?", *Methodos,* XV (1963), also criticizes Baier, as well as Hospers (*Human Conduct,* Chap. iv). Nielsen argues that one can answer the question 'Why be moral?' only by deciding what sort of person one wants to be. H. A. PRICHARD's classic "Does Moral Philosophy Rest on a Mistake?", *Mind,* XXI (1912), also in his *Moral Obligation* (Oxford: The Clarendon Press, 1949), attacks the very attempt to give arguments for being moral.

A different account of the relation of morality to self-interest, which does not provide self-interested arguments for being moral, is found in David P. Gauthier, *Practical Reasoning* (Oxford: The Clarendon Press, 1963). And an important discussion of the relation of morality to the social interest is found in W. D. FALK's "Morality, Self, and Others," in H.-N. Castaneda and G. Nakhnikian, eds., *Morality and the Language of Conduct* (Detroit: Wayne State University Press, 1965).

E. CAN MORALITY BE JUSTIFIED AS RATIONAL?

This question is not explicitly examined in our readings, although some of them presuppose the rationality of morality. An affirmative answer is returned by NIELSEN, "Is 'Why Should I Be Moral?' An Absurdity," *Australasian Journal of Philosophy,* XXXVI (1958). A. I. MELDEN relates morality to being reasonable in "Why Be Moral?", *Journal of Philosophy,* XLV (1948). NARVESON attempts a rational proof of utilitarian morality in the last chapter of *Morality and Utility.*

STEPHEN TOULMIN examines the place of reason *within* ethics, denying that one can give a rational justification *of* ethics, in *The Place of Reason in Ethics* (Cambridge at the University Press, 1950). P. S. WADIA's "Why should I be moral?", *Australasian Journal of Philosophy*, XLII (1964), agrees with Toulmin against Baier that this is not a philosophical question.

The classic rejoinder to those who seek a rational ground for morality is found in DAVID HUME, *A Treatise of Human Nature*, Book II, Part III, § 3, and Book III, Part I. Hume did not deter Immanuel Kant from offering the classic attempt to found morality on reason, in the *Groundwork of the Metaphysic of Morals* and the *Critique of Pure Practical Reason*.

F. FUTURE DEVELOPMENTS

Anyone interested in pursuing our suggestions about the use of game theory in clarifying questions about morality and rational self-interest will find R. DUNCAN LUCE and HOWARD RAIFFA, *Games and Decisions: Introduction and Critical Survey* (New York: John Wiley & Sons, Inc., 1957) indispensable. R. B. BRAITHWAITE's little book *Theory of Games as a Tool for the Moral Philosopher* (Cambridge at the University Press, 1955) attempts to use game theory to explicate good sense, prudence and fairness.